ATHENS RISING

ATHENS RISING

A tale of Harmodius and Aristogiton

William Mott

iUniverse, Inc.
New York Lincoln Shanghai

Athens Rising
A tale of Harmodius and Aristogiton

iUniverse, Inc.

For information address:
iUniverse, Inc.
2021 Pine Lake Road, Suite 100
Lincoln, NE 68512
www.iuniverse.com

ISBN: 0-595-30198-3

Printed in the United States of America

Dedicated to

Miss Phillips, Mary Renault, and Karen

A history teacher who shared her love of Ancient Greece, a writer whose time-less fiction enchanted my youth, and a sister who delighted in sailing the wine dark Aegean and scaling the Acropolis with her older brother.

Wreath'd in myrtle, my sword I'll conceal,
Like those champions, devoted and brave,
When they plunged in the tyrant their steel,
And to Athens deliverance gave.

Belov'd heroes! Your deathless souls roam,
In the joy-breathing isles of the blest;
Where the mighty of old have their home—
Where Achilles and Diomed rest.

Hymn,
In honor of Harmodius and Aristogiton

An ancient ode attributed to Callistratus

This translation by Edgar Allan Poe published in the
Southern Literary Messenger, December 1835
Publisher TH White, Richmond, VA

Acknowledgement

The lines quoted from the Iliad are from a wonderful new translation
generously placed in the public domain
by
Ian Johnston
Malaspina University-College
Nanaimo, BC
Canada

Preface

Democracy, or _demokratia_ as the ancient Greeks knew it, evolved over several centuries. Athens, like her neighboring sister city-states, first came to power as a monarchy. But sometime around the 11th century BC, her citizens rose up and overthrew the rule of kings, choosing instead to place the reins of their governance in the hands of the landed nobility…an aristocracy. For the next 400 years, a small group of highborn men—elected from within their own class and given the title _archon_—shared the religious, judicial, and military leadership responsibilities of a king.

In 594 BC, at a time when Athens' economy was crippled by the corrupt, nepotistic legacy of this centuries-old aristocratic rule, the Athenian statesman Solon was elected archon. Beginning with a series of land reforms, Solon set out to right the mistakes of his highborn predecessors. Canceling the debts of farmers who had been reduced to virtual serfdom on their own land, Solon restored economic stability to the lower and middle classes. Turning a critical eye to the Athenian constitution, Solon then pushed through reforms that made income and property ownership, not birth, the sole qualification for holding public office. Satisfied that he'd returned stability to Athens' government, Solon retired to spend his final years traveling around the Mediterranean.

In Solon's absence, a disturbing trend—the rise of private armies—crept into Athens' already turbulent political atmosphere. Pisistratus, leader of an up and coming faction, used the pretext of a spurious attack on his person to petition the city for a sizable increase to his bodyguard. In 560 BC, his personal army seized the Acropolis—at this time a mighty fortress surrounded by a scattering of temples all standing on the highest point of the city—and Pisistratus had himself declared *Tyrant*. Meaning 'king' to the ancient Greeks, the word 'tyrant' was largely free of the negative connotations we give it today.

It was during the *tyranny* of Pisistratus that Athens rose to become a great military power. A generous patron of the arts and beloved by the Athenian population for the great wisdom of his rule, Pisistratus continued the reforms of Solon until his death in 527 BC.

Unfortunately, wisdom and benevolent rule are not always inherited traits.

In this long evolutionary progress toward democracy, the Tyrant guilty of abusing his powers would often serve as a catalyst in the volatile transition from aristocratic rule to the rise of popular assemblies and the first truly democratic governments.

This is the story of one such violent transition...

Prologue

The shutters had been left open allowing the cooling breezes off the Saronic Gulf to freshen the bedroom. Still dark outside, the restless woman—long awake but still lying abed on her couch—stared up out the small window cut high in the wall searching for a familiar constellation. Propping herself up on one elbow, she craned her long slender neck. Yes, there it was…Cassiopeia. Cassiopeia the queen…left to hang upside down in the heavens as punishment for her notorious vanity.

Helena smiled to herself recalling that day so many years ago when her brother, catching sight of her staring at her own reflection in a bowl of water, had teased her with that wicked name. "Little Cassiopeia…Little Cassiopeia…I fear your vanity will bring about a tragedy!" She could still hear Harmodius' mocking adolescent voice stinging her ears, reducing her to sobbing tears. Tears he'd laughingly wiped away with the edge of his tunic before lifting her up in his strong arms and carrying her outside the farmhouse. Seating her on his lap, he'd pointed up at the clear night sky toward the lop-sided outline of proud Queen Cassiopeia…the woman whose vanity had so offended the gods that they'd sent a monster to destroy her kingdom. Counting off the constellations one by one, he regaled her with the famous tale of the hero Perseus and his magical flying horse Pegasus who, with the decapitated head of the hideous, snake-headed gorgon Medusa, turned the monster to stone and saved the kingdom.

"Well, little sister," he'd crowed, "…at least you're no Medusa!"

Remembering the gentle tease of his voice, Helena felt a painful tug in her chest.

There was a quiet scratch at the door. "Mistress?"

"I'm awake, Rebia…you can come in."

The door opened and Helena was surprised to see Mila, the ancient family nursemaid, come shuffling in carrying a bowl of fresh water in one hand and a small oil lamp in the other. Hopping off her couch, Helena ran over and relieved her of the heavy bronze bowl. Setting it carefully so as not to disturb its contents on the table under the window, she frowned at the old woman. "Dearest Mila, you're far too old to be carrying such heavy things about. Where's that scamp Rebia this morning?"

Mila laughed. "My years may give me the appearance of frailty, little sparrow, but I promise you…there are a good many years left in these spindly arms and legs." She smiled wistfully at her mistress, revealing many more gaps than teeth. "Today being such a special day I wanted to see to your needs myself…" she shrugged her shoulders "…so I told that lazy child that she could sleep in this morning." Moving with a familiar briskness Helena had come to identify with her childhood, Mila scuttled about the room lighting the twisted wicks of several tiny clay lamps set high in narrow niches on each of the four walls. "Now, quickly…" she called over her shoulder "…come over and wash yourself and then we'll see what we can do with that hair." Handing her mistress a clean towel, she placed the lamp on the table and turned her attention to folding the light woolen blanket on the couch.

Leaning over the bowl, Helena dipped the cloth in the water and began sponging the back of her neck. "It *is* a special day, isn't it Mila? I can't stop thinking about my brother…especially all those years growing up together on the farm."

Mila carried the blanket over to an old pine chest that had been in the family since Helena's grandmother was a child. Raising the rusty iron clasp, she carefully placed the blanket inside and then lifted out a small black lacquered case. Peeking inside, she nodded her head approvingly before bringing it over to the table and placing it next to the washbowl. Relieving Helena of the sopping wet rag, she began scrubbing between Helena's shoulder blades. "Harder little sparrow…or you'll never get clean!"

Recalling that very same admonition from her own childhood years—as well as from the nursery the night before where Mila was bathing the twins—Helena couldn't resist a chuckle, "Oh Mila, don't ever change!" Lifting the lid on the black box, she pulled out a polished bronze mirror with an exquisitely carved ivory handle wrought in the shape of a willowy papyrus stem. "Do you remember when he gave me this?" she asked. "He brought it all the way back from Egypt."

Mila pulled a stool over to the table and sat her mistress down. "Such a lovely gift, how could I forget it? Harmodius always had such good taste..."

There was another soft knock at the door. Carefully shielding Helena's nakedness with her own body, Mila called out, "Come."

Diokles peeked his head into the room. Seeing his wife already seated at her dressing table, he smiled and entered. "Up already? But my dear, the ceremony won't be for hours yet."

The nursemaid bowed her head, stepping to one side as he approached and kissed Helena on the cheek. Looking up into his still handsome face, Helena smiled back. "I want everything to be perfect today. Perfect for Harmodius and perfect for Aristogiton."

Diokles ran his fingers through her luxuriant black hair, stopping to gently knead the soft skin at the back of her neck. "Everything will be just fine my darling...you know old Cleisthenes will see to that." Taking note of the still perfect swell of her naked breasts—even after the birth of the twins—he felt a warm stirring in his loincloth. Tilting her chin up, he gazed fondly into her clear almond-colored eyes. "Gods...you're even more beautiful than on the day we married."

Helena sighed. "Ahhh...always such a flatterer. Take care Husband, or you'll bring Aphrodite's jealous wrath down upon us all!" Turning her attention to the black box, she began removing her collection of brushes, makeup jars, and pencils, setting each in a neat line on the table in front of her. "Are you going to the Gymnasium this morning?"

Diokles reached down and picked up his wife's mirror. For a moment his gaze seemed to be lost in the distance as he stood fingering the detailed carving of the handle. "Ah yes...Egypt!" he sighed. "The endlessly flowing Nile...those towering pyramids on the Giza plateau..." the lines on his forehead bunched together as he struggled with a memory "...and that Persian devil...now, what was his name?" Diokles eyes sparked with an unexpected fire. "Ah yes, of course...Baobil...that was it. Baobil the eunuch." He chuckled as he winked at his wife. "Now that, my dear, was an adventure!" Flushing, he carefully placed the mirror in Mila's waiting hands before nodding his head and answering his wife's query. "Yes, my dearest, straight away to the Gymnasium...I was just peeking in on my way out."

Helena furrowed her eyebrows. "You won't be late coming back, will you?"

Bending over, he kissed her affectionately on the back of the neck. "Of course not. I'll be home at least an hour before the Dedication ceremony." Turning to Mila, he grinned at the flustered old crone. "Do your best today, old woman. After all, I want *all* the goddesses—not just Aphrodite—burning with envy as they gaze down on my wife's incomparable beauty from high on Mount Olympus!"

As he turned and left the room, Mila quickly spat three times on the floor, clapped her hands twice, and turned in a circle, all the while fumbling with the mirror and clutching at the terra-cotta amulet hanging around her wrinkled neck. "Ohhh…such impiety…such impiety!" she groaned. "The gods will surely bring the whole house down around us all!"

Helena couldn't help smiling at her superstitious ways. "He's a man, Mila. Men are born to be impious."

Setting the mirror down on the table, Mila waved both her hands in the air in a double-fingered salute meant to ward off the evil eye. Helena used this opportunity to retrieve her heavy, wooden-toothed comb from the box. Handing it over her shoulder to the scandalized serving woman, she picked up the mirror and began examining the current state of her face. "My hair, Mila…we were going to do something with my hair."

"Of course mistress…" Starting at the back, Mila began gently combing out all the tangles and snarls. "May I suggest a single plait down the back?"

"That will be fine, Mila." Eyeing the mirror, Helena still found some satisfaction at the creamy white reflection staring back…spending ones' life indoors did much to keep the complexion pale. Returning the unopened jar of white lead back to the box, she instead took up the precious tiny bronze container of mulberry rouge. Placing a single dot on each cheek, she began rubbing it in with her fingertips, blending until the edges merged with her natural skin tones. "Men…I'll never understand them." She said with a sigh. Peering at her old nursemaid in the mirror she raised a single irritated eyebrow at the old woman, "Why *do* they spend all that time at the Gymnasium, Mila? Do you know?"

Mila rocked back on her feet, her giggles edged with irony at the age-old question. "Do you even need to ask, little sparrow? The old ones go to ogle the young…and the young to ogle back at the old…and all for what?" She crossed her eyes and gritted her teeth as she attacked a particularly stubborn knot. "But you have nothing to worry about, little sparrow…your man has been besotted since the day he first laid eyes on you!"

Helena chuckled to herself. "Yes…yes he has." Diokles had thankfully long outgrown the adolescent crushes so popular with Athenian youth. And as for finding himself another eromenos…well, in all their years together she'd never known him to show even a passing interest in boys.

"Of course, when he was younger your husband certainly had a fine time larking about with that good-looking rascal Tylissus!"

Tylissus...Helena sucked in a breath, her face flushing red as Mila's casual mention of her husband's eromenos brought a profusion of long-suppressed adolescent memories crashing down around her. Sensing her mistress' distress, Mila rested a placating hand on her shoulder. "Forgive me, lady...that was a foolish thing to say. I'm nothing but a silly old woman whose tongue should be cut out and pickled."

Helena drew in a steadying breath before reaching back and patting the old, gnarled hand. "Nonsense, Mila. Tylissus should be remembered as a hero. We should be happy for *all* of them today. This celebration belongs as much to him and Nicias, as it does to Harmodius and Aristogiton." Dipping a finger back in the rouge pot, she spread a thin coating over her lips as she turned the conversation away from uncomfortable memories. "As always, Mila...we have much to be grateful to Lord Cleisthenes for."

Mila bounced her head up and down. "So true, mistress...so very true." She wedged a hairpin in place. "I thank the gods every night before I go to bed that your wily father caught the Archon's eye all those years ago. He's been your family's protector ever since."

Startled, Helena turned around and stared at the jabbering old woman. "What are you saying, Mila? I know that Cleisthenes has always been a good friend to our family...but that doesn't mean he was..." Her eyes narrowed as she scanned the old woman's face for the truth. "Oh, Mila...you're not implying that old Cleisthenes and my father were...no, you can't be serious!"

Mortified, Mila covered her mouth in embarrassment. "I told you," she moaned, "...it should be cut out and pickled!"

Laughing, Helena reached over and pulled her hands away from her mouth. "Tell me, you silly old goose...I want to know everything! Father and Cleisthenes were *lovers*?"

Mila bobbed her head from side to side, holding her stomach as she cackled. "Oh, mistress...if you could have seen them in their youth! Such a handsome couple! Of course, this was many years before your father met your beautiful mother. Even then, that young Cleisthenes was quite the catch—rich, powerful...already a leader in the Assembly. At the gymnasium the older boys used to line up to try and catch his eye. And it was there one day that he saw your father wrestling in the palaestra..."

"The gymnasium...always the gymnasium." Helena sighed.

Licking her dry, cracked lips, Mila grinned at her charge. "Men will be men, my dear…and your father was no different than all the rest." Pulling up a stool alongside her mistress, Mila continued her story. "Even in his youth, Cimon was a proud man…one who'd never make the first move." She winked slyly at Helena, "You know how your father could be!" The old nursemaid leaned forward and rested her elbows on her knees. "With these kinds of relationships it's usually the *erastes*, the older boy, who acts as the aggressor. But even though the younger Cleisthenes followed him around like a love-sick puppy, our Cimon wouldn't believe a boy of such high family and standing could be interested in a mere landowner's son."

"What happened next?" Helena was intrigued. No one had ever talked to her this way about her father's youth before.

"Well, my dear…soon the gifts and love poems began arriving at your grandfather's door. Night and day…week after week…gold rings, baskets of fresh fruit, even a heavily embroidered *himation* from Corinth. Finally, your grandfather had had enough and, taking his son aside, he told the stubborn Cimon that all this romantic foolishness must come to an end. The very next day Cimon went to the gymnasium and, cornering the gawking Cleisthenes, demanded an end to it all." Mila leaned forward and lowered her voice to a whisper. "And the way I heard it from one who was there and actually saw it happen…this little upstart told your father that he would only agree to stop bothering him if Cimon would consent to receiving a single kiss!"

"Well?" prodded the impatient Helena. "What did Father do?"

"He agreed of course. One kiss and…"

"And?"

Mila sat back on her stool, her hands slapping her knees as she cackled. "And they were inseparable for the next four years!"

With a loud 'harrumph' Helena turned back to the makeup case sitting on her dressing table. "I don't believe it, not a single word! If it's true, why have I never heard this story before?"

Mila waggled the comb at her mistress. "Ah, men! How they love to keep their secrets." She stood up and slowly stretched the kinks out of her back before returning her industrious fingers to the job of plaiting her mistress' hair. "And I'll tell you this, my sparrow. Cimon loved his eromenos so much that, when it came time for him to marry, rather than distress the poor love-struck boy, your father waited a full year until Cleisthenes had settled on a wife for himself, before marrying your mother."

Helena held the mirror up to her eyes, carefully searching for any tiny crows feet along the edges. "Well...perhaps there's some truth in what you say. That would certainly explain why the great Cleisthenes has always acted like a second father to Harmodius and me."

"Oh it's true, all right...every word." The old nursemaid tapped the top of her mistress' head with the comb. "You don't think Mila would ever tell tales to her little sparrow?"

Helena ignored the question as she set about applying a whisper of charcoal to her eyebrows. Frowning back at her reflection, she sighed wistfully. "Mila, you've lived for so many, many years...in all that time have you ever found yourself wishing you were born a man?"

Mila paused in her work. "What a silly question, sparrow. The gods fashion each of us from the same clay...men and women alike. Why then should I not be satisfied with my lot?"

Helena crooked her head to one side. "It's not that I'm unhappy with my lot, Mila. It's just that...well, sometimes I grow jealous of this bond men share with one another...especially the erastes and eromenos—the young lover and his beloved. While we women are confined to the household giving birth and raising children, men have the freedom to walk about the world in the company of whomever they please. And that's not all. You know as well as I that there's a special bond between fathers and sons...something that doesn't exist between any Athenian and his daughter. Why, I've see it in my own husband's eyes when he looks at our young Hylas."

Now it was Mila's turn to frown. "You are being foolish Helena, all fathers love their daughters. They create a special place in their hearts whenever fortune send a daughter along...just as Cimon did when you were born."

Helena responded with a raised eyebrow. "My brother used to tease me about father wearing mourning on the day that I was born!"

"Oh, that Harmodius!" Mila shook her head fondly, her eyes filling with salty tears at the memory of Helena's too handsome, black-haired scamp of a brother. "He could be such a rascal when he was young!" The old woman tightened her twisting as she reached the end of the plait. "He was pulling your leg, little sparrow. Pisistratus, our beloved tyrant, had just died. Everyone in Athens...in all of *Attica* in fact, was dressed in mourning on the day you were born!"

"I know, I know...I've heard that story a thousand times before." Helena held the mirror high up over her head for a final inspection of Mila's tidy handiwork. "Even so…I'll bet things were quite a bit different on the day when my dear brother was born!"

Smiling sadly at the back of her mistress' head, old Mila was almost overcome as bittersweet memories of that long ago happy day came flooding back. "The day our Harmodius was born." She smiled. "Yes, little sparrow…now that was a day I'll never forget!"

CHAPTER 1

The next-door neighbor's dog barking at two morning larks scuffling over a crust of bread out in the street woke Cimon with a start. The sun hadn't quit risen over the hills yet and the early morning chill caused him to reach out for his wife's naked shoulder. The other side of their bed was empty. Suddenly wide-awake, he propped himself up on one elbow and whispered into the dark, "Philippia...is it time?"

A sound of muffled groaning came from the far corner of the room where Cimon's wife was crouched over a chamber pot. "Yes, Cimon...my water's come. I think we should send for the midwife."

Cimon jumped up off the wool-stuffed mattress and, stumbling through the dark, reached for the door. Flinging it open, he called out to his sleeping manservant, "Wake up Platon...it's time! Bring fresh water from the kitchen and the lamps, bring all the lamps...and send Mila for the midwife."

There was a rustling noise across the courtyard followed by a sleepy response, "Right away, Master...right away."

Cimon left the door ajar and returned to his squatting wife. "Does everything feel alright?" he asked nervously. This was their first child and the two innocents were more than a little afraid of the ordeal ahead. Kneeling next to her, he wiped the sweaty hair off Philippia's brow with the edge of his hand.

Her breath came hissing from between her lips as a contraction rippled through her belly. "It's fine, my darling. But go now...you shouldn't be in here...this is women's work."

Cimon bit his lip. He didn't want to risk bringing calamity down upon the entire household by intruding on the birthing ritual...but he cringed at the thought of leaving his wife squatting here all alone in the dark on the floor of their bedroom. "Let me at least stay until Mila comes back with the midwife." He couldn't see her response, but a moment later felt the warmth of her lips brushing against his cheek.

"A few minutes more, Husband...I'm sure the goddess won't mind."

❧   ❧   ❧

The sun was already nearing the top of the ancient olive tree growing in the center of the family's private inner courtyard when Cleisthenes' appeared at his old erastes' house. Seeing the look of sheer panic in his old friend's eyes as a harried serving woman came bustling from the bedroom with a jug of soiled water to empty out into the street, he took Cimon by the arm and led him forcefully toward the front door. "Come now, my brave 'father-to-be', enough of this pacing. You need a drink!"

As they strolled to a nearby tavern, Cleisthenes tried not to smile at poor Cimon's obvious preoccupation. "I'm sure all will go well..." the agitated father kept mumbling under his breath, "I'm sure of it! My wife is young and strong, there's been no bleeding, we've made all the proper sacrifices...and today couldn't be a more propitious birthing day."

Cleisthenes raised an eyebrow. "Propitious...why yes, I suppose so. Our great overlord Pisistratus will be honored to hear that your wife has chosen to give birth during his great Festival of Dionysus!"

Ignoring Cleisthenes' sarcasm, Cimon vigorously nodded his head. "Yes...the god Dionysus. If all goes well with the birth I shall go off to the theater district first thing tomorrow morning and sacrifice a ewe on the Vine God's altar."

Cleisthenes laughed as he wrapped a muscular arm around his former lover's shoulder. "And I shall be there at your side sacrificing a pair of spotless doves in honor of your new son!"

"A son!" Stopped dead in his tracks, Cimon turned to stare into the sea green eyes of the most pleasant folly of his youth. "Do you really think it will be a son?"

Clapping him on the shoulder with a coarse laugh, Cleisthenes stealthily reached under Cimon's tunic. Before his friend could squirm away, he cupped the two low hanging balls in the palm of his hand and crowed: "From this vigorous duo?" He gave them a playful squeeze. "How could it be anything *but* a strapping boy?"

The sun was edging its way toward the mountains in the west when the two men, a bit worse for an afternoon drinking, stumbled back up the street to find Mila waiting, her arms crossed in mock irritation, on the front stoop. When she saw her master, her eyes brightened and she ran forward to meet him.

"He's here, young master…he's here!"

"Who's here, Mila?" Cimon shook his head, trying vainly to clear away some of the purple haze that accompanied too many cups of unwatered wine. "Has someone come to see me?"

"Men!" Planting her fists on her hips, Mila grumbled in exasperation as she nodded her old woman's head. "Yes, Master…someone's here to see you. *It's your new son who's here, that's who!*" She grabbed him by the arm and pulled him straight into the house leaving Cleisthenes to follow behind like an overly excited puppy dog. As they made their way through the courtyard, Cimon was greeted with shouts of joyous felicitation as the household servants bustled all around him. The sight of the open bedroom door looming ahead brought a sudden—but welcome—sobriety to his cloudy mind. Entering the room, he waited for his eyes to adjust as the niche lamps scattered about the room's walls were lit against the encroaching twilight. His wife—looking freshly scrubbed, but exhausted—was laying on their bed…a tiny bundle wrapped in fleecy sheepskin held close to her breast.

As her husband slowly approached, Philippia looked up and smiled, her face glowing with an almost mystical radiance. Without a word, she handed him the bundle. Holding the child in his arms, Cimon carefully unwrapped the sheepskin and revealed the tiny body sleeping soundly inside. At the sight of the miniature penis, Cimon felt his heart skip a beat. "A son…" he whispered, his eyes aglow with pride. "You have given me a son."

Behind him, the midwife quietly cleared her throat. Carefully handing the baby back to his wife, Cimon turned to find the old woman standing with a bundle of bloody rags, sheets and cloths in her arms. With the smug satisfaction of a job well done, she shared his pride as she smiled at him. "Congratulations, Lord. Your honored firstborn is a son." Then, with the slightest bow of her head, she held out the filthy bundle. "But remember…your house has been polluted by the birth. To appease the goddess, you must take these things straight away to the Temple of Artemis and dedicate them at her shrine."

Solemnly nodding his head, Cimon hoisted the bundle under one arm, even as he untied the small purse at his belt and handed it over to the old crone. "With the thanks of my entire household for this felicitous treasure you've delivered here today." Without another word, the midwife accepted his gift, bowing low to Cimon and his wife, and quietly left the room.

Turning back to his wife, he smiled down at her with grateful eyes. "I won't be gone long, dearest wife. To the temple and back with Hermes winged shoes to speed my way!" He reached down, squeezed her hand with affection and was gone.

Crossing the courtyard, he found his old *eromenos* waiting patiently for him near the olive tree. "I was right then?" Cleisthenes eagerly asked. "It is a boy?"

Cimon nodded, smirking at him with a father's special pride.

Reaching over his head, Cleisthenes snapped off a leafy olive branch. "To hang over your front door so that everyone in Athens will know that you have been blessed with a son!"

Arm in arm, the two men left the house—one making his brisk way to the Temple of Artemis, there to appease a jealous 'virgin goddess' averse to all things sexual between man and woman by offering up the remnants of his wife's bloody labor…the other to spread the happy word of his beloved Cimon's good fortune throughout the city.

❦   ❦   ❦

The weeks following Harmodius' birth were filled with celebrations and ceremonies…most of them strictly dictated by centuries-old Attic tradition.

Five days after consecrating the boy's birth linens at the Temple of Artemis, Cimon welcomed his closest friends and family members into the central courtyard of his home to witness the *Amphidromia*—the ceremony that would introduce his infant son to the family's household gods. Lifting the wriggling boy in his arms, he carried him from room to room, finally ending in the alcove adjoining the kitchen where the family's hearth was always kept aflame. Invoking the goddess Hestia, patroness of hearth and family, Cimon lifted the boy high over his head and ran around the hearth three times. Then, laying the child on the dirt floor in front of the fire, he stood aside as relatives and friends stepped forward to place tiny charms and votive offerings all around the bawling child. It was hoped that these prayers and tokens from family, friends and neighbors would ward off the evil eye and bring the boy a long life of good fortune. Solemnly raising his arms in a silent appeal for the goddess' protection and favor for his son, Cimon picked up the offerings and one by one tossed them into the blazing flames. Retrieving the squalling infant from the floor, he kissed him tenderly on the forehead and returned him to his wife's waiting arms. With a boisterous clap of his hands, he led his guests back into the open courtyard where a great feast had been laid out.

Five days following the ceremony of the Amphidromia, Cimon—with the ever-enthusiastic Cleisthenes tagging along as primary witness—carried his son up the steep hill of the Acropolis to the enclosed precinct of the ancient Temple of Athena where the boy's naming ceremony took place. It was there, following another Greek tradition, that Cimon named this child, his first-born son, after the boy's grandfather—Harmodius.

The infant Harmodius grew into a robust and healthy toddler, his sparkling brown eyes a living reflection of the continued prosperity enjoyed by both family and city-state during these final, golden years of the tyrant Pisistratus' rule. While some in Athens chaffed under the autocratic nature of the Pisis-trade regime, few could deny the wealth and stability twenty years of peace had brought to the thriving city. Even Cleisthenes, whose aristocratic family had maintained a long time grudge against the Pisistrades, looked the other way when the aging tyrant sought to appoint his two young sons—Hippias and Hipparchus—as his joint heirs-apparent.

Shortly before Harmodius' third birthday, his father decided that the boy, having successfully survived the most dangerous years of early childhood, was now ready to be enrolled in the family's *phratry* or clan. Each autumn during the final weeks of *Pyanopsion*, life in Athens came to a halt as citizens prepared to celebrate the Festival of Fatherhood—*Apaturia*. And this year's Apaturia was to be a special one. In addition to the usual three days of ceremonies and sacrifices to Zeus the protector of the phratries, followed by the enrolling of children and newly married wives into their respective clans, the Archons had decided to honor the Tyrant Pisistratus with a new title—"Father of the City". Great feasts were planned and, even though the Festival of Dionysus was still several months away, actors were summoned from all over Greece to perform their comedies and tragedies in the newly completed theater built into the side of the Acropolis—a gift from Pisistratus to his beloved city.

"Can you say *Gephyrai*, little one? Geph—ear—aye?"

The little boy holding tightly to his father's hand as they followed the bustling crowd of morning shoppers slowly making their way toward the Dipylon gate, smiled shyly and stuttered, "Geffer...geffffer."

"That's right...very good Harmodius, that was very close. Try it again...Geph—ear—aye," each syllable enunciated with the polished skill of a professional orator.

Harmodius' forehead crinkled in concentration until he forced out an approximation of the word: "Gef—errr—RAY!" The last syllable shouted with all the enthusiasm of a surprise victor in Zeus' sacred games at Olympia.

Cimon, beaming with pride, reached down and swept the excited child up into his arms. "Perfect!" he laughed. "Perfect! Gephyrai...and that's the name of our family's clan." They passed into the shade under one of the two great arches of the old city gate and came out on the other side in an area known to one and all as the Potter's Quarter. "One day very soon *you* shall be a member of the Gephyrai clan...just like your mother and I." He tweaked his son playfully on the nose before setting him back down on the ground. "Now come along my little man...I promised your mother we'd be home before the noon meal and we have some important shopping to take care of before that."

The night before, as Cimon and Philippia, lay side by side on their narrow bed, his wife had drawn close and tickled his ear with the tip of her tongue. "Dearest husband," she teased, "I have happy news for you...I think I'm with child again." The frenzied joy of their lovemaking that night could be heard all the way across to the servant's quarters. Afterwards, exhausted but still too excited to sleep, Philippia had leaned across her husband's chest and whispered, "I must take an offering to the Temple of Demeter...perhaps a small statue of her daughter Persephone? Yes...that might please the goddess."

Cimon, hearing the ageless wisdom behind her words (after all, at times like this it certainly couldn't hurt to show proper appreciation to the Goddess of Fertility), dutifully nodded his head. "First thing in the morning I'll take our little scamp out for a walk to the Dipylon...and we'll see if we can't find something worthy of Demeter."

❦   ❦   ❦

The district just outside the Dipylon Gate was filled with makeshift stalls crowded in between the more permanent dwellings—houses in the back and shop fronts facing the street. As they strolled along, Harmodius kept rushing ahead of his father, the whole time jabbering away like a little monkey as he pointed at the different craftsmen and their hard-working slaves bent almost double over the whirling pottery wheels and heavy mortar stones. One shop specialized in ornately carved grave markers, while the next in brightly painted terra-cotta urns; here a sculptor sat chiseling a marble block into the graceful head of Apollo, while just across the way a slave, sitting in the shade of an old, torn awning, held his sharp knife over the side of a large commemorative *krater* and carefully incised the beard of a Trojan warrior.

Cimon and Harmodius stopped for a few minutes, watching this man as he completed the final touch up work on this magnificent masterpiece. The earthenware krater was nearly three feet tall with two enormous, flamboyantly curling handles attached to the top rim. Like most Athenian pieces of the period, the many decorative figures on the body had been painted on with a special clay—one that, after firing in the kiln, left them black against the oxidized red of the background. Detail work, such as the beard on this warrior, was completed by incising the final creation with a sharp knife all the way down to the red clay underneath.

"Hector?" inquired Cimon.

The slave looked up with a pleased smile. "No, lord…this one here is Prince Paris…he of the roving eye. And the lady Helena is here on the reverse." He flipped the krater around with a practiced hand and revealed the finished beauty on the other side.

Cimon smiled, "Ah…a wedding gift then?"

The artisan nodded his head. "Yes, noble lord."

Cimon couldn't help sighing at her beauty as he examined the legendary Helena of Troy stepping naked from her bath. "Excellent work…a true artist."

The slave bowed his head. "Thank you, gracious lord."

Cimon could sense that Harmodius was beginning to fidget so, picking him up in his arms, they continued on their ramble. A mere two stalls down from the krater artist, Cimon found just what he'd come looking for. Lined up on several wood plank shelves were a number of clay figurines…some left the natural dun color of the rich Attic soil, while others were brightly painted to mimic the colors of the living world. As Cimon and his son stood perusing his inventory, the stall keeper—his hands dripping with wet clay—eagerly stepped forward.

"Can I be of assistance, good sir?"

Cimon slowly let his head nod as his eyes carefully scanned the rows of merchandise. "I'm looking for a votive offering…a Persephone, if you have one."

"Ahh…I have just the thing!" The merchant quickly wiped his hands on his clay-splattered apron before leaning past Cimon and snatching a beautifully decorated figurine off the back shelf. "Persephone…done in the Cretan style. You see…she's even holding a half-eaten pomegranate in her hand." He passed the diminutive goddess over to Cimon who, turning it over and over in his hands, examined it for flaws.

The long-haired figurine was painted wearing a blue and green flounced skirt cinched tight at the waist, her green blouse left open in the Cretan style to emphasize the fertility of her two bountiful breasts. One hand held out a sheaf of wheat, symbol of her goddess-mother Demeter of the Harvest…in the other she held the fateful piece of half-eaten fruit that had doomed her to spend half of each year with the dark god Hades in his Shadow Kingdom.

"She's perfect…" said Cimon with a note of satisfaction in his voice, "this one will do just fine!" Handing the miniature Persephone back to the merchant, Cimon reached inside the bag of coins tied to his belt.

☙   ☙   ☙

As the two shoppers were turning to leave, Harmodius tugged nervously at the edge of his father's chiton. "Give, Papa…please?" he asked, covetously holding his hand out and eyeing the pretty figurine tucked under Cimon's arm.

Cimon raised a skeptical eyebrow. "Are you sure you want to carry her, Harmodius? If you drop her or break her in any way…the gods will be very angry with you." He got down on one knee and looked his son in the eye. "And not just you, my little One…they might turn that unfortunate anger on your unborn brother or sister as well!"

Even though Harmodius' eyes grew round as saucers, he continued holding out his grasping fingers and nodding his head. "Big boy," he said, proudly thumping his hand against his chest, "Carry pretty thing home…" he held out his hands and waited.

Just then, a noisy disturbance a few stalls down the way caught Cimon's attention. Without giving it another thought, he passed the statuette over to his son, picked him up in one arm, and wandered over to see what all the commotion was about.

A group of young men barely out of their teens and each wearing the expensively dyed himation of an aristocrat draped over chitons cut fashionably above the knee were crowding around the stall of the krater artist. One of them, the ringleader so it seemed, had the slave by the frayed collar of his tunic and was screaming in his face. Cimon could see that the poor man, his face white as marble and his eyes staring desolately at the ground in front of him as he stood pressing his beautiful masterwork protectively against his side, was nearly speechless with terror.

"Where's my cow head, you ass...my father's cup? Cephus promised me that it would be ready today." He punctuated every other word with a bone-rattling shake. "The Festival of Fatherhood is next week and I won't have anything to give him!"

"I...I'm sorry great lord...my master was taken ill today and is resting at home. I...I know nothing of any such cup. Perhaps if you could describe it, I might..."

The young man's fist suddenly shot forward striking the slave on the side of his face and knocking him to the ground. A woman standing behind Cimon gasped even as one of the man's companions stepped forward and put a restraining hand on the aggressor's arm. "Easy brother...easy." The cautious man glanced warily over his shoulder at the growing crowd. "No need to cause a scene with this...this *nothing*." He spit contemptuously on the ground missing the slave by an inch.

The angry man shook off his brother's hand. "That's easy for you to say, Hippias...you already have a gift for Father." To emphasize his angry disappointment, he savagely kicked out at the magnificent krater still clutched protectively in the fallen slave's arm and shattered it into a hundred pieces.

Furious at this man's callous disregard for those of a lower station than himself, Cimon set his son down on the ground behind him and stepped forward. "Was that really necessary?" He reached past the two arguing brothers and helped the horrified slave to his feet. Still holding the broken handle of the wedding krater in his hand, the poor man looked devastated. "This man is not the cause of your troubles." Stepping between the slave and his attacker, Cimon smiled coldly at the two men. "If you wish recourse for your missing cup, perhaps you would have better luck seeking out the merchant from whom you originally ordered it...this man's master."

The aggressor's nostrils flared at the disapproval in Cimon's voice, but before he could react, his brother Hippias once again placed a cautionary hand on his arm. "This good citizen is correct, Hipparchus..." his smile was forced as he nodded in the slave's direction, "...we have erred here today. In our overly hasty desire to bring some small pleasure to a most revered father, we have violated the public's decency. And..." he turned a withering glance in Cimon's direction "...as this good citizen suggests, perhaps it would be best to go now and seek out the merchant at his home...I'm sure we'll find your missing cup waiting there." With a showy gesture, he took a handful of silver coins out of a leather purse strapped to his waist and dropped them in the dirt at the slave's feet. "For your trouble...slave."

Without another word he took his brother's arm, roughly pulling him away from the scene and, followed closely by their companions, they disappeared into the crowd...but not before the one called Hipparchus peered back over his shoulder to gave Cimon a particularly icy glare.

His mouth suddenly dry, Cimon had the unsettling feeling that he'd just been marked for some future reckoning. As the crowd around him disbursed, Cimon was left to stare after the two men in appalled disbelief. "Hippias and Hipparchus..." he thought, "...the two sons of our beloved Pisistratus...and the younger no better than a common thug." Bending over, he retrieved the scattered coins from the dirt and handed them to the slave with a disgusted shake of his head. "I'm sorry...your krater was a truly beautiful work of art." The poor man, his hands shaking, rubbed at the tears running down both cheeks as he gazed forlornly down at the shattered remnants of more than a month's labor. Little Harmodius, still standing obediently off to the side where Cimon had left him, came running over to take his father's hand. Sweeping him up with his muscular arms, Cimon turned to leave. "Come little one, I'm afraid our noon meal will be growing cold."

They hadn't gone very far when the bedraggled slave suddenly came running up behind them. "Please, kind sirs...accept my thanks." He pressed something into Cimon's hand. "I have nothing to give but my labor...perhaps you will find some pleasure in this small token?" With that, he bowed low and vanished back into the crowd. Cimon looked down and found a single large shard of the broken krater lying in the palm of his hand. Turning it over, he smiled to himself at the still undamaged representation of fair Helena of Troy stepping naked from her bath.

Holding it up for his son to see, Cimon laughed. "Have I ever told you the tale of the most notorious woman the world has ever known…a beauty so seductive that two great nations went to war over her?"

Shifting Harmodius to a more comfortable position against his shoulder, the two shoppers headed back up the lane toward the Dipylon Gate and home.

A week later, during the Festival of Apaturia, Harmodius was duly enrolled in the Gephyrai Clan. Afterwards, a small group of close friends gathered at Cleisthenes' villa to celebrate this all-important step on the young boy's road to full manhood and citizenship in the Greek world. That very same night, a great feast was held high on the Acropolis to honor Pisistratus as 'Father of the City'. Among the many fine gifts graciously received from the invited well-wishers, sycophants, and family members was an exquisite *rhyton*—a painted terra-cotta drinking cup…this one in the shape of a calf's head with an elegant golden hoop hanging from each ear.

Six months later, the 'Father of the City' died peacefully in his sleep.

Hoping to prolong the many years of prosperity that Attica had enjoyed under the rule of her benign tyrant, the archons met with the other city elders and together decided to honor Pisistratus' final wish. Turning to the eldest son Hippias, they begged him to assume the heavy mantle of authority worn for so many years by his famous father. Appointing his younger brother Hipparchus as co-tyrant, the two men declared a yearlong period of mourning for the entire city. Following a magnificent state funeral for the 'Tyrant of Athens', Hippias and Hipparchus wasted little time before polluting public policy with their own high-handed personalities. While continuing to adhere to the principal elements of Pisistratus' statecraft, subtle—but disturbing—differences between father and sons soon began to appear.

Cimon took one final look around the room and, satisfied that everything was safely packed away, went off in search of his wife. He found her resting in the courtyard under the olive tree, the newborn baby nursing at her breast while little Harmodius sat cross-legged at her feet playing a game of *knucklebones* with old Mila.

"Are you off then?" she asked.

He smiled and nodded his head. "Yes…but I'll be back early. I want us to make an early start in the morning." He settled down on the bench next to her for a moment, watching in amazement as the most beautiful child in the world sucked hungrily away at her rosy nipple. "She is truly something, this daughter of ours…and by far and away the most beautiful…"

Mila looked up from her game and quickly made the sign to ward off the evil eye. "Be careful, good master…the gods might be listening!" she whispered.

Cimon laughed. "Don't worry, Mila. I think the gods have their hands more than full keeping a watchful eye on our Hippias and Hipparchus!"

Philippia frowned. "Oh husband, I wish you wouldn't say such things."

"Sorry, my dearest." He leaned over and playfully kissed her neck. "But whenever I see you nursing our precious little Helena, I can't help but fall under the spell of her beauty and…" he grinned "…just like poor besotted Paris of old, all common sense flies straight out the window."

He teasingly nudged Harmodius with the tip of his sandal. "This little scamp was right to insist that we name her after that infamous Trojan hussy!" He smiled, remembering back to that sunny day three short months ago when, after a long and difficult labor, Philippia finally gave birth to this perfect girl-child. Harmodius, after taking one look at the little beauty, had run straight to his room and retrieved the shard of pottery bearing the naked Helena painted on one side from its special hiding place. Ever since hearing the tale of the Trojan War on that walk home from the Potter's Quarter, Harmodius had been obsessed with the story—Paris and Helena, Menelaus and Agamemnon, Achilles and Patroclus…heroic warriors and passionate lovers were all he talked about. And right then and there, standing over his newborn sister's cradle, he had insisted that she bear the name of the pretty lady in the picture.

Yielding to his son's prescience, the new addition to the family—who by rights should have been named Xanthippe after an old widowed sister of Cimon's father—found herself instead named after the most infamous beauty of all time…Helena of Troy.

Smiling to himself as the pleasant memory faded away, Cimon kissed his wife's forehead, affectionately brushed a fingertip along the downy soft cheek of his little daughter, and stood up. "Well, I mustn't keep Cleisthenes waiting." Leaning over, he ruffled Harmodius' thick black hair. "Keep a good watch over the house while I'm gone tonight, my little Achilles."

⚜   ⚜   ⚜

The conversation at Cleisthenes' dinner party—a weekly ritual of friendship since long before the two men had parted as lovers—was in danger of devolving into a one-man tirade against the city's worsening political situation. Cimon, reclining on his feasting couch, appeared to listen politely...but in truth, his mind was drifting. From time to time he leaned forward on one elbow and helped himself to a carrot or a radish or a piece of honeyed flat bread from the little table set in front of him...all the while keeping his eyes fixed on the increasingly incensed features of his beloved 'erastes'.

"I tell you, the news spread like wildfire! It was the talk of the gymnasium this morning, dammit! First Iphicrates and now, of all people, poor Cleophan!"

Cimon's ears pricked to attention. "What about Cleophan?"

Cleisthenes' eyes went wide as he popped a salted sardine into his mouth and swallowed it down in one gulp. Swinging his hairy legs around the edge of his couch, he sat up and leaned toward Cimon. "You haven't heard the news then?"

Cimon, calmly dipping his fingers into a small silver washbowl and wiping them on a clean towel, shook his head.

"Well," Cleisthenes suddenly lowered his voice so the servants standing near the open doorway wouldn't hear. "You must have heard that old Cleophan got into it with Hipparchus over next year's *Plynteria*. The two had a very public argument right there in the Assembly when Cleophan sought to reject Hipparchus' outrageous plan to hold public theatrical performances during the celebration of the cleaning of Athena's temples."

Cimon sat up, reflexively adjusting his himation as he did. "You must be joking! What ceremony is more solemn than the Plynteria? The city's goddess, already distracted by the ceremonial cleansing of her temples, will most certainly have her eyes turned away from the city's protection. Why would anyone want to draw the attention of harmful spirits and the like by holding theatrical performances at such a precarious time?"

Cleisthenes shook his head. "It's unheard of, I know!"

"You mentioned Iphicrates. Don't tell me our co-tyrants have taken it upon themselves to once again replace..."

Cleisthenes cut him off with an angry wave of his hand. "It's worse than Iphicrates. Not only was Cleophan replaced...this morning, Hippias' personal guard showed up at Cleophan's front door. He was put on a donkey and escorted right out the city gates…exiled from Athens for two years!"

Cimon jumped up off his couch, his fists clenched in anger. "That's outrageous! Cleophan is a model citizen…an excellent administrator. Why, the old man's been on the council for as long as anyone can remember. It's preposterous! They can't just toss him out on his ear like that…"

"Oh, but they can…and they have." Cleisthenes shook his head. "These days, few in the city are willing to speak up against the high and mighty 'Sons of Pisistratus.'"

Cimon took a deep breath, wringing his hands as he fought to bring his anger under control. "So, my friend, tell me the rest of the news…who is it that's been appointed to take over poor Cleophan's duties? Another sycophantic pup I suppose?"

"Not this time…" Cleisthenes reached down and helped himself to a handful of dried figs from Cimon's table. "It appears that Cleophan's position will remain vacant for the time being." He rolled his eyes in exasperation. "Hipparchus has graciously taken it upon himself to personally supervise this year's Plynteria."

With a resigned sigh the two men sat back down, this time side by side on one of the couches. Cleisthenes tossed a fig over to Cimon, "Dark times, are they not my friend?" he muttered before popping one into his own mouth and chewing half-heartedly on the sticky sweet treat.

Cimon gazed down at his hands for a moment, nervously gathering his uneasy thoughts together. "I have some news of my own, Cleisthenes. First thing tomorrow morning I'm taking my family off to Araphen…we're moving out to the farm."

"What? You're not serious!" Cimon could tell from the hurt expression on his friend's face that he'd been taken by complete surprise. "I'll grant you things are bad in Athens…but they're not *that* bad."

Cimon stood up and walked over to the expansive window overlooking the *agora* and its long colonnaded *stoa* far below. He watched in silence as the sun disappeared behind the low hills in the west before clearing his throat and offering up an explanation. "There was an incident, Cleisthenes…something that happened a few months back…something I never told you about." With a sigh, he turned back to his oldest friend. "At the time, I thought it was a little thing…but now…" he stopped, chewing thoughtfully on his lower lip, "well, the truth is…I fear I may have inadvertently put my family in danger."

Rejoining Cleisthenes on the couch, he recounted the story of the day he and Harmodius had gone to the Potter's Quarter in search of an offering for the goddess Demeter…and of the bitter words he'd crossed with the brutish sons of Pisistratus.

❈   ❈   ❈

"Unfortunately, I didn't realize who they were until it was too late…and even then, my outrage was so great that I suspect I would have given it little thought. I mean really, the two sons of our benevolent Tyrant…" he grunted, "…and totally lacking in any sense of decency. Even so, I assumed they would be no more above the law than any other citizen of Athens." Turning to his friend, Cimon's expression was grim. "But that look…the one Hipparchus gave me just before disappearing into the crowd." He raised his eyebrows in alarm. "I'm sure of it now, the man was marking me for later."

Cleisthenes' growing concern that his beloved Cimon and family might be leaving Athens for good obscured his true feeling of distress at this disturbing news. "But, this was nothing, Cimon…a mere incident…and one quickly forgotten. I'm sure that if you ran into him today that hotheaded young popinjay wouldn't even recognize you."

Cimon smiled sadly even as he shook his head. "And so I myself had hoped. But just last week, stopping in at the gymnasium for a quick massage, I happened to pass by Hipparchus exercising with a group of his cronies in the wrestling pit. As he came up for his second wind, I saw one of his friends nudge him with an elbow and point off in my direction. Even as the light of recognition sparked in those cold eyes I felt an icy chill on the back of my neck."

Cleisthenes jumped up. "Did he say anything? Did he call you over?"

Cimon shook his head. "No…he just smiled at me. Smiled…and then turned his attention back to his wrestling partner. Assuming the position, he placed his hands on his opponent's shoulders and whispered something in the big brute's ear before turning and nodding his head in my direction." Cimon snapped his fingers. "Just like that…I felt myself marked all over again."

Cleisthenes pounded his fists on the edge of the couch. "You're right, of course…this *is* very bad news. Why, even now that bastard could be arranging for…for an 'accident' to happen to you. In truth, you should have left the city at once." He stood up, his face noticeably paler in the flickering lamplight, and began pacing in front of the open window. "You're a brave man, Cimon…brave, but sometimes a bit foolish. I cannot believe you walked all the way up here tonight without so much as an escort by your side!" With that, he shouted out for his servants. "Don't worry, my old friend…I'll have my man follow you home tonight. And in the morning I'll send two of my best fighters to accompany you and your family all the way to Araphen."

Before the two men parted, Cleisthenes promised monthly reports by way of passing merchants as the political situation developed in Athens.

The two men grasped arms in a tight bear hug. "Take car of the little ones…and don't let them forget me!" Cleisthenes had tears in his voice.

Kissing his old eromenos on each cheek, Cimon whispered in his ear. "I shall miss you…light of my distant youth."

CHAPTER 2

"Son of warlike Peleus, you must hear this terrible
    news—something
I wish weren't so—Patroclus lies dead. Men are now fighting over
    the body.
He's stripped. Hector with his gleaming helmet has the armor."

Ambling along the old dirt road overlooking the sparkling blue waters of the Gulf of Petalion, Harmodius always paced his oration practice by marking it with the steady rhythm of his ambling gait as he slowly made his way home from morning classes at the village school. Had he been attending a real academy in Athens, a slave called a paidagogus—a man whose sole job was to keep an eye on his young master during the day—would have followed behind, prodding him along all the way home. But rural life in the sparsely populated countryside near Araphen was a different matter altogether. Slaves and servants couldn't be spared for such non-productive tasks when there was a large farm and household to run. So each day young Harmodius made the long walk to and from the Araphen's modest school on his own.

Stopping for a moment, Harmodius set his wax covered slate and wooden stylus on the ground and gathered up a handful of egg-sized pebbles. Wielding them with a powerful arm that belied his seven years, he punctuated each line of the Iliad's next stanza by sailing the stones off the cliff one by one, watching with delight as each one fell out into the crystal clear waters far below.

"A black cloud of grief swallowed up Achilles.
Scooping up soot and dirt with both hands, he poured it
on his head, disfiguring his handsome face,
covering his sweet smelling tunic with black ash."

When he was sure these two couplets were fixed in his head, he picked up one last rock and threw it as hard as he could out over the curling waves. With a sigh of regret he retrieved his writing tools from the dirt and resumed his meandering ramble home. Turning inland, a mile from the shore he came to the narrow lane that led up a low rocky hill to the family's residence. All of a sudden, Harmodius found his feet having to dodge around fresh, smelly, insect covered donkey turds. "Hmm," he thought as he brushed an annoying fly away from his face "…visitors."

As he entered the spacious front yard of the main house, he saw a line of pack mules tethered in the shade of the oak trees that peppered the property. A beleaguered house slave was carrying a leather bucket of water from one thirsty animal to the next, the impatient ones at the rear all the while braying irritably for their turn.

Little Helena, sitting cross-legged on the porch and playing with one of her rag dolls, dropped the toy on the ground and came running as her adored older brother called out: "Who's come for a visit, 'little turtle-face'?"

About to leap into his arms, the precocious five year old stopped short and frowned up at her grinning brother. "Don't call me that!" she cried with a sour pout on her face and a stubborn stamp of her foot. "I'm *not* an ugly turtle-face…"

Harmodius, tossing his school bundle to the ground, snatched his sister up by the arms and lifted her high over his head. "Who said anything about *ugly*? Turtles aren't ugly, sweetling…they're the handsomest of Poseidon's creatures! And so favored by the great Sea Lord that he allows them to dwell both in his watery undersea kingdom and on the dry surface world as well!"

Helena's glowering frown started to edge up at the sides. Hugging him tightly around the neck she whispered in his ear, "Oh, but they're so green, big brother. They're so icky…and so awfully, awfully green!" She scrunched up her nose.

Harmodius chuckled as he carefully set her back down on the ground. "Ahh yes…'icky and green'. As always you are right, my little…my *little princess*." He arched an eyebrow, "Is that better?" As she smiled and happily nodded her head, he bent over and collected his school things together. "Very well then, my little princess Helena…perhaps now you can tell me who's come visiting us with all these poor tired mules in tow?"

"Oh…it's just one of those men come to buy Papa's olives…someone new, I think."

"An olive oil merchant? Come from Athens?" Harmodius' eye's brightened.

"And this one brought a boy with him."

"A boy?" Harmodius scratched his chin. Olive oil and wine merchants were frequent visitors to the isolated farm—sometimes arriving alone, sometimes accompanied by an army of slaves and bodyguards—but Harmodius couldn't remember anyone ever bringing a child along before. Taking Helena by the hand, he returned her to the porch and her forgotten rag doll. Feeling a refreshing itch of curiosity in what had so far been a very routine day, he quickened his pace as he approached the front door.

Inside, he found his father and the merchant—a balding, heavyset man with long curling streaks of gray coloring a very full beard—seated across from each other at a trestle table set up in the home's sunny interior courtyard. The two men were lost in laughter as they enjoyed refreshing mugs of his father's most expensive Egyptian beer. Harmodius stopped in the doorway, bowing low to his father's guest as he patiently waited to be acknowledged.

After a few moments, Cimon set down his mug, wiped the foam from his lips, and rose from his bench. "Ah, home from school at last. Come my son…come over here and meet our honored guest." With an encouraging wave of his hand, he motioned the boy forward. As Harmodius approached the table, the red-faced merchant rose to his feet and turned to face the smiling lad. "Good friend Scopas, allow me to present my first born son…my boy Harmodius."

The old man beamed with pleasure as he stepped forward and grabbed Harmodius by the arms. "A fine lad, Cimon…a fine, fine lad. For once that rascal Cleisthenes wasn't exaggerating. Excellent stock," he winked at Cimon, "…just like his father." Harmodius felt a rosy blush rising to his face as the two men, laughing at a shared private joke, fondly clapped each other on the shoulders. Harmodius was about to quietly back himself out of the room when all of a sudden a beefy hand wrapped itself around the back of his neck. With a gut wrenching turn, Scopas the merchant swung Harmodius around on his heels and pushed him in the direction of the farthest corner of the courtyard. There, unseen until this moment in the shade of the portico was someone quietly perched on a low, three-legged stool. Shoving the embarrassed boy forward, Scopus crowed: "And this is *my* son…Aristogiton."

The handsome boy jumped to his feet and, as he stepped forward into the light, Harmodius was somewhat taken aback to see that his sister had been mistaken in her description. This wasn't any *boy* staring him down with those two cold, clear lapis-blue eyes…no, this tall, lean, serious-looking youth was nearly a man! The two continued eyeing each other for a few seconds more before each in his turn, politely nodded his head.

Scopas clapped a loving arm on Aristogiton's shoulder and pulled him forward. "My son has come along on this venture to learn the ways of the olive oil trade." Suddenly looking very tired, the old merchant closed his eyes and let out a long slow sigh. "Some day soon, I'm afraid...after I've gone on to join the lonely shade of his dear mother...Aristogiton will be left alone to run the family business."

Cimon joined them and, resting his own hand on Aristogiton's other shoulder, offered up a genial protest: "Tut-tut, friend Scopas...I'll wager that won't be for many, many years to come." Turning to Harmodius, Cimon curled an eyebrow toward the half-empty jug of Egyptian beer. "Boys...Scopas and I have important business to discuss..." gesturing with a subtle nod of his head in the direction of the open doorway, he prodded his son: "Why don't you take Aristogiton outside and show him around the farm?"

Before Harmodius could answer, Aristogiton raised a hand in protest. "Thank you, sir. But if you are going to be discussing my father's business, I would prefer to stay here and learn."

There was a moment of awkward silence before Cimon, clearing his throat, smiled and nodded his head. "Well of course, young man...if that is your wish. You are certainly welcome to stay inside with us and observe our...our *negotiations*."

"Thank you, sir." Aristogiton stepped back and quietly resumed his place in the shadows.

Something in Aristogiton's voice (was it a hint of condescension?) pinched at Harmodius' pride...after all, this merchant's son wasn't *that* much older...three, maybe four years at the most. Bowing stiffly to Scopas and Cimon, Harmodius felt his smile tighten as he responded: "That's alright, Father. I promised Helena that we'd have another go at fighting the Trojan War."

He began to back out of the room and then stopped. Bobbing his head in the direction of the shadowy portico, he couldn't resist adding: "If the young master has a change of heart, he will find us *children* playing out in the vineyards."

❧   ❧   ❧

Hunched over and dragging her makeshift spear behind her, Helena scampered along between the long, low rows of vines, careful to hop over the tiny cabbage and lettuce shoots sprouting up in the rich red soil between the neatly-grooved furrows. Stopping to catch her breath, she carefully stood on tiptoe and peeked over the top of a grape vine. Harmodius was still several rows over, his father's great bronze helmet completely covering his head as he poked his wooden sword between the branches of a vine.

"I know you're here, my little Hector…I can smell you!" Harmodius' feeble attempt at a fearsome war growl was largely defeated by his high-pitched soprano voice. Thrusting his sword arm again and again, he jabbed between the vacant branches until the repeated motion knocked the heavy, too-large helmet off balance and Harmodius went sprawling on all fours. With his narrow eye slits askew, and fearing that Helena/Hector was creeping up on his now defenseless position, Harmodius scrambled about on the ground for his fallen sword. Suddenly, a firm hand gripped him by the arm and, in one sweeping motion, lifted him to his feet. Panicked and still blinded by his off-kilter helmet, Harmodius fanned his arms out in alarm.

"Whoa there…hold still my brave Achilles."

Harmodius felt the dusty wooden hilt of his practice sword pressed back into the palm of his hand and a moment later two strong hands grabbed hold of his helmet and carefully righted it on his head. Able at last to peer through the eye openings, Harmodius was surprised to see Aristogiton's handsome face grinning back at him.

"Or perhaps I'm mistaken. Perhaps this is *not* the unstoppable hero, Achilles." The merchant's son was rubbing his chin in mock consideration even as his two piercing blue eyes took a moment to scrutinize Harmodius from head to toe. "Hmm…if not the Achaean chieftain, then who else…" His deliberation suddenly turned to wide-eyed comprehension. "Why, of course…that ill-fitting armor gives you away." He gave the helmet a solid rap with his knuckles. "Not Achilles then…but the loyal Patroclus, friend and lover of the great warrior! The beloved Patroclus who borrowed his lover's armor to face-off with the Trojan Prince Hector!"

Before Harmodius could respond, Aristogiton took hold of his shoulders and twisted him back around. "Be on your guard, loyal Patroclus…" he shouted, the exuberance of his laughter ringing in his voice, "I fear our treacherous Trojan enemy has used this parley to his advantage. Behold, the formidable Hector is at hand!"

Helena had used the cover of Aristogiton's unexpected appearance to sneak up behind her unsuspecting brother. With a quick thrust through the vines, the blunted olive branch she was wielding as a spear, poked him in the belly and sent him reeling backwards into Aristogiton's waiting arms. "Die Achilles...die!" she screamed as she jumped through the bushes waving the olive branch spear in triumph over her head.

Solemnly lowering his voice, Aristogiton held the body of the fallen warrior against his chest as he nodded to the jubilant conqueror. "Bravely done, Prince Hector...bravely done." Fighting to catch his breath, Harmodius could feel Aristogiton's heart pounding against the back of his neck as he sprawled up against him. Before he could respond to his sister's sneak attack, he felt himself lowered to the ground by Aristogiton's two strong arms.

Helena was cavorting around the two boys like a crazed harpy, whooping and hollering as she celebrated her unexpected victory. Kneeling next to the 'fallen' warrior, Aristogiton looked up at her with a twinkle in his eye. "Ahh...but have a care, Trojan Prince...I fear you've been deceived!" With the practiced hand of a warrior, Aristogiton grabbed hold of the helmet by the cheek pieces and slid it back off Harmodius' head. "Yes, mighty Hector...it's not the brave Achilles you've slain on this memorable day...it's his compatriot and lover, Patroclus!"

Helena's wild victory dance came to an abrupt halt. Crossing her eyes in irritation, she gave the poor creature feigning death at her feet a swift kick in the side. "Who's Patrocleese..." she whined. "Harmodius told me he was playing Achilleees!"

Harmodius opened one eye and squinted up at his pouting sister. "I'm not Achilles!" he hissed. "Our honored guest is correct...I'm only the loyal Patroclus disguised in the armor of the Great Warrior." He rolled his eyes back in his head and with a bubbling gurgle in his voice screamed: *"And now you've run me through...and my shade cries out for vengeance!"*

Without another word, our 'fallen hero' tossed his wooden sword up in the air where the merchant's son deftly snatched it. In almost the same movement, Aristogiton scooped up the helmet and placed it firmly on his own head. Waving the sword in the air, he scowled down at the petulant Helena with a ferocious sneer. "Foolish Trojan...you've killed my beloved Patroclus! Tremble in your boots...for now you'll have the *real* Achilles to contend with!" Growling like a lion, he took a threatening step forward. The poor girl screamed, threw her spear down in the dirt and, turning like a shot, disappeared back between the vines…with Aristogiton—looking more like a great hulking bear than any mighty Greek warrior—lumbering noisily along after her.

Harmodius, howling with laughter, propped himself up on one elbow and watched with delight as the eye-catching 'Achilles' chased the miniature squalling 'Hector' through the twisting rows of his father's vinyard, all the way up onto the front porch and straight into the house.

An excited Harmodius spent the rest of the balmy afternoon escorting his young guest around the family's vast farmstead. He proudly showed off his father's vineyards and the many olive, apple and fig groves; the many fields sown with millet and corn and the ones left fallow; the gently sloping hillsides dotted with sheep and goats grazing lazily away on the short scruffy grass. As the sun began its tired dip towards the western hills, the two boys finished their long day together down at the beach. Stripping off their dusty tunics, they took a cleansing swim in the calm, crystal clear waters of the Gulf of Petalion.

Returning to the house, they found the evening meal already being set up in his mother's flower garden behind the kitchen. In honor of his guests, Cimon had ordered the cook to slaughter one of his plumpest piglets. Even now, as darkness settled in around the quiet countryside and the torches and braziers were lit against the starry night, the honey-glazed animal was roasting away in his freshly dug, rock-lined pit. Eschewing the separation of the sexes so elemental to more formal Greek occasions, Cimon invited his wife and daughter to join with the men at this makeshift feast. To crown the extravagant meal, Cimon served everyone abundant quantities of the finest unwatered wine from the family's own vineyard…and by the time the last shreds of meat were being plucked from the greasy carcass, the younger heads were beginning to nod.

Waking late the next morning, the wine-dazed Harmodius sensed that the busy household had been long astir. Throwing a cloak over his shoulders to cover his nakedness he ran out onto the porch to find Scopas' mule train already loaded down with heavy jars of olive oil and ready to go. Cimon and the merchant were finishing up last minute business in the middle of the yard while Philippia and Helena waited patiently to say their farewells from the shade of an oak tree.

Aristogiton, tightening the last strap on a skittish mule, saw Harmodius—still obviously suffering the effects of last night's feast—standing bleary-eyed on the porch. Slapping the feisty mule on its rump, he walked over and joined his new friend. Holding him at arms length for a moment, he looked into the two bloodshot eyes and slowly shook his head. "Don't worry," he chuckled, "a few more years and not only will you grow into that oversized helmet of yours…but you'll be able to drink like a man and still wake up bright and cheery the next morning!"

Before Harmodius could stutter an objection, Aristogiton pulled him close and planted a formal kiss on both cheeks; a gracious thanks to his youthful host for a pleasantly hospitable afternoon and evening. Then, with a roguish wink, he turned and swaggered lazily back to await his father at the head of the mule train.

Boisterous handshakes, affectionate kisses, and repeated promises for a quick return, finally sent the jolly merchant and his son on their way. Before disappearing down the long road leading back to Athens, Aristogiton turned one last time and waved to the lone figure standing on the porch.

For the rest of that morning, even as the fuzziness in his head slowly cleared, Harmodius found his thoughts returning over and over to those two piercing blue eyes…eyes, he belatedly realized, that had sparkled with the same color as the crystal clear waters of Petalion.

That evening, following a more subdued meal than the one served up the night before, Harmodius went in search of his father. He found him sitting in the barn with a hand-held sharpening stone giving new edges to all the old sickles and reaping hooks. Sitting at his feet, he offhandedly broached the subject of the old merchant and his son. Heaving a heavy sigh, Cimon paused in his work and looked at his son.

"Well…I first met Scopas many, many years ago. He was an acquaintance of Cleisthenes and—once he and I were together—all of my new erastes' friends immediately welcomed me into their circle. Being the oldest of our little group, Scopas was the first to feel the hot sting of Eros' arrow…leaving his youthful companions for the marriage bed. And…well, I guess we didn't see very much of him after that…at least not for a few years."

Motioning his son to hand him over another sickle, Cimon continued his story as he scraped back and forth against the rusty blade.

"Scopas, like all good husbands, adored his wife and young son…so much so that Cleisthenes was always chiding him that his olive oil business was sure to suffer from the benign neglect. But all that came to an abrupt end on that fateful summer day when his poor wife died during a particularly virulent fever season." Cimon shook his head as he set the second blade on the ground and signaled for the next. "Fearing that Aristogiton would be left alone and destitute, he dutifully turned his attention back to his flagging oil trade. With a revitalized energy bordering on desperation, over a few short years he built his business back up to the very profitable levels it enjoys today."

Finishing the third sickle with a wide sweep of his arm, he dropped it in the pile next to the others and stood up to stretch the kinks out of his back while Harmodius waited patiently to hear the rest of the story. Sitting himself back on the bench, Cimon gestured to Harmodius for the next implement. "But ill fortune seems to dog this genial man no matter which path he chooses. Just this last year, one of Cleisthenes' letters mentioned that Scopas had suffered some kind of seizure while on board ship returning from his annual trading expedition to Crete. The poor man was laid up for months trying to get his strength back." Cimon tested the fourth sickle with the edge of his thumb and, satisfied it would do, tossed it on the ground with the others. "Hand me that last one there, Harmodius."

Wiping the sweat from his forehead, he spit on the stone, bent over and began whetting the edge of the last blade. "And now, even though he's back nearly as good as new, the poor fool has become obsessed with his own death. He's convinced himself that Hades' dark chariot will be paying him a visit someday soon…and this plays on his fear that the boy Aristogiton is still too young…that he won't be ready to take over the business." He looked up at his son. "That's why he brought him here yesterday…he's trying to introduce him to all of his old customers." He gave Harmodius a reassuring smile and chuckled. "But from all I could see, the boy is a natural…he has a shrewdness of character that would be the envy of *any* merchant," his smile widened to a mischievous grin, "and he's certainly not lacking any of his father's good humor." With a dull clang, the last sickle joined the others on the ground. "I'm sure that, whatever future the Fates have in store for dear old Scopas and his family, the boy will manage just fine."

Later, as the two made their quiet way back toward the lamp lit house, Cimon stopped his son for a moment to gaze up at the star-filled sky. Suddenly, the stillness of the night air was disturbed by a rustling of leaves as a mother deer and her two fawns—each little more than a foot in height and seemingly oblivious to the presence of humans—passed through the yard not five feet from where they stood. Harmodius, holding his breath at this amazing sight, slipped his smallish hand into Cimon's larger work-callused grip. As the three deer moved away on up the hillside, Harmodius felt the tension in his father's grasp loosen, and a moment later the two exhaled their breaths in almost perfect unison.

"Now that's something you'd never see growing up in Athens!" He leaned over and whispered: "Quick, look up at the Moon and say a prayer to the huntress...the lady Artemis must be close at hand!"

Harmodius mumbled something under his breath and then, hoping to keep this precious moment alive, spoke up in a hushed voice of his own: "Did you see her eyes...the doe's I mean? They were so big!"

Cimon couldn't help chuckling at the excited animation in his son's face. "Yes, my boy...they *were* quite big. Almost as big as..."

"As big as Aristogiton's eyes!" cut in Harmodius, his excitement getting the best of him.

Cimon's chuckling turned into a single half-embarrassed snort. Slowly he turned and gave his beloved only son a long, appraising stare. Still just a youth...not quite the adolescent ready to leave school and attend a true gymnasium. Even so, for the very first time the father saw his son as something other than a helpless child. Smiling with something akin to relief at the blameless innocence still shining from the boy's youthful eyes, Cimon circumspectly nodded his head. "Yes, Harmodius...as big as...as Aristogiton's."

Resting an arm on his son's shoulder, the two turned back toward the welcoming light streaming from the open shutters on the porch. Keeping his voice as casual as possible, Cimon couldn't resist a gentle prod: "But tell me boy, I seem to have forgotten. Those two great eyes...Aristogiton's I mean...they weren't brown like the doe's, were they?"

Harmodius pulled his father up short. "Why they were wonderfully blue, of course...as blue as the morning sea!"

Cimon sighed. "Ah yes, 'wonderfully blue'...of course, how could I have forgotten?"

As they continued on their stroll it suddenly came to him that, at least in body, young Harmodius *had* grown. Sometime in these last few months—or had it been years and he just hadn't notice them passing—the boy's head had gone from barely reaching Cimon's waist to now being almost level with his shoulders.

"He'll be ready to attend gymnasium sooner than I thought..." a bittersweet notion "...and that will mean returning the family to Athens."

Athens...

Sudden memories of a brutalized slave in a potter's stall and a long ago quarrel threatened to shatter the serenity of the quiet evening. Running his fingers through the thick black hair sweeping across Harmodius' forehead, he pushed the uneasy thought aside. With an affectionate swat on the boy's behind, he steered his son ahead of him into the house.

"But no, perhaps not quite yet…"

❧   ❧   ❧

The late afternoon was unusually cold, even for autumn, but the accompanying downpour proved little threat to the boy's practiced concentration. These days, Harmodius was able to recite five complete cantos from the Iliad each morning and afternoon as he made the long walk to and from school. Having consigned the entire epic to memory almost a year ago, he figured he was able to complete a recitation of the entire poem nearly once each month.

As he made his way up the muddy track to the family farm, his *chlamys* pulled up and over his head against the rain, he heard Helena calling out to him. Peeking out from the sodden edges of his rain-soaked cloak, he saw her waiting impatiently on the porch…a waxed tablet and stylus having recently taken the place of her old rag doll in the center of her lap. "Gods, how she's sprouting up…" he thought as he picked up his pace, smiling at the sight of his young sister's dogged determination to learn.

"Is father back yet?" He called out sidestepping a muddy puddle. Two days ago Cimon had received a cryptic message from his old friend Cleisthenes summoning him to a secretive meeting in Athens. Taking one of the horses, he'd grabbed a loaf of fresh bread, packed an extra tunic in his saddlebag and galloped off, promising his ever-fretting wife that he'd return before the end of the week.

"Not yet." Helena's lips curled down in a familiar pout, "…and I've been sitting here waiting for you all afternoon!" Her scold turned to a half-giggle as he stepped up under the porch overhang and began shaking the water off his body like a rain soaked puppy.

"I'll be with you in a just moment, little annoying one." Shrugging off his chlamys, he made a point of shaking it out in her face. Her half-giggle turned to a feigned scream of outrage as she leapt backwards in an unsuccessful dodge from the chilly spray. Sweeping past her, the grinning Aristogiton called over his shoulder: "Let me go find something dry to put on…then I'll come back here and we'll resume your lessons."

As he tossed her his school pack, she responded with a surprisingly enigmatic smile. "Well don't take too long, big brother…my honey cakes won't stay warm forever." Lifting the edge of a cloth covering a plate sitting on the windowsill, she coyly fluttered her eyelashes as the smell of warm, honey-sweetened barley wafted through the air.

Licking his lips, Harmodius felt his empty stomach yelp in anticipation, even as he grinned back at his sister, "You've been cooking again!"

Helena's eyes beamed with immodest pride. "Yes, Mother helped me…I've been practicing all morning, and this is the best batch of the bunch!" She picked up one of the sticky little crumb cakes and wafted it under his nose. When he moved forward to take a bite, she slyly pulled it back. "Ah-ah-ah…not until we begin my lesson."

Harmodius scowled playfully. "Always the temptress! Someday I fear you'll drive some poor man to distraction with your scheming wiles…just like your legendary namesake!" With a final ruffle of his damp hair, he turned and disappeared into the house leaving a trail of rainwater behind him.

Pressing her stylus into the soft wax, Helena carefully copied the simple letters from Harmodius' tablet onto her own.

"G—E—P—H—Y"

She sounded out each letter slowly and clearly as she inscribed them into the wax. Satisfied, Harmodius rubbed out the first five letters with his thumb and then neatly wrote down the last three letters of the word: R-A-I

"R—A—I" repeated Helena as she dutifully copied them out, careful to imitate the exact shape of her brother's notation. "Geph-y-ra-i…" she said, stating each syllable with a slow, studied precision as she carefully sounded out the difficult word. "Gephyrai…Gephyrai…" she looked up just in time to catch the last of the honey cakes disappearing between her brother's voracious lips. "Gephyrai…that's a funny word. What does it mean, Harmodius?"

"*What does it mean?*" His attempt at familial indignation was somewhat defeated by the sight of several sticky barley crumbs hanging from his chin. As Helena reached across and wiped them away, he reproached his student. "Why, it's our family name of course…the name of our sacred clan. *We* are the Gephyrai!" He punctuated this latest important brotherly life lesson with an overtly masculine thump of his fist against his chest.

"Oh…" Helena arched an eyebrow "…I didn't know that." Twisting her knees around, she tapped her stylus against the edge of her tablet, her lips twisting together into something resembling pique. "But then, dearest brother, why would I—*a mere girl*—know anything about our family's clan?" Bending over, she ignored him for a moment as she concentrated on using smaller letters to re-scrawl the entire word across her tablet. "Tell me, Harmodius…" she passed the tablet over for his inspection, "…why hasn't anyone spoken to me about the family's clan before now? After all, I am a Gephyrai too, aren't I?"

Harmodius, licking the last of the honey from his fingertips, did his best to ignore the all-too-familiar edge of frustration creeping into her voice. "Well yes," he said, "I suppose you are…at least for the next few years." Picking up his own tablet, he rubbed out the 'RAI' and wrote out a new word for her to copy. "You see, little dove, when you get married you will no longer belong to the Gephyrai tribe. Instead, you will be enrolled into your husband's family. With your own household to manage, you—and of course all your children—will naturally take the name of your husband's clan."

Notorious for her stubborn streak, the prepubescent Helena suddenly stomped her foot and angrily threw her stylus to the ground. "But…but I don't want to belong to another family! I'm a Gephyrai and I want to stay a Gephyrai!"

Harmodius was beginning to see the wisdom behind the Greek custom of not educating their womenfolk. When he'd approached his father with the idea of teaching Helena to read and write, Cimon had rolled his eyes and shook his head. "It'll be a waste of time…yours and hers," he said. "That headstrong creature will have better luck snaring a suitable husband if she spent more time at her loom…or working with her mother in the kitchen!"

And perhaps his father was right…

To his surprise Helena's mulish scowl suddenly brightened. "I know what I'll do!" she cried out. "What if I *marry* a Gephyrai? Then I won't have to change my name…I won't have to be a somebody else!"

Eager to get the stalled lesson moving once again, Harmodius decided to agree with her. "An excellent idea, little pomegranate seed…excellent…" (Although he couldn't resist stating the obvious) "Of course, by limiting yourself to male members of the Gephyrai clan, you'll seriously be reducing your pool of prospective husbands." He shrugged his shoulders indifferently. "Ahh…but what matter that when you can hang onto the family name!"

Helena was still a touch too young to appreciate her adolescent brother's sarcasm. "Thank you, dearest Harmodius…it *is* an excellent idea! I knew you'd agree with me."

Tapping on his slate with the tip of his stylus, he tried to once again bring his tiny class back to order. Passing the new lesson over to his eager sister, Harmodius waited for her to resume her copying. With an embarrassed giggle, Helena bent over and retrieved her discarded stylus from the dirt. Screwing her eyes together in concentration, she set back to work.

"C—A—D—M—U—S"

Diligently duplicating her brother's blockish characters, she spoke each letter aloud before sounding out the whole word. "Cadmus…cadmus." She looked up, her stubborn temper promising a quick return visit. "Now what's a cadmus supposed to be, Harmodius? Really! When are you going to teach me how to write words that mean something…words I already know like rain or wind or…or *lamb*?" She covered a sudden giggle with the back of her delicate hand. "Baby lambs are so sweet, big brother…why can't I learn how to write 'baby lamb'!"

"It's not 'what's a cadmus'…it's 'who's Cadmus.'"

Rolling his eyes and crossing his arms (and for a moment, looking amazingly like his always skeptical father), he pushed on. "You were just whining about wanting to stay a Gephyrai for the rest of your life…" picking up the slate from her lap, "…so I thought you should know where our clan came from. Here…" he tapped the name etched into the wax, "Cadmus the Phoenician…the founder of our famous tribe."

An unexpected flicker of interest appeared in Helena's eyes. "Cadmus…" she held her own tablet up and stared at the word as she carefully sounded it out "Cadmus…the Phoenician?" Leaning forward, her elbows resting gently on her knees, she waited for her brother to continue.

Laying his slate to one side, Harmodius wrapped his fingers behind his head and settled himself back against the wall of the house. "Yes…Phoenician. The Gephyrai clan originally came from a distant land far across the Aegean Sea. Hundreds of years ago our ancestor, the brave Cadmus, led our forebears from Tyre across the windswept seas to the kingdom of Boeotia…" he pointed vaguely to a land off toward the northwest "…not very far from here in fact. And it was there that they founded the famous city of Thebes." Harmodius picked up his slate and turned it toward his sister. "And *this* is the great treasure he brought as a gift for the Greeks…writing."

Helena's eyes grew owlishly wide. "Writing?" she asked, her usually high-pitched tone dropping to a near whisper at the import of his suggestion.

Harmodius nodded his head. "Yes, writing." He began etching the letters of the alphabet across the top of his tablet. "The Phoenicians are famed throughout the world as the inventors of the alphabet. Before Cadmus and the Gephyrai came to Greece, the art of writing was unknown here."

"The Greeks…they must have been very grateful to Cadmus."

Harmodius shook his head. "Well…yes and no. For many years Thebes thrived as the center of Greek culture and learning. But a few generations passed and the great grandson of Cadmus, none other than the ill-fated King Oedipus…" he scratched his chin "…you remember, the one who had the misfortune to kill his own father and marry his own mother?" His sister, spellbound by this fascinating recitation, silently nodded her head. "Anyway, when King Oedipus' tragic crimes came to light, he and the tiny Phoenician colony were expelled from Boeotia."

Helena looked horror struck. "Oh, but that's terrible! After giving them 'writing' they were all sent away?"

Harmodius smiled. "Ahh…but there's a happy ending for the Phoenicians. The sacred city of Athena, the goddess of knowledge, offered Oedipus and his followers sanctuary. They were even given a special section of the city to live in and call their own. And that is how the Gephyrai finally came to settle here in Attica."

"An honorable people…" Helena slapped her stylus down on her slate. "I will definitely wait for a Gephyrai to come woo me!"

Laughing, Harmodius shook his head and once again set his stylus in motion crawling across the smoothed waxen face of his tablet. "Enough history for today, we have just enough time before supper for one last lesson. Pay attention now, little scamp…and I'll show you how to write 'baby lamb.'"

That evening, just as the servants were clearing away the supper dishes, all heads turned at the sound of horse's hooves galloping up the path toward the house. Harmodius grabbed a lamp from the shelf and, with his mother and sister following close behind, ran to the front door. As hoped, it was the family patriarch Cimon returning from his short visit to Athens. Hearing the sound of his arrival, a slave came running from the barn and took the reins of the heavily breathing animal from his master's practiced hands. Jumping down off his rain-slickened horse, Cimon ran the last few paces through the mud to the refuge of the covered porch where his family stood waiting. With everyone trying to talk at once, he pushed them on ahead of him, back into the house where a servant was waiting with an armful of towels.

Thoroughly dried off—and with a fresh tunic thrown over his travel-weary body—he rejoined his anxiously waiting family in the dining room to bring them the latest news from the city. As he took his seat at the table, a servant placed a large bowl of thick, hot lentil soup and a freshly baked loaf of round bread in front of him.

"I have wonderful news..." he said between hungry bites. "Our very own Cleisthenes has been elected Archon for the year!"

"But how can that be?" asked Philippia. "The Alcmaeonid family—and especially Cleisthenes—are the bitterest rivals of the Pisistrades! Have things changed so much in Athens that Hippias would accept an Alcmaeonid on the ruling council?"

Cimon shrugged his shoulders. "Apparently so..." He tore off a hunk of bread and dipped it in the flavorful soup. "There's been growing dissatisfaction in the city...trade has been off for more than a few years now...and taxes are climbing. In a gesture of goodwill, Hippias has replaced a number of his old cronies with respected men chosen from all parties." He reached across and lovingly squeezed his wife's hand. "Cleisthenes was his nod to the Alcmaeonids."

Philippia looked doubtful. "And what of Hipparchus?" she asked.

Cimon's smile widened...this was the best news of all. "Cleisthenes has assured me that Hippias is keeping his brash younger brother on a very short leash these days. After a number of embarrassing incidents—most of them involving boys too young to know better and angry fathers seeking compensation before the law—he and his clique have been barred from the city's gymnasiums. Hipparchus resigned as co-tyrant and Hippias has him keeping his nose to the grindstone managing the city's religious festivals."

"Then...you think it's safe to return home?" Philippia looked unconvinced.

Cimon stood up. "Come over here, son." He motioned Harmodius to stand by him at the head of the table. Almost matching his father in height and stature, it was clear how much the boy had grown over these past few years. "Dear wife...can you have any doubt that it's well past time for our boy to be enrolled at a true gymnasium? At his age, what kind of an education can we expect him to receive at that hopeless school in Araphen?"

Philippia stared at Harmodius, looking more like his father every day…and, for a disconcerting moment felt his all too brief childhood slipping away. Biting back her fears, she dropped her gaze and nodded her head. "Yes, dearest…as always, you are right. It's long past time the boy met others of his age and received the proper education due a young man at an Athenian gymnasium."

Cimon gave her a reassuring nod as he resumed his seat.

"Very well then," he smiled, "it's all settled. As soon as I can organize things here on the farm, we'll pack up the old cart and return to Athens. In the meantime, I'll send some of the servants on ahead to make sure everything is ready for our homecoming."

That night, few in the household found sleep a trouble-free visitor. Cimon and his wife lay awake talking as he sought to dispel any lingering fears about Hipparchus and the Pisistrade regime. Little Helena tossed and turned in her narrow bed, wild imaginings of a city she had virtually no memory of haunting her childish dreams. And, staring up at the ceiling from his wood-framed bed, Harmodius couldn't quell the racing of his heartbeat as one word kept repeating itself over and over in his fevered mind:

Gymnasium…

CHAPTER 3

On the 11th anniversary of Harmodius' birth, Cimon proudly led his only son through the narrow, winding streets of Athens, bypassing the rocky hill of the Acropolis, on their way to the Temple of Olympian Zeus situated closer to the city's southeastern wall. It was customary for boys entering puberty to offer up the toys of their youth as tokens of their burgeoning manhood. In a brief, but solemn ceremony, Harmodius consigned his favorite spinning top, a miniature painted horse with four tiny wheels made of clay, and his old wooden play sword, to the flames burning on the open altar in front of the great ivory and gold statue of the mighty thunder god.

Leaving the gloom of the temple behind them, Cimon and his son turned on to a street that lead through an open gate in the city' stout protective wall and out toward the small *deme* of Diomeia. There, situated on a low wooded hillside along the banks of the Ilissos River was the enormous gymnasium complex known as the Kynosarges. Spread across several acres, the gymnasium proper was located at the center of a great park filled with running tracks, discus fields and shaded walkways. As the two visitors made their ambling way down the wide gravel path leading toward the great building housing the actual gymnasium, Harmodius couldn't help but marvel at the vast numbers of people working and playing at various activities throughout the park.

And much to his surprise…they all seemed to be quite naked.

"A Greek who hasn't trained at the gymnasium will never find true acceptance among his peers," his father was saying. Nodding his head, Harmodius watched spellbound as a heavily muscled youth, glistening with sweat from head to toe, took a deep breath and spun twice around before letting a flat stone discus go sailing through the air. As it fell to the earth with a dusty thud some distance down the course, a small group of older men, admiring him from the sidelines, cheered his throw. With a modest blush rising on his cheek, the youth turned and gratefully accepted a towel from one of them.

"…And always keep in mind that the gymnasium is a place for intellectual stimulation as well as physical exercise." Just then, as Cimon and his son were passing through a shady grove of ancient elm trees, Harmodius heard what sounded like muffled laughter. Peeking through the lush overgrowth, Harmodius could just make out the shadowy figures of two men—naked as all the rest—entwined tightly in each other's arms. At first he thought they might be wrestling, but closer inspection revealed lips seemingly locked in a kiss…even as their free hands groped at each other's privates. Cimon put a hand on his son's shoulder and pushed him along the path and away from this intimate scene. Clearing his throat, Cimon stifled an embarrassed chuckle, "It's not polite to stare, Harmodius."

As they left the shade of the trees and approached the great square building at the center of the park, Cimon turned off the path and led his son over to a group of benches lining a man-made pond. Seated side by side, Cimon scratched his chin for a moment before turning and looking the boy straight in the eyes. "As I was saying, son…the gymnasium is a place for physical exercise…" he looked down and studied the hairs on the back of his hands for a moment, "…and by that I mean all kinds of…er, 'physical exercise.'" He gestured toward the expansive marble edifice in front of them, "Here in this building…" then spread his arms wide "…and on these grounds…" he smiled as years of happy memories came flooding back, "…you will learn to *fight* like a man, you will learn to *think* like a man, and you will learn to *love* like a man." He slowly turned and nodded his head back in the direction of the hidden elm grove.

Following his father's gaze, Harmodius suddenly realized exactly what he was getting at and almost immediately felt an unwanted rosy blush of his own coloring his embarrassed cheeks. Swallowing back a nervous gulp, he managed a half-hearted show of enthusiasm with his answer: "I understand, father. And I will work hard to make you proud of me."

Cimon took hold of Harmodius' hand. "You needn't work to please me, my son…I'm your father and I will *always* be proud of you. And you needn't work to meet the expectations of others. If you approach these years at the gymnasium as a priceless opportunity to better both your mind and body, others will recognize the honesty of your efforts…and your reward will be their undying friendship and love."

With a final reassuring squeeze of his son's hand, Cimon released his grip and stood up. "Come along now…it's time we paid a visit to the *palaestra* and the *ephebeon*." Leading the boy back to the well-traveled dirt path, the two approached the great four-sided structure as Cimon regaled his son with the history of the famous Kynosarges Gymnasium.

"While this building itself was erected not long ago—during the final years of the tyranny of the great lawgiver Solon—this location has been the site of a gymnasium in one form or another ever since the time of Homer. Sacred to the mighty warrior-god Heracles, the polis originally set aside the Kynosarges for military training. Over the years sections of the forest were cleared away as running tracks, wrestling pits, and exercise areas were added to the site." He motioned toward a grove of trees from whence the sound of rushing water could be heard. "Of course it was the convenience of the River Ilissos—close at hand for bathing following a strenuous workout—that finally established the Kynosarges as one of the city's most popular gathering spots."

Stopping at the foot of the wide steps leading up to the main entryway, Cimon pointed to the larger-than-life marble statues of Heracles and his lover Iolaus flanking either side of the doorway. "Not far from here," he nodded off toward the right, "down that path and through those trees, are three temples dedicated to Heracles, his mother Alcemene, and of course Iolaus. For one week each spring, worshipers come to Diomeia from all over Greece to celebrate the Festival of Heracles. During that time the Kynosarges is so crowded with aggressively competitive naked men that…" he smiled at another distant memory "…well, the very air seems to buzz with the god's divine energy." Cimon's smile turned to a grin as he started up the stairs with the gawking Harmodius tagging along behind. "However, as we are still many months away from the next festival…the energy today should be a bit more subdued."

The heat from the bright Mediterranean sunshine dispersed as they passed through the gymnasium's great bronze doors and moved into the cool marble-columned interior. An alcove off to their right led to a changing room where slave-attendants assisted Harmodius and his father in divesting themselves of their clothing. Before leaving the room, Cimon handed the attentive men a small gratuity and then exchanged a few more coins for a small bottle of olive oil.

Like most Greek children, Harmodius had been raised with a healthy respect for nudity. The numberless statues and paintings, so common around the public spaces of a wealthy city like Athens, almost always portrayed the gods and heros—both male and female—without the benefit of any clothing.

And as the concept of undergarments was largely unknown to the Greeks, their short-skirted chitons and the flimsy draping of their open-on-the-side himations more often than not exposed the male genitals to even the most casual of onlookers. Even so, the still youthful Harmodius found this first display of mass public nudity vaguely unnerving…and at the same time, oddly fascinating. As the two strolled side-by-side through the covered peristyle surrounding the great open workout arena at the center of the building, it was all Harmodius could do to keep from covering his private parts with a nervous hand every time they passed someone else coming the other way.

The Kynosarges gymnasium was built in the form of a perfect square, the perimeter consisting of a four-sided, twin colonnaded peristyle. The outer walkway housed changing rooms, cubicles for massage and meditation, a small library, open arcades where philosophers met and exchanged ideas with their students, and an indoor bathhouse complete with both heated and cold soaking pools. A recent innovation, the Kynosarges' bathhouse had become a popular gathering place for the city elders to relax and exchange gossip at the end of a long day conducting business in the Agora. The hardier, younger athletes, who preferred much of their exercise out of doors anyway, were more than happy to leave the luxuries of indoor bathing to their seniors, favoring instead a brisk dip in the time-honored mountain waters of the Ilissos River.

The inner colonnade had been left open and undivided, serving double duty as both the *xystos*—a workout and training area reserved for older men who were more interested in maintaining their strength and skills than in the heated, testosterone-fueled activities of the *ephebeon*—and an all-weather, covered running track.

The open space at the center of this great double colonnade was the heart of the gymnasium—the ephebeon…the training area reserved for Athens' youth. With its natural dirt floor and extensive areas set aside for the different athletic and military exercises, the ephebeon was a hive of activity. Young, hard, naked bodies sprinted along 50 meter racing tracks, boxed with leather-wrapped fists, and long-jumped in soft sandy pits with heavy hand-weights thrown out in front of them to add distance to their vaults. Sword blades flashed in the sunlight as young men sparred with one another, while on the far side of the dusty enclosure, several others lined up to heave 10-foot long javelins, the small, leaf-shaped iron spearheads driving deep into the straw-backed targets. Gathered at the very center of the ephebeon could be found a constant crowd of cheering men and boys surrounding the gymnasium's palaestra, the area reserved for that most popular of Greek combat sports—wrestling.

As Harmodius somewhat reluctantly followed his father down the wide steps from the shady porch of the peristyle onto the sun-filled arena floor of the ephebeon, the boy couldn't keep from catching his breath at the sight of all these well-tuned, oil-covered, hard-muscled young bodies working in such close proximity to one another. Gazing with adolescent fascination on their various activities, it soon became apparent that there was a good deal more going on here than just athletic exercise. A congratulatory peck on the lips following a successful parry and thrust turned into something more sensuous…a joking squeeze of a buttock or a tweak of a nipple brought a flushed smile in response…the roaming hands of an overly-friendly backrub…an intimate whisper in the ear. Everywhere he turned, Harmodius saw excited eyes filled with admiration, envy, ambition, and desire…and to his growing horror he realized that many of those very same eyes were turning in his direction.

"Take a father's advice and just ignore them."

Harmodius looked up with a start. Cimon was standing at his side, his expression an exercise in discretion as he appraised the situation.

"For the time being, that is." He reached over and gave Harmodius' unexceptional bicep a playful squeeze. "The more you visit the gymnasium, the more you'll see these grow in size." He touched a finger to Harmodius' chest. "And this will mature as well…" without any warning his hand suddenly moved down and, to Harmodius' utter mortification, cupped the boy's testicles, "…and these too." He laughed gently at his son's red-faced discomfiture. "In the coming months you will see and feel mysterious changes in both your body and heart…changes that will mirror your maturity as an Athenian citizen." He raised an eyebrow in the direction of a young lifter who, dropping his stone weights to the ground, had turned to stare rather avariciously across the dusty expanse at Harmodius. "And don't worry about these others. You will know when it's the right time to involve yourself in all that…all that *business*." The overly muscled lifter looked just about ready to make his move, so Cimon—wrapping a protective arm across Harmodius' shoulder—pulled him away in the opposite direction. "Come on, boy…let's go practice some javelin throws."

As they slowly made their way across the ephebeon floor Harmodius could feel his heart racing as handsome young men nodded in his direction and then turned back to whisper in one another's ears. Stumbling over his own two feet, he caught a good-natured chuckle echoing from somewhere behind him as he let his father direct him through the sweaty, jostling crowds.

Hefting a spear in each hand to find the proper balance and weight, Cimon tossed one over to Harmodius. "Here…try this one."

As he walked over and placed his toes just behind the throw-line, Harmodius had the uncomfortable feeling that every eye in the ephebeon had turned in his direction. Taking several paces backward, Harmodius joggled the shaft in his hand as he searched for the proper balance point. Confident that he was ready, he nodded at his father, drew the spear back behind his shoulder and, taking three giant leaps forward, let it fly. To his horror, it missed the straw bale target by several feet and actually caused one hapless onlooker to jump out of the way as it skidded to a noisy stop against the marble portico steps.

Blushing red to the very tips of his ears, Harmodius was surprised when the only person within earshot laughing at this wild throw was Cimon…and it was clear that his father's genial chides were more to break the tension than anything else. "Don't worry…" Cimon said as he walked over and retrieved the errant shaft, "…before you know it, you'll get the hang of all this." With a knowing wink, he gestured in the direction of the other athletes as he tossed the spear back to his waiting son. Returning to his place along the sidelines, Cimon added: "A week from now, you'll have settled in and the gymnasium will become like your second home. And those others…they'll have forgotten that you're the new boy…you'll be just another citizen come to train his body and mind with the other young folk of Athens." Raising his fist with a virile shake, he smiled proudly at Harmodius. "Now then, my boy…let's show them how a Gephyrai son truly wields his spear!"

Harmodius' first morning at the gymnasium passed in a dusty haze of running, jumping, lifting, and tossing. After this strenuous workout, Cimon went with his son to one of the many massage rooms located in the outer colonnade. Handing the attendant the small bottle of olive oil, Cimon and son climbed up on the wide wooden table and spent the next half hour being oiled, sanded, rubbed, pounded and pummeled. With any threatening knots and stiffness having been duly attended to, the boy and his father sat up and spent a few moments taking a dull-edged *strigil* to one another. As they scraped the remaining oil and dirt residue off their arms and legs, the two shared a hearty laugh recalling the incredulous expression on the poor spectator's face when Harmodius' first javelin throw went wild and almost clipped him on the ankle.

A luxuriant immersion in the heated pool, followed by a quick plunge in the cold pool, left the two feeling refreshed and ready to face the world.

As they walked back home through the bustling Athenian streets, shopkeepers and customers were busily finishing up their final transactions of the morning before closing up shop and returning home for the afternoon meal. Stopping at a fruit seller's stall, Cimon bought a handful of figs to share with his son as they continued on their way.

Removed from the curious stares of the ephebeon, Harmodius felt ready to question his father about some of the more curious things he'd seen that morning. "Father..." he wiped a sticky trickle of fig juice from the corner of his mouth, "I think I understood what you were saying about...well...about men sometimes taking older lovers at the gymnasium...before they marry, I mean." He hesitated a moment, probing his father with a questioning glance before continuing: "Like you and...and Lord Cleisthenes?"

Cimon smiled and slowly nodded his head.

"Is that what all those men were doing...the older ones I mean? The ones who seemed to spend the entire morning watching us from the steps of the peristyle?"

Cimon frowned. While not exactly the time or place he'd planned for this conversation, it would have to do. Tossing him another fig, he answered: "Let me try and explain something to you...something about the moral nature of our society, Harmodius." He rested a hand lightly on his son's shoulder. "The most important thing to any Greek citizen is protecting the integrity of his family's name. And to do this...to ensure the paternity of his children, the virtue of his womenfolk must never come under suspicion. This is why your mother's life is largely confined to the rooms inside of the home—her familial responsibility to raise her children and supervise the household's activities. And this is also why your little sister is no longer allowed to run freely about in the streets...and will most certainly never be allowed to attend an Athenian school." He shook his head and let out an exasperated sigh as he recalled this current bone of contention ruffling the serenity of the household. "With the exception of a few carefully chaperoned festivals each year, most wives and daughters are content to protect their chastity behind the walls of their homes...and in this way, the paternity of their children is never brought into question."

Cimon paused for a moment to let this all sink in. Tossing the last of the figs in his son's direction, he brought his index finger to rest against his lips—the image of pensive reflection—before finally clearing his throat and continuing.

"Men, on the other hand, don't share these same societal strictures. The golden years of our youth are spent out and about in the public world…much of that time devoted to the training of mind and body to glorify, defend, and honor our revered city-state. Parents dutifully relinquish control of their children to the culture of the gymnasium, the young now turning to their peers and elders for further education and experience. These can be turbulent years for a youth: his first brush with independence…awkward growth spurts of the body…new, largely unexplored feelings and emotions." As much as he hated to admit it, Cimon could feel color beginning to flush his own cheeks even as he heard the stiff, clumsy words come stumbling from his mouth. "And since the generous god Dionysus has…er, seen fit to saddle men with a more…uh, 'priapic' nature than womankind." He frowned as a look of confused consternation crossed his son's face. "Well, boy…these didactic relationships…the pairings that form in the gymnasium…well, they often have a…a sexual side to them." He stopped, glancing down at the wheel ruts cut into the graveled street as he fished about for the right words. "It's important, Harmodius, to realize that since most Greek men don't marry until well past their 25th year, the 'eromenos/erastes' relationships of the gymnasium serve a dual purpose. Through them we grow into emotional manhood, learning how to love and be loved. And at the same time, the sexual temptations of youth that might lead to the ruin of a woman's virtue are held at bay until marriage."

"Eromenos? Beloved?"

"Yes…the 'beloved'…the 'sought after'…in most cases, the younger in these intimate relationships. The eromenos is wooed and won by the elder erastes. And in time, as the eromenos approaches his own manhood, he will often become an erastes—a 'lover'—in his own right." He smiled to himself as he recalled the chaotic emotions of his own youthful peccadilloes. "And I think you'll find that, if the time ever comes, there's as much pleasure in the wooing…as there is in being the wooed." Raising a hand, he instructively ticked off three fingers. "First comes the 'learning love' of adolescence…second comes the 'teaching love' of young manhood…and finally, upon reaching full maturity, comes marriage and the sacred love of a wife. And with that," he snapped his fingers, "you have your own children and the cycle begins all over again."

Harmodius took a moment to let this all sink in. Having been exposed since early childhood to countless obviously enamored male couples walking arm in arm through the streets of the city, and familiar with his father's own past intimate relationship with Cleisthenes, none of these concepts were particularly new or troubling to him. In an odd way, now that he'd seen how the thing actually worked, he felt much as he had when first exposed to the casual nudity of the gymnasium earlier that morning—it was vaguely unnerving...but still strangely fascinating.

"I think I understand, father..." he arched an eyebrow, "...and those older men watching from up on the peristyle...when the time comes, I should choose from them for my erastes?"

Cimon was touched—and somewhat alarmed—at his innocent son's ingenuousness. "No, no, no Harmodius, you don't go shopping for an erastes like a...a cabbage in the market place...and certainly *not* from those old geezers gawking about on the porches of the colonnade." He laughed. "While your erastes will most certainly be a bit older and more experienced than you...he shouldn't be *that* much older." They turned onto the shady lane that led up the gently sloping hill to the family's city house. "Four or five years at most...that's what you should be looking for. Anything older than that is...well, it may be acceptable in Sparta or Thebes, but it would certainly be frowned on in Athens. Those men lolling about on the porches are idlers with too much time on their hands. Most have never married...or even worse, have grown bored with their poor wives..." he shook his head, "...either way, they're an affront to civic duty and something to avoid. No, Harmodius...mark my words, it's best not to get mixed up with that crowd. Take a father's advice and stick with the chaps closer to your own age...the boys who work out on the ephebeon floor."

Harmodius tapped the arm on his shoulder. "Look, Father...someone has come to visit."

Cimon gazed up the street and saw that it was old Cyrus, Cleisthenes' gray-bearded Persian manservant, who was sitting on their front door stoop passing the time in idle chatter with the family's nursemaid Mila. "Cleisthenes..." he murmured under his breath as they drew closer.

Seeing her master approaching, Mila jumped to her feet and sprang forward on surprisingly agile toes for one so old. "Master..." she cried out, "...the Archon Cleisthenes has been waiting for you for nearly an hour!" Cyrus had risen as well and was standing off to one side with his hands clasped in front of him and his head tilted in deferential obeisance.

Cimon picked up his pace as he approached the door. "Important business, Cyrus?" he asked the dark-skinned servant.

Cyrus' wizened head bobbed up and down. "Oh yes, master Cimon. We have received some sad news from Crete..."

✴   ✴   ✴

"And to think he still made the difficult voyage to Crete twice a year, each spring and each fall. Insisted on it! Even after that most recent seizure left him rigid on one side, forcing him to leave the running of the day to day business in the hands of his steward." Cleisthenes' eyes clouded over and he spat out the word. "Hah! Steward!" He banged his fist on the table. "Damn the gods…Scopas should never have trusted that filthy scoundrel."

Cimon refilled the two cups sitting on the table. "I can't believe he's really dead…"

Cleisthenes took a healthy swig of the lightly watered wine and set his cup back on the table. "The news only came to Athens this past week. Scopas and his boy had taken a shipload of his finest olive oil to Phaistos on the southern coast of Crete…" he winked an eye and tapped the side of his nose "…his best clients he always used to say. And to old Scopas it wasn't work, it was more like a vacation." Cleisthenes sighed and then took another sip. "Apparently, their ship had docked in port and, as he was stepping off the gang plank, he seized up again—just like before—falling backward, straight into the water. That young buck of his, Aristogiton, he jumped right in after him…got a nasty scar on his cheek for his trouble." Cleisthenes shook his head. "But it was too late. The old man must have hit his head on the side of the ship. The poor fellow was on his way to Hades before they could even fish his lifeless body out of the water."

Cimon suppressed a shudder as he called out for more wine. To his surprise, Cleisthenes put a restraining hand on his arm. "Dionysus be damned, old friend, we should go easy on the wine. We'll need our wits about us before this day is done."

Nodding his head, Cimon waved the servant away. "So tell me again…his boy's in trouble…Aristogiton?" His eyes narrowed in concentration as he searched his mind for an elusive face. Harmodius, until that moment sitting quietly at the two men's feet, suddenly shifted his position and in so doing joggled a long-forgotten memory. "Aristogiton…why of course. If I'm not mistaken the boy has big round eyes, like a doe's eyes…and their blue as the 'waters of the morning sea'." He favored his son a wry smile, but Harmodius' seemed to have forgotten his juvenile infatuation from so long ago. "I believe we only met once…and it was quite a few years back. If I'm not mistaken, Scopas brought the boy along with him on one of his many trips out to Araphen."

Cimon scratched his head. "Gods…that must have been more than three or four years ago. I'm not sure exactly…but it was some time before all these seizures finally broke his health." He shook his head. "Even then he was worried about the future…afraid that death was stalking him…hounding his heels. He told me that he'd brought the boy along to show him the ropes…introduce him to his best customers…that kind of thing. I remember him going on and on about preparing young Aristogiton to take over his business in case anything happened to him."

Cleisthenes' eyes lit up. "Now that's exactly what I needed to hear!" He joyously clapped Cimon on the shoulder. "You'll be the boy's salvation!"

❋　　　❋　　　❋

"You might as well come along then, Harmodius…if you're old enough to attend gymnasium, you're certainly old enough to observe the Athenian law courts in action. Run change into your finest clothes and you meet us on the way. We'll be walking in the direction of the Agora."

Harmodius scrambled to his feet, ran to the house fountain and haphazardly splashed water on his face, before hurrying to his room to dig through the cedar chest at the foot of his bed for his finest embroidered himation. He was still trying to drape the folds and pin them into place with a small onyx broach—a birthday gift from his sister Helena—as he rushed out the front door and ran up the street after his father and Cleisthenes.

The two men hadn't gotten far before Harmodius spotted them. Running up alongside, he carefully matched their oversized gaits and pricked up his ears to catch any stray details he might have missed about Aristogiton's lawsuit.

"No, I don't think I remember him," his father was saying. "It was so long ago…after all, it was only a few months after you and I got together at the Kynosarges that you introduced me to Scopus." His father sounded doubtful.

"But surely you must remember his younger brother," answered Cleisthenes. "A hideous brat…always trailing along spoiling for trouble, following Scopus about wherever he went. A skinny little whiner with shifty eyes…and a compulsive liar to boot!"

Cimon's eyebrows shot up. "Skinny…and a liar? Of course, now I remember the little rascal. Scarecrow…Heron the Scarecrow…wasn't that what we used to call him?"

Cleisthenes nodded his head. "The very same! And while he may have joined us here in the middle ages of life, he's still managed to retain all those same disgusting personality traits of his youth. He's still bent on making trouble for old Scopus…even after the poor man has taken his one-way ferry ride over the icy River Styx." Cleisthenes pinched the bridge of his nose, rubbing at an ache forming between his eyes. "No sooner had our young Aristogiton returned from Crete, bereft with the news of his father's untimely death, then the skinny little weasel wormed his way over to the city clerk's office and made a claim to his brother's estate."

"But young Aristogiton…wasn't he Scopus' only son and therefore his only legal heir? How could Heron think to circumvent the city's laws of natural inheritance?"

Cleisthenes shook his head with disgust. "Oh, he's a crafty one, he is. The only thing of any worth in Scopus' entire estate is the old export business. And as the boy has yet to reach his full maturity—however worldly wise and experienced he might be—Heron has sniffed out this window of opportunity. He's applied to the courts for guardianship of the business."

"But the magistrate wouldn't overturn a legal will just because of the age of the inheritor!" Cimon's voice fairly rippled with outrage.

"That's just it…he shouldn't have." Cleisthenes lowered his voice to a near whisper and Harmodius had to lean forward to catch the next few words spoken into his father's ear. "Collusion, my dear friend…collusion, pure and simple. When the naïve boy answered yesterday's summons, he went into the courts fully expecting an open and shut case." Cleisthenes gritted his teeth to control his indignation. "No better than a lamb being led to sacrifice."

"*You're not saying that a city magistrate was bribed?*" Harmodius' father sounded truly scandalized.

Cleisthenes shook his head. "No, I don't think so…at least not the magistrate, thank the gods. But Heron brought three witnesses forward to testify against the boy—two of them were clients of Scopas and the third was that deceitful ingrate of a slave who'd been acting as his steward for these past few years." Cleisthenes spit on the ground in disgust. "The two merchants testified that they'd heard Scopas expressing reservations about his son's ability to run the business." He frowned. "Of course they were quite vague about specific times and places…but, with no one there to refute it, damning evidence just the same!" His eyelids narrowed and his lips pursed together in an irritated grimace. "Then that sniveling slave stepped forward and told the court that in recent months he'd been witness to growing conflicts between the father and son." Cleisthenes took a deep breath and once again lowered his voice to a near whisper. "The deceitful cur actually had the gall to tell the magistrate that he'd

seen the boy beating the old man!" Cleisthenes nodded his head at the astonished look on Cimon's face. "Yes, those were his very words: '...he beat the
poor old man senseless.'"

"But that's impossible! If there were troubles between father and son, why
would Scopas have brought the boy along with him on his last voyage to
Crete?" Cimon shook his head. "It doesn't make any sense, my friend."

Cleisthenes sighed, anxiously rubbing at the deepening furrows on his forehead. "Even so Cimon, with times the way they are...the shaky economy...the
nasty trouble over in Persia..." he shook his head. "In truth, a successful trading company is far too important to the city's financial survival to run the risk
of allowing it to fail. And with that kind of testimony, what could the magistrate do but rule in favor of a trustee to oversee Scopas' business?"

"But they must be lying...it can't be true," Cimon shook his head angrily.
"It can't be, I tell you. I know it's been some time since I met the boy, but he
was devoted to his father...*and to the business as well.* All those years ago when
they came to visit our farm and the old man and I sat talking shop over a cool
jug of Egyptian beer, even then the boy insisted on perching right alongside us
on a little stool...hanging onto every word his father uttered...almost as
though he were hearing direct pronouncements from the Oracle at Delphi! We
finally had to shoo the poor lad outside with the other children so that the old
man and I could reminisce about the 'good old days'!"

Cleisthenes' grim scowl had almost softened to a half-smile. "Those words
are music to my ear, old friend. Thank the gods on high Olympus that I was in
court on my own business yesterday...or we might have been too late to save
the boy. I recognized the lad right off and when I saw what was happening—that dazed look on the poor boy's face as the magistrate issued his verdict—well, you can just bet I stepped forward and immediately invoked
Solon's right of appeal." His smile blossomed into a Cheshire grin. "You should
have seen the looks on all their faces! Heron turned redder than a beet! And
those so-called witnesses of his...well, I can assure you that their eyes grew
wider than honey pots as they darted about the room with all the desperation
of shades looking for the quickest escape route from Hades!"

Cleisthenes' mirth was infectious. As Cimon joined his old erastes in a
hearty bout of laughter, Harmodius could feel the exhilaration building in his
chest. With confident steps the three entered the Agora and twisted their way
through the swarming crowds of late afternoon shoppers. Cimon and Cleisthenes, their two heads bent together as they worked out a final strategy, left

Harmodius to stand alone in an alcove at the rear of the courtroom as they proceeded down the main aisle to take seats on a bench up near the front.

Harmodius, scanning the crowd from his hidden perch at the back, was hoping to recognize Aristogiton. He remembered something about meeting the boy on that single, long ago day back at the farm…but for some reason, had trouble recalling his face.

A moment later, Harmodius' breath caught in his throat as a strapping youth with piercing blue eyes and an angry red scar running up from the edge of his jaw line, passed by him less than an arm's length away. A shiver ran up his spine accompanied by the vague memory of two muscular arms pulling him to his feet, his father's war helmet all akimbo on his head even as those same blue eyes drolly scrutinized him from head to foot. Before he could open his mouth to say something, the young man passed him by, striding boldly down that same central aisle taken just moments before by his father and Cleisthenes.

❧   ❧   ❧

"Here he comes…"

Hipparchus stepped back into the shadows before turning to watch as the Archon Cleisthenes, with another man walking close by his side, entered the courtroom and took seats down near the front. Keeping a scowl hidden from his companion's view, Hipparchus reached out and grabbed the frightened man's arm. "I told you to stay calm."

"How can I stay calm?" hissed Heron, *"He's an archon for god's sake!"*

The errant brother of Athens' reigning Co-tyrant tightened his grip until the other man whimpered in pain. "Nothing will go wrong if your men just keep their wits about them!"

Hipparchus' little fiduciary adventure had taken an unfortunate turn yesterday when Cleisthenes, swooping down like a veritable 'deus-ex-machina', made a last minute appearance at the hearing and invoked the boy's right to an appeal. What had started as an easy mark—a small monetary investment in exchange for a silent partnership in one very lucrative oil exporting business—had grown considerably more costly with this new development. Last night, their two already well-paid 'witnesses' had panicked at the prospect of perjuring themselves in front of an entire room full of jurors. Only a hefty increase to an already excessive bribe had kept them from 'disappearing' before today's appeal. In moments, what had started as a petty investment had swollen into something his present purse could ill afford. As he released his hold on Heron's arm, Hipparchus felt his teeth beginning to grind at the thought of losing all that money.

"Look there, Hipparchus...it's the brat!"

The two men watched from their hiding place at the side of the hall as Heron's nephew Aristogiton entered. Scanning the jostling crowd until he caught sight of Cleisthenes, the boy straightened his shoulders and lifted his head high before making his confident way down along the wide central aisle to join the archon and his friend up near the front. The sight of that very short tunic and those young muscular thighs moving with all the swagger of an Olympian racer making his way to the starting line, gave Hipparchus a moment's pause. "After this is all over, I wouldn't mind a piece of that ass..."

Heron, a nasty smirk spreading across his face, choked back a high-pitched shriek. "Aphrodite be damned...how can you think of sex at a time like this?"

"Go on, worm..." the dissolute brother of Athens' overlord gave Heron a rough shove back out into the open courtroom, "...it's time you took your place at the front with the others." As Heron stepped forward he heard Hipparchus hiss a final warning. "And don't screw this up..."

Feeling the sudden chill of a trickle of sweat running down the center of his back, Heron timidly joined his three fidgeting witnesses up near the front of the hall. Hipparchus, meanwhile, gave his youthful adversary one more avaricious look before quietly slipping back into the shadows to watch the proceedings from his hiding place.

"Too bad about that scar..." he thought.

In Athens, the law clearly stated that whenever private citizens brought grievances against one another, the *anakrisis*—or preliminary hearing—was heard before a single court magistrate. Having affirmed their oaths of honesty, the magistrate listened to the testimony given and, if the evidence weighed heavily on one side or the other, his decision was usually accepted as the final verdict. However, since the judicial reforms of the Tyrant Solon nearly a century before, Athenian's had been guaranteed the right to appeal any magisterial decision before a full jury. The number of jurors varied from trial to trial—Athenians trusting the maxim that the larger the jury, the less chance for a suborned outcome. Any male citizen over the age of 30 could sit on a jury and—as trials were one of the few day-to-day entertainments available to the average Athenian—juries often numbered in the hundreds. On this particular day to hear the case challenging Scopus' will there were well over two hundred jurors present in the courtroom.

Silence spread across the hall as the magistrate, a balding, heavyset man with a perpetually sweat-covered forehead and three ponderous chins rolling down to his chest, waddled into the room. Seating himself on the dais directly across from the jury, he picked up a scroll sitting on a table at his side, unrolled it and in a stentorian voice proceeded to review the evidence from the day before. Having been given a passing familiarity with the basics of the case, the witnesses were then recalled one by one to restate their testimony before the jurors.

Initially, all went much as it had the day before. The two merchants stood up, each in their turn, and repeated their so-called 'damning testimony' concerning Scopus' distrust of his son's business abilities. Astute observers who'd been in attendance at yesterday's anakrisis might have noticed a newfound reticence to their testimony—words more carefully considered, an uncomfortable evasiveness when questioned by the jury. On the other side of the aisle, Aristogiton turned to nervously glance over his shoulder at Cleisthenes and, in return, received stoic smiles and nods of reassurance.

Then it was Scopus' steward—the slave Bustades—turn to be summoned from the witness bench. With far less to lose than his two perjuring co-conspirators, he approached the jury with an air of smug confidence. A mocking half-bow to his superiors, the slave opened his mouth to speak and was immediately cut off by a loud shout from behind. Spinning around, he saw that the archon Cleisthenes had risen to his feet and was signaling to the magistrate for a 'point-of-order'.

Tamping with an already damp handkerchief at the sweat on his cheeks, the magistrate held a puffy hand up to put a hold to Bustades' testimony. Noting the presence of the Archon, with a ponderous nod of his head, he signaled for Cleisthenes to continue.

"Honored Magistrate, Citizen-Jurors...I apologize for interrupting these worthy proceedings, but in the interest of Athenian justice I must point out that the man about to give testimony is a *slave.*" As Cleisthenes directed a damning finger in Bustades direction, the slave felt all his smug self-confidence draining away. "And the law clearly states that if the defendant is a citizen, then a slave's testimony can only be given while under torture..."

The magistrate scratched his three chins for a moment, his eyes narrowing to slits as he considered the validity of Cleisthenes' point of law. After a moment he nodded his head. "You are, of course, most correct, honored Archon." He smiled blandly at Cleisthenes. "The court thanks you for keeping us…er, on our toes." Turning to the boy Aristogiton, he waved a questioning hand in the air. "Is it the defendant's desire to hear this slave's testimony under torture?"

Before the boy could stand and answer the magistrate, Heron jumped to his feet and shouted. "But hold, Honored magistrate…it's not true! This man is not a slave! He was given his freedom in my brother's will. Here…look here, my lord…these are his manumission papers!" He shuffled up to the dais and bowing low, placed a scroll in the magistrate's expansive lap, before hurriedly scuttling back to his bench.

For a moment the magistrate sat scowling down at the tightly wound scroll…and then, using two nimble, long-nailed fingers, he picked it up and dropped it on the table next to him without so much as favoring it with a single glance. His eyes slowly moved across the room until they locked on Heron. "This man, you say…this man was freed in your brother's will? This same *will* that you are here today contesting in this courtroom?"

Heron felt the color draining from his face. "Why…uh…yes, Honored Magistrate, that would be correct. Of course…er, I am not contesting the…not the entire will, Honored Lord…just the portion dealing with my brother's olive oil…"

"Enough!" The magistrate raised a threatening hand for silence. "Either you accept the merchant Scopus' will as it stands…and in that case the court will acknowledge that this *person* is a free man…" he pointed a thick finger at Bustades, his head now bent over in utter terror as his two trembling knees visibly knocked against one another, "…or you continue with your challenge to this boy's inheritance," he nodded at Aristogiton, "…thus temporarily invalidating the entire will until this case is resolved."

Heron, his hands contritely wringing together, bowed to the magistrate several times. "A thousand pardons, Honored Sir…a thousand pardons. Of course I wish my case to proceed…but…is it really necessary to torture this poor soul to elicit his…"

"Very well then." Ignoring Heron's sputtering objections, the magistrate turned his attention back to Aristogiton. "Once again, young man, I ask you…is it your wish that this slave's testimony be taken under torture?"

Before Aristogiton could offer up any response, the whole room suddenly echoed with a loud thunk as Bustades dropped to the floor in a dead faint. Summoning two guards with an impatient waggle of his finger, the magistrate sat rolling his eyes and twiddling his thumbs together as he waited for the slave to be revived. Finally restored to a semblance of consciousness by a painful kick in the side, and now propped in place between the two burly guards, Bustades immediately began moaning and crying out, begging the court to spare him from any torture. His panicked entreaties ignored by the disgusted magistrate, the frightened man unexpectedly began to recant his earlier testimony.

"I lied…" he screamed over and over, "…please don't hurt me…not torture…please, I beg of you…don't torture me…I'll tell the whole truth! My good master loved this dear boy. He told me so time and again. And all he wanted was for the lad to take over the business!" Tears came streaming down the poor fellow's cheeks. "The master was always so good to me…he trusted me so…oh, why…oh, why did I ever get involved in all this…" his cries ended in an ear-piercing howl as his knees began to buckle under him. Grabbing him by the arms, the two guards struggled to keep him upright.

The magistrate slowly got to his feet, the utter disgust on his face evident to everyone in the courtroom. "Shut that creature up…" he grumbled to one of the guards. After the man had brutally clamped a hand over Bustades' mouth, the magistrate raised his voice so the entire courtroom could hear. "This man…" he shouted, "this *slave*…has lied while under the most sacred oaths of law. As he's already given conflicting testimony in this case, torture would be useless in bringing us any closer to the truth." The relief on Bustades' face lasted less than a moment, as the magistrate's next words sealed his fate. "For committing the crime of perjury against a free citizen of Athens, I order that he be taken out and executed—his throat to be slit, his tongue to be cut from his head and burned on the altar of the Temple of Jupiter, and his perfidious heart to be cut out and fed to the crows nesting near Athena's Temple on the Acropolis. The remains of his naked body are to be tossed outside the city walls, there to be devoured by whatever carrion eaters can stomach his deceitful soul."

With an irrevocable slice of his hand he dismissed the guards who dragged their horrified prisoner, kicking and screaming, from the great hall. Turning to resume his seat, the magistrate waited impatiently for the noise in the great hall to quiet. With order restored, the magistrate turned his attention to the jury. "Good citizens, it appears that you must now render a verdict based solely upon the testimony of the two *previous* witnesses…" he looked over his shoulder at the whispering figures on the front row benches and cocked an eyebrow, "…unless there's someone else?"

Aristogiton jumped up. "Yes, Lord…I do have a witness."

With some effort, the magistrate stifled a weary sigh as he took the edge of his handkerchief and wiped at the beads of sweat trapped inside the folds of his copious chin. "Very well then...let him step forward and address the jury." Without further prompting, Cimon stood up, slid past Cleisthenes, and walked over to stand in front of the jury box. After speaking his oath of truthfulness before all those present, in a loud, clear voice he began his testimony:

"Citizens...I am called Cimon...Cimon, the son of Harmodius and grandson of Cimon of the Gephyrae clan. I met the merchant Scopus many years ago, first as a worthy opponent in the wrestling pit at the Kynosarges and then again in later years, as a satisfied client of his flourishing export business." He paused for a moment to let his long history and close association with Scopus strike home with the jury.

"At my farm near the town of Araphen I have several large groves of olive trees and for many years now I have carried an exclusive contract..."

❦   ❦   ❦

Hipparchus, sequestered in his cubbyhole at the rear, had watched in a blind fury as the slave Bustades was dragged screaming from the courtroom. Convinced that their case was lost, he pulled his chlamys up over his head and was about to sneak out the back of the building in search of a cheap bottle of wine to mollify his anger, when the sight of Cleisthenes' friend walking boldly up to the witness stand brought his exodus to an abrupt halt.

There was something familiar about the man...something familiar and...disturbing. With a quick step back into the shadows, he let his chlamys fall back around his shoulders and listened intently as the man began to speak.

"Citizens...I am called Cimon...Cimon, the son of Harmodius and grandson of Cimon of the Gephyrae clan. I first met the merchant Scopus..."

That voice...

Hipparchus chewed on his lower lip as he wracked his brain to recall the last time he'd seen that face and heard that self-assured voice. He could almost feel a hint of a memory from long ago niggling at the back of his head...but in a most aggravating fashion, it continued to elude him. As the forthright witness made a vigorous case in the boy's defense with his account of the old merchant and his son paying a visit to a farm out in the countryside, Hipparchus had an epiphany. The image of a cow-headed drinking cup suddenly blazed forth in his mind's eye...the very one he'd bought all those years ago for the Festival of

Fatherhood. And with that same image linking to the sound of this witness' voice, the rest came flooding back.

The lazy fool of a pottery merchant…his missing cup…a sniveling slave lying in the dirt with a bloody nose…and the haughty young fool who'd had the nerve to come to the slave's defense.

"Of course…" he thought, "the marketplace outside the Dipylon Gate. My father's drinking cup…that stupid slave and the citizen who challenged my right to…"

The blood rushed to his face, the heat of humiliation burning his cheeks as he recalled that cold, mocking voice and those scorn-filled words aimed at slighting his dignity.

'Was that really necessary? This man is not the cause of your troubles…'

The stinging words rang in his ears as though it were yesterday.

And now, after all these years, here he comes again…come to the rescue of yet another pathetic stray. "And once again at my expense…" The words smoldered in his mind as he struggled to focus his attention on the man's damning testimony. It was clear to even the dullest wit in the crowd that the Bustades' travesty—coupled with the obvious sincerity of this new witness—had swayed the jury over to their side. Even that fat pig of a magistrate was leaning forward in his seat, listening raptly as the cursed man recounted a tale of a promise made:

"…And the next morning, as we were loading the mule train for the trip back to the city, Scopus took me aside, begging me once again to honor his wishes concerning his son Aristogiton." It was clear to Hipparchus that this Cimon, son of Harmodius—his eyes slowly surveying the members of the jury with an earnest gaze—had them in the palm of his hand. "Fellow citizens, I grant you that this happened almost three years ago. But even at that much earlier age, Scopus believed his son had already acquired the skills and strength of character necessary for successfully running the family olive oil trade." The witness turned back and nodded toward the boy. "I have no doubt that, should you see fit to reinstate the pertinent codicils of my friend Scopus' will, Aristogiton will do his father…and our glorious city-state…proud."

There was no point in waiting for the outcome…

Even as Hipparchus pulled the nondescript chlamys back up over his head and slunk quietly from the cavernous building, he could hear the echo of the 'pebbles of exoneration' being dropped into the great bronze urn as it was passed from one juror's hand to the next.

Outside on the steps of the law court he found his associates throwing dice against one another in the shade of the porch overhang. Taking a particularly mean-faced one aside, he pulled him over behind a wide column where they could watch the expansive courthouse door without being seen by the perpetually milling crowds. As they stood waiting, he whispered a series of orders in terse, clipped sentences to the surly henchman.

The fool Heron's bumbling miscalculation with that gutless slave would end up costing him a great deal of money that day...the bribes alone could have fed a large family for months. But settling up with that sniveling weasel could wait...at least, for the time being. For the present, his mind had turned to settling an older score.

Moments later, the trial having come to an ending, the courthouse began to clear out. Pulling the thuggish man in close to his side, he whispered: "Watch closely now..."

There they were...the arrogant Cleisthenes walking arm-in-arm with that scar-faced pup Aristogiton...the well-wishers pummeling them on all sides with boisterous cries of congratulations. Broad smiles on beaming faces as they exited the building verified a verdict in their favor...and brought another cold rush of anger roiling up inside Hipparchus' chest. And then, crowding out behind them and bringing up the rear of the little group...

"That's him! That one there...he's the one...the man with the young boy at his side!"

For a second, Hipparchus found himself distracted by the sight of the long ebony locks of gently curling hair falling over the slender neck of the youth walking at Cimon's side.

"A bit too young," he thought to himself, "but verging on a beauty that someday soon will be ripe for..."

With an angry shake of his head, he pushed the lascivious thought from of his mind. Wrenching his gaze from the boy walking at Cimon's side, he grabbed his henchman by the arm and slipped a few coins into his open hand.

"The man...his name is Cimon...go and follow him. See where he lives. Use discretion. Find out everything you can about him from his neighbors and then report back to me as quickly as possible." As the man was about to start off, Hipparchus had a sudden afterthought and called him back. "I heard him say something about a farm out in the countryside...near Araphen I think." With a quick nod of his head, he sent the man on his way.

As the father and son moved off down the steps of the courthouse, Hipparchus watched with pleasure as his burly minion—keeping a discreet distance behind them—pursued his quarry into the teeming crowd. Leaning back against the stony-cold pillar, he let out a long sigh and for the first time all afternoon felt a thin smile stretching across his face.

"Ahh…" he mused to himself, "what could be more satisfying than settling up an old score?"

＊　　　＊　　　＊

The weeks immediately following the trial were hectic ones for Aristogiton. Now the sole director of his father's business, there were delayed inventories to be filled, merchants to be visited, and newly contracted orders to be sent on their way. Aristogiton had hoped to express his gratitude to Cimon and his family long before this, but instead found himself constantly pulled back to the warehouse to settle problems that had been left unresolved since his father's untimely death.

Finally the day came when everything seemed to be in place…slaves and workers were busy at their assigned tasks, the latest shipment of export goods bound for the islands of Naxos and Delos had sailed from the harbor at Piraeus the day before, and Aristogiton at last found himself with his afternoon free. Following a brisk workout and a relaxing soak in the heated pool at the Kynosarges, he returned home and dressed himself in his finest chiton. Lifting a heavy jug of the finest Egyptian beer in his arms—he hadn't needed Cimon's testimony to jog his memory of that still fondly recalled visit to the Araphen countryside all those years ago—he made his way through the early evening streets of the city in search of Cimon's house.

As he walked along it occurred to him that, as much as he'd wanted to thank Cimon for saving the day at his appeal, Aristogiton was also looking forward to reacquainting himself with that fine looking son of his…the boy called Harmodius. On that afternoon, as they were all leaving the courthouse, the two had only a moment to shyly nod at one another before the boy and his father had been swept away by the jostling crowds. Feeling a nervous lump settle in his throat, Aristogiton found himself pondering the promise of that developing young body coupled with the honest intensity shining from those two smiling brown eyes. And, gods…then there was that long, curling black hair that fell ever so lightly over his shoulders. Was this really the same child he'd teased so ruthlessly about his father's oversized war helmet on that hot day in the olive grove at Araphen?

Aristogiton, reaching what he thought was the street where Cimon and his family lived, was about to turn the corner and start up the hill when, in the fading light of sunset, an old woman with a black himation pulled up over her head, shuffled past him and turned up the street ahead of him.

"Excuse me, old mother…" he called out, "I am looking for the house of a man named Cimon…I was told he and his family live somewhere nearby?"

Aristogiton heard a gasp as the woman stopped dead in her tracks. After an uncomfortable silence, she slowly turned back and peered at him through the growing darkness. A torch had been lit on the lintel of a nearby doorway and in the flickering light Aristogiton could see that the old woman had been crying.

"Yes," she finally said, her voice trembling with emotion, "…just up this street a ways." A single tear ran down the hollow of her withered cheek and dropped onto the dusty road at her feet. "But, good sir…my master Cimon…he is no more."

"No more?" Aristogiton shuddered as the color drained from his face. "You mean that Cimon…Cimon, the close friend of the archon Cleisthenes…this same Cimon is…is dead?"

"The very same." With a solemn nod of her head, the old woman wiped at another tear with the back of her hand. "Foully murdered, he was…out on the road to Araphen…by scurrilous robbers who lured him from the city with a false tale of a fire at the family's farm." Her voice caught in her throat and Aristogiton touched her arm with a sympathetic hand. "They stabbed him in the back, they did…then they stole his horse and left him naked and dead by the side of the road." Her halting voice had become a low moan as she held up a gnarled fist clutching a sprig of parsley in it. "My mistress sent me to the market so we'd have a little parsley to sprinkle on his…his grave. He is to be buried in the morning."

Aristogiton was stunned.

Memories of the miserable days at sea mourning his father's lifeless body, even as it slowly corrupted in a great barrel of brine in the hold of the ship returning from Crete, came flooding back to haunt him. For nearly a week he'd spoken to no one…had taken his spare meals and spent his anguish in the seclusion of the dark, damp hold. And at the time, he'd been grateful to be left alone with his grief.

As he looked up the dark street, he pictured Cimon lying cold and stiff on his wooden bier, the boy Harmodius standing at his father's side with his palms held out in supplication to the gods, the beautiful face twisted in anguish, his dazzling black hair cropped brutally short in mourning…and all of a sudden the heavy jar of fine Egyptian beer became an awkward weight in his arms.

A cold touch on his shoulder woke him from this reverie. "Good sir…if you like I can show you the way. Will you follow me to the house?"

Aristogiton took a step backward, his eyes dropping shamefacedly to the ground. "No…no, I have no wish to disturb them now." He shifted the jug to one side. "I'll…I'll make my delivery on a more suitable day." With a brusque nod of his head, he turned away and disappeared into the looming night before the old woman could call him back.

CHAPTER 4

Harmodius scratched his head in frustration…try as he might, the figures from the farm's earnings just weren't coming out right. The oil lamp sitting on the edge of the table sputtered for a moment causing the shadow of his stylus to dance from wall to wall. Shrugging his shoulders to release the knots in his neck, he took a sip from a cup of diluted wine and, with a world-weary sigh, started at the top of the row of figures one more time. Halfway down the wax tablet he let out a grunt of satisfaction when he found his mistake. With the last month's income and outlay finally balancing, he closed the account register and pushed his chair back from the table.

Cleisthenes had done his work well…

Two years had passed since Harmodius' father had met his untimely end. And in all that time the murder, as well as the identity of his assassin, had remained a mystery. Given the sequence of events, there were still too many unanswered questions crying out for an answer.

A few days after the business concerning old Scopus' estate was settled, Cimon had received a frantic message—purporting to be from the farm's manager at Araphen—saying that a terrible fire had destroyed the family's barn and several of the nearby outbuildings. The letter writer sounded both confused and frightened as he urged Cimon to come at once and deal with the disaster in person.

The very next morning, as the sun was edging over the eastern horizon, Cimon kissed his wife and children goodbye, tied a pack carrying some food and a change of clothes to his saddle, mounted a horse borrowed the night before from Cleisthenes, and headed off at a gallop toward Araphen. Halfway there, just outside the tiny village of Phyla, his unknown assailant had ambushed the unsuspecting Cimon. Several hours later a passing traveler came upon Cimon's naked corpse laying face down in a muddy ditch by the side of the road.

Early the next day Cleisthenes himself personally rode out with a large retinue to bring the broken body of his one time lover home to Athens. When the farm servants and slaves were summoned back to the city to attend Cimon's funeral, to everyone's great surprise it was discovered that there had never been a fire at Araphen…the original letter had been a ruse. The family's poor, confused manager, insisting that no such message had ever been sent from the farm, nearly committed suicide on the spot for having been the nominal cause of his master's death if the good Philippia hadn't forcefully intervened.

Without a standing police force to investigate such crimes, and lacking any obvious clues or witnesses to the act, little could be done to pursue justice in the case of Cimon's murder. In the end, the mystery of the absent fire was shrugged off with most agreeing that Cimon had most likely been the unfortunate victim of one of the numberless highwaymen then plaguing Attica's rural roads.

Following the funeral, Cleisthenes dutifully took it upon himself to place Cimon's wretched young family under his protection. Just eleven years old at the time of his father's death, the old erastes saw to it that Harmodius mastered the workings of his father's farmstead, thus ensuring at least a measure of financial stability for the family. Little my little, the bereaved household removed their mourning garb and once again moved forward. Harmodius resumed his education at the Kynosarges and Philippia, taking her daughter's domestic education firmly in hand, saw to it that each month a small portion of their income was set aside for Helena's future dowry.

A year later, in 519 B.C., the political scene in Athens was thrown into turmoil when the tyrant Hippias decided the time had come to reassert his control over the floundering city-state. Adversaries who'd been given ostensible positions of power in his earlier show of good will were, one by one, stripped of their titles and sent back into ignominious retirement. As corrupt sycophants and hangers-on took their places controlling more and more of the city's important municipal offices, the few voices of reason that rose up against the excesses of the Tyrant soon found themselves impeached from office under fabricated charges and, in many cases, stripped of their lands and sent off into exile. Unjustly charged with 'corruption in office', the archon Cleisthenes—following his own sham trial—was himself cast out of the city. Few friends had the courage to show up in court when the vilified Cleisthenes was sentenced to exile on the island of Crete for ten long years. But Harmodius, the grateful son of Cimon, was in the forefront of this minority of well-wishers.

By the time he'd reached his thirteenth year, Harmodius had settled into a confident routine as head of the family household. Twice a year, at planting and harvesting time, he would ride out to Araphen to personally oversee affairs on the family's farmstead. The rest of the year, with the day-to-day administration of the farm left—as it was during his father and grandfather's lifetimes—in the experienced hands of an on-site manager, Harmodius was free to continue his education in Athens. Each morning, as the city streets and markets were coming alive with noisy activity, he'd stroll through the town, picking up friends and admirers all along the way as he headed toward the high-towered gate leading out to the quiet deme of Diomeia and its' famous gymnasium—the Kynosarges.

Adolescence burst upon his unsuspecting body like a fever, and Harmodius found himself growing increasingly interested in the other naked, sweaty young men working out alongside him on the open fields of the ephebeon. Interested, yes. At times, he might have even admitted to an attraction or two. But, whereas others his age were busily yielding to the temptation of their own passionate pairings, Harmodius found himself not quite ready to commit to any serious relationship. Time and again he would hear an echo of his father's sage advice ringing in his ear and tactfully withdraw from any perceived attention before it got out of hand. His mind and body—both flourishing under the strenuous tutelage of the many philosophers, orators, and athletes at the Kynosarges—assured him that, although he had many admirers longing to claim him as eromenos, the right one had yet to come along.

Of course, that's not to say that he wasn't pursued…

❀   ❀   ❀

Harmodius crossed the small room that had served as his father's office, carefully returning the waxen slates containing the farm's monthly accounts back to the corner shelf resting against the eastern wall. Stacking them on top of last month's records, he returned to the table that now served as his desk and retrieved the flickering oil lamp. With the household long abed, an occasional snore coming from the servants' quarters was the only thing that threatened to intrude on his private thoughts as he crossed by lamplight under the old olive tree still growing in the central courtyard. He reached out and affectionately touched a gnarled limb of the old tree—that very same tree he'd played under as a child—before heading off to make one final check that all the windows and doors were secured tightly before retiring for the night.

As he was about to joggle the bolt on the front door, he thought he heard a noise just outside…almost like someone had stumbling up against the front of the house. A moment later there followed the muffled, but still obvious sounds of nervous voices giggling. Curious, he reached for the bolt just as a heavy-handed fist slammed up against the door. The earsplitting knock was so loud that it made Harmodius jump backward. Even as he reached out to slide the locking bolt back, he could make out the sounds of panicked feet scrambling away down the street. Pulling open the heavy door, Harmodius ran out into the lane after them, his head turning in both directions in a vain effort to catch sight of the late night mischief-makers. And, as on too many nights before…he was disappointed to find his tormentors had already vanished from sight. Rubbing his forehead in frustration, he groaned and turned back to find his mother standing in the open doorway, a snowy white wool blanket wrapped across her shoulders to ward off the late night chill.

"Goodness…I'm sure that even your late father, as handsome as he was, never knew such popularity in his youth!" She favored him with an ironic smile as she pointed a telling finger down at a large woven straw basket full of luscious, ripe fruit leaning haphazardly against the side of the front steps.

"Sorry, Mother…I'm sure they didn't mean to disturb your sleep." He shook his head in frustration. "I'll see what I can do to put a stop to all this foolishness in the morning."

Philippia's eyes opened wide as she laughed at the embarrassment on her exasperated son's face. "Oh, no…don't do that, my little man. Youth and beauty are such fleeting things. The day will arrive far too soon when you'll find yourself longing for all these little…attentions."

"Very funny, Mother…" he grumbled under his breath. With a heavy sigh, Harmodius stooped over, picked up the loaded basket and followed her back inside the house. Balancing the awkward load in one arm, as he turned to reset the bolt on the door, Philippia reached past him and plucked a golden plum from the top of the tasty assortment.

"Besides…" she continued with an impish gleam in her eyes, "out-of-season fruit isn't easy to come by these days. And I do so love a good ripe plum before retiring in the evening!" With a quiet laugh, she turned towards her bedroom and, tossing the plum up and down in her hand, disappeared into the darkness.

✤   ✤   ✤

"Was there any message?"

Harmodius pulled two shiny succulent apples from inside his chiton and passed them to Tylissus who in turn tossed one over his head to Nicias, the red-haired lad lagging along at the rear of their little troupe. "Of course...hidden away at the bottom of the basket," he answered with a bored tilt of his head. "A short message...written on Egyptian papyrus."

Nicias gasped. The apple now all but forgotten in his hand, he ran to catch up to his friends. "By Hera's sacred rump!" He whistled in Harmodius' ear, "Do you know how expensive that stuff is?" Harmodius turned away and gave Tylissus an all-too-knowing look. "Cleon gripes for days whenever his father invests in a new shipment."

A month earlier, after a somewhat abbreviated courtship, Harmodius' oldest school chum Nicias had accepted Cleon, the son of a prosperous trader, as his erastes. The only one of the three inseparable friends to have so far made his match, Nicias was one of brash identical twin sons born to impoverished working-class parents, the owners of a small armor repair shop just outside the city walls. Initially shunning the besotted Cleon's overtures—largely because of the difference in their social status—Nicias feigned indifference to his many lavish gifts. The good-natured red head claimed to have been finally won over by a single passion-filled kiss when cornered one afternoon under a shady pine tree in the Kynosarges Park. From that day on, the two were practically inseparable...and Nicias had developed a surprising interest in the value of things material.

"Never mind what it was written on..." his mouth so full of juicy pulp, Tylissus could barely be understood. "Tell us what the note said!"

Pulling a last hidden apple from the pouch of his loose-belted chiton, Harmodius held it up to his eye and carefully examined the dark red, as yet unbroken skin. With his friends hovering anxiously on either side to hear exactly what had been written on his little hidden love missive, he chose instead to help himself to a bite...sadistically savoring the fruit's sweet-pungent, woodsy flavor.

"Come on, you donkey's ass! Tell us!" Tylissus pummeled Harmodius on the shoulder and a chunk of the apple almost caught in his windpipe. Coughing it up, he spit it out and wiped the juice drippings from his lips with the back of his hand.

"Oh, all right!" Harmodius' eyes narrowed in mock-annoyance as he shrugged his shoulders. "It really didn't say all that much, you know…just a few trite phrases…and no signature or seal."

"And they were…" Nicias squeezed his arm.

Harmodius sighed. "*Think of me, handsome one…and save an apple for your sister.*"

Tylissus and Nicias each grabbed hold of an arm, roughly jerking Harmodius to a halt in mid-step. "*Diokles!*" Their high-pitched screams cascaded off the surrounding houses as they jumped about in the air laughing and shouting his name over and over again.

"Diokles." Harmodius finally affirmed with a somewhat chagrined shrug of his shoulders. It was common knowledge around the Kynosarges' playing field that on a certain morning several months ago when the tall, gangly-limbed Diokles first spied the handsome brother and his fair young sister shopping together in the agora, Eros had been laying in wait with *two* arrows notched in his bow. And while there was little doubt that Diokles' current obsession was wooing the spectacular Harmodius for his eromenos, many suspected he already had an eye out for his future bride. And the ebullient Helena—who at twelve years of age was already taking on the pleasing adolescent roundness of womanhood—had become an added distraction.

"And?" asked Nicias.

"And what?" Harmodius shook off the two restraining arms and helped himself to another bite from his apple as they continued on their way toward their morning workout at the Kynosarges.

"And…did you save the little princess one of your precious apples?" Nicias loved a good joke.

Harmodius' upper lip curled with the distain of an older and wiser brother. "I'm afraid there were only three apples in Diokles' gift basket. One for you…one for Tylissus…and," he took one last noisy bite from his own apple before tossing the core high into a tree branch where a chittering squirrel deftly caught it between two tiny gray hands, "…one for me and my little friend up there!" He bowed graciously to the little ball of animated fur who took this as a signal to disappear around the other side of the tree. "I'm afraid that if my sister wants an apple, the 'little princess' will have to see to her own harvest!"

The echo of their ribald bantering followed them as they passed under the Diomeia Gate. A few minutes later, as they entered the expansive grounds of the Kynosarges, Tylissus turned to Harmodius and, in a somewhat off-hand manner, asked: "So…what *are* you planning on doing about Diokles?"

Harmodius shrugged his shoulders. "Don't know…" his forehead wrinkled in thought. "I've tried to be polite, to let the infatuated fool down gently…but he doesn't seem to take any notice of my total lack of interest."

"Well you know…persistence isn't necessarily a bad thing." replied Tylissus.

Harmodius stopped and gave him a sidelong glance. "No…" he took a deep breath and let it out in a long, exasperated sigh. "But unfortunately the wretched Diokles has of late gone well beyond *persistent*." Straightening his shoulders, he took two leaping skips before performing a perfect cartwheel in the sand. Turning back to face his friends he added: "By the gods, his little escapade last night even got my mother up from her bed!" Vexed, he shook his head in disgust. "So I think it's time I put an end to all this business with Diokles once and for all.

"You're not going to hurt his feelings, are you?"

The unforeseen edge in Tylissus' voice caused Harmodius and Nicias to turn and look at him in surprise. Staring at his curly-headed friend, Harmodius' eyes screwed together as he tried to read Tylissus' face. The nervous boy opened his mouth to say something more…and instead, slowly dropped his head against his chest to stare forlornly down at his sandal straps.

Setting two hands squarely on his hips, for once Harmodius resisted the urge to curl up a sardonic eyebrow. "What's going on here, my friend? Is there some special reason why I should go easy on that imposingly oafish Diokles?" He tilted his head to one side and grinned. "It couldn't be that there is perhaps…something going on between you two?"

Tylissus looked up, his face flushed as he stubbornly shook his head. "No…" he almost shouted the word. Then, with a careful modulation of his cracking voice, he mumbled, "…not really."

Unconvinced, Nicias came creeping around to Tylissus' other side. Resting his chin on a shoulder, he whispered in his ear: "*Not really?*" With a sidelong glance and a mischievous twinkle in his eye, he winked over at the grinning Harmodius. "What kind of an answer is that? Come on, speak up little Tyty…it's time to tell Harmodius the truth."

Tylissus, his face burning under their relentless gaze, shrugged him off with a mulish shake of his head. Intrigued by this unexpected turn of events, Harmodius plopped himself down on the ground at their feet and smiled up at his friends. "All right then, you two…I'm not moving from this spot until I know exactly what's going on!"

Nicias scampered around to kneel at Harmodius' side. "If he won't tell you, I will!" he hissed. Before Tylissus could stop him, Nicias had blurted out that their curly-headed friend had been nursing a secret unrequited crush on Harmodius' Diokles for these past several weeks.

Looking up into the pained expression on the humiliated Tylissus' face, Harmodius slowly shook his head and favored him with a sheepish grin. Reaching up, he grabbed hold of his wrist and yanked, pulling the flustered Tylissus down onto the grass next to him. "Little fool, why didn't you say something? If I don't want him...and I certainly don't...what's to stop you from going after him?"

Unable to come up with an answer, Tylissus just shook his head and shrugged. Laying a sympathetic arm across his shoulders, Harmodius pulled him close and kissed him on the cheek. "Forgive me, friend...I've been insensitive. Diokles is a fine man...handsome, intelligent, well mannered and...er, persistent. And you, good Tylissus, are his match in every way." His eyebrows drew together in affected consternation as Harmodius added with a chuckle, "Well, perhaps you're not quite as persistent." Ruffling his fingers through the tight, closely cropped curls, he took his chin and turned his head so that they were looking into each other's eyes. "Is there something...some reason you felt unworthy to pursue this erastes in your own right?"

"But it's you who've caught his eye..." Tylissus protested.

Harmodius laughed and patted him gently on the cheek. "Silly boy, that's nothing. No doubt I'm just a passing infatuation...another pretty face prancing around the ephebeon to him." With a look of blithe disregard he shrugged his shoulders before adding with a loud snort. "And besides, you haven't forgotten my sister Helena? For all I know, I'm nothing more than a stepping stone to his future marital bed!" He scrunched his nose up at this. "And there's something uncomfortably Egyptian about that whole line of thinking!"

Even the red-faced Tylissus couldn't resist joining in the laughter at the mocking irony in Harmodius' voice. As they slowly got back onto their feet, Harmodius reached over and chucked his friend on the shoulder. "Seriously, Ty...you are mistaken if you think there could ever be anything between he and I. The good Diokles knows nothing of the real me." Narrowing his eyes, his solemn smile slowly transformed into an impish smirk. "*Just as he knows nothing of the real you...*" With a deft hand Harmodius reached under and adroitly flipped Tylissus' chiton up in the air to reveal a surprisingly oversized appendage hanging between his legs. "You know, my 'not-so-little friend', we've all heard the whispers from the other athletes as you sashay across the ephebeon floor. I don't think you quite appreciate the *enormity* of your…virtues."

Nicias, howling in laughter at Tylissus' red-faced embarrassment, reached over and made a grab for the one-eyed snake dangling between his friend's two well-muscled thighs. With the dexterity of a dancer, Tylissus knocked his hand away and elbowed him in the side, even as he modestly covered himself up.

"You see…" Harmodius smirked, "few men can resist such a wonder!" Rubbing his hands together, he winked at Nicias. "I think it's high time we introduced Tylissus' greatest asset here to my *persistent* suitor, don't you?"

"What do you mean?" Tylissus sounded wary.

Harmodius scratched his chin in thought. "Well…I have an idea that might, with a little bit of luck, bring peace to *all* our minds." Reaching over, he patted them both on the cheek. "Come along, my fellow athletes…it's off to the ephebeon." Placing a well-muscled arm over either fellow's shoulder, he directed them back onto the path. "And if the good Diokles is hanging about, as I'm sure he will be, here's what I mean to do…"

A natural athlete, whenever Harmodius took to the ephebeon floor for javelin practice or a few laps around the jogging track, or to strengthen his sword arm in mock skirmishing with his friends, you can be sure that admiring eyes turned in his direction. The cinched waist and broad shoulder muscles honed by countless throws and takedowns in the palaestra, the firm buttocks and beefy thighs taut from racing and the long jump—and especially the long curling black hair that reached clear down to his shoulder blades—often left men breathless at the sight. "The image of an Achaean Warrior fresh from the sack of Troy…" they'd whisper to one another, "…an Apollo", "…Achilles himself brought to life."

A vigorous competitor, Harmodius' workout was long and hard so that whenever challenged on the playing field, he rarely endured the humiliation of defeat. Whether racing around the track, or wrestling in the palaestra, or tossing the heavy stone discus out in the open meadows surrounding the gymnasium…Harmodius rarely came in second.

But on that particular morning…

✤   ✤   ✤

You could hear the whispers from the porch as Harmodius' third and final javelin went wild, missing the straw target altogether. "Damn…" he said, angrily pounding his fist against the open palm of his hand. "I don't know what's wrong with me today. My throws were way off the mark, boys." With a curt bow and a gracious smile, he playfully squeezed the bicep muscle on the victor's arm and in a loud clear voice said, "Bested by the better arm and the better eye…the match is yours Ty."

Arm in arm, in seemingly casual conversation, the three conspirators made their way across the ephebeon floor as Harmodius surreptitiously scanned the other athletes working out or lounging idly up on the portico. Keeping a smile fixed on his face, he turned to Tylissus and mumbled under his breath, "Look, there he is…over near the palaestra." With the slightest nod of his head he pointed toward the spot where Diokles was standing alongside the edge of the wrestling pitch.

Unusually tall for a Greek, his head was bent in animated conversation with another naked athlete when he glanced over and thought he caught Harmodius gazing back in his direction. A pleasant smile spread across the breadth of his face as he straightened his back, brushed the hair off his forehead, and politely nodded. Pretending to ignore him, Harmodius turned to Nicias and snorted, "Gods, we *are* in luck today! Isn't that your Cleon over there…talking with Diokles?" Nicias didn't answer; instead his eyes lit up as he stood on tiptoe and waved excitedly at the erastes who'd turned to see what had drawn Diokles' attention away from their conversation. "Love…" grumbled Harmodius as he grabbed hold of Nicias' arm to keep him from racing off. "Hold on there one moment, my friend…" he hissed in his ear "…don't forget you have a job to do. Remember, Nicias…if you keep their attention focused on the palaestra we'll be half way there!" Impatiently bobbing his mop of bright red hair, Nicias shook off Harmodius' restraining arm and trotted off to join Cleon and Diokles.

A moment later, Harmodius took Tylissus' by the arm and dragged him toward the wrestling pit. "I'm not too fond of losing, Little One…so this is your lucky day," he murmured under his breath. "For the sake of the gods, make the most of it!" Turning toward the corner where Diokles, Cleon and Nicias were standing, Harmodius raised his voice loud enough to be heard by all, "And now, my young stallion…having bested me at the javelin, would you care to test your fortunes in the ring?"

Unaccustomed to this kind of attention, the red-faced, wide-eyed Tylissus could only shrug his shoulders and mumble, "I don't think this is going to work, Harmodius…"

Slapping him hard on the buttocks, Harmodius laughed and took hold of his arms. "Excellent!" he shouted as curious onlookers began to gather along the edge of the palaestra. "Oil me up then…" Wrenching him around, he plunged Tylissus' palms into the wide vat of fresh olive oil set up next to the wrestling pit and, turning his back, waited for the nervous boy to rub him down.

The oil of the olive was an essential element of Greek style wrestling. Coating the entire body, wrestlers hoped to elude the iron grip of their opponents by slipping and sliding away. At the same time, powerful strength developed in the fingers and hands to offset the lubricating effects of the oil. To see two fine wrestlers going at it—grasping each other about the waist, twisting in and out of each other's grips, heaving naked bodies high into the air before slamming them down onto the dust of the palaestra floor—now that was a sight that thrilled even the most urbane Athenian heart.

Harmodius may have been an excellent wrestler, but he was a cunning showman as well. Two hard muscled, glistening bodies circling the ring, he got the pulses of the crowd racing when he suddenly bellowed like a bull and attacked his opponent with an unexpectedly gutsy bravado…only to be tripped up by Tylissus' seemingly well-placed foot. In no time at all, the two grappling men were locked in each other's arms, rolling around on the ground as the fine brown dust coated their oily backsides. Aware of the modulating hum and roar of the crowd as champions were cheered and bets were placed and re-placed, Harmodius could sense that the exact moment for maximum effect was drawing near. Taking Tylissus to the ground with a sudden twist of his arm, it looked as though he would surely win. As the throng lining the palaestra waved their arms and shouted out their glee or dismay, Harmodius drove Tylissus' shoulder toward the ground…all the while muttering under his breath, "Push back, you fool! Push back against me!" With an almost Herculean effort that brought a throat-ripping roar from Tylissus' usually timid lips, the frustrated 'paramour' thrust his back up, flinging Harmodius roughly over on his side. Jumping on top of him, Tylissus pressed him to the ground with a body slam that set Harmodius' teeth rattling in his head. The tables turned, it was now Harmodius pressing up against the relentless forces of gravity, the muscles and weight of Tylissus' lean oiled torso, and the uncaged motivation of his puppy love. Straining his neck muscles until his eyes bulged, he held out until a sizeable puddle of oily sweat had dripped from his cheeks on to the dirt beneath his head (thus ensuring a not too humiliating drubbing) before crying out in defeat as his shoulder sank to the ground.

After the good-natured shouting and backslapping had died away, most of the crowd drifted back to their own activities. Tylissus and Harmodius were left alone sitting on the edge of the palaestra, scrapping the oily dust residue off each other's torsos, arms and legs with their strigils. Hearing Nicias' nattering voice approaching from behind, Harmodius suddenly clapped a hand on Tylissus' knee. "Well, my twisted little Heracles…" he shouted good naturedly "…that's twice in one day you've taken me down. Will you not give me one final chance for satisfaction…out on the race course?"

Leading a tiny procession out of the gymnasium and across the pine needle scented grounds to the racetrack, Harmodius made quite a show of working out any post-wrestling kinks in his shoulder, arm, and leg muscles. Tylissus, walking close by his side, kept casting furtive glances over his shoulder to make sure Diokles was still tagging along. Nicias and Cleon, traveling at their own ambling pace with their arms entwined and heads tilted together in conversation like two old women, kept Diokles engaged with intimate whispers and the occasional bawdy joke.

"I should never have eaten that sour apple this morning…" Harmodius moaned aloud as he rubbed at his stomach "…too much fruit slows you down." He playfully nudged Tylissus in the side. "I'm sure that's the only reason you bested me in the palaestra."

Tylissus elbowed him back. "That's not funny!" he scowled. "You're going to hurt Diokles' feelings."

Harmodius leaned over and ruffled his hair, at the same time mumbling in his ear, "I'm *trying* to hurt his feelings, you idiot!"

Before Tylissus could think of a response, Harmodius spun around and faced the others. Walking backwards, he continued prattling away: "I've got an idea…" his fingers snapped crisply in the cool morning air, "…let's make this a *real* race." He narrowed his eyes in thought. "But to do that, we'll need a prize…something worthwhile…something to strive for…to give it our all." He scratched his head in thought. "Something of value…" his eyes lit up "…or perhaps *someone*…yes, that's it…one of *you* can act as our prize…rewarding the lucky victor with a lover's kiss!" As the others caught up, Harmodius surprised them all by slipping an arm around Diokles' waist. "Good friend Diokles…Cleon here, being otherwise occupied, simply won't do as our prize…" he smiled self-effacingly up at his overly-tall 'would-be erastes' "…is there any chance you might offer yourself as the prize at our finish line?"

From the look of sheer joy on his face, Harmodius thought Diokles would faint dead away. "Why of course, young lord. It would be an honor to be your prize. What was it you suggested…a kiss for the winner?" He winked at Harmodius, who gave his waist an intimate squeeze in return.

"A kiss…oh, yes!" he answered, his finger tapping thoughtfully against his lower lip. "But perhaps something more?" Diokles' eyes grew even wider with lustful anticipation. "My friend Tylissus and I have already had quite a workout this morning. Perchance, after the sweet reward of your gentle kiss, you'd consider accompanying the lucky winner down to the Ilissos?"

"An excellent idea!" Diokles was almost bubbling with enthusiasm. "A long, leisurely bath together in the fresh mountain waters of the river." He held up his two great hands, "And a massage…I am known for my skill with these hands!"

Harmodius stared at the two giant paws, "Yes…" he laughed, "I'm sure you are!" As they reached the edge of the sprinting track, Harmodius eased his arm free. "It's settled then…a lover's kiss, followed by a bath and massage…*for the winner.*"

Nicias walked over and leaned himself between the two naked racers. "My father always used to say that 'a big one' brings you luck in any race." Before Tylissus could react, Nicias reached around and grabbed hold of the healthy member dangling loosely between his legs. Holding on long enough for Tylissus' penis to react with a natural thickening, he released it with a cackling "whoop" and nimbly ducked away from Tylissus' flailing fist.

For an awkward moment, all eyes turned and focused on the mortified racer's slowly rising cock. As he tried to hide it with his open hand, Harmodius took him by the arm and pulled him up to the starting line. "You're a silly ass, Nicias!" Harmodius called over his shoulder…following it with a private conspiratorial wink. "Never mind him," he whispered to Tylissus, "concentrate on winning the race." Raising an eyebrow he added, "And don't forget…a kiss and a bath for the winner!" Tylissus tried to hide his eagerness with a shamefaced nod of his head.

Try as he might, Diokles found himself unable to tear his startled eyes away from the colossal penis head bobbing up and down as the red-faced Tylissus stepped up to the line. Licking his lips as growing confusion riddled his face, Diokles looked over at his beloved Harmodius before letting his gaze wander back again to settle on the almost upright penis of the other boy. Loudly clearing his throat, Harmodius got his attention and impatiently nodded toward the far end of the track. Blushing, Diokles smiled and turned to jog the length of the track…there to wait impatiently for his champion to come claim his prize.

Assuming their respective starting positions, Harmodius called over his shoulder: "Be a good fellow, Cleon…break loose from that red-headed satyr of yours and come give us a start!"

The race was over before it had scarcely begun. Harmodius, with a convincing stumble off the mark, allowed Tylissus to take a lead he never relinquished. At the finish line, the bewildered Diokles waited for the two contestants to catch their heaving breathes before nervously stepping over to Tylissus, bending down and chastely kissing him on the lips. "For the winner…" he said with a shy, somewhat flustered smile. Removing himself a step back, he found his curious gaze trapped by the unexpected fire burning in the eager boy's olive green eyes. Stepping forward once again, he looked down at Tylissus with a questioning smile spreading across his face. "Forgive me, intrepid victor…but that was an unworthy kiss. You deserve a better prize than that." This time folding his great arms around the winner's back, he pulled him forward into a much more intimate embrace. Eventually breaking apart—and without so much as a 'fare-thee-well' to the bemused Harmodius—the two slowly turned and, hand in hand, disappeared off into the trees…off toward the banks of the Ilissos River.

"Well," Harmodius heaved a bemused sigh as he retraced his steps to Nicias and Cleon at the starting line, "They could have at least *thanked* me!"

For the next few months Harmodius avoided the Kynosarges during the usual morning hours, choosing instead to time his workout at the gymnasium for later in the day…well after the worst of the noontime heat had passed. The budding relationship between Diokles and Tylissus, begun that fortuitous day on the racing track, was slowly firming into a true erastes-eromenos bond. And for that reason Harmodius felt it would be, at best, importunate of him hanging around the ephebeon—a distracting reminder of past 'amours'—during the hours they were most likely to be in attendance.

Besides…these days, spending time with Nicias and Tylissus—each so recently smitten by Eros' delicately barbed shaft—left him with a hollow ache in his gut. Hunting about the field of prospective suitors, the handsome son of Cimon and Philippia had yet to meet a man who left him feeling weak at the knees. Perhaps this change in his daily routine—exchanging the familiar morning faces at the Kynosarges for a fresh new slate in the afternoon—might at last reveal a man worthy to be called 'erastes'.

Harmodius' first week of afternoon workouts had barely passed before a fresh round of older men began plying him with unsolicited love-offerings. Fresh baked pastries, a wide metal-studded leather belt, a basket of dried herbs from the colonies in Sicily…with each new arrival on his doorstep his mother would raise a pert, questioning eyebrow which he would answer with a glum shake of his head.

None of these men stirred his heart.

Carefully stepping from the hot pool, Harmodius accepted a towel from one of the attendants and quickly dried himself off. As he was leaving, an older man whose hair was thinning back from his forehead and whose insistent foot he'd painstakingly dodged under the water, leaned over the edge of the bath and whistled. "Such delicious thighs, young one. I'd love to pry them apart some afternoon."

Harmodius smiled with compassion down at this most recent of vulgar tormentors. "Gentle sir…I'm afraid you'll need more than that limp sausage of yours to gain entrance to these sacred portals!" With a firm slap on his right buttock, he turned and left the room…the sympathetic howls of laughter from the other bathers ringing in his ears.

As he strolled the length of the open colonnade, the mirthful echoes died away to be replaced by the sounds of muffled voices rising in friendly argument from the many symposium halls. Passing through the library, he rounded a corner and came to the area where the philosophers and sophists of the Kynosarges held their open-air classes. In the two years he'd been exercising his body at the gymnasium, Harmodius had made a point of attending symposiums, debates and lessons at least three times a week in an earnest effort to apply his father's dictum for a well-rounded education. The esoteric lectures of the gray-bearded philosophers—interminable elucidations on the true character of mankind and his dubious place in the cosmos—usually left him reeling with headache. He much preferred the more practical sophists with their emphasis on politics, music, mathematics, geography and astronomy—all the things a well-rounded citizen would need to manage the running of a simple farmstead…or the government of a bustling city-state.

Harmodius couldn't help smiling at the all-too-familiar sounds as he passed by each group. In this room he caught fragments of the seemingly eternal argument over the true natures of fire and air; over in this one, a young sophist was expounding on the geometrical disposition of the triangle; and over here a young student seemed bent on haranguing his teacher with the latest conundrum of logic:

"But dear master, you persist in teaching us that only 'unchanging' things can truly exist in nature. And now we hear word from our brother scholars across the Aegean that the latest Ionian philosophy teaches that, in its natural state, *everything* changes!" Harmodius could almost picture the questioner's lips curling down in a teasing frown. "Now really, master…as budding philosophers, if we are to accept both ideas as truth…well then, wouldn't that mean that *nothing exists!*"

Harmodius found himself slowing to a stop. There was something oddly familiar about that voice…no, not the voice exactly…it was more the caustic tone that harkened to something visceral in Harmodius' past. Resting his cheek up against one of the cool marble pillars, he leaned forward and listened as the flustered teacher sought to defend himself.

"No, no, no, my dear boy…I fear you're missing a fine point here. You keep insisting that two diverging philosophies must, as a matter of course, meet somewhere in the…"

The insubordinate voice cut him off: "Yes, yes good master…but now consider this. You yourself will one day grow old and make the lonely journey to the realm of the Underworld, your body *changing* from warm flesh to wind-blown dust, vanishing forever from our earthly domain. Therefore…being something in nature that clearly changes, your very body is in violation of the tenets of your own philosophy! Wouldn't this then mean that *you yourself* do not exist?"

"Philosophy…" Harmodius thought with growing chagrin. He could almost picture the frustrated teacher rubbing at the wrinkles on his forehead, groaning at the paradoxical noose being slowly twisted around his neck.

"But master…I think you'll agree that the most bitter truth to swallow…"

Harmodius couldn't help grinning…this boy was truly relentless.

"…Lays in the very nature of your body's mortification. In rotting away, haven't you inconveniently proven the *Ionian theory?* I mean, really…as far as they are concerned, since your deceased body goes through the physical state of change…both you—and therefore your beliefs—*must exist!*" The mirthful sounds of spirited laughter came echoing from the room at the off-key proposition posited by their clownish classmate.

His curiosity piqued…Harmodius took a step forward into the noisy alcove where the flustered teacher was trying to rein back the high spirits of his students and waited a polite distance away for the pedagogue's recognition. Shushing the raucous group with a brusque wave of his hand, the teacher smiled and signaled him forward. "Have you come to join our symposium, young man?" he asked.

Harmodius bowed his head, placing a silver coin in the red ceramic bowl at the philosopher's side. "Yes, good master. As I passed by out in the hallway my ears were intrigued by the…er, fascinating twists and turns of your philosophy's logic. With your kind permission I would learn more of this curious nature known as…'existence.'"

The sallow-cheeked, white-haired old man beamed with pleasure at the handsome youth's well-mannered words. "And your name, my good young man?"

"I am called Harmodius…Harmodius, son of Cimon."

"Well then, Harmodius, son of Cimon…you are welcome to enter our little circle of academics." Peering past Harmodius' shoulder, he flicked a gnarled finger. "You there, my silver-tongued headache-maker…slide over on that couch of yours and make room for this fellow truth-seeker." He closed one eye, giving him a stern glare as he shook his head. "But have a care, Aristogiton…I don't want you whispering any of your subversive ideas in his poor, innocent ears!"

"Aristogiton?" Turning, Harmodius found himself face to face with the waggish pupil with the vaguely familiar voice and too-cutting wit. As their eyes met, each nervously sought out something familiar in the other's face. When his teacher impatiently cleared his throat, Aristogiton blushed and quickly slid over to make room on his twin reclining couch. Moving as if in a dream, Harmodius—his knees suddenly quivering like a jellyfish—approached the warm indentation made by Aristogiton's body.

"By Olympian Zeus…" he thought with a lovesick sigh, "…they really are the same color as the crystal waters off the Petalion coast."

CHAPTER 5

Following that first symposium, Harmodius and Aristogiton loitered about the changing room for nearly an hour, locked in a fevered debate over the philosopher-teacher's rigidly traditional line of existential reasoning. By the time they left the now nearly deserted gymnasium building, they were conversing with the ease of old friends. A lone slave, waiting near the entrance with torches to light any stragglers on their way back to the city, was their first indication as to the actual lateness of the hour. Passing under the shadowy arch of the Diomeia Gate, Harmodius screwed his courage together and asked a question that had been nagging at him ever since renewing his acquaintance with the handsome son of Scopas.

"I know that running that import-export business of yours must keep you on the road quite a bit." He scratched his chin in thought for a moment before continuing on. "I'm also well aware that my family still has substantial contracts with you...we ship a fair quantity of our olive oil to the outer islands in your cargo holds." Harmodius was suddenly glad that the night's shadows hid the nervous blush rising to the tips of his ears. "And, well..." Struggling with his mounting frustration, he finally screwed his shoulders together and blurted out: "I guess I'm just a little curious as to why it is, in all this time, we've never actually seen you in person? Not since that day of the trial when your uncle contested the legal right of your inheritance." He made no effort to hide the disappointment in his voice. "Whenever contracts are renewed or consignments collected, it's always one of your representatives who comes to pay a call at the house."

He turned to face his newfound friend and, in the flickering torchlight, almost missed the color draining from Aristogiton's face. Afraid that he'd offended his new friend, he reached out and placed a reassuring hand on Aristogiton's arm all the while shaking his head. "I'm sorry…that was foolish of me. I've said something that's upset you."

"No, no…not at all." Embarrassed, Aristogiton looked down at his feet. A moment later he turned away and, raising his head, he stared off into the distance, down the empty street up ahead. "It's just that your innocent question reminds me of a deep shame that I bear…a grievous oversight that rests solely with me." He turned and looked at Harmodius, his eyes glistening with unshed tears. "You see…I *should* have called in at your house…and years ago! In fact, I did try once…shortly after the trial." He shook his head in obvious distress. "I wanted so much to thank your father for saving my inheritance." He looked down at the ground again. "And I think I wanted to see my handsome Patroclus once again…"

Harmodius felt his heart skip a beat. Drawing in a long, slow breath to calm his voice, he waited before asking: "But what happened, Aristogiton? Why didn't we ever see you?"

Aristogiton shook his head. "I was already too late…" The pain in those simple words was almost too much for Harmodius to hear. "In the weeks immediately following the trial I found myself overwhelmed with new responsibilities, often sleeping the night through on a rickety cot set up in my office. The slave Bustades—yes, that same sniveling fool they executed for lying at my hearing—had for months been fiddling with the firm's bookkeeping to hide large shares of the profits…siphoning off whatever he could get away with into his own purse, I suspect. It took all my time and energy just to begin setting these things to right again." He rubbed his forehead and sighed. "Finally, a night came when I had a bit of time to myself. I stopped in at the marketplace and bought the finest jug of Egyptian beer I could find—certainly a small recompense for the great service your father had rendered at my trial…" he half-smiled at a long ago memory "…I seemed to recall it as something of a favorite of his." The smile slowly disappeared as he continued. "In any case, as I was making my way toward your house, I happened upon one of your servants…a poor old woman distraught with grief." The anguished expression on his down turned face told the rest of the story. "The news that your father was dead…that he'd just been murdered and his lifeless body was lying there…" he swallowed and shook his head "…well, it was all so unexpected that I didn't know what to do." His body sagged up against the side of a house, his head sinking to his chest. A moment later he spoke, his voice ragged with tears. "Without thinking, I turned and stumbled back home. Your poor father was dead and to my eternal shame I'd never even thanked him!" His shoulders were shaking so hard that Harmodius barely heard him utter: "And it was this same disgrace that kept me from ever again showing my face at your house…"

Harmodius stood staring at him for a moment, unsure how to react to this poignant outburst. He was somewhat surprised to find that, while a strong part of him wanted nothing more than to sweep the distraught man into his arms and kiss these old troubles from his mind, something else…something deep in his gut…held him back. "This man has a terrible pride…" he thought to himself. In the end, he contented himself by simply reaching out and giving Aristogiton's arm a consoling squeeze.

"It's all right…there is nothing for you to feel any shame over," he said. "My father saw the whole-hearted thanks beaming from your face that day at the court when that fat magistrate stood up and ruled in your favor." He smiled as he nodded his head. "It's quite true…he told me so himself as we were leaving the building." Taking him by the arm, he pulled him forward. "Come now, my young friend…the hour is late and I'm afraid my mother and sister will be holding the evening meal for me." The two men picked up their pace and by the time they'd reached the edge of the Agora where their paths home parted ways, Harmodius had eased the conversation back to the more humdrum topic of the Kynosarges.

"You know, Ari…" he said with an innocent twinkle in his eye, "…I wasn't kidding you. Now that I've switched my workout to the late afternoon, I need to find a reliable…er, sparring partner." Harmodius, nearly substituting the word 'sex' for 'sparring', felt his mouth go dry as he stumbled over these last few words. He took a deep breath to steady his nerves before continuing his case. "Truthfully, I need someone to keep me on my toes…to help me maintain body and mind in peak form." He reached across and half-jokingly felt the firm bicep muscle on Aristogiton's arm. "A well-rounded athlete and a studied academic…someone like yourself." Biting his lower lip, he added. "A true son of Athens that I can hope to one day measure up to."

The sudden flush coloring his cheeks led Harmodius to suspect that Aristogiton had caught the hidden sentiment behind his words. Aristogiton stood silently for a long moment, his fingers self-consciously stroking the jagged scar on his cheek as his eyes made a calculated appraisal of the boy standing in front of him. Harmodius, aware that he may have pressed him too far, kept a nonchalant smile firmly locked in place. After all, in some quarters the very tenor of his words could have been taken as nothing short of a proposal that the two become erastes and eromenos!

Heaving a loud snort, Aristogiton smiled gently and reached across to merrily punch him on the shoulder. "It would be my pleasure, son of Cimon." Trying not to be too obvious, Harmodius released the pent-up breath he'd been holding inside. "After all, it would be a shame for us to lose contact with one another...after all these years, I mean." Nodding his head, Aristogiton smiled thoughtfully. "Yes, I would like nothing better than to reacquaint myself with you...er, and your family."

Harmodius grinned back at him. "Excellent!" A sudden thought occurred to him. "And why don't you come along and join us for dinner tonight? I'm sure my mother and sister would..."

Aristogiton shook his head. "No...I think not." He raised an eyebrow. "But another night...soon? Next week, perhaps?" His smile broadened. "I look forward to seeing your gracious mother again..." he scratched his chin "...and your little sister...Helena, isn't it? Does she still suffer from delusions of Trojan grandeur?"

Harmodius' laughter echoed against the whitewashed walls lining the deserted street. "Oh, not exactly. My dear little Helena may no longer fancy herself as Prince Hector reincarnated...but that hasn't kept her from asserting dominion over the entire household!"

Aristogiton clutched his arm, his guffaws blending with the younger man's as he leaned forward and kissed Harmodius gently on both cheeks. "Until tomorrow then...at the Kynosarges. We'll meet again in the changing room and..." the glint in his eyes was pregnant with promise, "...and get right to it."

❦   ❦   ❦

"I remember him as being a rather shy boy, sweetly devoted to his father..." Philippia clapped her hand to her cheek and sighed, "...oh, but that was so many years ago."

"Shy? Sweetly devoted!" Helena jumped up from the table and circled around to where Harmodius was crouched over his bowl of warmed-over lamb stew. "Mother, please! He was a villain...a monster...and at twice my age, a bully to boot. Don't you remember? He chased me screaming right into our very front door!"

Harmodius snuck a glance at his mother and rolled his eyes. "Aren't you forgetting your part in that playful venture, Little One? After all, hadn't *you* just given me a painful poke in the stomach with that toy 'spear' of yours?"

Helena, incapable of looking truly contrite, shrugged her shoulders and plopped down next to him on the bench. "Oh, I suppose so…" She slipped an apologetic arm through his, nearly bumping the wooden spoon from his hand. "Sorry, my dearest 'Patroclus'…in the heat of battle I mistook you for someone *important.*" She rested a cheek on his shoulder and sighed. "Although, I must admit…if memory serves me right, the merchant's son was quite handsome…yes, that much I do remember. And there was something about his eyes…"

Harmodius rested his chin on the palm of his hand. "Yes…he has very nice eyes."

"Oh?" was all Philippia needed to say. Harmodius looked up to find a hint of a smile on his mother's face suggesting that, in her own maternal way, she'd somehow fathomed out his secret crush. Feeling the heat tickling the tips of his ears, he suspected that his cheeks were blazing bright red. After a moment, Philippia stood up, walked over to his other side and kissed him on the forehead. "I'm happy for you, my son. I have no doubt that your father would have approved of your choice.

"His choice?" Helena echoed, suddenly regarding her brother with suspicion. "His choice for what?"

Harmodius, dropping his spoon into the empty bowl, reached over and pinched his sister on the cheek. "Nothing you need concern yourself with, Little One!"

She shook his hand away and angrily pounded a stubborn fist on the table's edge. "But I want to know!" she cried out, a nasty scowl darkening her usually amiable face. Taking her by the arm, Philippia stood her up, walked her back to the other end of the table, and sat her back on her own bench.

"No one likes a spoiled child, dearest," she whispered in her daughter's ear, "and if you keep scrunching your face up like that, you'll have the wrinkled eyes of an old woman before you are even thirteen!"

"Yes," crowed Harmodius, "and then how will you ever snare a husband?" Mirroring her pout, he couldn't resist adding: "By the gods…what ever would that besotted swain of yours—my poor friend Diokles—think if he'd seen you like this?"

Helena, her knuckles white with rage, tried to hop back up out of her seat, only to be held firmly in place by Philippia's tightening grip on her shoulder. "Don't you ever mention that faithless traitor to me again, dear brother!" Her eyes narrowed. "And, oh yes…" she hissed. "Don't think I missed that note at the bottom of his little gift basket…"

Philippia shook her head. "Your father tried to warn you, Harmodius…you should never have taught her how to read!"

Helena held out an expectant hand and stamped her foot under the table. "Where's my perfect apple?" she demanded. "Diokles told you to save me the best one and I want it right now!" The fact that Harmodius—his grin hidden behind his hand—was obviously trying to keep his laughter in check provoked his sister even more. "I want my apple, Harmodius!" she raged, "Diokles promised me the best one in the basket…and I want it right now!"

"That will be quite enough, Helena…" The steely admonition in her mother's hushed voice brought Helena's burst of anger to an abrupt end. "It's very late and you're overtired. Kiss your brother 'good-night' now, and then go straight off to bed. If you wish to question him about your missing piece of fruit, you can do so in the morning…and in a more ladylike manner. For now…good night, my dear." She leaned her cheek down and waited for a kiss.

With the shrug of a penitent, Helena slowly rose from her bench, kissed her mother on the cheek and then slouched over to her brother's side of the table. "I'm sorry I lost my temper, Harmodius…" She leaned forward to buzz his cheek, her back conveniently blocking her mother's view as she hissed in his ear: "*and I'll have that cursed apple you owe me, Brother!*" Before Harmodius could think to back away, she gave his earlobe a painful nip.

Harmodius, feeling a bit guilty—after all, he *had* given away the apple meant for his sister—grimaced in pain even as he held his tongue. Satisfied that she'd made her point, Helena spun back around, curtsied low to her mother, and went skipping off to bed.

"I'm sorry Mother, that was all my fault. It was selfish of me to take all of Diokles' apples." Philippia smiled benignly as she stood up and returned to sit at the side of her only son. "I promise you…first thing in the morning I'll go to the market place and buy her the biggest apple I can find!"

"What *am* I going to do with you two?" she sighed, ruffling his hair. "Goodness, your jealous little sister certainly has a long memory." She patted him on the arm. "You know dear, she doesn't really care about that apple…it's that boy Diokles that she's angry with. It was bad enough when she first caught his eye and found out that it was you she would be in competition with. In her simple mind, she's always assumed that, with her wheedling ways, she can get whatever she wants from her ever-dependable older brother." Philippia shrugged her shoulders. "She assumed that, with Diokles safely tagged as your erastes, it would be a simple matter of reaching a suitable age before she stepped forward to take possession of the befuddled young fool." She opened her hands and gave him a wry smile. "Now, however…" she stifled a chuckle, "now there's that other boy to deal with. I'm afraid she doesn't fully understand how these things work between two young men…how this romance sprang up so suddenly between your friend Tylissus and her Diokles." She sighed once again. "And the whole thing's left her in an unpleasant mood for weeks now."

"Gods…I fear that's all my fault too." Although he was careful not to mention it, Harmodius cringed at the very thought of all the household havoc that might have ensued if he, and not Tylissus, *had* accepted Diokles' tepidly romantic overtures. "Don't worry Mother…I don't think our pretty Helena has much to worry about. While Diokles is most certainly devoted to his new eromenos, it's been pretty clear from the very beginning that he's the type who, once he passes on into adulthood, will want nothing more than to marry a good-hearted Athenian maiden and set about raising his passel of future warriors for the glory of our city-state!"

"I do hope you're right," she groaned as she shook her head. "Whenever your Helena has her heart set on something…"

Harmodius squeezed his mother's hand. "Have no fear, mother…I hardly envision a life of spinsterhood for our feisty little beast!"

The two sat laughing for a moment, each quietly enjoying the intimacy of the other's company. Turning to face him, Philippia tilted Harmodius' chin up with the tip of her finger so that she could gaze directly into his eyes. "And now, shall we speak of another erastes and eromenos? Have you news to share, my son?" That prescient smile had returned. "I sensed something had changed the moment you stepped inside the front door tonight. Shall we turn our talk back to this new boy…this Aristogiton?"

For a moment the deep blush on his cheeks betrayed his embarrassing depth of feeling. But even hearing his mother speak Aristogiton's name aloud had filled Harmodius with such a euphoric rush, that he found himself pushing back from the table and jumping to his feet, his eyes shining with excitement as he bobbed his head up and down. "Oh yes, Mother…" he bubbled, "He's the one, I'm sure of it! He's definitely the one!"

Philippia clapped her hands, the infectious joy of this—her son's first love—filled her with a mother's pride. "Oh, Harmodius…I'm so happy for you…so happy! If only your father were here to share this moment…" Her eyes grew moist as she bit her lower lip and quickly looked away. Not wanting to spoil the moment, she stood and took him by the arm, pulling him in the direction of the atrium. "Come…let's go outside to the garden. It's such a lovely night and the stars are so bright. I want you to sit with me under our old olive tree—it was your father's favorite spot—and tell me everything that happened today!"

After so many impatient months of adolescent disappointments, mismatched signals, and unwanted advances, Harmodius could barely keep his newfound enthusiasm in check. He rattled on to his mother about how, at the first sight of this breathtakingly handsome youth stretched out like a lazing lion on his couch, toying with his prey—the befuddled old philosopher with his pretentious reasoning—he'd suddenly felt his knees go all wobbly. His eyes glazed over as spoke of lingering behind together in the changing room, neither wanting to bring an end to this first meeting. "I got him to promise to be my exercise partner, Mother...we're to meet again at the Kynosarges tomorrow afternoon."

"Exercise partner?" Philippia frowned. "Hmm...that doesn't sound particularly roma..."

"Oh, I'm not going to rush this thing, Mother." Harmodius' brows knit together as he stroked his chin in dutiful contemplation. "Aristogiton has had a difficult time of it...with his mother dying when he was so young, and his father passing away and leaving him with all that mess in the courts. And now here he is, still a tender age and single-handedly left to run the family business." He shook his head. "I don't think it's ever occurred to him that he's entitled to his share of happiness in this life." Harmodius looked at his mother with a sly grin. "And I intend to be the one who enlightens him."

Philippia smiled back. "I know you've only just met again after all these years..." she kept her voice even, not wanting her natural maternal concern dimming the obvious exhilaration her son felt for this man "...but in all this chit chat between you two tonight, did Aristogiton ever give you any indication as to what *his* feelings were...I mean his feeling towards you?"

Harmodius pitched his voice to sound more confident than he felt. "Oh...there's definitely something there all right." He nodded his head. "Yes...I'm sure of it." His eyebrows wrinkled together. "But he's so painfully shy...and more than a bit self-conscious about that old scar on his cheek. I don't think he's ever considered having an eromenos-erastes relationship before."

"Goodness," his mother covered the surprise in her voice with a nervous giggle, "then you two haven't actually spoken of a relationship yet?

Feigning a yawn, Harmodius shrugged off her query with a twitch of one shoulder and a nervous shake of his head. "Oh...I suppose I dropped a few hints along the way. Nothing specific, mind you…just enough to let him know that I'm interested…and available."

Philippia clucked her tongue. "Be careful that you don't move too quickly with all this, Harmodius. Remember what the old Aesop warned…'slow but sure wins the race.'"

"'*Slow but sure*'…my sentiments exactly, Mother." His eyes narrowed in thoughtful rumination. "Aristogiton has great pride and, I suspect, quite a stubborn streak about his responsibilities." A devious smile curled the edges of his lips. "Perhaps rather than trying to accomplish this all on my own…it might be best to enlist a little aid from my friends." Standing and stretching his arms over his head, he leaned down and brushed his mother's cheek with a 'good night' kiss. "After all, I think I'm owed a favor or two…"

With a wink of his eye he was off to bed, anxious to cast his night spirit to wandering along the shore of lover's dreams.

❦   ❦   ❦

Harmodius was right about one thing…Aristogiton could be very stubborn. No matter which tack he tried—flattery, an off-hand, innuendo-laden remark, subtle and not-so-subtle flirtations, an indiscreet hand sliding up a well-oiled thigh in the wrestling ring, untold numbers of post-workout back rubs…even the numerous small tokens and gifts left behind in his locker—failed to shake Aristogiton from his modestly aloof pose. One after-noon, a few weeks into their workout routine, Diokles and Tylissus showed up at the Kynosarges. Running into them out at the discus throw, Harmodius made a great show of introducing his two close friends as a 'couple'. The very next day, it was Cleon and Nicias' turn to make their appearance at the gymna-sium. Bemused by Harmodius' efforts, Aristogiton smiled and nodded politely when meeting the two couples; seemingly oblivious to any implications the obviously besotted relationships might be hinting at.

Even so, it wasn't long before the once-introverted Aristogiton found him-self a regular in Harmodius' tight little circle of friends. In addition to exercis-ing together, they could often be found sharing meals at one another's houses, taking classes with the same sophists and philosophers in the open arcade of the Kynosarges and, when the blustery month of Elaphebolion arrived, they enjoyed each other's company at the countless religious ceremonies and theat-rical festivals held to celebrate the city's annual Dionysia.

Growing up an only child in the hectic world of his father's export/import business, Aristogiton had never experienced true friendship with a boy his own age. And now this good-natured face from the past, this almost-too-handsome-for-his-own-good son of the man who'd once saved his inheritance, had reentered his life...casting aside in a single afternoon all the carefully crafted isolation he'd encased himself in after his father's untimely death.

Still, there were times he felt his emotions at war with one another.

While he certainly relished the joyous hours spent in the company of his new friends—especially the longhaired, glib-tongued Harmodius—every minute spent away from the ever-pressing needs of his father's struggling business left him riddled with guilt.

Even so, Aristogiton continued to find time each day for Harmodius and his friends. And it would have been the happiest of times for him...except for one thing. Alone in his bed each night, Aristogiton found himself envying the intimate physical relations between the lovers Tylissus and Diokles, and Cleon and Nicias. After dinner, when the two nuzzling couples went off together and Harmodius and he parted to go their separate ways, Aristogiton couldn't help wishing that the brown-eyed Adonis whose muscular legs he pinned so devotedly to the ground during countless sit-up repetitions—and whose amorous advances were becoming increasingly difficult to ignore—was more than just his friend.

Perhaps if he'd had the money to afford a trustworthy servant...someone skilled in running an export business...someone much like the old family retainer who so judiciously administered Harmodius' country farm...

Perhaps then he would have had the time to pursue matters of the heart.

"Are you almost done there? We're starting to draw a crowd..."

Harmodius looked over his shoulder and saw that most of their fellow athletes had stopped working out and were gathering in small groups along the edges of the palaestra, waiting impatiently for their weekly wrestling bout to begin. "Almost done..." he mumbled as he rubbed his olive oil covered hands down the center of Aristogiton's chest and back up under his slightly raised arms. Leaning forward, he whispered into his opponent's ear: "Here now...why don't we give the old boys something to *really* snigger about..." Before Aristogiton could respond he felt one of Harmodius' oil-slickened hands slide around to his backside to lodge comfortably in the crack between his buttocks.

If it had been anybody else, Aristogiton would have wasted little time vehemently swatting the intruding hand away, the provocateur risking a blackened eye or worse for this obscene liberty. However—and much to his surprise—Aristogiton found himself enjoying the intimate sensation of Harmodius' fingertips gently massaging his buttock muscles. Content to let the errant hand rest there for a few moments, Aristogiton was acutely aware of the hoots and whistles coming from the increasingly boisterous crowd. Smiling good-naturedly, he turned his head and kissed the brazen boy on his oily cheek before slowly backing out of Harmodius' embrace and striding manfully over to his corner…there to await the start of their match.

In the months they had been working out together, Harmodius and Aristogiton had fallen into a comfortable routine—boxing on Tuesdays, running laps on Wednesdays and Thursdays, and wrestling in the open air palaestra on Saturday afternoons. This last activity in particular had become quite a crowd pleaser, as the two handsome boys—a near match in both strength and stature—never failed to put on a good show. Having a natural affinity for the strenuous grips, lifts, and throws of the ring, neither boy ever willingly conceded defeat, the winner on most days having to be determined by the first to achieve three successful throws rather than a pinning to the ground. Their clean style and polished skills were so admired by the more serious Kynosarges competitors, that the names 'Harmodius' and 'Aristogiton' were soon alluded to whenever talk turned to the chosen athletes that would be representing Athens at the next Olympic Festival.

They were well into the afternoon's match, Aristogiton having thrown his opponent once and Harmodius returning the favor twice, when a sudden hush in the usually animated crowd caused the longhaired contender, hastily wiping the sweat from his eyes, to steal a glance over his shoulder…and thereby neglect Aristogiton's fast approaching hip. Before he knew what was happening, he'd been flipped over backward and was laying face down on the sandy arena floor. The match now tied two and two, Harmodius spit the bits of oily grit out of his mouth as he wryly accepted Aristogiton's proffered hand and hopped back to his feet.

Crouching over and reaching across for Aristogiton's powerfully muscled upper arm, Harmodius assumed the face-on stance for the tiebreaker round. But his preoccupied opponent, staring past him at a sudden clamor rising from the midst of the oddly subdued crowd, gently shook him off. Turning to see what had gotten everyone else's attention, Harmodius watched as the milling crowd silently parted in two. A small company of obviously inebriated revelers accompanied by several fearsome looking bodyguards made their unobstructed way to the front of the palaestra.

For a long uncomfortable moment, no one spoke or moved…then a thick waisted merchant—a notorious lecher known around the Kynosarges for the inordinate amount of time he spent lingering in the shadowy corners of the bathhouse—stepped forward and bowed low to the tall man at the center of the new arrivals.

"Allow me to welcome you to the Kynosarges…*Co-Tyrant* Hipparchus." he cried out, emphasizing the Pisistrade's newly restored title, "Welcome to our humble palaestra…and a thousand congratulations on your recent elevation!"

As people heard the shocking news—the whispers quickly traveling to all four corners of the open palaestra—the subdued throng came alive with buzzing chatter mixed with groans of stunned disillusionment. Few at the Kynosarges had yet heard the news from the morning's Council of 400 gathering, where the tyrant Hippias—continuing his aggressive reassertion of political control over the city—had rescinded all earlier restrictions against his profligate brother. Not only were he and his companions no longer barred from public gymnasiums…in a sweeping gesture of misplaced filial trust, the title of co-tyrant had been restored to the loutish Hipparchus.

"Better lock up your sons!" one wag hanging near the back shouted out.

The sounds of muffled laughter erupted from the crowd. Hipparchus chose to ignore the pointed remark, although several heads bobbed and weaved in an attempt to avoid eye contact with his heavily armed bodyguards as they scanned the crowd for the foolhardy culprit. Haughtily stepping onto the arena floor with a skinny, blond haired youth—the sparse, fuzzy down on his pubic areas attesting to an embarrassingly recent budding of adolescence—hanging tightly on his arm, Hipparchus accepted the mumbled congratulations of the few other sycophants in the crowd.

"My friends and I were looking to watch some sport today," he said with a genial lilt in his voice, "something invigorating and masculine to help us celebrate this most auspicious of days." His words were addressed to the crowd; even as his avaricious eye turned to linger over the oily, sweat covered body of the shorter of the two standing wrestlers. "And I see we've come to the right place." When no one responded, he turned to his clinging companion. "And who do you think will win this match, my little cock-tease? Beauty…" he nodded toward Harmodius, "…or that beast over there?" As their newly appointed co-tyrant pointed in his direction, Aristogiton was sure he could smell the rancid wine on his sour breath clear across the arena floor.

The wispy-haired creature, frowning at the word 'beauty', wriggled his arm loose from Hipparchus and ambled over to slowly circle behind the two naked wrestlers. He was just about to reach for Harmodius' bicep when a hand shot out and grabbed him tightly by the wrist. "If you so much as *touch* him," muttered a grim-faced Aristogiton under his breath, "I'll break your arm in two…"

With a high-pitched squeal the blond creature snatched his wrist free and scampered back to his master. "His scarred face may not be pretty to look at, my lord…but I'll place my money on 'the beast'." He rubbed at the tender red mark on his wrist and laughed.

"The beast it is…" Hipparchus turned to his friends. "And I, of course, will take 'the beauty' for my bet." Lifting his purse, he let his eyes scan the crowd. "Will anyone else take my wager?" he shouted out.

Aristogiton had seen enough. "We're finished here," he announced in a loud voice, his disgust evident to all standing around the open ring. Taking hold of Harmodius' shoulder, he began leading him off the palaestra floor.

"Hold there, Beast…just where do you think you're going?" Hipparchus' stony glare silenced the buzzing crowd.

Aristogiton stopped in his tracks, pausing just long enough to get his temper under control before slowly turning back to face his inquisitor. "I'm a free citizen of Athens, *Co-tyrant*…" the word dripped with sarcasm, "…what business is it of yours where I go?"

Caught off guard, Hipparchus' already wine-swollen face turned an even darker shade of red at the blunt disdain in Aristogiton's voice. "My apologies…*citizen*. We meant no offense to your sensitive civic pride." Turning away, he leaned over to the fat merchant still hanging about near the edge of his company and, raising a single eyebrow, pointed off in Aristogiton's direction.

The sycophant bobbed his head up and down, answering in a low, tremulous voice: "Aristogiton, Lord…Aristogiton, son of Scopas…a deceased oil merchant."

The words 'son of Scopas' dashed through him like a bracing, cold winter shower dispelling any remaining wine-muddled haze from Hipparchus' calculating mind. With a newfound clarity, his head swung slowly back around, his eyes narrowing as he studied the suddenly familiar face. Of course...the scar. He felt his mouth go dry. How could he have forgotten that humiliating day in the courtroom...and that fool—this same boy's uncle Heron—dragging him into his misbegotten swindle for that damned import/export business? Hipparchus' hands balled up into two tight-knuckled fists. There was still an accounting to be made here...

Acutely aware of the agitated crowd waiting expectantly on all sides, Hipparchus forced himself to draw in a calming breath before noisily clearing his throat. "Well, young Aristogiton...son of Scopas," a tight smile slowly stretched across his face, "...once again, please accept my apology and...go about your business. We will seek our entertainment elsewhere."

Aristogiton and Harmodius turned to leave.

"Hold one moment...*son of Scopas.*" With an imperious wave of his hand Hipparchus sent one of his spear-wielding bodyguards to block their departure. "While I've given *you* leave to depart, I would have a private word with your most worthy opponent...the young 'beauty' at your side." As he flashed a leering smile at Harmodius, his skinny blond companion, still slouching at his side, howled and stomped a jealous foot in the sand, only to be cuffed across the face by the back of Hipparchus' hand. "Take this annoying creature back home...now!" he growled to one of his associates as he pushed the protesting boy away. Amidst shouted objections of innocence followed by hysterical wails of apology, someone stepped forward and, grabbing him by his skinny arm, dragged the boy screaming from the Kynosarges.

Harmodius looked nervously at Aristogiton...suddenly feeling more frightened for his friend than himself. Holding his arm tightly, he leaned over and whispered, "Don't worry my friend, I can deal with this pompous..."

Aristogiton, his face white with fury, shook off Harmodius' restraining arm and took a bold step forward. "I already told you, *Co-tyrant*...as a free citizen, I don't need yours or any man's leave to depart!" His nostrils flared with anger. "And as for this 'beauty' at my side..." he turned and gestured back to Harmodius, the blazing fire in his eyes leaving the boy breathless, "...the crude and lascivious insinuation of your manner and tone are an insult to both my lover and I...and to every other erastes and eromenos here!"

Harmodius started at these unexpected words—lover...erastes...eromenos. Suddenly oblivious to everyone else around him—the enraged co-tyrant, his scandalized cohorts, and the tension-filled mob—Harmodius stepped forward and encircled Aristogiton with his arms. His face radiant with love, he stood on tiptoes and kissed his erastes on the lips with an almost swooning passion. "Aristogiton speaks the truth, my lord…as all can witness here." Tears threatened his eyes as he addressed the entire crowd. "This man *is* my erastes…and will be for all the years left to me on this earth. And even after that…when we are lost and wandering in the eternal shadowland of Hades, his shade will forever be entwined with mine."

Aristogiton, still in somewhat of a daze at the recklessness of his foolhardy denunciation of the new co-tyrant—and now, even more so by Harmodius' unexpectedly forceful response—gently placed the palm of his hand under his new eromenos' trembling chin and, pulling him close, ardently returned his kiss.

The entire Kynosarges, frozen in a moment of stunned silence as all eyes fixed on this affectionate tableau, seemed to heave a collective sigh.

And then, from a far corner of the crowd someone called out: *"He's right! Is this the respect we show our love-pledged couples…our young erastes and eromenos?"*

Hipparchus' head swung in the direction of the voice, his eyes searching the crowd for the rabble-rouser…but before he could signal to his bodyguard, someone else at the other side of the stadium responded with: "Shame!"

A moment later another voice, this one closer to the front, repeated the cry: "Shame!"

And then another athlete picked up the stinging rebuke…and then another…and another. Soon the whole arena shook with the deep throbbing rumble of: "Shame! Shame! Shame!"

Hipparchus blanched in alarm as the reproachful cries came raining down on him from all sides. Unnerved, he looked to his cohorts for support and saw that they were lost in their own cowering fear. With a nervous chopping motion of his hand, he signaled to his bodyguards to close rank around him and, using them to clear a path through the howling mob, the scowling co-tyrant of Athens made his ignoble exit from the Kynosarges.

With the attentions of the crowd following Hipparchus out of the gymnasium, Aristogiton turned to Harmodius and tugged on his oily dirt-covered arm. "Come on, *my little eromenos*…we need to have a talk…someplace private." Harmodius, nodding his response, followed him as he led the way through the churning, boisterous crowd, up onto the covered porch and then out through a small door in the side of the building. Still naked and oily from their aborted wrestling bout, Aristogiton sought out a small rarely used foot-path at the back of the building that led down to a sandy beach along the edge of the Ilissos River.

Carefully wading into the icy, knee-deep waters, for the next few minutes Aristogiton and Harmodius silently took turns scrubbing the dirt and oil off of each other's skin. The finely ground sands of the Ilissos, rubbed against the body with the palm of a hand, served in place a strigil...and left their hides clean and tingling with its earthy abrasiveness. At some point during this play-ful fourhanded 'scrub down', Harmodius found himself wrapped in the taller boy's well-muscled arms. Without a moment's hesitation, he smiled, looked deeply into Aristogiton's questioning eyes, and whispered, "I really do love you..." before kissing him lightly on the lips. Feeling the fire rush up his arms as he pulled his erastes in closer, he took a chance and kissed him once again, this time invitingly parting his lips to receive Aristogiton's cautiously probing tongue. As the kiss deepened, their hands began to glide excitedly over each other's water-slick bodies. When Aristogiton settled his wandering palms against the two well-rounded buttocks of his willing partner, and Harmodius' eager fingers began massaging the foreskin of his lover's fully erect cock, the two boys wordlessly waded from the water and lay down side by side in a grassy hollow along the beach's edge.

As Apollo's golden stallions relentlessly dragged the flagging sun chariot westward towards their distant nightly repose in the stables out beyond the Pil-lars of Hercules, the two young lovers, Aristogiton and Harmodius, bound their lives together in an act as timeless as the Olympian Gods.

Selene's silvery, crescent-shaped crown had paused to rest for a time in the constellation of the crab when a single blade of grass, fiendishly tickled under his nose, brought Aristogiton back to the world. Opening his eyes to the moonlit sky, the sleepy young oil merchant could scarcely make out the shad-owy outline of the handsome face peering down at him from a few inches above.

"Are you cold, my love?"

Aristogiton shook his head. The flattened grass beneath his body was still warm from their feverish lovemaking, and a balmy spring breeze off the Saronic Gulf did much to keep the night's chill away. Pulling Harmodius' face down, he offered another lingering kiss before shifting on his side and raising himself up on one elbow. Without waiting for an invitation, Harmodius slid his body in closer, nestling his head in the crook of his erastes' arm and waiting patiently for Aristogiton to speak whatever words preyed on his mind.

At first Aristogiton was content to remain silent, his mind dwelling on the near perfect nature of the erastes—eromenos relationship. And while this seemingly unquenchable passion for the youth resting so trustingly in his arms had suffered through a rather abrupt birthing in the palaestra today, he had little doubt that any inconsequential words of validation he might offer up were unnecessary between them. At that first touch of Harmodius' lips pressing against his, Aristogiton had felt the uncompromising hand of destiny clutching at his heart. An attachment—though the words had been left unspoken until now—that was clearly shared by the beautiful boy lying at his side.

From this night forward their love for each other, spoken or not…simply was.

Even so…there *was* something troubling him.

"Beloved," he said, his eyebrows furrowing together in a tightly knit arch over his pale, sea-colored eyes, "There's a fear gnawing at my gut that I may have committed you…er, us…to a dangerous path this afternoon…" a shadow seemed to cross his face "…with our new co-tyrant, I mean." He bit his lip and slowly shook his head. "Perhaps I should have curbed my tongue with Hipparchus. Instead, I lost my…"

Harmodius snorted, "The man's a pig! An arrogant, self-important pederast who got just what he deserved!"

Aristogiton smiled gratefully as he sighed. "That well may be, Harmodius. But in truth, as much as it was by the love I feel for you, my outburst of temper today was fueled by selfish thoughts of stupid pride." He pulled him in tightly against his chest. "And in my haste to satisfy a personal grudge, I foolishly brought *you* under the co-tyrant's dissolute gaze."

"Grudge?" repeated Harmodius.

Releasing his eromenos from his hold, Aristogiton rolled onto his back and gazed up at the stars. After a moment, he took a deep breath and continued: "One day last summer, I accompanied an old family friend and my gracious benefactor—the Archon Cleisthenes—down to the boat docks at Salamis Bay…" he turned and looked at Harmodius, his head still resting easily on his outstretched arm, "…to see the great man off on his undeserved exile to Crete. Anyway, as we two stood waiting next to the pier for his possessions to be loaded onto the ship, Cleisthenes shared a piece of information that had recently come his way." He reached across and took Harmodius' hand in his.

"It seems that the scheming Hipparchus was somehow involved in my uncle's scheme to defraud my father's will."

Harmodius sat up. "Why that foul, crooked snake…"

Aristogiton pulled him back down onto the grass. "Tut-tut, my young champion. Cleisthenes had no real proof…just an errant rumor that had come to him by way of a disgruntled bathhouse pretty boy." Turning back on his side, he felt some of his uneasiness relax as Harmodius' hand reached over to stroke his firm, hairless chest. "Rumor or not, the archon, in his wisdom, decided to tell me anyway…as a warning." Covering Harmodius' roving hand with his own, Aristogiton gave it an affectionate squeeze.

"A warning?" Harmodius echoed, careful to keep his tone offhand.

"Yes." Aristogiton grew introspective for a moment as he carefully weighed the wisdom of sharing the rest of the story that Cleisthenes had revealed on that long ago day.

Impatient, Harmodius tweaked his nipple and before Aristogiton could think to react beyond an initial gasp of pleasure and surprise, the boy jumped to his feet and bounded over to the tree line where he waited with a sassy grin on his face for his lover to catch him. Rising slowly to his feet, Aristogiton hunched over and quietly circled around the trees, catching him in a bear hug from behind. Ruffling Harmodius' soft, raven colored hair with his fingertips, he pushed a handful off to the side so that he could cover the back of his neck with light nipping kisses.

Meanwhile, Harmodius maintained his sympathetic pose…doing his best to sustain an air of calm indifference as he waited to hear what Cleisthenes' warning words were all about.

Instead of finishing his story, Aristogiton grasped one of his arms and spun him around face on. "It's grown quite late, Harmodius…and I for one, don't intend to spend the entire night out here naked in the woods with some sex-mad youngster chasing after me through the trees! Not when I have a nice warm bed…a bed big enough for two, mind you…" he added, winking a lecherous eye "…waiting at my home." Taking him by the hand, he led him back through the trees onto the path. "I think if we bang hard enough on the front door of the gymnasium, we should be able to wake up one of the attendants to help us retrieve our clothing and then…"

"Now wait just one moment, my secretive friend." Harmodius held his hand tightly as they dodged hanging pine branches on the overgrown path. "What about Cleisthenes?"

Now it was Aristogiton's turn to force a semblance of nonchalance back into his voice. "It was nothing of consequence…really. I should never have brought it up." Seeing the stubborn look in Harmodius' gaze, he shrugged his shoulders. "Well…if you must know. It seems that the crooked Hipparchus, in exchange for an equal share in the business, gave my uncle the money he needed to move the case against my father's will forward…" he paused, taking a deep breath. "And when things didn't go as planned," the saliva in his mouth dried up as his throat threatened to constrict, "well…people disappeared."

Harmodius stopped, wrenching Aristogiton to a faltering halt next to him. "People disappeared? What do you mean…what people?"

Trying to look unconcerned, Aristogiton shrugged his shoulders. "My uncle, for one. And a client…one of the oil merchants who'd testified against me at the trial…the fat one who nearly fumbled his testimony on that second day. At the time, I was so tied up trying to restore some sanity to my father's business, that I was pretty oblivious to things going on around me. I remember hearing the slaves talking one day about Uncle Heron packing his things and supposedly moving off to the island of Paros." Aristogiton rubbed at a knot of tension building in the back of his neck and Harmodius obliged by lending a kneading hand. "I didn't really give it any thought at the time…I was just glad to be rid of the old goat."

"And the merchant?" Harmodius asked.

"He was a client…well, after the trial, an ex-client. I heard the news from another merchant when he and his ship were lost at sea…and with a very expensive cargo of Delian wine I might add." He rolled his head to one side so that Harmodius could reach a particularly tender spot. "Mmm…that does feel good."

Harmodius shook his head. "I'm confused, what's so terribly sinister about someone moving away…or for that matter, the tragedy of an unforeseen ship-wreck."

"Oh, nothing sinister to the casual observer. But when Cleisthenes heard about certain discrepancies in the story from that talkative 'bath boy', he decided to conduct an investigation of his own. Imagine his surprise when he discovered that my Uncle Heron had never arrived on Paros…and in fact, no record could be found of him ever leaving Athens by ship…for anyplace." Aristogiton groaned with pleasure as Harmodius' probing thumb found a particularly tense muscle.

"Well then, what about the missing merchant?" Harmodius blew several breaths of concentrated warm air on the spot before kneading it with his knuckles.

"Now that's the really interesting part of the story. It seems that the tale our 'bath boy' had come crying to Cleisthenes about concerned a particularly nasty falling out with Hipparchus over a promised commission on some stolen jars of *Delian wine* our co-tyrant was trying to unload…and just days after the merchant's ship supposedly went missing."

Harmodius finished his labor of love with a gentle peck on the neck and stepped back as Aristogiton, purring with pleasure, rolled his head easily from side to side. "Gods…how I needed that! A lesson to remember, my boy…never doze off under the midnight stars without the benefit of a pillow resting under your head!" Setting a firm hand back on Harmodius' shoulder, he pushed him on ahead up along the shadowy pathway.

"So I take it that the Archon was warning you that Co-tyrant Hipparchus is not only a bounder and a cad…it seems that the man also traffics in some pretty dodgy business affairs on the side." He peeked a reproachful eye over his shoulder. "And the moral of the story is that, rather then goading him on, we would both be wise to steer clear of him and his company?"

Aristogiton grinned sheepishly. "Well, yes…I suppose that's the gist of Cleisthenes' warning."

Harmodius halted dramatically in mid step. "But what's this? Is that the smell of smoke in the air?"

Aristogiton stopped, lifted his head and sniffed. "I don't smell anything…"

"Oh, yes…I'm sure of it!" Harmodius elbowed him playfully in his side. "I think it's all those bridges we just burned behind us!"

Aristogiton frowned as he pushed him on ahead. "Very funny…"

❧   ❧   ❧

Harmodius wound the narrow leather sandal strap around his ankle and tied it off. Yawning, he leaned up against the brightly painted marble statue of Heracles flanking the side of the gymnasium doorway and waited for Aristogiton to finish dressing.

Lacing his own sandal straps tightly around his calves, Aristogiton looked up at him. "I've been thinking…"

"Yes?" Harmodius stifled another yawn and, crouching down at his side, rested a balancing forearm on his shoulder.

"How would you like to take a little trip with me?"

"A trip?" his eyes lit up. "Where to?" He offered Aristogiton his hand and helped him to his feet.

"My ship is set to make a run to Naukratis next week…"

"Naukratis!" Harmodius grabbed him by the shoulders and spun him around. "You mean Egypt? We're going to Egypt?"

Aristogiton brushed the dirt off the backside of his tunic. "Yes, it's time someone attempted a reopening of trade with the Greek mercantile colonies in the Nile Delta." He shrugged his shoulders. "Why shouldn't it be me?"

Harmodius frowned. "I know the war in Egypt is over…but what about the new Persian overlords? I've heard they're none too fond of Greeks."

Aristogiton grinned. "It took poor old Cambysis nearly three years to track the last pharaoh down, ending his short-lived dynasty and bringing the Land of the Nile under the heel of Persian rule. Word coming from the East has it that, for all his ferocious power, the Great King is himself dead…murdered by his own grasping relatives on his long journey back home to Persepolis. Now that the family squabbles have died down, a distant cousin of Cambysis—a young warrior named Darius—has taken possession of the Peacock Throne. And it's this same Darius who is feverishly working to return a sense of stability to the farther corners of this wide-flung empire." Aristogiton greedily rubbed his hands together. "And stability means trade…"

"Naukratis…" Harmodius shook his head in amazement. "In my wildest dreams I never thought that one day I'd be journeying over the Great Sea to visit the Land of the Pharaohs…to sail up the mighty, life-giving Nile!"

"And don't forget the Pyramids…"

"The Pyramids!" Harmodius clapped his hands together, fighting to restrain himself from jumping into the air. "What an adventure it will be!"

"Fine Greek olive oil has always been favored by the Egyptians…especially as a base for their many cosmetics. If my ship is the first to arrive in Naukratis, I should have no trouble getting several talents of gold and an entire hold full of Egyptian corn in exchange!"

The two men gathered their things together into a single bundle and started down the Gymnasium stairs. Halfway to the bottom, Harmodius paused and tapped Aristogiton on the back. Frowning, he asked: "Good friend, this trip to Egypt…it doesn't have anything to do with Hipparchus, does it?"

Aristogiton chewed on his lip for a moment before looking down at his feet and answering: "Well, yes…and no." He peeked up and favored his eromenos with a reassuring smile. "This trip *has* been in the planning stages for some time now. But, in all honesty, I hadn't decided whether to accompany the expedition myself or to send a factor in my place…not until now." He scratched his chin as he avoided Harmodius' penetrating gaze. "Since we've had the timely misfortune today to cross Hipparchus' path, I think our wisest course would be to follow Cleisthenes advice and…"

"I know, I know…'steer clear of him and his company.'" Harmodius groaned in disgust.

Aristogiton placed a reassuring arm around Harmodius' shoulder. "Yes, my love. If we leave town for awhile…"

"Leave town? You mean run away from Athens…all because of some brutish bully who needs his phallus lopped off by a good whack with the axe?"

With a resigned sigh Aristogiton started them both moving back down the stairs once again. "We'll only be gone for a few months, Harmodius. Just long enough for today's 'incident' in the palaestra to be forgotten. After all, Hipparchus was already half-drunk when he arrived here at the Kynosarges…" he shrugged his shoulders, "…who knows what he'll remember about today. And these next few months will be rife with even more festivities, more celebrations, more bouts of all-night drinking with cronies and sycophants as he *commemorates* his 'grand' ascension to the Athenian Tyranny. By the time we return from our lucrative little voyage, the names Harmodius and Aristogiton will mean nothing to our *'Co-tyrant'.*"

The derisive tone of Aristogiton's voice saw a smile slowly spreading across his lover's troubled face. Thoughts of treading Egypt's sun-baked desert sands at the side of this magnificent man threatened to overwhelm his stubborn Athenian pride. Looking into Aristogiton's sparkling eyes, he had little trouble convincing himself that an adventure at sea might not be such a bad thing after all.

"Well…" he finally said, "…considering the prudence of our exiled archon's warning, I suppose a few months at sea wouldn't be such a bad idea."

Relief washed over Aristogiton like a warm spring rain. "I know," he cried out, "why not turn this into a real holiday? We'll invite your young friends to come along to Egypt with us and in that way strip Athens bare of all it's handsomest men…now that ought to teach the randy Hipparchus a lesson!" Both men laughed. "Besides, the southern routes can be tricky this time of year, so I'll need a brawny crew to help me wrestle with the stubborn winds of the borealis." He flexed an arm, showing off his own bulging bicep. "And who better to lend an arm than your muscle-bound friends Tylissus and his Diokles?" He kept an eagle eye measuring Harmodius' growing enthusiasm as he rushed on. "And Cleon…his family has long been known for their admirable trading skills. He and his little scamp Nicias can keep a sharp eye on all the business dealings once we've reached Naukratis!"

"Imagine it…" the threat of Hipparchus obviously forgotten as Harmodius' eyes grew wide with anticipation, "…a ship crewed by three pairs of lovers! We'll be the envy of the high seas!"

❧   ❧   ❧

Passing under the Diomeia Gate, their ideas and plans for the upcoming trip to Egypt echoing excitedly off the high arching walls, the two young men reentered the central precinct of the night-deserted city. By the time they crossed through the empty agora, exhaustion from all the day's excitement had finally taken its toll and the two fell into a companionable silence. Coming at last to the intersection where the two men usually parted for the night, there was no hesitation on Harmodius' part as they turned in unison up the long narrow street that led toward Aristogiton's house.

Along the way, Aristogiton did his best to assuage a nagging guilt about keeping one last secret from his Harmodius. "I was a fool to bring up old Cleisthenes' warning," he angrily told himself. "It's one thing to tell the boy about the disappearance of my Uncle Heron and that perjuring merchant…" Aristogiton felt his stomach take a sickening lurch, "…but I came so very close to revealing Cleisthenes' suspicion about his father's…"

"Hey! Haven't we just passed by your door?"

Startled, Aristogiton looked up and saw Harmodius standing in the street looking back over his shoulder at the front door to his house. "Oh…sorry." He said with half a chuckle. "It must be the lateness of the hour…my mind seems to have drifted away."

He pulled out his key and, quietly unlocking the front door, held it open for Harmodius. Lighting a taper from the glowing embers of the hearth, Aristogiton lit the wick of an oil lamp and, hoping not to disturb the sleeping servants, quietly led the way through the darkness to his bedroom at the back of the house.

Much later, his arms wrapped tightly around his sleeping eromenos, Aristogiton came to a decision. To protect both the boy and his family he would keep his painful secret for a few months longer…but only a few. Eventually, Harmodius would know of Cleisthenes' suspicions concerning his poor father's murder…but not from Aristogiton. No…this dangerous news must come from—and be duly tempered by—the old archon himself.

"Yes, this time I'll let Cleisthenes do his own dirty work…"

As he drifted toward sleep, his thoughts turned to the coming voyage to Egypt…

"And who knows…" he thought "…on our way home, perhaps a stop on the island of Crete to replenish our water supply…and maybe pay a quick visit to an old friend in his lonely exile.

CHAPTER 6

"Shouldn't we lower the sail, Aristogiton?"

Diokles groaned as the ship soared up and over another swell. He covered his mouth with the back of his hand to keep from losing the remnants of a light morning meal as he stumbled over to the side of the rain swept ship.

Aristogiton ran over and held him around the waist as he finally let loose and puked over the railing. "Easy there big fellow." He looked over his shoulder back toward the stern where Tylissus and Harmodius were fighting to keep the tiller steady. "Over there…" he shouted as he pointed to the starboard side, "…aim her for that trough!" Harmodius acknowledged him with a terse nod of his head, the spray from the rain flinging off his forehead in all directions as he and Tylissus struggled to move the steering oar. Hauling Diokles back down onto the deck, Aristogiton wiped the foul-smelling spittle off the corner of his mouth with the edge of his soaking wet tunic before grabbing the end of a rope and tying one end around the green-faced man's waist and the other to the single mast at the center of the ship. Hoping to distract the seasick man, he pointed at the half-furled sail. "I'm trying to keep her trimmed at half sail so that we can use this little storm's blustery winds to help shorten our trip."

"*Little storm?*" Diokles moaned.

Aristogiton offered a sympathetic smile. "I'm guessing we've already cut off a day or two of sailing time in these last few hours alone." Diokles suddenly grabbed his side as a cramp bent him nearly in two. Looking desperately into Aristogiton's sympathetic face, he rolled his eyes and reached for the rail once again. "Sorry old boy…" Aristogiton held him steady as he dry-heaved over the side. "It won't be long now," he pointed to a single shaft of light breaking through the churning black clouds far behind them. "Look there…the squall's almost over."

Checking the safety rope one more time to make sure that Diokles was securely anchored to the deck, he patted him reassuringly on the back before stumbling across to the heaving port side and grabbing hold of the rope ladder that led down into the ship's cargo hold. Plunging into the tight darkness under the ship's deck, for a few uncomfortable moments Aristogiton felt a slight queasiness of his own at his sudden loss of a visual horizon. Listening to the almost musical clinking of his valuable cargo—the tightly knotted cargo of olive oil amphorae tapping gently against one another to the rhythmic sway of the storm's thrust and pull—Aristogiton eventually got his bearings and his belly under control. His eyes finally adjusting to the murky shadows, he spotted Cleon off to one side, zealously baling the runoff rainwater out through one of the oar holes with a large oaken bucket. "Are you doing all right?" he called across the darkness. Without losing his rhythm Cleon gave him an exhausted smile, brushed his hair out of his eyes, and nodded his head. Hanging onto the rope ladder, Aristogiton leaned in closer to his ear, "Surprisingly good sea legs for such a city-bound business man!" Grinning at the tired fellow, he added: "It won't be much longer now…" and he pointed topside, "…the storm's breaking up in the north!" Patting his shoulders with a bit more gusto than he'd used on the tender Diokles, he shouted, "I'll take Tylissus place at the tiller and send him forward to give you a hand with the buckets." Too worn out to muster any kind of verbal reply, Cleon nodded his head one more time and kept right on baling. "Good man!" Aristogiton called over his shoulder as he turned and scrambled back up the ladder.

Tylissus, ever the clown of their motley group, made a sour face when Aristogiton told him to go below and help bucket out the bilges. "But Captain, I'm a much better top man than a bottom!"

Harmodius, the first to catch his double meaning, laughed as he made room for Aristogiton at the tiller, "That's not what I've heard, you rutting she-goat!" He had to shout in Tylissus' ear to be heard above the squeal of the shrieking winds.

Taking his place, Aristogiton nudged Tylissus on his way. "Get along now, you scamp! And watch your footing, the salt spray and all this rain have left the deck in a pretty dicey condition." Slapping him on his soggy backside, he added as an afterthought: "Why don't you stop and give that poor erastes of yours a cheering word before you head below deck!"

For the first few minutes after he'd hustled Tylissus on his way, Aristogiton focused his attention on locating a steady cadence for keeping the ship's tiller in line with the rough sea's continually rolling motion. Rising up and gliding down from trough to trough, the ship soon picked up even more speed under her captain's expert hand. Watching Aristogiton's bulging shoulder muscles as he directed the steering oar first this way and then that, Harmodius quickly matched his partner's measure and, adding his own strength to the tiller, soon had the ship's course bending to his lover's will.

During one particularly hair-raising swell when the entire ship seemed to leap up and over, right out of the water, Aristogiton couldn't help grinning at the bleak expression clouding Harmodius' face as he clung to the tiller for dear life. Aristogiton reached over and, resting a sympathetic hand over his, gave it a cheering squeeze. "If these winds keeps up," he chuckled, "we'll be in Egypt in no time at all!"

Harmodius responded with a terse nod of his head, even as he silently uttered a prayer to the volatile sea god Poseidon that these powerful winds would die down, the drenching rains would dry up, and this sudden rebellion in his stomach would pass on before he humiliated himself in front of his erastes.

"Perhaps little Helena was right after all…" he groaned to himself as the ship began another long, slow lurch toward the crest of yet another towering wave and the shuddering wooden planks under his feet squealed their protest.

"Oh Mother, please…don't let him go! Make him stay home here with us! That boat's so tiny and the great open sea so frightening…I know he'll be lost…they'll all be lost…they'll drown in the sea, I'm sure of it!" Helena's chin quivered and hot tears streaked her waxen cheeks as the horrifying picture of her handsome brother and his friends disappearing beneath mountain-high waves on the stormy Middle Sea passed before here terror-stricken eyes.

"Helena…sister…there's nothing to worry about." Harmodius, flustered by her hysterics in front of Aristogiton, gave his mother an imploring look.

With a sigh, she walked over to her daughter and placed a calming arm around her shoulder. "Hush now, Dearest. As Harmodius says, there's nothing to worry about." She smiled as she took a corner of her himation and gently wiped at Helena's tears. "Your brother is the head of the household now. And whatever decisions he makes, we are duty bound as mother and sister to obey him." She motioned for Aristogiton to step forward and she took hold of his hand. "And look here, child...if anything were to happen at sea, our Harmodius has a protector." She squeezed his hand. "You see the love in his eyes, Helena? Do you think this brave man would let anything happen to our boy?"

Helena turned her head and, with a sniffle, looked up at the tall man who, all those years before, had chased her willy-nilly through the sunny vineyards at Araphen. Suddenly grabbing his arm, she entreated him: "Oh please Aristogiton, you won't let anything happen to him...you'll see that Harmodius returns safely to us?"

Aristogiton knelt down on one knee and gently patted her cheek. "Don't worry, my pretty Trojan princeling," Helena half-smiled at the memory of that long ago day, "your brother and all his friends will be safe in my care. My father trained me well. I know the southern shipping lanes like the back of my hand and the *Thetis* is a sturdy, water-tight craft...she's voyaged the Middle Sea many times in the past and I'm confident she'll see us safely to Egypt and back again."

"Enough now, child..." Philippia helped Helena to her feet "...I wish to speak with your brother in private. Why don't you go to the marketplace and purchase a good luck charm for his trip?" She walked over to a small camphor box on a high shelf, retrieved a silver coin from the family's household money, and handed it to the young girl. "And for goodness sake, take Mila with you! You're well past the age when girls should be wandering about the city unchaperoned."

After Helena had gone on her way, Philippia turned to her son and rested a cool hand against his cheek. "You will be careful, won't you?"

Harmodius reached up and tenderly covered her hand with his. "Of course, Mother. I won't take any risks and I won't do anything foolish...I promise!"

She smiled at his confidence and, turning away, resumed her seat in front of the old loom. As she picked up her shuttle and began weaving it back and forth through the red and black wool threads, she reflected on the enormous change these last few months had worked over her son. Almost overnight, he'd matured into a fine example of Athenian manhood...much of it due, no doubt, to his erastes Aristogiton. With a twinkle in her eye, she noisily cleared her throat causing her son and his friend, their heads joined together in discreet whispering, to look up. "No secrets now, you two...not from Mother!" With a peremptory wave of her hand she summoned them to attend her. "Why don't you bring those stools and come sit here by me. I do have a number of questions...and not just about this sailing adventure to Naukratis, mind you…" Harmodius felt the color rush to his cheeks as her always perceptive eyes sought out the core of his innermost thoughts.

❄   ❄   ❄

As much as he admired his mother's sometimes too candid attitudes and encouraging chatter about his relationship with Aristogiton, in the end he did keep one thing from her. After much discussion, the two men had decided that any mention of their recent altercation at the Kynosarges with the new co-tyrant Hipparchus would only exacerbate an already tricky situation and needlessly unsettle his family…and at a time when neither man would be present to placate their concerns. Besides, they told themselves, as long as the two men were away from the city; Harmodius' family would surely to be left in peace. After all, it was inconceivable to any honor bound Greek that a man's womenfolk might be used as pawns in a game of personal retribution.

In the end, Harmodius summoned his steward and two strong field hands back from the farm at Araphen to keep an eye on things in the city while he and Aristogiton were away in Egypt.

When the day of their departure came, everyone climbed into a mule drawn cart for the short trip down to the bustling seaport of Piraeus. Scheduled to cast off with the late morning tide, their precious cargo of olive oil filled amphorae had been loaded into Thetis' hold the night before. To conserve space for their precious payload, Aristogiton had decided to forgo the use of extra rowers on this trip, instead relying on the winds and currents to carry him and his gentlemen crew of five to and from the coast of Africa.

❄   ❄   ❄

"I don't understand it…where could they be?" Harmodius, gazing up at the eternally transiting sun, made a nervous estimate of the time. "If they don't show up soon, we'll miss the tide!"

Aristogiton sniffed the salt air, clapped him reassuringly on the shoulder and laughed. "Don't worry so much, my little friend. The tide hasn't turned yet…there's still plenty of time."

Harmodius turned his eyes back toward the dusty road coming from the city, his consternation almost palpable to the others standing with him on the wharf. A moment later Diokles and Tylissus, their gear safely stowed below deck, hustled down the narrow wooden plank to join the small company wait-ing to see the Thetis off.

"No sign of them, yet?" Diokles asked.

Harmodius shook his head. "Didn't you see them at the gymnasium yester-day?" Tylissus nodded his head. "Did Nicias mention anything to you at all…about a problem with the trip…or maybe some trouble between him and Cleon…anything at all?"

Diokles and Tylissus, both looking equally perplexed, shook their heads in almost perfect unison. "No," answered his weasel-faced friend, "when we parted company, they were sitting out under the trees cooing like two turtle-doves in heat." He scratched his head, "I'm sure Nicias' last words to me were, 'see you at the ship…' or 'see you at the wharf…' or something to that effect." He looked to his lover for confirmation and the older man nodded his head up and down.

Suddenly, the drum of hoof beats in the distance shattered the morning calm and an excited Aristogiton shouted out, "Here they come!" All heads swung around to see two men on horseback—one with his brazen shock of red hair flying out in all directions—come galloping down the city road. Nicias, the thin lines of sweat etching through the road dust on his face, actually jumped off his horse before it had come to a full stop. Tossing the reins to Har-modius' cart driver, he bent over to catch a breath before standing and facing his anxious friends.

"Disaster!" he cried out before anyone could put them to task for their tar-diness. As he raced over to his friend's side, the dumbfounded Harmodius saw that fresh tears were crossing tracks with the dirty lines of sweat on Nicias' face. "Disaster…" he repeated, this time more a faltering croak than a despair-filled cry.

As Harmodius held him steady by the arms, he gazed over his shoulder and was dismayed to see that there was no traveling pack tied to Nicias' saddle. "What is it, Nicias? Why are you late? Tell us what's happening here?"

Nicias took a feeble swipe at his eyes before dropping his head in shame. "I…I'm so sorry Harmodius. But something's come up…I can't go to Egypt with you." As his quaking words spilled forth, his voice fell away until he could barely be heard.

Aristogiton, now suddenly two men shy in his already tiny crew, came over and rested a reassuring hand on Nicias' quivering shoulder. "It's alright, Nicias…why don't you stop and take a few deep breaths, get your wits about you, and then tell us all what's happened."

Nicias, nodding his disheveled red head, swallowed the sour tasting saliva in his mouth and let out a long exasperated sigh. "It's my accursed brother…"

"Your brother? You mean Demoritus…your twin?"

His eyes glaring with disgust, Nicias spit out his answer. "The very same!"

All those gathered on the docks that day had heard the amazing story of the old armorer's twin sons—as alike in their ruddy appearance as two seeds sprouting from the same pomegranate…and yet, with personalities as unalike as the shy prairie hare from his cunning cousin the mountain fox. An incorrigible mischief-maker, Demoritus had already been summoned before the city magistrates on numerous occasions for scandalous incidents involving public drunkenness and street brawling.

Crestfallen, Nicias wiped at his eyes with the grimy back of his hand, "The City Guard came to our house last night…and they took him away…again." His voice was shaking as he slapped at the dust on his bare arms. "It seems that when he and his friends were on their most recent binge…they thought it would be funny to piss it all out on the steps of the Temple of Ares." He chewed on his lower lip for a moment, his face blanching at the utter humiliation his brother had brought upon his family's humble name. Dropping his eyes to the ground once again, he forced himself on. "The magistrate is furious…this time he's talking of adding a charge of 'sacrilege' to the indictments for public drunkenness!"

Her audible gasp caused all heads to turn in unison as Harmodius' mother broke her way into their tight circle. "Good gracious no, not a charge of *sacrilege!* If his case goes before the Archon Basileus, your brother Demoritus could be facing exile for life…or even execution! Why, the poor child could be flung to his death off the highest wall of the Acropolis!"

Harmodius looked over to where Cleon was tying his own overworked horse to the rickety cart's railing next to Nicias' panting mare and couldn't help noticing that, while his friend's saddle had been noticeably bare, this one had an overfull leather pack strapped securely to the side.

Stepping forward, Cleon wrapped his arms protectively around his teary-eyed eromenos' shoulders. "Yes, Lady…these are most serious charges" he said, acknowledging Philippia's dire warning, "and that fool Demoritus most certainly faces the possibility of execution for his inexcusable act of impiety." A surprising insistence colored his voice as he turned Nicias' around to face him. "And that is all the more reason why we should *both* remain behind in Athens. Demoritus will need whatever support he can find—my effort as well as yours—to overcome his perilous situation."

Nicias angrily shook his head and wriggled out from Cleon's embrace. "No!" he barked as he brushed his lover's hands to one side. The entire group fell silent at the harshness of his response. Embarrassed by his overwrought reaction, Nicias dropped his hands and sighed. Lowering the volume, but maintaining the intensity of his voice, he continuing forcefully on: "We've already discussed this, dear Cleon. I will remain behind in Athens to attend to Demoritus' legal troubles, as is my duty to my family. You however, owe a responsibility to our friends here…" he attempted a consoling smile "…and to me, your fickle eromenos. As hard as this separation will be, I must insist that you go along to Egypt with the others. Your much needed strength, wisdom and resolve will go far to covering my absence on Aristogiton's worthy crew."

Distraught, Cleon had the crestfallen look of the worn down. "But…" he tried again.

Nicias remained firm. "No, Cleon…it's impossible. The Thetis just might be able to make sail with one less crewman. But with the both of us missing, she'll never even make it out of the harbor." He turned to Aristogiton for confirmation and the ship's captain nodded his head in affirmation. "Besides…" Nicias continued, his poignant smile turning into an impish grin, "…I'll not have you mooning about the city for the next three months…all because you've missed out on the mercantile adventure of a lifetime!"

For a long moment Cleon stared into his lover's intractable eyes…and then, gritting his teeth with resolve, he nodded his head. "Very well, my heart-song…if that is your wish."

Before Cleon could change his mind, Harmodius ran over to his horse and untied his traveling pack. Tossing it to Tylissus and Diokles, he motioned for them to get back on board the ship. Turning to the anxious well-wishers waiting alongside the Thetis to see them off, he clapped his hands in the air. "Our tide is turning, my friends…the time for farewells is at hand!" Grabbing hold of Nicias, he pulled him in tightly, kissed him on both cheeks and whispered: "I'm afraid things just won't be the same in Egypt without my nimble, little redheaded monkey scampering at my side, old friend." Nicias, clearly spent from his trouble-filled night with Demoritus and the private battle with Cleon, found himself at a loss for words. As if reading his thoughts, Harmodius gently added: "And you have my solemn promise, Nicias…I will look after your Cleon. We'll keep him so busy tallying his figures and haggling for bargains with the Naukrates, that he'll barely have time to miss you." He grinned mischievously, "Well…at least not very much." Without another word, he turned to the waiting Aristogiton and, winking a conspiratorial eye, whistled to get him moving. "Beloved…" he called out, "perhaps you could assist our good friend Cleon up the gangway?"

Aristogiton, catching his meaning, nodded and winked back. As soon as the parting lovers finished with their final embrace, he obligingly took hold of Cleon's arm and, without another word, led him away toward the embarking ship.

"I'll cast off her lines and be right behind you…" Harmodius called after him. As he turned to bid his mother and sister an affectionate farewell, to his surprise, it was his mother and not his sister who suddenly began spouting tears. With an affectionate hug and a quick stream of reassuring words, he did his best to kiss them all away. Turning to Helena, he found his sister holding out a small silver chain with a tiny, painted ceramic figurine dangling from its end.

"It's supposed to be Thetis…you know, the sea nymph…the goddess mother of Achilles…" she raised her eyebrows, grinning shyly "…and we all know how important the Myrmidon leader is to you." She held it up for his inspection. "See here…she has a fish's tail instead of legs." Lifting it high over his head, she carefully placed the amulet around his neck. "And since your Aristogiton's ship is called the Thetis, I…well, I just thought it might bring you luck on your voyage." Her last few words flew out in a tear-stuttering rush.

Kissing her on both cheeks, Harmodius felt his stomach do a sudden flip-flop of anticipation as the finality of it all set in. "Thank you, my dearest sister. I promise to wear it until we all come safely back home. And on that joyous day, you and mother will accompany me to the Temple of Poseidon…and together, we'll place this precious amulet of yours at the Sea Lord's feet…a thank offering for our safe return from mysterious Egypt." Anxious to be on his way, he squeezed Helena's arms one last time before releasing her to her mother's care. With a final wave of his hand, he ran to loosen the remaining hawser lines from the wharf.

"And though it matters little to me…have a care that that fickle simpleton Diokles returns in one piece…" Helena called out after him "…and don't forget to bring me back something pretty from Egypt! Something pretty and expensive!"

Waving to them all one last time, Harmodius' excitement bubbled over as he scrambled up the gangway. With Tylissus bending over at his side, the two used the sturdy plank to push off from the wharf before hauling it back on board. As the morning breezes billowed out the sail, the slow moving ship began inching its way towards open water. Running back to take his place alongside the handsome Aristogiton at the tiller, the last thing Harmodius heard as they pulled away from the dock, was the sound of his mother's scolding voice:

"'Bring me something pretty!'" she admonished the sobbing Helena, "Oh really, daughter…sometimes you're too much for words!"

❦   ❦   ❦

"Africa…"

He heard a seductive voice calling to him from far away.

"Wake up Harmodius, we're here…open your eyes and take your first look at the desert kingdom of the once mighty Pharaohs."

An easy hand ruffled through his hair…and then two salt-cracked lips gently brushed against his cheek. Opening his eyes, he was momentarily taken aback to see Aristogiton staring into his eyes from little more than an inch away. "Are you awake, my lazy one?" his mellow voice was lighter than a whisper. Harmodius nodded his head. He moved to sit himself upright when a sudden halting pain shot up through his neck causing him to gasp. "Easy there…" Aristogiton skipped around behind and began rubbing at the tender kinks and knots in his stiff neck and back, "…I'm afraid you fell asleep at the tiller."

Harmodius looked down and saw that, while his left arm was still carelessly draped over the long steering oar, his right hand was tangled around Helena's ceramic amulet as though he were clutching it for dear life. He slowly loosened his fingers, turning his head to first one side and then the other, his muffled groans catching immediate attention from Aristogiton's kneading fingers.

"The storm…" he mumbled.

"Blew itself out last night." Aristogiton, leaning forward and redoubling his efforts, dug into a particularly tender spot with both thumbs. "I'm sorry to say that you slept through the worst of it!"

Harmodius looked down and saw that, like poor seasick Diokles, he too had been haltered to the Thetis' railing with a short line of rope. As his numb, fumbling fingers struggled to loosen the knot at his waist, Aristogiton finished up his massage and handed him over a dipper of fresh water. Harmodius used the first sip to rinse out his mouth, neatly spitting the stale residue over the side of the boat. The next few sips obligingly refreshed his parched throat. And the last portion he dumped over his head to clear away any remaining fog from his groggy, sleep-muddled night.

"Is he awake yet?" Tylissus, resembling a skinny-legged mountain goat as he came hopping over the coils of rope cluttering the deck, had a chunk of strong-smelling cheese in one hand and a piece of unleavened bread in the other.

"Just…" answered Aristogiton.

"Well then, 'master sea-legs'…get up off that bony ass of yours and come take in the first glorious sight of land!" Tylissus swallowed the last bite of bread, tossing the leftover cheese across to Aristogiton, even as he grabbed Harmodius by the arms and wrenched him to his feet. If anything, his poor legs—bent all night in one position at the knees—were even stiffer than his back and neck had been. Ignoring his howls of protest, Tylissus dragged him forward to the prow of the ship as Aristogiton, resuming his place at the tiller, laughed at the sight of two storm-bedraggled ragamuffins.

Holding to Tylissus' arm for balance as he leaned out over the rail, Harmodius gazed in fascinated bewilderment at the palm fringed coastline—a blazing golden, sand-covered beach stretching off in seemingly infinite flatness from horizon to horizon. As the ship edged in closer to shore, Aristogiton shifted the tiller until the Thetis turned and was running eastward in a parallel course. "Hey you two! Keep a sharp eye on the waters ahead…" he called out to them, "…and let me know when the coloring starts to muddy. That'll be the red silt drifting out from the Nile delta…and the first sign that fabled Naukratis is at hand."

The sun was approaching its noontime zenith when the waters all around them finally began to exchange their crystalline, opalescent blue-green tint for a murkier, reddish-bronze colored sheen. Within the hour, brightly colored sails from numerous small fishing craft began appearing close to the horizon. Their keen-eyed owners, catching sight of the heavily laden trading vessel coming towards them out of the west, immediately turned homeward, racing each other back to port…each hoping to be the first to deliver the welcome news of the arrival of a Greek merchant ship to the trade-starved city.

Following them into the westernmost arm of the delta, Aristogiton used the breezy offshore winds to push his craft upriver against the Nile's slow moving current. By the time the slow-moving Thetis swung past the great stone break-water—her sail lowered and her four crewmen each manning an oar as she drifted toward a waiting berth alongside a vacant dock—the entire city had turned out to welcome them.

✦   ✦   ✦

The fabled glory days of Egypt's Old and New Kingdoms—the golden age when formidable rulers bearing the sacred names of Thutmose, Amenhotep, and Ramses led their armies across the desert to create a great empire ruled from their elegant capitals along the ever verdant banks of the Nile—had come to an ignoble end in 945 BCE with Egypt's own brutal conquest by her fierce Libyan neighbors.

Following centuries of chaotic civil wars and foreign invasions—Egypt had enjoyed a brief return to self-rule under the pharaoh Psamtik I. A minor king from one of the lesser delta city-states, Psamtik employed Greek mercenaries from Ionia to expel the invaders and accomplish his miraculous reunification efforts. Setting himself as sole ruler on the throne of Egypt, Psamtik rewarded his Greek army—at the same time, isolating their foreign ways from the rest of his kingdom—by allowing them to settle in the quiet delta village of Nokratj. Eventually chosen by default as the sole trading center between his kingdom and the rest of the Mediterranean, Naukratis—as the Greek settlers came to call it—soon became the economic hub of all Egypt.

Psamtik's heirs—and the city of Naukratis—thrived for nearly one hundred years, growing rich and complacent trading Egyptian corn for Greek olive oil, wine and silver until, overwhelmed by the Persian Cambysis and his mighty war machine, Psamtik's Dynasty came to an abrupt end in 525 BCE. Having sided with their Egyptian benefactors against the ruthless Cambysis, the Greek residents of Naukratis quickly found their trading privileges curtailed by Egypt's new overlords.

Distracted by palace intrigue and rebellions in the farthest corners of his enormous Empire, Cambysis' administration of Egypt suffered from rampant corruption, undergoing a period of serious decline until his successor, Darius I, came to power. In an effort to bolster the legitimacy of his own rule, Darius had the old satrap of Egypt summarily executed and set about restoring confidence in the new Persian regime. Reinstating Naukratis' earlier trading privileges, Darius allowed word to spread throughout the lands encircling the Mediterranean that Egypt was once again 'open for business'.

And so it was that Darius' newly appointed satrap—only recently arrived from the court at Persepolis—came himself, racing down the Nile from Memphis, as soon as word reached him that this first over-laden trading vessel had arrived at the port of Naukratis.

❦   ❦   ❦

"There now, stroke him gently on his flanks. And use a soothing voice when you talk to him…and don't forget to rub his ears, he likes that!" Baobil's toothy smile was infectious as he carefully handed the two loose reins up to Harmodius' outstretched hands. "Now then, lean back. No, my young lord, further…much further…and hold tight!" With a whooping yell punctuated by guttural clicks of his tongue, Baobil took his heel off the camel's forearm and the animal lurched forward, rising gracefully off the hot desert sands. Swaying wildly from side to side, the hairy beast ambled off on its own accord to take his place alongside the others in the waiting caravan line.

Aristogiton, Diokles, and Tylissus having—with varying degrees of success—completed their own initiations to this exotic form of desert travel, laughed heartily from their precarious perches high above the sun-bleached desert floor as a white-faced Harmodius, fighting to keep his balance on the ungainly creature, put on a brave face. The camel sidled into position and Harmodius, ignoring the ribald jibes of his friends, carefully leaned forward to rub his hairy mount's twitching right ear. Just as the young Greek novice was beginning to relax, he felt a deep rumble pass under his legs…followed a moment later by a noisy, gaseous fart exploding from his camel's behind. The look of abject embarrassment blushing on Harmodius' face brought a fresh round of heckling from the rambunctious group…at least until the acrid animal smell drifted in their direction and their boisterous hooting turned to sickened groans of revulsion.

Satisfied that everything was well under control, Baobil turned his attention to the last camel and rider. Leading a particularly tall beast over to a slightly green-faced Cleon, Baobil—once again flashing his trademark toothy grin—tapped on the hairy calluses covering the animal's knees and brought the obedient animal down to rest on all fours.

"You're next, oh gracious lord…" he whispered in that oddly seductive, singsong voice.

Cleon took one look at the seemingly benign, great humped monster and vigorously shook his head. "Oh no…I don't think so. I…I'm sure I've had a change of heart about all this." Casting an imploring glance in Aristogiton's direction, he took a stumbling step backward, all the while nervously shaking his head. "If it's all the same to you Aristogiton, I think I'll stay behind here in

Naukratis. After all, someone should be here to keep an eye on the ship and…and, after all, I don't really have any great desire to see the…"

Baobil, his lips turned down in a pout and his two sharp eyebrows raised in feigned distress, cut him off with a curt slap of his riding stick against the side of his billowy pantaloon. "You question the security of your cargo? Do you doubt the word of my master, Greek?" he demanded in that same singsong, twittery voice.

Cleon raised both hands in protest. "No, no…not at all. I mean…er, that's not what I meant to say. It's just that…well, in truth I don't think that I can…"

Baobil's good-natured smile slowly returned and, as Cleon continued his rambling protestations, he quietly unstrapped the wood framed cradle from the camel's back, replacing it with an even more convoluted contraption. Throwing heavy blankets here and there over the structure, he turned back to Cleon and, for a curious moment, stood studying him from head to toe. Finally, hushing all objections with a stern tap of a finger against his lips, he bowed low to the Greek and grinned.

"Nothing to worry about, gracious lord. Today, you and I will ride together."

❦   ❦   ❦

The visit to Naukratis had been a huge success for the Greek travelers.

Immediately upon his arrival—and much to the dismay of the local merchants—the Royal Satrap stepped forward and made the first bid (and a most generous one at that) on Aristogiton's precious cargo of olive oil, forcing the others to enter the auction at a much higher level then they would have preferred. In the end a bidding hysteria from the dearth of trading goods set in and Aristogiton received almost triple the price he'd anticipated from the sale.

The rest of that busy week flew past as the young Athenians were feted by the town's preeminent citizens—an odd mix of Ionian Greek, Egyptian and Persian—all brought together in bustling Naukratis by their worship of various gods and goddesses of commerce. Almost nightly, at elaborate feasts and parties held in spacious open-air villas and whitewashed townhouses along the banks of the Nile, Aristogiton and his crew enjoyed the gracious largess of their hosts.

Having expressed a desire to see the famous sights of Egypt's Old Kingdom, especially the fabled Pyramids, before setting sail for home, the travelers were delighted when the Royal Satrap clapped his hands together and ordered up a special caravan to transport them south through the desert to the ancient capitol of Memphis. On the night before their departure for the Giza plateau, the beaming Satrap—dining aboard the Thetis as a guest of his visitors—informed the travelers that he would personally vouch for the safety of the ship and their belongings until their safe return from Memphis. And, as an added gesture of goodwill, he offered up the services of his right-hand man, his 'beloved Baobil'—a facile linguist fluent in Greek, Egyptian, and Persian—as translator and guide.

❋   ❋   ❋

As sweltering as the desert could be during the long daylight hours, the sudden cold chill of the night invariably caught travelers by surprise. Huddled under thick woolen blankets around a blazing fire of dried brush and camel dung, the five Athenians ate a nourishing stew of mutton and vegetables cooked in a pot of savory spices with unfamiliar names, complemented by long thin pieces of flatbread dipped in honey flavored yogurt, and all of it washed down with jars of the finest Egyptian beer cooled in the shallow waters of the Nile.

"I tell you…I think the man was fondling me!" Cleon, his eyebrows pinched together in consternation, peered over Diokles' shoulder to make sure that Baobil was still far away across the camp directing the slaves as they assembled their low slung sleeping tents for the night.

"Oh come now, Cleon…you're imagining things." Harmodius moved to rest a reassuring hand on his shoulder but Cleon angrily shook it off.

"I am not imagining things!" He reached down and grabbed at the braided waistline of the heavy Persian pantaloons he'd been given to protect his thighs from the rough, bristles of the camel's hairy body. "I'm telling you, he somehow managed to undo the knot I put on these godforsaken things before we'd gone even half a league today…and the next thing you know, he had both hands buried deep inside!" Cleon tore off a strip of the flat bread and dipped it furiously into the yogurt pot. "And the way that smelly beast kept weaving us back and forth…well, I didn't dare do or say anything…it was all I could do to keep from falling off and breaking my damned fool neck!"

"So…what you're telling us is that you just sat back and enjoyed yourself, letting our gracious host Baobil play with that tiny 'thing' of yours all afternoon?" Tylissus, leering at him from across the fire, reached over and popped a chunk of meat into Diokles' waiting mouth. "You lucky dog!" With a wry chuckle he turned to the others and couldn't resist adding: "Or perhaps our friend here has been dreaming that it was his absent Nicias riding up there behind him on that camel…and not some Persian 'fancy boy'!"

With a quick jerk of his head, Tylissus deftly dodged a sticky remnant of flat bread that came sailing at him from across the flames. "That's not funny!" Cleon growled.

Aristogiton held up his hand. "Now wait a minute, you two…I think Cleon here may be onto something." Lowering his voice and leaning in toward the fire he whispered, "Haven't you all observed some rather unusual things about our Persian guide? The birdlike voice…the graceful movement of those long limbs when he walks…and his skin, have you noticed how smooth his skin is?"

"He certainly has an *ageless* quality about him," added Harmodius. "Sometimes when I look over at him he seems like a mere child…and then moments later, I'll look back and think I'm seeing a wizened old grandfather!"

The others silently nodded their heads. Scratching his chin, Diokles asked, "Do you remember what the Satrap called him on that night before we left Naukratis? 'My own beloved Baobil'…"

Cleon's eyes suddenly grew round as plates. "You don't think he's a…a…"

"Shhh…" Aristogiton waved his hand. "He's coming over."

Baobil approached the fire and, circling around to the far side, crossed his legs and settled gracefully onto the ground just behind Cleon. "Is the evening meal to your liking, happy Lords of Greece?" he asked.

Tylissus, taking a swipe with the back of his hand at the rich mutton juice dripping down his chin, nodded his head. "Oh yes, Baobil…it's delicious!" Stuffing another piece of bread in his mouth, he grinned and added: "Cleon…why don't you slide over a bit and let our host in to enjoy the fire?"

Glowering across the flames, Cleon scooted closer to Harmodius and Baobil silently slid himself into the vacant spot at his side. Holding his hands up to the flames, the Persian briskly rubbed them together and smiled. "Yes…that's very much better."

An uncomfortable silence settled around the campfire.

Dipping a piece of flatbread in the honey yogurt, Aristogiton offered it to their willowy Persian guide who accepted it with a smile and a graceful bow of his head.

"Baobil…"

"Yes, Lord?"

Searching for a more comfortable position, Aristogiton shifted his legs to one side. "You must forgive our rudeness. We are ignorant travelers, unfamiliar with the customs of your distant land. And well, not wishing to offend you or your gracious Master, we were wondering if we might ask…"

Baobil chuckled as he helped himself to a thin slice of mutton from a plate warming by the fire. "Fear not, oh 'Captain of the Thetis'…there is nothing that you or your gentle companions could say or ask of me that will give any offense." Licking the mutton juice off his fingertips, he arched a knowing eyebrow and posited: "Ah…but then perhaps I have already divined the nature of your curiosity?"

Intrigued, Aristogiton nodded his head, politely waiting for him to continue.

To everyone's surprise, Baobil reached over and took hold of Cleon's hand. "Here, friend Cleon…run your hand along my face…" and so saying, he rubbed Cleon's hand against his cheek. "Soft…no? Beardless…and smoother than any skin shaved by even the sharpest of razors." Cleon, somewhat unnerved, tugged his hand away. "And look here…" Baobil pulled his shirt up and over his head revealing a completely hairless torso. Then, lifting an arm, he exposed a hairless armpit for all to see. "And here as well…" Hopping to his feet, before anyone could protest, he undid the tie on his pantaloons and let them drop them to the ground.

Now, while it's an eternal truth that Greeks are notably blasé in their attitudes concerning nudity, there was an unnerving something about this sudden frank display of the guide Baobil's very naked brown, hairless, and goose bump covered body standing before the open fire that had them all fidgeting in their seats.

"That's really not necessary, Baobil…"

The naked Persian turned a melancholy face toward Aristogiton. "Oh, but it is, gracious Captain of the Greeks…for you see," he reached down and lifted his large uncut endowment in one hand, "while I may have a hairless body and a somewhat higher-pitched voice than most men…I am not the monster down below that many believe my kind to be."

Even though they were shamed by his bluntness, none of the Greeks could resist leaning forward to study the emasculated nature of their Persian guide. And while it was apparent that in the long years since his delicate gelding, his now empty scrotum had shriveled up against his body…the castration had in no way affected the size or performance of the magnificent member which, to their amazement, grew hard and even longer as Baobil held it out for them all to see.

"A eunuch…" whispered Tylissus, his mouth hanging open as he stared at the alien sight with a mixture of horror and admiration. "By all the gods…"

Baobil's bittersweet laugh touched them all. "Yes," he responded, "by all the gods, indeed…a eunuch." Suddenly shivering in the clear night's chill, he retrieved his shirt and, bending over, pulled his pantaloons back up. Retying them securely around his waist, he quietly resumed his seat next to the dumbfounded Cleon. Hoping to restore some of the bodily warmth stolen by his brief exposure, he held his hands out closer to the flames, smiling somewhat sadly as he told them his story.

"When I was but a boy, a bit younger than you Lord Harmodius, my old master—a noble prince of ancient Babylon—was so enamored with the youthful beauty of my face and the graceful sweep of my arms as I ran singing about his palace, that he couldn't bear to part with them. One day he asked me if I would sacrifice my manhood on the altar of love…and, without hesitation, I submitted myself to the temple surgeon's blade." Baobil dipped another slice of flat bread in the yogurt jar before continuing.

"As I grew older, my besotted master, wishing to improve upon my rather adolescent skills as a lover, sent me off to study with the famous priestesses at the Temple of Ishtar. From these very accomplished ladies I learned the delicate arts for pleasuring a man…" he turned and smiled at Cleon, "techniques and skills that I have used over the years to bring untold delights to the many men I've served…all the while slowly improving my own position in this sometimes brutal world." Baobil, turning to stare into the fire, took a long, slow breath before letting it out as a weary sigh. "But I digress…

"Before I could share the wonders of my newfound skill with my old master, he and his entire family were slain as decadent Babylon fell to the marauding Persians. A spoil of war, I found myself allotted to the household of one Aryandes, a general in the conquering army. I served my new master for many years and, when the great Cambysis' conquered Egypt, it was this same lord—my master Aryandes—who was honored with the title of Satrap over the new province. Suddenly, I found myself thrust upon a reluctant camel's back, right alongside all my acquisitive lord's other treasures, for the long caravan ride across the barren Sinai…to be relocated here in the great palace at Memphis."

Baobil shrugged his shoulders. "Ahh, but I fear my Aryandes (a rather ineffectual lover, in any case) was a far better general than he was a bureaucrat." A shadow crossed his face…accompanied by a rather grim chuckle. As the others watched in fascination, he slowly ran his thumbnail across his neck. "Displeasing our new Great King Darius with his bounteous ineptitudes, I'm afraid he recently forfeited his foolish head."

"And that, I take it," piped up Harmodius, fully mesmerized by this most unusual man, "is how you came to reside in the household of the current Royal Satrap!"

This time, Baobil's responding laughter was filled with hearty warmth. "Exactly right, my young lord. And I'm pleased to say that my current master is not only a skillful administrator, he's a very talented lover as well…a most sensible man who makes much better use of my…er, many *other* talents than did my previous lord. Hence, the wisdom of his unselfishness in parting from me for this brief period of time…so that I may act as your peerless guide through the desert!"

This time, everyone joined in the laughter.

Cleon, somewhat moved by Baobil's forthcoming nature, cleared his throat. "If I may, I have a question of my own for you, Baobil. These past few days when we were riding together on the back of that filthy animal…you, uh…" the flush on his face grew even redder in the flickering light of the campfire. "Well, you took some…er…rather personal liberties with…uh, with my…er…"

Baobil's toothy grin gleamed white in the guttering light. "Ah, yes…" he purred, "…and you have a fine one…quite impressive for a Greek!"

Cleon covered his eyes as he shook his head in chagrin. "Yes…but why did you…why were you so…"

"Ahh…" said Baobil, finally discerning the true nature of his question. "Rest assured, it was nothing personal, my lord. Merely one of many relaxing techniques I've learned over the years to distract and calm the apprehensive." He reassuringly patted him on the back of his hand. "It was quite clear on that first day that you were frightened of my animals…so, by taking your organ into my care, as it were, I sought to ease your mind away from this most irrational of fears." He studied Cleon's face for understanding. "This wasn't a wrong thing to do…was it, lord?"

Gesturing to the others, he added. "And unlike you're obviously coupled friends here…you *are* traveling on this journey alone, are you not? And if so, I thought it my responsibility to…"

Now poor Cleon was truly flustered. "Yes…that is, I mean no!" First he found himself nodding his head, and then shaking it in equally vigorous denial. "I mean yes, it wasn't necessarily a wrong thing for you to do…er, because I *am* traveling alone. But…but you see, I'm really not alone…I'm with someone else…er, that is, back at home there's someone there waiting for me."

Baobil's look of concern changed to one of relief. "Ah, then all is well with us…because I too have my beloved Lord Satrap waiting back home for me!"

Tylissus tossed a sticky crumb of bread across the fire. "You see, Cleon…I told you there was nothing to it!"

Before their old argument could begin anew, Aristogiton rose to his feet, stretched his arms out, and yawned. "It's growing late, my friends…and no doubt we've another long day in the saddle to look forward to."

Baobil reached his arms out for balance and lithely got to his feet, in the same graceful movement, bending over to assist Cleon up off the ground. "Not so long now, my friends, not so long. We should reach our destination—the eternal, white walled city of Memphis—well before noon tomorrow. And you'll be pleased to hear that, once there, most of the ancient sights favored by visitors are but a short horseback ride from the city."

"Including the Pyramids?" whooped Tylissus as he danced around his yawning Diokles.

Baobil laughed, "Most certainly, my rambunctious lord…in fact, the Great Pyramids are already close at hand!"

"Horses!" exclaimed Cleon. "A sensible beast, thank the many gods! And special praise to our own Poseidon, the creator of horses, for this greatest of gifts to my poor camel-bruised backside!"

A final round of good-natured laughter followed as the Greeks moved off toward their respective tents. With a practiced wave of his hand, Baobil summoned the servants over to tend to the fire and clean up the remnants of their evening meal. The two low tents shared by Aristogiton and Harmodius, and Diokles and Tylissus were closest to the campfire and, by the time Baobil caught up with Cleon, the others had all disappeared inside for the night.

"Excuse me, my Lord Cleon?" he called out in a whisper, lightly touching his arm with an outstretched finger. Startled, Cleon spun around and found himself almost face to face with the same dark-skinned man who'd been so adept at massaging his love-starved genitals for these past days. Even in the darkness, Baobil could see him still flushed with embarrassment. Before he could speak, Baobil took his hand and, bowing low, pressed it against his cheek. "Lord…I have a great favor to ask of you." Cleon opened his mouth to speak, but Baobil, still clinging tightly to his hand, rushed on. "In truth, I have never lain with a Greek before…and you would be doing me both a great service and a great honor by allowing me to share your tent...on this, our last night in the desert."

Cleon snorted, his voice sputtering, "You want to...*what?*"

"I have lived my life proudly sharing what special gifts I have with soft, perfumed Babylonians and hairy-backed Persians. Now, for this one night under the stars, I have a longing to know what it feels like to lay in the arms of a virile Greek...someone handsome...like yourself." With the raise of a single eyebrow, his familiar grin took on a more lascivious hue in the soft white light of full moon. "And in exchange, My Lord, I'll happily share with you the many secret skills of lovemaking I learned at the hands of the priestesses of Ishtar. Magical wonders that promise to delight and tickle all five of the senses." He winked at the now dumbfounded Cleon. "Techniques and secrets that, once learned, I guarantee will titillate and thrill that lucky young man waiting for your return home to Athens." Before Cleon could open his mouth to object, Baobil leaned forward and began smothering his lips with soft kisses, his lightening tongue working its way in to do an exotic dance against the very backs of Cleon's teeth.

Feeling himself alone and adrift in the silent desert—and uncomfortably aware of an insistent stirring between his legs—what little resistance Cleon had left, drained away into the star-filled night. Without a word, he allowed the Persian eunuch to take his arms and pull him down, in between the flaps of his waiting tent.

CHAPTER 7

The first site of Egypt's newly restored capital city Memphis left the visiting Greeks wide-eyed and speechless. Perched atop their camels on a high dune overlooking the rich, green Nile Valley below, the fabled city stretched out before them in all its sun bleached, timeless glory. The whitewashed walls, blinding in the noonday glare, enclosed a thriving metropolis easily ten times the size of their native Athens. And even from this distant vantage point one could see that the capital was a beehive of activity, with web-like scaffolding crawling up the sides of monumental construction projects all over the city.

As the camels resumed their trouble-free loping pace down the rocky trail leading to the outskirts of the city, Baobil related the story of how Egypt's last pharaoh, Psamtik III, having been defeated at Pelusium by Cambysis' army, fled here to Memphis to make his last stand against the Persians. Hoping to spare his beloved city from the ravages of a lengthy siege, Psamtik opened wide the gates and led his troops out to battle. Wounded in a hail of Persian arrows, Pharaoh Psamtik could only watch in horror as the voracious conquerors tore through his beautiful white walls and sacked his once-proud city.

Later, as Cambysis surveyed the terrible damage wrought by his army—and perhaps feeling a little guilty at the wanton destruction of such timeless monuments and temples—he embraced his new possession as though it were a precious jewel. Setting massive reconstruction projects in motion, the Great King—and after him, his successor Darius—envisioned an Egyptian capital that would rival Babylon and Persepolis in size and splendor.

❧   ❧   ❧

Arriving in front of the gates to the governor's palace, with a few words from Baobil, the visitors were shown to their elegantly appointed quarters in spacious rooms fronted by wide canopy-covered verandahs overlooking the gently flowing Nile.

Each morning for the next week, Baobil arrived at their rooms to escort them to the palace stables where, once mounted up, they would head out to explore the vast city and its multi-faceted environs. Acting as their guide, Baobil took them to the famous necropolises of Saqqara and Dahshure on the city's outskirts to view early attempts at Egyptian pyramid building. Day after day, they stood in the sand gawking up at countless structures, some built as giant, step-like platforms laid one atop another, and others that shot nearly straight up out of the desert floor only to bend in halfway up and converge in a single bronze-capped point at the top. As they lazed in the cool shadows cast by these ancient monuments to the dead, Baobil filled their heads with stories of hidden funerary treasure storehouses and the ever-present tomb robbers that lusted after them. At noon, with the sun nearly overhead and the heat almost unendurable, the boisterous sightseers would race each other back to the governor's palace and the relative coolness of its thick, clay-covered walls. Following a light meal and a nap through the worst heat of the day, the travelers would venture back out, this time on foot, to see the wonders of the inner city itself.

On one of these late afternoon forays, the travelers paid a reverential visit to the city's largest monument, the Great Temple of Ptah—dedicated centuries before to the patron god of Memphis and a near rival in size and grandeur to the famous lotus-columned Temple of Amon-Ra at Karnak. With Baobil as their guide, they were admitted into the sacred precinct where the Apis Bull, the living incarnation of Ptah himself, was housed. A great black beast with a white diamond on his forehead and the outline of a vulture marking his back, the Apis Bull was venerated as the "Spokesman of Ptah" and, upon his death, was mummified with the same pomp and ceremony as his brother gods—the pharaohs. The Greeks gazed in wonder when ushered inside the giant underground vault deep beneath the sanctuary where one day the current Apis Bull would rest alongside his thousands of mummified taurine predecessors.

Still speechless as they pondered the sight of this underground city of mummified animals—each stacked neatly one against the other in great torch lit rows—Baobil finally led them away, back up into the dim, but reassuring light of the main sanctuary. Wandering through the temple's cavernous hypostyle hall with its nearly one hundred brightly painted, hieroglyph-covered columns, they eventually passed out into the courtyard where the massive pylons commemorating the reign of the temple's most ostentatious benefactor, Ramses II, were casting their longing shadows toward the east. Reaching the great bronze gate to the temple complex, Harmodius pulled Baobil to one side and asked him if there would be time for a quick visit to the city's marketplace.

❀   ❀   ❀

"You see, Baobil...I promised my sister I'd bring her something special from Egypt...a gift..." he said with an embarrassed grin and a shrug of his shoulders, "...something truly unique and...well, memorable, I suppose."

"No need to worry, my young friend." reassured Baobil, his shiny-toothed smile a familiar beacon to them all over these past few weeks. Turning his head, he glanced westward toward the orange-pink blush coloring the twilight sky and his smile suddenly drooped downward. Wrinkling his brow in consternation, he cried out: "But, dear me...the time has escaped us! My master the Governor returns from his tour of the Delta cities with the setting of the sun and I...we...should be on hand to greet him." He gnawed on the back of his finger for a moment. "Forgive me, Lord Harmodius. I fear the marketplace—a most mystifying warren of stalls, shops and insistent vendors at the best of times—can be more than a little overwhelming to the novice shopper." He cocked a knowing eyebrow, "And I'm afraid your reputation as wealthy Greek merchants will have preceded you...making it all the worse."

Harmodius tried to hide his regret. "Well, of course we still have one more day in Memphis...perhaps tomorrow we'll find the time."

Baobil raised both hands in the air, forcefully shaking his head. "Ah no, my dear friends...impossible! For you see, I've saved the best for last!" Grinning with infectious anticipation, he clapped Harmodius on the shoulders. "Tomorrow we ride out to the Giza plateau and at last make our pilgrimage to the Great Pyramid."

Tylissus looked confused. "But I thought we've already seen the pyramids...lots of pyramids...do we really have to go out again in all this heat just to see more of the same?"

Baobil narrowed his eyes as he waggled a scolding finger. "Young Lord, the pyramids of Saqqara and Dahshure are puny things...mere toys in the sand when compared to the mighty burial place of the ancient pharaoh Khufu! It's a truly exceptional sight that can't be missed!"

Seeing the disappointment on Harmodius' face, Baobil grew thoughtful for another moment before at last regaining his radiant smile. "I think I have a solution, my lords. You must allow *me* to arrange for all your purchases! If you will trust me this one last time, I guarantee that my servants will procure the finest treasures in all of Memphis for you and your loved ones back home. Fitting keepsakes to commemorate your all too short stay with us here in Egypt."

Aristogiton sounded skeptical. "I'm afraid that would be too much to ask. You and our host, the gracious Lord Governor, have already overwhelmed us with your many kindnesses and generosities…treating us as though we were visiting potentates rather than the simple traveling merchants we really are." He felt Harmodius tugging on his arm. "But it's also true that, having tarried here in Egypt for too long, we must soon be on our way north again or run the risk of losing the seasonal winds back to Greece." Relenting, he took Harmodius' arm and smiled at Baobil. "Perhaps in this case, it would be best to accept your kind offer…" now it was his turn to cock an eyebrow, "…but with the understanding that all *gifts* are to be paid for directly from my purse!"

Acquiescing, Baobil—looking more than a little slighted by Aristogiton's words—made a noble bow at the waist. "Of course, noble Captain of the Greeks…I wouldn't think of offending your sense of obligation."

And that was the only lie that the eunuch Baobil ever told his Greek friends…

For one last time Baobil served as guide when, early the next morning he led his travelers north on horseback along an ancient desert track to the heights of the wide, wind-swept Giza Plateau. The Greeks spent their entire day wandering among the lush Nile-watered temple gardens and maze-like necropolises ringing the three brilliantly white limestone faced pyramids of the centuries dead pharaohs Khufu, Khafre, and Menkaure—still, and for many centuries to come, the tallest structures ever conceived of and built by man. And it was here that the Greeks received their final lasting impression of the timeless nature of the land called Egypt. As the sun passed into the west, the weary travelers made their silent farewells to the ancient land, lingering nearby for a last reflective hour between the eternally frozen arms of the wind-scarred yet still affectingly enigmatic Sphinx.

Returning on horseback to the Governor's Palace, the Greeks found preparations for a final night of feasting in their honor well under way.

✻   ✻   ✻

The torch lit great hall of the governor's palace was a cacophony of sound as lute and sistrum players, harpists and drummers, naked dancing girls with tiny bronze bells tied to their fingers and toes, found themselves competing against the excited hubbub of animated nobles and merchants, each anxious to make one last favorable impression on their visiting Greek guests.

As he stared at the sapphire colored wine goblet in his hand, a delicate creation of the finest blown glass he'd ever seen, Aristogiton could sense a subtle hint of desperation in the air…commercial anxiety brought on by too many years of war and too long a dry spell for Egypt's trade-hungry merchants.

Unlike formal Athenian dinner parties where men and women feasted in separate rooms reclining on narrow couches facing one another in a tight circle, their Egyptian and Persian hosts were content to throw enormous goose-feather pillows about the room, their guests—men and women alike—finding places on these makeshift floor seats and eating from heavy silver trays as they were passed about the room by an army of naked servants. On a low dais at the front of the hall, their host—the High King Darius' Chief Governor of the Satrapy of Egypt—sat with the trusted Baobil nestled at his side, each in turn feeding the other from a flat golden platter of sweetmeats and fresh fruit slices. The governor was clearly pleased with Baobil's insightful handling of their foreign guests, smiling and nodding his head to each of them in turn several times throughout the long evening.

At one point in the middle of their meal, Baobil whispered something in his master's ear. Receiving the governor's blessing with the slightest nod of his head, Baobil stood up, walked down onto the main floor and, much to everyone's surprise, took a place on the pillow where Cleon was sitting alone eating his solitary meal. Blushing, Cleon nervously looked toward the dais to find the unconcerned governor pointedly ignoring them both as he picked at his food. Turning to one side, he saw his smirking traveling companions furtively whispering to each other behind the palms of their hands. Trapped by his own embarrassed discomfort, Cleon stared down at his lap until the ever-patient Baobil, calmly leaning over to his side, whispered something into his ear. A few moments later, the two were lost in laughter; eating and conversing like long-lost old friends.

As the feasting ended and the scattered remnants of food and drink were silently cleared away, a gong was sounded throughout the hall. On cue, the guests and musicians fell obediently silent as the portly governor rose laboriously to his feet. Clapping his hands together, he took pains to look pleased with himself as a large ebony trunk with the intricate, ivory-inlaid carving of the Greek ship 'Thetis' set on the lid, was carried in by two muscular Nubians and placed in the center of the room directly in front of his honored guests.

"Captain of our brave Greek sailors…" the governor motioned for Aristogiton to rise. "This box contains small gifts of our appreciation…and that of our gracious master, the High King Darius…mementos for you and your fellow crewmembers of your all too brief visit with us here in Egypt. Our wish for you all is a safe journey home…and we pray that the many benevolent gods who watch over the lands of Egypt, Persia, and Greece will favor us with many future visits from you and your fellow countrymen." Aristogiton opened his mouth to respond, but a silent shake of Baobil's head kept him silent. The governor continued: "Our one true wish is that, as tales of your commercial success here spread throughout your homeland, other Greeks will respond favorably to our desire for friendly commerce with the tradesmen of your land…and journey across the Middle Sea to enjoy Egypt's open-handed generosity."

Taking his cue from Baobil, Aristogiton bowed low at the waist, remaining in this position until the shuffling tread of the retiring governor disappeared from the room.

Later that evening, Baobil had the ebony trunk carried to Aristogiton and Harmodius' suite where everyone gathered around to see what treasures it contained. Carefully lifting the ivory-inlaid lid off the chest, Baobil began passing around delicate blown glass bottles of perfume, small folded papyrus packets containing exotic Egyptian cooking spices, jars of fragrant unguents and priceless myrrh, large folds of the finest pure white linen, rolls and rolls of the highest quality writing papyrus and, resting on a cushion at the bottom, a tiny wooden box with five golden rings—each having the name of the Great King Darius carved in a hieroglyphic cartouche in the center of a perfect lapis stone.

Seeing the look of vexation on Aristogiton's face, Baobil sought to forestall his objection with a dramatically penitent sigh. "Gracious Captain, you must forgive this small deception. Try as I might, there was no way I could persuade my master to suppress his overly generous nature. And the mere suggestion that you might prefer to *pay* for his wonderful 'gifts' would, I'm sure, have scandalized the entire court with your...er, ingratitude." Dropping his head to his chest, he shrugged his shoulders despairingly. "If you cannot find it in your generous heart to accept these humble 'trade offerings'...well, I'm afraid the ripples of imperial displeasure might be felt all the way back to Persepolis and my master's master!"

Aristogiton, blushing at his own obstinacy, quickly acceded to the wisdom of Baobil's words. "As always, your advice shines like a beacon in the night, friend Baobil...guiding us along the surest path towards..."

Baobil giggled. "Tut-tut, noble Captain. I fear you've been lingering among my kind for far too long...you're beginning to spout the willowy phrases of an experienced courtier!"

Aristogiton, turning an even brighter shade of red, joined with the others as they laughed at Baobil's joke.

Pulling his gold embroidered robe close around him, Baobil bowed and took a step backward, moving toward the door of the suite. "And now, dear friends...the hour grows late and I'm sure you will be wishing to get an early start in the morning. A local merchant, seeking favor with my lord, has offered the services of a swift sailing craft to return you downriver to the Delta and the city of Naukratis..." he grinned, "...a journey, I suspect, that you won't find nearly as taxing as our overland camel ride!" With a wave of his hand, a slave stepped forward and replaced the lid on the ebony chest. "The servants will see to it that the Governor's gifts, as well as all your other things, are safely stowed on board before your departure." He smiled, bowing once more, and was just about to take his leave when all of a sudden he stopped in the doorway. Raising a finger in the air, he cried out: "One moment," he snapped his fingers together, "I almost forgot the most important thing!"

Turning to a slave waiting in the hallway, he motioned for the small leather-bound package the man was holding tightly against his chest. Beaming from ear to ear, Baobil called Harmodius over. "You expressed a desire to take home 'a special gift' for a lovely young sister." He held the packet out to him. "And I have personally conducted an extensive search to the very depths of the palace treasury for something truly special...a trinket that might be pleasing to a young woman of culture and station." As he handed the packet over, he pulled on the old leather tie string and the stiff leather covering fell away to reveal a polished bronze mirror with a long ivory handle carved in the shape of a papyrus stem.

Harmodius gasped as he held up the mirror and stared at his own golden reflection in the ancient speculum. "But, Baobil…this is really too much! It's so beautiful…the artistry…so beautiful and so…"

"Ancient?" added Baobil with a sly lift of his eyebrow. Answering his own question, he smiled as he nodded his head. "Yes, quite old and quite rare indeed." Carefully returning the precious mirror to its well-loved leather covering, Harmodius tried to push it back into the Persian's hands, but the courtier politely refused to accept it. "Many, many years ago…centuries, indeed…this very mirror belonged to a great lady, a queen of Egypt, a woman reputed to have been the most beautiful who ever lived. The temple archives tell us that she was married at an early age to an ugly, misshapen man who, upon assuming the double crown, spurned the many gods of this land in favor of a strange belief in one god." He reached out and tapped the back of the mirror. "Look here, etched onto the backside is the symbol of this strange 'one god.'" Harmodius held the mirror up to the light and could just make out the worn carving of a small golden sun disc with numerous shafts of light spreading out in all directions. Each of these sunbeams ended in a tiny benevolent hand bestowing the gift of life upon its worshipers. "They called their god the Aten…" said Baobil, "…and worshiped him by praying in great roofless temples open wide to the Sun."

Harmodius passed the mirror around the room and, as each in their turn studied the exquisite craftsmanship and the odd little etching on the reverse, he asked Baobil. "And did she come to love him…this ugly pharaoh?"

Looking past him, Baobil caught the eye of Cleon as he answered. "Oh yes, young Greek…and that is my favorite part of the story. This great woman had a heart as strong and powerful as her great beauty…she saw past his poor monstrous exterior and found the hidden beauty buried away inside him."

"What happened to them," asked Tylissus, "…this ugly pharaoh and his beautiful queen?"

"Lost to the ravages of time I fear," he answered with a sad little sigh. "The Queen Nefertiti is still remembered for her great beauty. But her husband's name has vanished…obliterated from the temple walls and commemorative pylons by those same vengeance-seeking priests of the gods he'd so willfully spurned…expunged even from the sacred Pharaonic rolls for his terrible blasphemy against this superstitious land. Today, the poor man is all but forgotten in his own kingdom."

The mirror was returned to Harmodius and he carefully wrapped it back in its ancient, cracked-leather carrying case. Before he could try one last time to return the priceless item to Baobil, the Persian clasped his hands together and bowed low. "I pray you will accept this special gift...and not, this time, from my royal master...but rather, from a humble servant who has been most honored to have shared this all too brief time together in your company."

Without raising his head, Baobil backed quietly out of the room and disappeared down the torch-lit hallway.

Three days later, as their well-appointed merchant vessel slowly turned into the expansive harbor of Naukratis, the travelers were surprised to see that, in their short absence from the bustling city, three other ships had arrived from Greece, come south to trade-hungry Egypt with their own shipments of olive oil and wine for the country's new Persian overlords. As promised, a small contingent of the governor's personal guard was standing at attention, stationed on the dock where the fully loaded Thetis lay quietly resting at anchor. With their help, all the personal belongings from their trek to Memphis, along with the heavy ebony gift-trunk from the governor, were safely stowed below deck.

Less than an hour after their arrival in Naukratis, Aristogiton once again seated himself at the helm and the Thetis weighed anchor, turning back out onto the gently flowing waters of the Nile, this time heading north with the current through the twisting delta channels...back toward the open sea and home.

With the rich pungent smell of salt tickling their noses, the Greek travelers unfurled the great square sail of the Thetis to catch hold of the rising winds blowing north off the delta. Securing the rigging, the four sailors gathered around the steering oar to hear Aristogiton's plan for their voyage home.

"Nothing fancy, I fear. We'll just keep her safe and steady on a northwest heading and in a week or so...possibly a bit more...we should catch sight of Crete."

"Crete?" asked Harmodius. "Will we be stopping on Crete?"

With an oddly forced smile, Aristogiton curtly nodded his head and stared past Harmodius toward the open sea. "Yes...um, I think we'll put in for a few days at Phaistos. Just long enough to stretch our legs and refresh the water casks."

Something evasive about his response left Harmodius with the disquieting feeling that there was more to 'Crete' than just a simple stretch of the legs and a few water casks in need of refilling. For a moment, as he sought an answer in his lover's eyes, he felt as if he was gazing into the unreadable hollows of an actor's mask. Before he could put the question to him again, Aristogiton reached past him and poked Cleon in the stomach. "So, friend Cleon...now that we're safely away, were you planning on sharing your little secret with us?"

Cleon frowned. "Secret? What secret?"

Tylissus crowed as he waved a waggish finger in Cleon's face. "Oh, come off that high horse Cleon, everyone knows that you were up to something with that randy Persian eunuch! Now that we're alone you have to tell us everything. We're all dying to know, what was it like making love to a..."

"None of your business, you little scamp!" Cleon's voice cracked even as he turned away in a huff, ready to take his secrets and retreat to the seclusion of the furthest cubbyhole below deck. Before he'd gone two steps, Diokles grabbed his arm and pulled him up short.

"Oh no you don't!" he said, swinging him back around to face the others. "This is something we *all* want to hear!"

"Yes," Tylissus took hold of his other arm, "do tell us Cleon...was it more like being with a man...or a *woman*?"

Cleon, held firmly in place between the two of them, remained obstinately silent. "And what of those notorious Priestesses of Ishtar..." Aristogiton, studiously avoiding Harmodius' persistent gaze, joined with the others in prodding the silent curmudgeon, "...Baobil must have shared some of their celebrated sexual 'techniques' with you!"

At the mention of the Babylonian's name, passion-filled memories began to soften the uncompromising hardness on Cleon's face. After another awkward moment, he shook his arms free and grumbled: "Oh let me go, you two. We're on a ship, for god's sake...I'm not going anywhere!"

Tylissus and Diokles reluctantly let loose their grip and resumed their seats on the wobbly wooden bench opposite Aristogiton and the steering oar. Heaving a sigh, Cleon crossed his legs, and plopped down on the wooden decking at their feet. "Yes, alright then...I confess it's all true...the pretty Persian boy, the mystical secrets of Ishtar...all of it."

Aristogiton and the others leaned forward, eager to hear the tale. "That last night on the caravan...around the campfire...that's when it happened, isn't it?" he asked with a lascivious grin.

Cleon looked down at the rough calluses on his work-hardened hands and felt a quiver in his stomach as he fondly recalled the strange softness of Baobil's intimate touches. "Yes," he said, unable to hide the slow smile creeping across his face. "That was the night…and then again later on…in the palace."

"In the palace! You and he were together in the Palace?" Harmodius scratched his head in amazement as he tried to recall the sleeping arrangements in Memphis. "And no one saw you?"

"The place is riddled with secret passageways." Cleon grinned as he shrugged his shoulders. "Baobil nearly gave me a stroke on that first night when the wall next to my bed slid open and there he was…naked as the day he was born!"

Tylissus laughed. "Gods…I would have loved to have seen that!"

Cleon sighed. "Yes, gelded or not, our little Persian had the body of a race-horse…"

Tylissus leered as he leaned over and whispered to his lover, "Yes…but who rode whom that night?"

Diokles nudged him with a sharp jab of his elbow. Turning back to Cleon, he licked the salt off his lips. "So, was it…was he…I mean, was it very different from…well, you know what I mean…different from what *we* do?" Flustered, Diokles gestured between Tylissus and himself.

"Oh yes…" Cleon's eyes glazed over. "It was *very* different. Incredible, in fact…yes, that would have to be the word for it. The man seemed capable of the most amazing feats!" Absentmindedly, he reached up and began rubbing at a tender spot on his left nipple.

For an achingly long moment the only sound heard on the gently rolling deck was the crisp flapping of the sail as it caught and held the cooling offshore winds. Each man, lost in his own oriental fantasy, found the oddly parochial-seeming practices of Athenian sexuality suddenly lacking.

Unable to bear it any longer, Tylissus cleared his throat and said: "Well?"

Cleon blinked, then looked up at him. "Well what?"

Exasperated by his friend's obtuseness, Tylissus slapped his forehead in mock annoyance. "Well, aren't you going to tell us what he did to you? You know…share some of those mysterious techniques and exotic positions known only to the Eastern 'professionals'?"

Frowning, Cleon tapped his index finger against his lips as he pondered his friend's request. "He wasn't a '*professional*', Tylissus." After a moment he smiled and shook his head, "And no…I don't think so." Tylissus opened his mouth to protest and Cleon brushed him off. "It's only fair that I save this hard-earned knowledge for my dear left-behind Nicias. After all, the poor chap did miss out on quite an adventure and, like Harmodius' sister, perhaps he too deserves a special gift…"

In a single movement, everyone rose to their feet shouting out their disappointed entreaties and objections.

Cleon waited for the good-natured uproar to die down before shrugging his shoulders and adding: "And besides…it's not really something one can just *describe* to someone and make it all work. There are tricky things you have to be *shown*…motions and movements that need to be demonstrated…intimate touches…things like that."

Tylissus jumped up shouting, "Me first!"

Cleon laughed as he held his hands up in mock defense. "Oh no, I don't think so, you horny little rabbit!"

Diokles, rolling his eyes and shaking his head from side to side, pulled his overly rambunctious lover back down onto his lap. Unwilling to lose out on this rare opportunity, the four wayward lovers continued with their wheedling and cajoling, begging the ever complacent Cleon to share the Persian eunuch's sexual secrets with them.

Satisfied that his friends had suffered enough, Cleon finally relented. Standing, he stretched his arms high over his head, took a deep breath and muttered: "Oh, very well…" Before Tylissus could jump to his feet again, Cleon took Harmodius by the hand and pulled him to his feet. "But Harmodius first. I'll need to ease into all this and, well…I'm afraid Tylissus would wear me out before we'd even started!" Turning to the dumbfounded Harmodius, he smiled encouragingly at the wide-eyed, open-mouthed boy hanging loosely onto his hand. "Come boy, we'll go below now. After we've finished…*then* you can send Tylissus down." Grinning at Aristogiton and Diokles, he added: "Don't worry…I'll be taking a long turn at the tiller tonight. And then my pupils…" he squeezed Harmodius' hand and winked over at Tylissus, "…*they* can become the teachers."

As Cleon and Harmodius crossed the deck toward the ladder that led down to the cargo hold, the good-natured hoots, whistles and howls of their salacious compatriots rang in their ears.

And whatever unformed question Harmodius had neglected to voice about the forthcoming stop on the island of Crete, disappeared in a buzz of nervous anticipation.

❧   ❧   ❧

Cleon leaned back against the railing, keeping a steady arm wrapped around the tiller as he gazed up at the star-filled sky. By holding the crab constellation sited just over the right-hand corner of the sail, Aristogiton had assured his novice sailors that their course would remain true for a speedy landfall on Crete. Facing a long, quiet night ahead of him, Cleon shrugged the kinks from his shoulders and shifted his butt to accommodate the slight hollow of the wooden steering bench. As he adjusted the tiller heading slightly to the left, the sound of a throaty moan echoed up from down below. A moment later he felt a thump under his feet as an overenthusiastic lover cracked his head up against the low-slung ceiling of the ship's hold. The painful sound of that wallop was followed almost immediately by a muffled yelp, quickly hushed by fits of embarrassed giggling.

"Good man, Tylissus…" Cleon whispered to the night, his smirk tempered with a teacher's pride.

❧   ❧   ❧

Far to the north, in a well-appointed villa overlooking the slumbering polis of Athens, another man stood on his balcony staring up at the stars. But unlike the randy, fun-loving sailors on the Thetis, this man was coldly indifferent to the natural beauties of the cosmos. As he stood there half-listening to the droning voice of a hired thug, he allowed his fingers to tap impatiently against the stone parapet. A single word catching his attention, his fingers stopped their patter and he looked over his shoulder at the dirt-covered brute reading from notes jotted onto a wooden-backed waxed tablet.

"A sister, you say? The boy has a sister?"

The obsequious lackey bowed his head. "Yes, my lord…"

The man turned around and snatched the tablet from the reader's scar-covered hand. "Her age?" he demanded, as his eyes carefully scanned the almost illegible scribblings on the tablet.

"It's right there, my lord…" the toady moved to point a single dirt encrusted finger at the wax, but the shriveling look on his master's face made him pull back. Bowing his head again, he muttered: "Thirteen, gracious lord…the girl is just thirteen years of age on this past seventh of Gamelion."

"Thirteen…" Hipparchus drew in a deep breath, smiling as the adolescent number resonated in his ear. "A ripe age…to be sure."

"Her name is Helena, lord."

"Helena…" the word tickled like a luscious crème filled pastry as he rolled it around his mouth, "…little Helena." His thoughts now elsewhere, he carelessly tossed the tablet back to his spy who nearly fumbled it to the ground. "By Aphrodite…if the vixen has half the beauty of her smug, older brother…" he wet his lips with the tip of his tongue, "…well then, she would most certainly live up to her infamous namesake's reputation."

Hipparchus turned away from the unnoticed beauties of the star-filled night. Leaving his private ruminations on the balcony, he returned with his servant to the spacious, second story room that served as his office. Picking a small leather bag of silver coins up off his cluttered desk, he slowly held it out to the fawning man. "It's the sister…" his eyes narrowed in anticipation at the thrill of this latest diversion, "…yes, I'm sure of it…she's the key to bringing that wretched family to their knees." His spy stood unmoving under his master's baleful gaze, a quivering hand half out-stretched in greedy anticipation. After a tortuously teasing moment had passed, Hipparchus sighed and tossed him the purse. "Now…if you bring me something about this girl…a scandal, an indiscretion, anything…there will be double this amount…and more." Without another word, he dismissed the spy with a curt wave of his hand. Turning around, he stared at his desk, seemingly lost in a fretful consideration of the enormous pile of work facing him.

Crossing behind, he took his seat on the comfortably cushioned chair and pulled the oil lamp closer so that he could read more easily. Even as he sorted through the stacks of papyrus scrolls and wax-covered tablets, humiliating thoughts of that wretched day at the Kynosarges Gymnasium confronting that pretty boy Harmodius and his surly-mouthed lover—a still-irritating thorn in his side—never receded far. As he tried to focus his attentions on the coming preparations for next month's all-important Panathenaia Festival, one part of his mind continually churned with delicious thoughts of settling scores.

"She's a child, after all…" the icy words echoed aloud in the empty room as he picked up a lead stylus and prepared to set to work, "…and children so often get into trouble."

CHAPTER 8

Eight days out of Naukratis harbor they saw the first indication that they were approaching Crete—a thin, curling line of smoke rising above the horizon. As the Thetis drew in closer, other fires were spotted burning inland from the shore. "Far too much smoke for simple hearth fires," said Diokles, "more likely some outlying farms have been put to the torch...and over there," he pointed to a black smudge clinging to a low hillside, "maybe even an entire village." He looked to his Captain for an answer, "Any idea what's happening here?"

Aristogiton looked grim. "Crete, I fear, has become a land of perpetual civil war" he answered. Pulling the tiller in tight against his shoulder, he dutifully kept the ship well away from the rocky coastline, turning away from the fires and skirting west along the southern coast of the long, narrow island. Shaking his head as the smoldering homesteads disappeared behind them, he wrapped his free hand around Harmodius' waist and pulled him in closer. "It's hard to believe that hundreds of years ago this war-wracked island nation ruled over a great seafaring empire," he snorted in disgust, "these days, she can't even field their own navy."

"What happened? What brought Crete to this state of...of ruin?" asked Harmodius, watching intently as the war-ravaged landscape rushed past, even as he reached for a blanket to ward off the chill of a sudden late afternoon drop in temperature.

Aristogiton looked up at the slate gray sky and frowned. "It looks like we're heading for some rain...why don't you go below and fetch the foul weather gear. When you get back I'll tell you all what happened and what kind of reception we can expect once we arrive in Phaistos."

The five mariners were tying the leather straps of their petasos—wide brimmed, felt traveling hats favored by Athenians in stormy weather—tightly underneath their chins when the first plops of rain began to splatter upon the deck. Even with her sail trimmed by half, the increasingly blustery weather still managed to move the Thetis westward at a frighteningly vigorous pace.

"Many years ago, the island of Crete was a nation blessed by the Goddess." Everyone had gathered around the stern of the ship to hear Aristogiton speak. "Ruled over by a great line of kings named Minos, Crete was a land celebrated to the farthest reaches of our Middle Sea for her modern ideas, productive farmlands and great fresco-covered palaces." Aristogiton raised an eyebrow to his listeners, "In fact, the stronghold known as Phaistos was second only in size, power and beauty to fabled Knossos, the immense palace-complex on the northern side of the island."

"Knossos…" asked Tylissus, his voice hushed with awe, "…the city with the Minotaur and the Labyrinth?"

Aristogiton nodded his head. "The very same."

Harmodius reached over and added his muscle to the wavering tiller as the Thetis plowed on through the growing swells.

"But that was all long, long ago…" continued Aristogiton, "…a century or more even before the great kings of Mycenae and Sparta went to war against Troy over the beautiful Helena."

"What happened to this great empire of King Minos?" asked Tylissus.

Aristogiton shrugged his shoulders. "No one knows for sure…a riddle of history lost to the ravages of time. All one can say with any surety is that empires rise, reach their zenith on the backs of their weaker neighbors, and then fall away into their own ignominious decline. Why, one need only look at the once unassailable Egyptian Empire…the supreme power on Earth for thousands of years…and today, this once mighty kingdom reduced to a mere fiefdom of Persia." He shook his head. "Here on Crete, the ancient cities have been reduced to mere shadows of their former glory day existence. Their once impregnable palace-complexes are today vacant, vine-covered ruins, destroyed in great conflagrations nearly a hundred years before mighty Agamemnon's fleet set sail from Aulis."

"Did they fall to invaders?" asked Harmodius.

Aristogiton smiled at him. "An invasion?" He shrugged his shoulders. "A warring nobility locked in internal conflict? Devastating earthquakes? Some other unknown natural disaster?" He shook his head again. "Unfortunately, our chronicles remain stubbornly silent on this haunting question." He motioned to Cleon for something to refresh his parched throat. As he drank, the others waited impatiently, their eyes scanning the rain-spattered coastline for signs of habitation. Swallowing the last drop of cold Egyptian beer, Aristogiton passed the empty cup back to Cleon, wiped his lips dry with the back of his hand, and continued his story.

"We do, however, know this much. For the last several hundred years this poor island has been torn apart by fractious in-fighting, her city-states existing in a seemingly perpetual state of civil war with one another, separating her even further from the rest of the world. Today Crete is a nonentity...an insignificant memory of the powerful kingdom she once was...isolated by the great churning sea that surrounds her."

Harmodius frowned, the unsettling memory of curling black smoke rising from torched outposts still fresh in his mind. "But, will it be safe for us to land here? I mean, if they're in the middle of this war with one another, shouldn't we try to restock our supplies at some other landfall...another island farther north, perhaps?"

Aristogiton seemed to ponder his question for a moment. "Well," he said, "I suppose we could turn back around and head east towards Rhodes...or, if we continue on this westward course, we could avoid Crete altogether and push on to the island of Kythera. Either way, our food supplies are already dangerously low." He glanced up at the glowering sky. "And if this weather works against us, we could be facing serious problems."

He settled back against the stern railing, pretending to close his eyes in thought as he waited patiently for their reaction...smiling to himself as each one in turn looked nervously over at the uncertain compatriot seated next to him. Finally, sitting up with a good-natured grunt, he sought to calm their doubts. "Don't worry, my brave fellows. We'll have no problems with the Cretans. This sad little country desperately needs whatever trade she can get. And since Phaistos is the undoubted commercial center of the southern coast, I'm sure she'll be more than ready to welcome us with open arms."

With each man's innermost thoughts turning below to the wealthy Egyptian cargo resting safely—for the time being—under his feet, no one responded to Aristogiton's reassurances. Their doubts persisting, the Captain needled them with a chiding laugh. "Oh, very well then! Once we reach Phaistos, the three of you can remain on board ship to keep an eye on our cargo. Harmodius and I will take care of the procuring on our own. We'll make all the arrangements for restocking whatever is needed for the voyage on to Athens and be back on board before you know it."

The mildly rebuking tone of their Captain's voice did the trick. Protesting their complete trust in Aristogiton's judgment, each now demanded a place with the shore party. After a round of friendly squabbling, it was agreed that only Cleon would remain on board ship, in charge of supervising the loading of the fresh water casks while Diokles and Tylissus accompanied Aristogiton and Harmodius into town.

As they rounded Cape Lithino and headed north into the choppy waters of the Bay of Messaras, the storm-heightened winds began to pick up even more, sending the Thetis flying across the water towards the safe harbor at Phaistos. As Aristogiton was about to send his tiny crew forward to trim the ship's sails even further, he murmured—almost as an afterthought—"And if things go smoothly tomorrow, perhaps we'll hire horses for a quick trip to Gortyn…it's a small town just to the north of Phaistos. An old friend of my father's makes his home there now and, if no one minds, I'd like to ride on up and pay my respects."

His companions eyed one another for a moment, and then each in his turn shrugged his assent. When no objections were heard, Aristogiton turned his relaxed grin on Harmodius' shining brown eyes, adding with a wink: "And I'd like very much for the old man to meet my handsome eromenos, as well…"

❦   ❦   ❦

The sun had long set beneath the cloud covered western skies as the harbormaster, pacing impatiently in the cold drizzle with his wood-backed waxed tablet held high over his head to ward off the worst of the stormy night, waited on the dock for the crew of the Thetis to run out its gangplank. Aristogiton sprang off the ship with a wide, friendly grin and a small purse clutched tightly in his fist containing a modest gratuity for the soaking man's trouble. Once informed that the Thetis had docked in Phaistos with the sole purpose of restocking her provisions and fresh water casks, the harbormaster scratched an appropriate note on his tablet, accepted Aristogiton's genial fee, and scrambled back to the dry warmth of his tiny office overlooking Matala, the quiet port of Phaistos.

The storm blew itself out overnight and, when the bleary-eyed crew of the Thetis awoke early the next morning, they found their energetic captain already disembarked in search of the local marketplace. By the time Harmodius was putting the finishing touches on their simple breakfast of meal cakes dipped in honey and a last few handfuls of Egyptian dates, Aristogiton was already making his way down the noisy pier with a line of heavily laden porters following in his wake.

In no time at all, the ship's nearly barren supply hold was restocked with fresh fruits and vegetables, the empty water casks exchanged for full ones, and Cleon—remaining as solitary watch on board for the next few days—was waving a brisk farewell as the others set off down the dock in search of horses to rent for the short ride to Gortyn.

The warm morning sun was still drying Phaistos' rain-soaked streets, misting the air like a diaphanous gray veil as Aristogiton, Harmodius, Tylissus and Diokles set off on the well-traveled road to Gortyn. And while their shrewd captain had had little trouble in acquiring excellent shipboard provisions for their long journey back to Athens, hiring local horses for the short upcountry ride had proven to be an entirely different proposition altogether.

❧   ❧   ❧

"By the sacred Earth Mother's seven teats...my backside is killing me!" groaned Tylissus as he tried to adjust the rough woolen blanket bunching up beneath him that was serving as a makeshift saddle. "Damn you, Aristogiton...these bowlegged beasts are impossible! They're meant for lugging jars of olive oil...not people!"

Aristogiton bit his tongue in an effort to keep the grin on his face hidden from the others. "Sorry, shipmates...but these old donkeys were the best I could do on such short notice." When Tylissus snorted his scornful response, Aristogiton lowered his voice and leaned across to the angry, red-faced boy. "And I would have a care with your words. Blaspheming in the eternal Earth Mother's name—by the way, she's known as the 'Earthshaker' around here—may not be a very good idea. She still has quite a large following on Crete."

"A thousand pardons to the Earth Mother if I caused her any offense...but this is really too much!" whined Tylissus. "Couldn't you have offered those greedy bastards more money for a few of their precious horses?"

Diokles reached across and, using the whisk end of his riding crop, gave him a playful, but sharp swat across his naked thigh. "Weren't you listening when the Captain told us that nearly every horse for miles around has been requisitioned by the local militia for their latest civil war?"

Tylissus yelped in pain. Narrowing his eyes at his lover's non-too-gentle rebuke, he glowered at them all. As their laughter stung his burning ears he slowly stuck out his tongue, all the while rubbing at the bright red mark rising on his thigh.

"Go easy on him, men...I think someone has been skimping on his sleep at night...abusing the famous 'secrets of Ishtar' I suspect!" Harmodius reached across and offered the pouting Tylissus a commiserating pat on the shoulder. "Come now, old friend, I think we're all in agreement here that these sorry beasts of burden may not be the ideal mode of transportation...but for once in your life can't you keep your mind off your precious ass?" He clucked his tongue as he made a sweeping gesture with his arm. "After all, you're missing out on some pretty spectacular countryside here."

The road to Gortyn climbed slowly from the sea, across the expansive Mesara Plain—covered at this time of the year with great sweeping fields of wildflowers—up into the foothills of the great mountain range that rose at the center of the island. The highest point, Mount Psiloritis—visible all the way from Phaistos in the south to Knossos in the north—still had snow covering its peak. With the heady scent of lemon and orange blossoms fading behind them, the well-groomed road from the Mesara Plain narrowed to a rocky country track as it left the poppy covered foothills and climbed into the mountains. As the noon hour approached, the rising heat of early summer was somewhat moderated by the increasing altitude of their climb. Twisting through a number of shady, oleander covered ravines; the rocky mountain track eventually reached a swift-running river, its narrow current carrying cold mountain snowmelt down to the ever-thirsty coastal towns. Turning to follow the river's course, the rocky trail widened out once again, eventually becoming a full-sized road as it climbed to the wide plateau that held the mountain stronghold of Gortyn.

❋   ❋   ❋

"Wait right here..."

Tossing the reins to Harmodius, Aristogiton hopped down off his donkey and, with a genial smile on his face, approached a group of indolent grandfathers gathered together on a shady porch to ogle the young serving maids as they came to fill their jugs with fresh water from one of the town's many cisterns. A few pleasant words were exchanged and then the gray beards were noisily conferring together before a number of helpful fingers pointed off down a narrow street that appeared to circle back around behind the city's modest hilltop acropolis. Nodding his head in thanks, Aristogiton gave them a friendly wave before returning to his waiting compatriots. "It's not far from here," he said as he took his donkey's reins in hand and turned to lead them on foot down the dusty street toward the acropolis. Reaching the same meandering river they'd followed into town, the visitors at last came around to a favored neighborhood of expensive looking homes dotting a scrub-covered hillside right beneath the town's acropolis. Counting each house as he passed by, Aristogiton pulled his animal to a stop in front of the third door. Scratching his chin, he gazed about in all directions.

"Well," he said with a nervous chuckle, "This must be the place…"

As the others gratefully hopped down off their doleful animals, carefully brushing the dust of the long journey off their travel-rumpled himations, Aristogiton approached the door and knocked. A few moments later the door opened a crack and a young woman with large, dark brown Cretan eyes peeked out.

"Is your master at home?" Aristogiton politely asked.

The woman, suspiciously eying the four bedraggled travelers, frowned, shook her head and, without saying a single word, slammed the door in his face. Caught off guard, Aristogiton took a surprised leap backwards, stifling another nervous chuckle as he glanced over his shoulder at his waiting friends. Shrugging, he stepped up to the door once again and knocked a bit more forcefully, waiting impatiently as a very slow minute crawled past. Just as he was about to take his fist to the door, he heard the sound of a voice calling from within and, before he could respond, the door was flung wide and an eager-faced boy came running out almost knocking him to the ground.

"You are come from Athens, my young lords?" he called out, running around to greet each one with an excited clap of his hands, "Come all this way to speak with my famous master?" When Aristogiton answered in the affirmative, the boy's smile widened even farther and he took a solemn step backward, bowing low as he quickly ushered them inside with an effusive wave of his hand.

"Please to follow me, my lords." The boy led the four travelers through several shady porticos of the spacious, well appointed home until they reached the rear of the residence and a narrow flight of steps that led up and out onto a canvas-covered rooftop balcony overlooking the entire Mesara Plain far below. As the Greeks lined the marble balustrade, gawking down at the breathtaking view, the serving boy quickly rearranged a group of chairs around a low table for their comfort. "My master is teaching at the gymnasium today and I've sent that foolish girl, Philina, to fetch him. Until he returns, may I offer you my master's hospitality?" Without waiting for a response, he disappeared back down the dark stairwell only to return moments later with a jug of wine wedged under one arm and a heavy tray laden with spicy sweetmeats and freshly picked fruit balanced precariously on his head.

"Look over there...isn't that our ship?" Diokles pointed off in the distance, down past the poppy-covered fields and the miniature bustling metropolis of Phaistos to the chalky white cliffs that surrounded the harbor town of Matala.

"Yes, I think you're right." Tylissus narrowed his eyes, shading them with the back of his hand. "That little speck of nothing down there...that has to be our Thetis!" Tylissus nudged him playfully in the side.

Diokles caught him around his waist and pulled him in close. "Well, well, well...I see that someone's mood is finally improving," he laughed as he ruffled his hair.

Smirking shamefacedly, Tylissus rubbed his saddle sore bum. "It's a bona-fide law of nature, my friend—the farther you keep me from that smelly, fly-infested, cantankerous old beast...the better my mood!"

"Wine?" asked Aristogiton as he sidled up to the railing with a clay goblet in each hand.

Gratefully accepting his offer, the two men returned to sit with Harmodius and his erastes at the al fresco feast set before them on the table.

"So, it's time to share the secret with us, good Captain..." invited Diokles between bites of a juicy orange slice, "...this mystery man that we've come so far to call upon...this 'friend of your father's'..." he looked around, noting the elegant surroundings, "...whoever he is, the man certainly seems to be doing well for himself." He gestured with his juice-spattered chin to the other posh homes dotting the scrub-covered hillside. "Tell us, Captain...just who exactly is this wealthy old fellow?"

Aristogiton felt Harmodius' hand tighten on his arm and, avoiding his lover's curious gaze, turned his vaguely guilty smile on the others instead. Washing a last bite of fig down with a healthy swig of watered-wine, he wiped his lips with a linen napkin, stood up and walked over to the railing along the edge of the roof. Looking south to the Bay of Messaras, he drew in a deep breath of the fresh mountain air before turning back to face their questioning stares.

"Well," he sighed, "I'm afraid I haven't been as forthcoming about our mystery host as I should have been. The man we've come all this way to meet today...the man who owns this fine house..." he dropped his chin to his chest for a moment and stared down at the thin layer of dust covering his sandals, "…well, this man is none other than our exiled Archon…"

"Why, Zeus and all the gods be praised…if it isn't young Aristogiton, the son of my old friend Scopas!" All heads turned in unison as a balding, heavyset man sporting a neatly trimmed gray beard skirting the edge of his dimpled chin, came clambering up onto the rooftop to join them. "So tell me, my boy…what news have you brought me from Athens?"

"Cleisthenes!" shouted Aristogiton as he ran over, his arms outstretched to greet his beaming host.

❦   ❦   ❦

"But the man's a convicted lawbreaker…a stateless exile…" whispered Diokles, "…do you have any idea how much trouble we could all be in if anyone were to find out that we stopped here on Crete specifically to meet with him?"

Diokles, Tylissus, and Harmodius lagged behind as old Cleisthenes, holding tightly to Aristogiton's arm for support, guided them through the twisting hilltop streets and alleyways of ancient Gortyn, proudly showing off his adopted home to his welcome visitors.

Harmodius frowned. "Have a care with your words, Diokles. It wasn't so long ago that this same 'stateless exile' was a well-respected archon, an honored citizen of our Athens…one of that too rare breed of aristocrats who found it in his heart to champion the cause of the common man over the privilege of his own class…and then duly paid the price for it!" His lips clenched together in a tight line. "And don't forget that, in his youth…this very same 'lawbreaker' *was* my father's lover.

Diokles blushed. "I'm sorry Harmodius, I misspoke. I have nothing but the deepest respect for the honored memory of your father." He scratched his chin, looking sideways to Tylissus for support. "And like your father, we all long for the day when the despotic Pisistrade brothers are driven from power…and men like the great Cleisthenes…" he smiled and nodded his head, waving to the old man who at that very moment was checking over his shoulder to see if his youthful guests were still keeping up "…are rightfully returned to their homeland, redressing the abuses of the past." He took a deep breath and shook his head even as he gave Harmodius a dubious sidelong glance. "But until that time, associating with known exiles—especially such a notorious one as Cleisthenes—well, no matter how you look at it, it's a rather dangerous game to play."

"Do you have any idea why Aristogiton brought us up here?" whispered Tylissus.

The furrows on Harmodius' forehead deepened, his thoughts returning as they had several times since meeting their host, to that first ardent night of lovemaking in Aristogiton's arms somewhere in the deserted gardens of the Kynosarges. "There is something odd about all this," he thought to himself even as he recalled the exiled Archon's cryptic words of warning about the dangerously high-handed nature of their new co-tyrant...the very same warning in fact, which had germinated the idea for this voyage across the Middle Sea. Suddenly feeling unsure of himself, he shook his head and answered quietly: "No...not really. That night we left Naukratis...that was the first time I heard any mention of stopping here on Crete." He stared on up ahead at the familiar knot of well-tanned wrestler's muscles defining his lover's strong shoulders, bent over now in intimate conversation with their still-spry host and, dropping his voice even further added: "But I have a sneaking suspicion that it might have something to do with our run in at the Gym with that cad Hipparchus."

❧   ❧   ❧

On the street up ahead, Aristogiton made use of these few moments alone with his old mentor to reveal the true purpose behind their visit. In quick, breathless phrases he recapitulated the unfortunate incident that day in the palaestra between the two wrestlers, Harmodius and Aristogiton, and Athens' newly appointed co-tyrant Hipparchus. Reddening with shame, he confessed to having shared Cleisthenes' admonitions about Hipparchus' dangerously volatile nature, but had shied away from any mention of the exiled archon's suspicions concerning Cimon's untimely murder. Fearing a hotheaded response from Harmodius—and unwilling to jeopardize the fragile state of their nascent romance—Aristogiton decided to hold off and let Cleisthenes himself determine whether revealing his suspicions concerning the father's tragic demise would cause more harm than good.

And all while keeping Harmodius at a safe distance from Athens...

Hearing the alarm in Aristogiton's words, Cleisthenes himself grew pale. Rubbing at the wrinkled skin on the back of his neck, he slowly shook his head in dismay. "Oh, my dearest boy...I fear in your haste to protect Harmodius, you've underestimated the lengths to which that monster Hipparchus will go to achieve his depraved desires. Even as I hear your story, I can feel his cold, insatiable grasp reaching out to us from across the sea. And not just for you and the boy..."

Aristogiton stopped short, his grip tightening around Cleisthenes' arm as his own complexion drained of color. Turning to face the old man, he stared deeply into his troubled eyes. "What are you saying, Archon?" he asked, a tremor quivering his voice.

Cleisthenes looked nervously back over his shoulder at the dawdling three-some fast closing the gap and, with a lowered voice hissed: "Why do you think old Cimon saw fit to remove his entire household to the countryside all those years ago?" Twisting his arm free, he urged the reluctant Aristogiton forward again, continuing: "He knew that with a murderous bully like Hipparchus placed safely above the law, no one was secure from his depredations...*even innocent women and children were fair targets for his corruption!*"

❋   ❋   ❋

"A free spirit, you say...a tomboy?" the co-tyrant Hipparchus' frown deep-ened to a glower. "And what girl-child in Athens, whose household lacks a father figure, doesn't grow up roaming the city streets unchaperoned?" He turned away from the man in disgust. "This is the best you could do with all the money I gave you?"

The spy, doubled at the waist in a suitably groveling posture, cringed at the ice in his master's tone. "There...there *was* something else, Lord."

"Well?" Hipparchus ratcheted up the impatience in his voice as he returned to sit behind his work-covered desk.

"One of the neighbors, Lord...she let slip that the entire street had had a good laugh at the family's expense when the girl Helena and her older brother found themselves in competition for the same lover last year."

Hipparchus looked up in surprise. "What was that you said?" he asked, a newfound glimmer shining in his close-set eyes. "The two were in love with the same man..." the previous impatience in his voice had been replaced by a delighted incredulity, "...you don't mean the merchant's son Aristogiton?"

The spy shook his head. "No, Lord...this was shortly before the boy met up with the merchant's son."

Hipparchus' eyes narrowed in a baleful stare. "Very well then...tell me, fool...who *was* this man?" The cold impatience was back with an all-too-familiar suddenness that made his agent shudder.

"The man's name was Diokles, Lord…a tall, gangly fellow with decent prospects, or so I've heard. He was aggressive for a time in his pursuit of the boy Harmodius…following him all around town, showering him with lavish gifts and tokens of love. And then," the man shrugged his shoulders, "just as quickly, he turned his attentions on another. Even so, this Diokles has retained close ties to the family." His lip curled up in a leer. "My forthcoming gossip hinted that rumor had him still carrying a mooning fascination for the sister."

"Hmm…" Hipparchus, looked up at the ceiling thoughtfully, folding his hands and resting them on top of a short pile of scribble-covered waxed tablets. "Perhaps there's something here after all…something in this trivial 'rumor' of yours that can be worked around to my benefit." With a distracted wave of his hand he dismissed the man without further payment.

Chagrined, the spy slowly backed out of the room. As he reached the door he stopped and with a larcenous grin added: "The neighbor did mention a rather noisy squabble over an apple…"

Hipparchus looked at him and sighed, suddenly bored with the whole conversation. Vaguely registering this final remark, he picked a single coin off his desk and tossed it to the grasping man. "We'll speak again later."

Turning his diverted attention back to the ever-growing pile of unfinished work for the upcoming Panathenaia Festival, he lifted the first tablet under his hand. It appeared to be a short listing of young girl's names, maidens from the highest-born families who, in the Great Procession, would be responsible for carrying the sacred *peplos* that would adorn the statue of Athena. As he scanned through the list of names, he was suddenly struck with an amusing thought. Using the ball of his thumb, he carefully rubbed out the name of the last girl on the list. Smiling dangerously, he began humming a merry tune as he picked up his wedge-shaped stylus and wrote in: Helena, daughter of Cimon.

❧   ❧   ❧

"And they treat you well here on Crete?" asked Harmodius.

Cleisthenes smiled at the innocent query from the achingly handsome, black haired youth, "Oh, yes…very well indeed," he answered. Releasing Aristogiton's arm he replaced it with Harmodius' proffered one, directing him around the corner of an unpretentious temple dedicated to Hephaestus, the gimp-legged God of the Forge. "Of course, it certainly doesn't hurt to have lots and lots of money at hand!" He grinned wickedly as he led his little group of sightseers up the wide marble staircase to the highest point of Gortyn's modest acropolis. Stopping at the top to catch his breath, he sat for a moment on a wide pedestal that supported a tall bronze statue of Apollo arm in arm with his chaste sister-goddess Artemis. As the four adventurers from Athens milled about him gawking at the sights, Cleisthenes reached out and, taking hold of their hands, pulled Aristogiton and Harmodius in close.

"I couldn't be more pleased to hear your wonderful news…erastes and eromenos." He eyed them both from head to toe. "And such a perfect match…" he couldn't hide the hitch in his voice: "…so much like your handsome father and I, Harmodius." He shook his head as delicious memories of his youthful paramour threatened to overwhelm the day's already over-taxed emotions. With a sigh, he let them go and rested back against Apollo's sturdy leg. "You've both grown into such fine, striking men…a tribute to our beloved city-state…and to the honored fathers who raised you."

"Tell us more about Crete…" prodded Harmodius, embarrassed by the older man's effusive praise "…and the disaster that befell her?"

Smiling sadly, Cleisthenes looked off into the distance. "Ahh yes…but there is little left to tell." Regret for beloved things lost still colored his voice. "One day a mighty sea power, unrivalled in her control over the waters stretching all the way out to the Pillars of Heracles…a gracious nation of brilliant thinkers and artisans ruled over by the crafty heirs of King Minos. And the very next, an unfathomable tragedy struck. No one knows exactly how it happened, but during my stay here, I've conducted my own studies at the ruins of Knossos in the north. It is my opinion that cataclysmic earthquakes followed by a huge tidal wave were the cause of this precipitous disaster. Overnight, this great maritime empire collapsed in upon itself leaving behind a sad little island of petty, ever-bickering city-states in its wake." He shook his head in disgust. "And to make matters even worse, in a vain effort to recapture the lost glories of their past, most of these foolish islanders came to embrace the cruel Spartan ethos as their model for society. Nowadays on Crete, everyone and everything belongs to the city-state…and everything for the sole purpose of conducting these endless bouts of civil strife."

"But if that is so…aren't you in mortal danger here after all? From all this constant warfare, I mean?" asked Tylissus, the concern in his voice sounding uncommonly sincere.

Cleisthenes smiled at him. "No," he answered. "They pretty much leave me alone to putter about as I like on the island. After all, the perpetual threat of mighty Athens' far-reaching arms—as well as the generosity of my seemingly bottomless purse—keep me, for the most part, safely out of harm's way."

Feeling somewhat refreshed from this brief rest, he hopped down off the cold marble plinth. "But come my boys, enough with this idle chatter. I've brought you all up here for a good reason." With an excited clap of his hands he headed them off in the direction of the acropolis' central square. "It's time I showed off the secret glory of my humble little 'home away from home.'"

Rounding a corner, he brought them all to a reverent halt in front of a modest open air temple with twelve standing stone tablets set up in a line under the shady expanse of its wide arcade. Leading them forward, Cleisthenes knelt before the first tablet and, running a fingertip across the tiny, deeply incised engraving, spoke to them in hushed tones. "The Law Code of Gortyn..." The others crowded forward, craning their heads to try and make out the tightly scrawled words. "Look here...see how it reads...the first line from right to left...then the next from left to right..."

"Well, at least the lettering looks familiar..." said Diokles, leaning over his shoulder with his eyes squirreled together in a comic squint "...but I can't seem to make out any of the words.

"It's written in an old Doric dialect, quite unique to Crete..." With an assist from Harmodius, Cleisthenes got back on his feet and stepped back so that the others could move in for a closer look. "If you sound each words out slowly, they should start to make sense..."

As the sun catapulted across the western sky and the shadows of the standing stones shortened, disappeared, and then began lengthening again in the opposite direction, the five Athenians spent the next few hours piecing together the intricate phrasings of this mysterious and marvelous ancient legal text—a law code that dealt with virtually every aspect of daily life in the austere society favored by the island's Dorian forebears. Each crime was clearly defined and, for their time, relatively humane punishments proscribed; rules for the sale and transfer of property were carefully delineated; even marriage, divorce and inheritance laws were presented in fascinating detail.

"The stones were set up here in Gortyn for a reason," pointed out their knowledgeable host. "Legend has it that it was on this very spot, after abducting the beautiful Europa in a fit of divine passion, the great Thunder God Zeus—still disguised as an enormous white bull with golden horns and a quite frightening bovine endowment—knelt down on his two forelegs and demurely released his terrified captive." The others laughed as he recounted the sometimes-ribald tale of the Rape of the Phoenician princess Europa, the subsequent birth of her demigod son Minos, and the founding of the Minoan Empire. Eventually his humorous lesson returned to the construction of this commemorative temple and the installation of the famous law tablets. "They are quite unique, you see…" he ran his index finger halfway down the dusty length of the third tablet, "…especially in how they seem to move in the direction of treating all classes of society on an equal footing before the law…even slaves!"

"Equal?" asked Tylissus, a skeptical grin crinkling the corners of his eyes. "Is that why a free man caught stealing from his neighbor is fined a mere 12 obols…while a lowly slave caught committing the same offence is required to forfeit 1200 obols as payback?"

"Ah, but don't you see?" Cleisthenes eyes sparkled with delight. "In Athens, if a slave is caught stealing, his hand is immediately severed at the wrist. Here in Gortyn, all he faces is a fine. And a fine is just that…money! What matters if one soul pays a little more than the other…just as long as no one is taken out and has their sorry arm lopped off! Not even a 'lowly slave'!" He slapped Tylissus on the back. "Now that's what I call *progress*, my boy!"

🍁   🍁   🍁

Later that night as they were all gathered on comfortable dining couches around Cleisthenes' munificent tables, their host kept the animated conversation swirling around the many political innovations and possibilities suggested by the Gortyn Law Code.

"Ah…if only Athens had adopted such a code," he sighed, "laws written to be obeyed by all men equally. No class distinctions, no special favors…just ordinary citizen respecting the rights of other ordinary citizens. Why, wouldn't that truly be a golden age for all mankind?"

"Yes…if only Athens had laws that put men on an identical footing…" Harmodius picked up a handful of dried figs and jiggled them thoughtfully on the palm of his hand "…then the despots like Hipparchus couldn't…"

Cleisthenes looked up and, with a throat-clearing cough, caught Aristogiton's eye. "Yes…that fornicator, Hipparchus…" the old man cut in, his eyebrows creasing together in a scowl. "Hipparchus and his thieving brother Hippias…the two of them…" he shook his head sadly, "…a bad business that." Picking up his own handful of figs, he tossed one straight into his mouth and chewed on it until all the sticky juice had run down the back of his throat. "I'm afraid you're right, Harmodius. Our beloved Athens will never know true freedom as long as these despots, surrounded by their mob of fawning sycophants and hangers-on, place themselves above the sacred laws." He paused, leaning thoughtfully back on his couch, waiting to see what Harmodius' response would be.

The young man's face blazed red as he angrily tossed his handful of figs back on the silver platter and sat up on his couch. "I hate him!" he said. "He spoke to me that day like I was a…a common *hetaera*!"

Sensing his agitation, Aristogiton looked to Cleisthenes for direction as he reached over and placed a soothing hand on Harmodius' arm.

A bit disappointed that, rather than appreciating the bigger picture presented by these two sons of Pisistratus—prime examples of the kind of despotism that should be dealt with by patriotic citizens—the youthful Harmodius was still fixating on the personal affront to his dignity…Cleisthenes studied the two lovers for a moment before reaching a critical decision. With a subtle, but sympathetic frown and a gentle shake of his head he silently expressed his resignation to Aristogiton.

And that was all…

With so many unknowns facing Harmodius and Aristogiton back in Athens, there seemed little point in arousing the boy's indignation further. If Hipparchus had already moved against Harmodius' defenseless family…well, he'd said as much to Aristogiton this afternoon and there was nothing more that could be done about that now. But if the tyrant had forgotten them…or at least chose to bide his time, awaiting their return home…well then, these last few weeks at sea would give them precious time together…a respite they were entitled to savor without Cleisthenes' baseless fears intruding into their intimate moments.

Of one thing the old man was certain…

There would be no mentioning of any possible involvement by the Co-tyrant in poor Cimon's death. Nothing would be more certain to seal this hot-blooded boy's doom.

❦   ❦   ❦

As Cleisthenes' excitable serving lad led the two guest couples to their respective sleeping rooms for the night, the old archon held Aristogiton back for a private word. Ignoring the confusion shadowing the young sea captain's face, Cleisthenes poured him a final cup of wine even as he reassured him that all would be ready for their early morning departure back down the mountain to the waiting ship at Phaistos' harbor.

"I know you are anxious to be away from here, but don't take foolish chances in your haste." He placed a sympathetically restraining hand on Aristogiton's arm, but then drew it back. "If Harmodius detects anything out of the ordinary in your behavior, he may come to suspect that you are holding something back from him. And that suspicion may damage his love for you."

Aristogiton took a sip from the goblet and then set it quietly back on the table. "And should I tell him nothing of his father?" he asked.

Cleisthenes solemnly rubbed his index finger along the dried, cracked skin of his lips. Finally, stifling a quiet groan, he sat back heavily on his couch.

"Nothing…" he muttered.

"Nothing?" asked Aristogiton, perplexed by the almost total resignation in Cleisthenes' response.

"Nothing." The old man repeated, this time accompanying it with a terse shake of his head. "Not unless you want to see the poor lad laid out on his funeral bier the very day after you arrive back in Athens!" Reaching across, he rested a restraining hand on Aristogiton's knee. "Think boy! There are some crimes so heinous, so offensive to their victims, that the poor souls can find no rest until vengeance has been duly sown and their harvest of blood reaped in full." Cleisthenes closed his eyes, rubbing them with his worn fingertips. "You saw his anger tonight…if your young lover were ever to suspect the Co-Tyrant's involvement in his father's murder, you can be sure that, as the night follows the day, Harmodius, possessed by a feverish madness, will gladly throw himself on Hipparchus' waiting sword."

Now it was Aristogiton's turn to rub his eyes in tired resignation. Even before he'd heard Cleisthenes' warning words, he'd known the truth of them in his mind. With a simple word of thanks, he stood and turned to follow his Harmodius to bed. Before he'd taken two steps, Cleisthenes was at his side holding him back.

"Don't worry, young Ari," he said. "Everything will work out fine. When you return to Athens follow Cimon's example…find some excuse to take the boy and his family off to the country for a while…at least until things resolve themselves in the city. After all, one can never tell which way the winds will blow when it comes to Athenian politics. Bide your time…after all, the despots Hippias and Hipparchus could fall as quickly as they rose. The important thing to remember is that, until they do, you must protect your lover and his family at all costs."

With a grateful smile, Aristogiton nodded his head, bending over to kiss his aging mentor on both cheeks, before disappearing down the lamp-lit hallway.

As his footsteps receded into the night, Cleisthenes returned to his eating couch, topped off his goblet of wine and, without bothering to cut it with the water pitcher, swallowed it down in one distracted gulp. "And until that time comes, dear boy…I only hope that you do a better job protecting them…than I did his poor lost father."

His quiet words echoed about the empty room.

CHAPTER 9

Anxious to be on their way, the bleary-eyed crew of the Thetis mounted their reluctant donkeys the next morning and left Gortyn well before the sun appeared over the eastern horizon. Under the forthcoming guidance of Cleisthenes' surefooted serving boy, they managed a swift return down the steep mountain pass to ancient Phaistos. With barely a word of greeting to their waiting comrade Cleon, Aristogiton had the ship's anchor raised and, that very same afternoon the Thetis set sail from the harbor of Matala.

Blessed with favorable winds and a strong current that swung sharply northward as it rounded the western tip of the Minoan island, the travelers made excellent time crossing the calm summer waters of the Middle Sea. Six days later the jutting, southern tip of the Peloponnesian Peninsula was sighted and, for the next hectic week, the Thetis carefully skirted north along the rocky coast of Laconia until she finally reached the open waters of the Saronic Gulf...and the final leg of her long journey home.

"What day is it, Ari...do you have any idea?" asked Harmodius as he rested his chin on his erastes' muscular, work-toughened shoulder. "All these endless weeks at sea have made me lose all track of time."

Aristogiton scratched his chin for a moment. "Let me see..." Sighting on the westernmost star in the crab constellation, he eased the tiller back a bit to keep the ship steady on its northwesterly heading. "When first we left Crete, the new moon was just rising in the night sky...that would bring us close to the noumenia of Hekatombaion."

"Hekatombaion?" Harmodius sat up; his wide eyes alight with disbelief. "It's already Hekatombaion? But it can't be that late! Does that mean we won't make it home in time to march in this year's Panathenaia?"

Aristogiton grinned as he shook his head. "Don't worry, my little Heracles, with any luck we should berth at Piraeus by tomorrow evening at the latest. If my reckoning is correct, the festival won't be starting up until a few days after that. We should be back in Athens with plenty of time to spare."

Harmodius sighed with relief as he slouched back against the rail of the ship and began rubbing Aristogiton's shoulders. "Good..." he said, "For some reason, these last few days I've been thinking of nothing else...to march proudly at your side, professing our sacred bond before the all gods and the entire city's population in Athena's great birthday procession." After massaging a last kink away, he leaned forward and rested his cheek against the smooth skin of his lover's shoulder blade. "Tell me, Beloved...do you think we'll be marching near the front with the champions of the Panathenaia games...or will we end up at the rear of the line with the ordinary soldier-citizens?"

Aristogiton snorted a strangled laugh.

Without a word, he reached behind and pulled Harmodius around in front of him, handing the tiller over with the practiced movement of a born sailor as he slid behind his eromenos and began returning the favor. As the tension flowed from Harmodius' shoulders, Aristogiton leaned forward and whispered in his ear: "Are you perhaps suggesting that we should enter the athletic contests...is that what you're trying to say?"

Harmodius grinned. "Well...I thought maybe if we got back in time, we could at least sign up to take a place in the wrestling matches." Eyelids blinking with feigned innocence, he peaked over his shoulder. "Tylissus says he's going to enter the pyrrhic dance contest...and he's enrolling Diokles in the javelin throw..."

Aristogiton rolled his eyes. "Oh, no...not the pyrrhic dance!" he howled. "Does that fool of a lad even possess his own suit of armor?"

"I heard that!" The voice echoed up from somewhere below their feet. A moment later, a head and two shoulders appeared in the forward hatchway as a flustered-looking Tylissus scrambled on deck, followed closely by his sleepy-eyed Diokles. "It was all his idea," he gestured with a backward thumb at his still groggy erastes. "All I said was that I wanted to march with the Champions this year...but that I couldn't decide which contest to enter. My 'all-knowing erastes' happened to mention that the city-fathers always seem to have trouble finding enough entrants for the Pyrrhic Dance...and well, since he's always admiring the way I move…and since '*anyone with half a head on his shoulders can dance in a full suit of armor*'—his words, not mine—I figured, why not!" Tylissus shrugged his shoulders. "He said he'd loan me all his gear and then it's up to me not make an absolute idiot of myself."

"Oh, don't let him fool you, he's dying to do it!" Diokles stifled a yawn with the back of his hand. "And besides, I *do* think it's something he'll be very good at it."

Tylissus nudged him gently in the ribs. "Of course I'll be good at it…" he shook his head, "…but then, according to you…I'm good at everything!"

Ignoring his petulant lover, Diokles reached across and placed both his hands next to Harmodius' on the tiller. With a nod of his head, Harmodius slid off the steering bench and Diokles took his place. Following his lead, Tylissus tapped Aristogiton on the shoulder, moving him out of the way so that he could slide in next to Diokles. "We weren't sleeping anyway," he said with an impish grin, "so we thought we might as well come up on deck and relieve you two lovebirds early."

Harmodius cocked a curious eyebrow. "Too much Persian love making?" he asked with his own lascivious smirk. "Baobil would be proud of you both!"

Tylissus rubbed at his aching backside. "You have no idea what two bodies are capable of in the cramped confines of a ship's hold!"

Harmodius sighed, wrapping his arms firmly around Aristogiton's waist. "Oh, I think we do…"

With a grateful stretch of his arms, Aristogiton squeezed Diokles' hand and pointed up at the stars. "Same heading as last night." he said. "And as we draw closer to port we'll be passing through the heavier trafficked shipping lanes. Be sure to call me back on deck if any other vessels come into sight."

With a playful ruffle of Tylissus' cowlicky hair, he turned to lead Harmodius to the hatchway below deck. "…'night, you two."

"And I'm not 'a fool of a lad'!" Tylissus called after them. "I'm at least a year older than Harmodius!"

      ✤   ✤   ✤

His striking red hair and excitedly waving arms stood Nicias out from the rest of the milling Piraeus crowd, waiting as the Thetis docked late the next afternoon. First up the narrow gangplank as soon as it touched ground, he fell into Cleon's waiting arms with an exultant whoop of delight.

"Three months!" he shouted. "You've been away from me for nearly three whole months!"

Cleon kissed him fervently on the lips, tears of joy threatening to well over onto his flushed cheeks. "I know…" he answered "…and it was unbearable!" He pushed him back, holding him tightly at arm's length. "But before we speak of anything else, tell me quickly…what of your poor brother Demoritus…is he safe…what happened at his trial?"

"Yes, yes…all is well here in Athens." Nicias' flustered answer sounded more like an exhausted sigh. "The charge of sacrilege was thrown out for lack of evidence. The fool was lucky this time. My idiot of a twin got off with a warning…a *final* warning. Any more mischievous episodes and the magistrate will be shipping poor Demoritus straight away off to permanent exile in distant Sicily!"

By this time the others had gathered around, each in his turn smothering their old comrade with hugs and kisses. "But how did you know our ship would coming in today?" asked a slightly bewildered Aristogiton.

Nicias blushed, looking down at his feet for a moment. "I couldn't stand all this unbearable waiting…" slowly his eyes traveled back up his lover's handsome length to rest finally on Cleon's smiling face "…not knowing if your ship had foundered…or if you'd been carried off by a host of blood-thirsty Cypriot pirates!"

Cleon clutched the back of Nicias' neck and pulled him until their noses bumped together. Gently wiping at his lover's tear-stained face, he sighed: "You needn't have worried so much, little scamp. We were all quite safe in the very capable hands of our good Captain Aristogiton."

"Even so…" Nicias' chin was still trembling, "…this entire month I didn't sleep a wink for all the worrying!" He turned away and pointed toward a large tenement building overlooking the wharf. "I finally took a room here in Piraeus so that I could be here everyday to keep a watch out for your ship."

Cleon's eyes suddenly lit up. "You have a room in Piraeus? Here? Now?"

Tylissus giggled, nudging his Diokles in the side. "With all the little tricks our good Cleon learned from master Baobil, I'm afraid our poor friend Nicias won't be getting much sleep this month either!"

"Baobil?" asked Nicias, his questioning eyebrows pinching together. "Who's Baobil?"

"Never mind Baobil…" Cleon took his arm and began pulling him back towards the gangplank, "I have an urgent need to see this room of yours!"

As eager as Nicias was at the prospect of at last spending a few private hours with his long-absent erastes, he found himself resisting Cleon's insistent tugs. Looking at the grinning faces all around him, he planted his fists firmly on his waist and held his ground. "Wait just one moment, *Beloved*. Before I step a single foot off this ship, I too have an urgent need…an urgent need to know just who this mysterious 'Baobil' person is!"

Harmodius laughed out loud as he clapped his hands down on the reluctant red head's freckled shoulders. "Oh, you have nothing to worry about, little satyr! Before this day is out, I guarantee you'll be running up and down the cobbled streets of Athens singing the praises of Egypt's most infamous eunuch!"

"*Eunuch?*"

Nicias gawped from one stupidly grinning face to the other and, for once in his life, found himself at a total loss for words. In the end, moved by the glassy-eyed desperation of Cleon's love-starved expression, and intrigued by the increasingly bawdy tone of his friend's tart jibes and taunts, he allowed himself to be dragged away…off the ship and across the wide wooden pier to his temporary—but most convenient—tiny wharf side hostel room.

❋   ❋   ❋

Anxious to greet his mother and sister, Harmodius hired men and horses to transport himself and Baobil's ebony trunk the short distance from the docks of Piraeus into central Athens. Promising to follow along later, Aristogiton remained behind to make sure that the rest of their priceless cargo would be safely conveyed off the ship and into one of the well-secured warehouses on the outskirts of the city.

Reaching the corner of his narrow street, he paid the two roustabouts from his heavy purse and sent them and their hired horses on their way. Hefting the heavy case onto his own shoulders, he could feel his anticipation bubbling up inside as he approached the front door to the old family home. Carefully resting Baobil's valuable trunk on the stoop, he leaned forward and rapped on the door's lintel with his knuckles. A moment later he heard the sound of hushed voices coming from inside as the tread of dainty footsteps came scampering toward the door. "It must be my darling sister," he thought with delight, "or perhaps one of the serving girls." But once the door was flung wide, to Harmodius' surprise it was neither servant nor sister waiting to greet him on the other side…it was his mother, wide-eyed and staring back at him, her two hands covering her mouth in amazement.

"But, what is this?" she cried out once she'd collected her scattered wits about her. "My dearest, dearest son, you've come home to us at last!" Tears of joy began streaming down her pale white cheeks. "Oh, but this is so unexpected!" She grabbed his hands and began pulling him inside the house. "Come in, my dear boy…come inside at once!"

Picking up the ivory-decorated ebony case, Harmodius followed her into the shadowy front hallway. "I didn't mean to startle you so, Mother."

Philippia clapped her hands smartly together and one of their ever-present household servants silently appeared at Harmodius' side to relieve him of his heavy burden. Smiling at her son, she took his face in her hands and studied it from side to side. "Goodness…you are becoming such a man! For a fleeting moment there, I thought it was your father standing at the door."

He leaned over and kissed her gently on both cheeks. Without another word, she led the way back to the rear of the house, back to the small sitting room where her omnipresent loom was set up against one windowless wall. It was in this quiet sanctuary that the women of the household held court, all the while sewing and weaving.

Retrieving the ebony chest from the waiting slave, Harmodius set it on the floor in front of his mother. "Wait until you see…" his irrepressible grin stretched from ear to ear "…I've brought such wonderful things from Egypt!" Frowning, he stood up and stepped out into the hallway. "But where's my greedy little sister?" he asked as he looked first to the left and then the right. "Where's Helena?" His eyes still glowed as he turned back to his mother. "As requested, I have brought her back something, not only pretty…but truly unique and special!"

Philippia slapped her cheek with one hand, wagging the other at her son. "Oh dear…" she said, "it was such a surprise seeing you standing there at the door just now that everything else simply flew right out of my head!"

"What is it, Mother?" Harmodius, feeling a sudden stab of concern, returned to her side and knelt down. "Has something happened to Helena?"

Philippia smiled, beaming with pride. "Oh, yes!" she cried out. "But it's something wonderful! An unexpected honor for the entire family…"

Assured for the moment that all was well, Harmodius—ignoring the ebony gift case—pulled up a stool and sat at his mother's elbow. "An unexpected honor?" he asked her. "Now you've piqued my interest, Mother. Why don't you tell me exactly what that little wood sprite has been up to all these months while I've been away at sea?"

"Well, it was quite sudden...in fact it all came about just three days ago." Philippia rested a quivering hand on her heart, her voice nearly breathless with excitement. "An official messenger arrived from the Temple of Athena Parthenos asking to speak with Helena's father. When informed that my poor Cimon had resided these many years on the distant shores of the River Styx, and that you—the elder of the household and her legal guardian—were away for an indefinite period, he asked to speak with me."

"Athena Parthenos?" repeated Harmodius, curious bewilderment evident in his voice. "But...what ever could they possibly want with our little Helena?"

Philippia could barely keep her words in check. "In truth, you won't believe it when I tell you! Your sister has been chosen from all the young girls in Athens as a candidate to carry the 'sacred peplos' in this year's Panathenaic Festival!"

Stunned, Harmodius' felt his mouth drop open as, for the briefest of moments, confusion ruled his face. As the veracity of his mother's words sank home, he stood up and wandered over to the loom, slowly running his fingers along the well-oiled wooden frame. "You're quite right, Mother...this *is* an honor...and a most unexpected one indeed." He bit the edge of his lip. "Especially since our family has neither the money nor the position in society, to warrant it." He returned to his stool, his brows furrowed in deliberation. "I suppose you asked why this unusual mark of respect had been accorded to us by our august City Fathers?"

Philippia nodded her head. "Do you think me a fool, my son? Of course I did." She squeezed his arm in reassurance. "I was as taken aback by this strange turn of events as you are. I even suggested to the Priestess' messenger that perhaps there'd been some mistake...that he'd come to the wrong house...or that he was searching for a different Helena." The firm shake of her head was emphatic. "But no, he swore to me that there was no mistake." Recounting the messenger's elucidation, she continued: "Someone at the temple complex had seen our Helena out shopping in the marketplace and, having remarked on her great beauty and poise, this noble personage..."

"A noble personage?" Harmodius suddenly felt himself go lightheaded.

"Yes...this nobleman then sponsored your sister's candidacy, bringing her to the attention of the High Priestess as a suitable maiden to carry the Goddess' peplos in the coming Great Procession."

"And did the messenger reveal who this 'noble personage' was?" Harmodius did his best to keep the growing unease out of his voice.

Philippia shrugged her shoulders. "No...the old man had absolutely no idea. And of course by this time Helena herself had heard the servant's gossiping together about the strange visitor and—well, you know how your sister can be—once she heard what had happened..." Philippia rolled her eyes in exasperation, "...well, from that moment on, there was to be no stopping her."

Harmodius rubbed his chin, trying hard to fit all the pieces of this curious puzzle together. "I still don't understand what all this means, Mother. Certainly Helena is an attractive child...and I suppose she has what some might call 'a certain poise'—and most young girl's burgeoning on puberty these days aren't usually known for that." His frustration suddenly erupted forth and, slapping his thighs with the palms of his hands he heard himself cry out: "Tell me truly, Mother...in all honesty...our Helena's a pretty little thing and sweet natured—at least most of the time—but have you ever considered her to be a 'great beauty'?"

Philippia sighed and, refusing him the answer he expected to hear, diplomatically shrugged her shoulders.

"And what about her age?" Harmodius stood up, pacing fretfully back over to the loom. "I know that on rare occasion girls *close* to her age have been chosen to carry the Sacred Peplos...but usually they're all much younger than Helena...mere children no older than seven or eight years!"

Philippia stood up and joined him at the loom. "Yes...well of course you're right, my dear. These very same questions plagued me as well." She placed a soothing hand on his shoulder. "Only this morning as she was leaving for the Acropolis to appear alongside the other candidates for the final selection by the High Priestess, I warned her to expect disappointment." Taking her son by the arm, she led him back to his stool. "Once they see how tall and gangly she is standing there next to all those younger girls...well, they'll most likely thank her kindly for appearing and send her on her way back home."

With the carriage of an aging aristocrat, Philippia resumed her own seat next to his and, waving one graceful hand, brought his attention back to the ebony box. "Just now, when you came knocking at the front door, I ran to answer because I thought it might be our Helena returning home in disappointment from the temple."

Somewhat mollified, Harmodius leaned over the ebony case, undid the golden fastenings and slowly raised the lid on Baobil's trunk. "You're right of course, Mother...and I suppose it is a formidable honor just to be asked to appear before the High Priestess as a candidate." With two hands, he carefully lifted Nefertiti's precious mirror—still swathed in its ancient leather wrapping case—up from its bed of folded linens at the top of the box. "And if they send her back home to us 'disappointed'," he gingerly passed the heavy object over to his mother's waiting hands, "this will certainly do much to raise her spirits!"

Philippia set the delicate object in her lap and was slowly undoing the cracked leather coverings when, all of a sudden, the shrieks of frenzied weeping and the distorted echo of sandal-shod feet running across the stone atrium floor came reverberating all the way to the back of the house. Harmodius was on his feet in an instant and, running to the open doorway, called out: "Sister!" just as Helena went sailing on past him, her head hunched over and completely covered by the folds of her shawl. Running straight back to her bedroom, she slammed the door behind her and threw the latch before anyone had time to react.

Philippia, shocked at this display of frenzied emotions from her usually unflappable daughter, quickly returned Harmodius' precious, still-unopened gift back to its linen bed and ran over to join her son standing in the doorway. Raising her own voice to a shout, she called out for the serving woman Mila to attend her. "It was old Mila who accompanied Helena to the Temple this morning..." she told her son, placing a tentative hand half-reassuringly on his shoulder "...we'll soon find out what brought about all these hysterics."

Still clutching two shiny, mother of pearl combs in her clenched fists—the ones she herself had placed in her young mistress' carefully coiffed hair that very morning...the same ones that had fallen to the street in Helena's frantic dash home—Mila came hobbling forward, deathly pale and out of breath.

"Oh Mistress!" she cried out falling to her knees. "Such a calamity has befallen our unhappy household!"

Each of them taking her by an arm, Harmodius and Philippia led the wailing woman over to the vacant stool. "Sit here, old friend. Breath slowly...try and calm yourself while I fetch a dipper of water." Harmodius ran to bring the old woman a cup of fresh well water from the tall amphora buried up to its neck in the dirt kitchen floor. By the time he returned, his mother had left the weeping Mila—still seated legs all akimbo on her lone wooden stool—and returned across the hall to bang on Helena's tightly barred door.

"Please, Helena dear...come out and talk to us. Tell us what happened at the temple. Nothing can be as bad as all that! And look here...did you see? Your brother has come home...he's back from Egypt...and with lovely gifts for us all." The mere mention of Harmodius only seemed to increase her hysterical moans.

Back in the weaving room, Harmodius watched with growing trepidation as Mila drained gulp after gulp of water down, all the while rocking, her voice a weird keening gargle as she attempted to maintain her stream of sorrowful lamentations. "Oh Master…it was a terrible thing that happened…so terrible!"

Unable to bear it any longer, Harmodius grabbed hold of her wrists, removing the almost empty cup from her quivering hands and setting it down on the floor. And then, taking her wrinkled face in his two hands, he held her motionless for a moment, fixing her with a somber stare. "You must calm yourself, Mila." He tried to use a calming, steady voice. "Mother and I need to hear from you exactly what happened at the temple today. You must tell us everything…" narrowing his eyes for added emphasis, "…everything" he repeated. Smiling, he released her face and slowly leaned back on his haunches, smoothing a sweaty strand of gray hair away from her cheek as he did. "That's better. Now then, Mila, tell us everything…why has Helena hidden herself away in her room? And why all these dreadful tears…what happened at the temple today that's upset my poor sister so?" Feigning incredulity, his eyebrows came together in a pointed arch over his nose. "All this commotion can't be over losing her place to a younger girl in that silly parade!"

"Oh, good Master Harmodius," Mila jumped up, waving her old, gnarled fingers in the air in the sign against the evil eye, her head shaking back and forth in dismay at his offhand impiety "…have a care, the gods are easily offended and they are *always* listening!"

Harmodius did his best to ignore this superstitious digression, instead focusing his stony glare on the old woman's teary, wavering eyes…impatiently waiting for an answer to his question. Eventually, the old woman choked back a single sob and settled herself back down on the stool. Reaching out, she grasped his hands and pulled them tightly into her lap.

"The day began so well…" she said with a shiver in her voice. "Shortly before the allotted time we arrived at the front of the Temple of Athena Parthenos, gathering there with the other expectant young girls and their followers. Soon a herald came out and, standing at the top of the stairs, he waited for the noisy hubbub to quiet. One by one, he called their names from his list and each in her turn entered the hallowed edifice. When your sister was summoned, we followed the other girls inside the temple, proceeding through several dimly lit antechambers into a great high-ceilinged meeting room at the rear of the sanctuary. Torches, burning brightly from fixtures along the four stone walls, augmented the shafts of light from the high, narrow windows near the roof of the room. Several young priests and priestesses stood in solemn attendance along the perimeter of the room mingling quietly with a goodly number of our sage City Fathers and other high-ranking members of the nobility. The room fairly buzzed with good-humored, but reverent whispers as the timid candidates were quickly lined up in the center of the room.

"The High Priestess, wearing her full regalia and carrying her ancient staff carved from the first olive branch, stepped forward and raised a hand in the air commanding silence. Smiling at the nervous candidates, she said a few encouraging words, uttered a prayer to the Goddess, and then began strolling up and down in front of the frightened young girls, inspecting each in her turn before moving on to the next. Several plain young things were dismissed outright, but somehow our young Lady Helena remained among the chosen." Smiling with pride, Mila rubbed at the tears staining her cheeks with the heel of her hand. "After this initial whittling process had been completed, the priestly acolytes stepped forward and began regrouping the candidates…this time by height—moving 'this one' over to stand next to 'that one', and 'that one' over to stand with 'those other two'—until there were several fairly balanced groups of four." The old woman licked at her dry, cracked lips. "This time, when the High Priestess stepped forward to speak with the remaining candidates, a nobleman followed at her side."

"A nobleman?" asked Harmodius. "What nobleman?"

Mila's eyes flashed with muted anger, "An important man…" she answered without hesitation, her lips twisting in a haughty frown. "Everyone bowed low when he passed by. He had a finely embroidered chiton draped ever-so-carefully over his shoulders and bright golden rings on each of his fingers."

"Did you hear his name?"

Mila thought carefully for a long moment before shaking her head. "No…" she said, touching a finger to her lips. "From where we servants were gathered on the far side of the room, you couldn't really hear very much." She hesitated for a moment. "But the woman in front of me nudged her friend and whispered something about '…the Co-Tyrant' as he passed us by."

Harmodius felt the color drain from his face. Rising off the floor, he turned away from the old family retainer, balling his hands into tightly knotted fists as he tried to regain control of his trembling voice. "The 'Co-Tyrant' you say?" his question was barely audible to Mila's old, careworn ears.

"Yes, Master…I believe those were her words."

"Go on, Mila…" he remained facing his mother's loom, his expression carefully hidden from the old woman "…what happened next?"

Mila took a deep, but halting breath. Punctuating her increasingly distraught words with dry, choking gasps, she told how the High Priestess had led this important man from group to group, introducing each candidate by her family name. "He smiled and laughed as he met each girl," she said, "…his voice gentle and encouraging as he stepped forward to utter a few kind words to each one." Mila shrugged her bony shoulders, shaking her head from side to side. "I couldn't hear what was said…but the sillier girls invariably responded with a giggle, while the others blushed shyly and contented themselves with a polite bob of their heads before gracefully stepping back into their place."

"And my sister?" The words came slow and deliberate.

Mila bit her lower lip and quickly dropped her head, staring down at the anxious hands wringing tightly in her lap. Alarmed at her sudden stillness, Harmodius swung around and, crossing back to the frightened serving woman, dropped to one knee in front her. Grabbing hold of her shoulders, he hissed: *"Tell me what happened next, Mila!"*

Stunned by the roughness of his voice, Mila looked up with a start. Her mouth flopped open to speak, twitched there for a moment, and then snapped shut again. Slowly turning her head to one side so that when she finally spoke the awful words she wouldn't be trapped by the terrible pain and hurt of his gaze, Mila answered:

"He said that your sister had no place there among the other young girls…that she had profaned her body…and that she was no better than a common street whore."

For what seemed like an eternity, the only sound heard in the house was Philippia's insistent tapping on the barred door across the hallway accompanied by her whispered pleas to the now-silent Helena. Eventually, Mila found her courage and turned to face the man she'd nursed from childhood still gripping tightly to her two frail, tired shoulders.

And what she saw turned her blood to ice.

The outrage she'd fully expected to see distorting his handsome youthful features was nowhere to be seen. Instead, she found herself staring on a look of hopeless abandon the like of which hadn't been seen in this unhappy household since the sorrowful day of his father's untimely murder. Reaching up, she carefully removed Harmodius' hands from her shoulders, clasping them together between her own weary fingers and bringing them down to nestle safely in her lap. Leaning forward, she whispered soothing words in his ear.

"Oh, my dearest boy, I don't know how or why this all came to happen today…what evil spirit was laying in wait for your darling innocent sibling in the sacred home of our city's most beloved goddess." Her voice trembled as she raised a withered fist in the air and shook it with all her feeble might. "And why this man, this…this cruel, cruel man said those things…made up those horrible charges against our precious Helena."

At the mention of his sister's name, Harmodius seemed to waken from his daze. Slowly, his look of bewilderment disappeared and was replaced by a chilling, steely-eyed determination. Time seemed to stand still in the quiet room as he studied the lines on old Mila's age-etched face. Then, swallowing hard to bring up enough moisture to wet his painfully dry lips, he carefully slipped his hands from between hers and stood. Looking down at her tired, tear-stained face, he waited for a moment, listening as his sister's tearful cries began once again in the other room. And then…

"I must know what this man said to her, Mila…" Harmodius voice cracked with pain, "…his exact words. Everything that you may have heard today."

Mila, chilled by the rage-filled eyes staring implacably down from his seemingly calm exterior, could only nod her head and obey.

"As he talked with each of the candidates, the man could barely be heard…his conversations intimate and private between the High priestess, the young girls, and himself. No one in the great hall was privy to these conversations. But when he at last came to you sister and her name was read aloud from the Priestess' list, he just stood there for a long moment studying her pretty, modestly down-turned face…almost as though he were searching it for something familiar. And this time when he spoke, he pitched his voice loud enough for all to hear.

"But my dear child, these very rumors are rampant throughout the city. Are you not the same Helena who has come to be known for her licentious behavior…cavorting openly with one Diokles of Agaron?"

Helena suddenly felt faint as all the blood pumping through her pounding heart rushed to her face.

"Speak up girl…" the same Co-tyrant, who only moments before had spoken so graciously to the other candidates, suddenly turned authoritarian and cold, his nostrils flaring with open distain as he peppered the girl with his humiliating accusations. "This Diokles—a man notorious for his depraved moral habits—is it not true that he pursued both you and your brother at the same time?" Hipparchus' eyes narrowed as his voice increased in pitch. "And isn't it also true that, possessed by some kind of degenerate longing to best your own sibling, you secretly acquiesced to your rutting suitor's blandishments and gifts, even yielding your most sacred virtue to his basest desires. Is that not so, girl?" His voice rang in her ears like a claxon on a bell. "Answer me, foolish child! Have you not had concourse with this man?"

Mortified by the coarseness of his accusations, Helena looked about in desperation as the other girls nervously sidled away. Before she could think to deny his malicious slanders, the Co-tyrant turned to the horrified High Priestess and sneered: "You see, Holy One…in her abject shame she cannot find words to answer my charge. Her disgraceful silence condemns her before this entire company." Snatching the tablet from the stunned High Priestess' hand, he pulled a stylus from the folds of his chiton and visibly scratched Helena from the list of names. Lifting the tablet aloft, he raised his voice so the entire assembly could hear his pronouncement. "The law is clear on this point…only maidens of the purest, unquestioned morality may seek to carry our Lady Goddess' sacred peplos in the Panathenaia." Pointing a condemning finger at Helena, he continued: "This wanton child is suspected of cavorting in a manner better befitting a common hetaera…a whore of the streets. She has no place here…standing at the side of these other young innocents…these true and pure daughters of Ath…"

Too late, Helena found her voice. "But, it's not true." She cried out, her voice faltering away in a sea of tears. "The Diokles I know is an honorable man…a good and loyal friend of my family…and I have done nothing with this man that would bring shame to…"

Ignoring her protests, the Co-tyrant angrily threw the tablet of names to the ground where the pieces shattered about her tiny feet. "You see, Holy One," he screamed out, as he stepped back in feigned revulsion, pulling the scandalized High Priestess along with him, "She admits to *knowing* this licentious man! Oh, sacrilege…sacrilege! This creature has profaned the very sanctity of our Virgin Goddess' Temple." Turning to the wide-eyed temple acolytes, he gestured sharply with his hand. "Remove this blasphemous stain from the Temple Precinct!"

Seizing the traumatized girl by her trembling arms, two acolytes dragged the silent, pale figure from the hall as the stinging buzz of accusing whispers shrieked in her aching head.

❦   ❦   ❦

"They dragged my innocent 'sweetling' out into the street and left her weeping in shame at the side of the Temple." Mila brushed a tear off her chin with the heel of her hand. "Before I could even reach her side she'd stumbled to her feet, her face covered in shame by the edges of her stole, and scurried away towards home."

As Mila spoke these last words, Philippia—frustrated in her efforts to speak with her distraught daughter—returned to the weaving room. "I don't understand," she said as she swept anxiously through the doorway. "What happened at the Temple today, Mila?" She turned to her son. "Harmodius...can you please explain to me what's happened here? Why all these hysterics over such a simple thing as not being chosen to carry..."

"It's unspeakable, Mother! That depraved pig...our so-called *Co-tyrant*..." the word fairly dripped with revulsion, "...he's gone too far." Ignoring the alarm in her eyes, Harmodius strode past her, "Stay here with Helena and the servants...I have to go out for awhile." Stopping in the doorway, he looked over his shoulder. "And keep the doors and windows bolted tight while I'm out."

Philippia opened her mouth, raising a hand to stop him, but before she could utter a single word, he was gone.

"Oh dear Mistress!" Cold, paper-dry fingertips brushing against the goose bumps on her arm caused the distracted Philippia to start with fright. Turning, she found poor old Mila doubled over on her stool, wiping at her dirt-smudged face with the edge of her tunic as tears overwhelmed her rheumy eyes. "What treacherous god have we angered so to bring such a terrible punishment down upon our heads?" she wailed.

"Co-tyrant...gone too far..." Harmodius' chilling words pounded in her head, filling her with a sickening dread. Seizing the old woman by the wrists, she dragged her to her feet. "Come along with me, Mila...I'll need you to help me get my daughter from her room." Pulling her towards the darkened hallway, she hissed over her shoulder, "And then you can tell me exactly what cursed words you filled my son's head with..."

❉   ❉   ❉

Running through the late afternoon streets, his mind a seething cauldron of anger and revenge, Harmodius was largely unaware of the crowds of people as he passed by. In his haste to be away from the suffocating atmosphere of his shame-filled home, he hadn't stopped to arm himself on his way out...which was probably for the best—as it had been illegal since the time of Solon to carry weapons openly in the city limits. With the present madness in his eyes and brandishing an unsheathed sword in his hand, it is doubtful that he would ever had reached the Acropolis before being stopped and questioned by one of the city bailiffs.

As it was, he came to the consecrated doors of Athena's many-columned temple unimpeded by anyone.

The temple porter, an old man with a slight hunch to his shoulders and a snowy white beard flowing nearly to his waist, was fitting wood-plank shutters over the windows for the night when the out-of-breath Harmodius arrived. Most Greek temples, deemed safe under the consecrated protection of their respective gods, left their doors and windows open to the elements...but as the basement level of the Athena's Temple doubled as the city's treasury, a number of basic security measures were taken each night.

Exhausted from his long run up the hill, Harmodius leaned against a pillar to catch his breath before approaching the doorkeeper. Before he could speak, the old man caught his eye and called out, "The Goddess' Temple is closing for the night, young man...if you wish to offer a sacrifice you'll have to come back in the morning."

Harmodius straightened up. "I'm looking for the Co-tyrant Hipparchus...I was told he was here visiting with the High Priestess."

The old man frowned. "Oh dear, I'm afraid he's long since gone, my boy. Back to those fancy digs of his over on the Areopagus, I suspect." The door-keeper pointed to a low villa-covered hill off in the direction of the setting sun. "He swooped in this noontime to select the 'peplos girls' for next week's big festival and then 'whoosh'" he whacked his hands together in a brisk sliding motion, "his 'high-and-mightiness' was off and away on more important civic business!"

Harmodius nodded tersely and was about to retrace his way down the temple steps when the old man suddenly called out: "Oh, but my goodness...you certainly missed quite a show here today, lad!" The doorkeeper slapped his cheek with the palm of his hand. "There was a girl in this morning's group…a pretty young thing, she was." Even with his back turned, Harmodius could smell the sour-breath as his waggish tongue clucked away. "But she was a rotten apple…or so they say." Harmodius cringed as the old codger's thoughtless words pierced his heart. "I'll say this much for that Hipparchus, he can certainly smell them out…has a regular eye for these things. Why, he picked the little vixen out without so much as a second glance…"

Harmodius shut his ears to the rest of the doorkeeper's thoughtless words as he raced down the steps and disappeared westward into the coming night.

The guard Leonidas slowly lifted himself on the balls of his feet at the same time arching his shoulders back in a restrained effort to ease the tightening in calf, thigh, and back muscles. Working his father's forge all those years had given him a handsome physique, but standing guard at rigid attention on an all-night shift was enough to test even the most athletic of bodies.

Nodding absentmindedly at the other faceless guard standing in the shadows opposite him, the bored young boy allowed his head to loll against the shaft of his spear as his mind strayed back to the day (was it really only a single week ago?) that his entire life was changed by the providential shattering of a horse's bit.

Riding past his father's smithy, the Co-tyrant Hipparchus and his entourage had been brought up short when the bridle on one of their horses broke loose and fell with a jangle to the street. Waiting in the shade of his father's awning for the simple repair to be completed, Hipparchus had spied the handsome lad working the bellows in the back of the forge. With a quick word in his father's ear, and a few coins to sweeten the offer, Leonidas' future had been sealed. The very next morning, the excited boy packed his few personal belongings together in an old, broken-handled straw basket, and began the trek across town to the luxurious villa nestled on the gentle slope of Areopagus Hill. As he was preparing to take his leave, his father had pulled him aside and told Leonidas what would be expected of him upon joining the Co-tyrant's household. A few nights warming the Co-tyrant's ample bed (not such a terrible prospect to a randy boy who'd never missed an opportunity to bend his backside over behind his father's smithy for a few extra pocket coins), and if fortune smiled, he might even spend a month or two as Hipparchus' favorite (his mouth had fairly watered at that prospect…after all, the Co-tyrant wasn't so terribly unattractive…even if his best days were long past). Then, once the Co-tyrant had finished with the lad, he'd been promised a secure position in His Lordship's household guard. Three meals a day, a roof over his head, and a modest, but regular, salary…now what underprivileged Athenian street youth would turn his nose up at that?

Unfortunately, Athens' Co-tyrant was notorious for the fickleness of his favors…

When young Leonidas arrived at the impressive villa with his broken basket of belongings tucked tightly under his arm, Hipparchus had already moved on, completely forgetting the handsome boy who'd caught his eye in the forge the day before. After handing the gate watchman the wooden chit Hipparchus had given his father, Leonidas was hustled inside…and straight down into the basement barracks of the villa. Before he had time to catch his breath, he found himself enrolled in Hipparchus' private militia and, as low man on the duty roster, allotted the hated 'sunset to dawn' posting.

The hated kinks invariably increased as the long night wore on; Leonidas shifted his tightening jaw back and forth, twisting his stiff neck from side to side to ease the growing pains, when a handsome lad suddenly appeared, running straight at him out of the darkness. Still new on the job, Leonidas found himself fumbling with his spear even as he jumped to attention while the young man, open-mouthed and anxiously trying to catch his heaving breath, stared up at the high walls surrounding the villa.

"Is this the home of the Co-tyrant…Hipparchus?" he finally managed to sputter. Leonidas frowned, detecting a disturbing note of panic in the lad's voice.

The nascent guard leaned forward and studied the man's face. There was a look of something—he wasn't sure what it was…anger, hurt, maybe even revulsion—radiating from his two powerful, bloodshot eyes. Before Leonidas could offer up an answer, his fellow sentry strode over from the opposite side of the gate and, holding his spear against the man's chest, demanded:

"Your business with the Co-tyrant?"

The man pursed his lips for a moment, staring down at the ground…and then, his voice seemingly back under control, carefully answered: "I wish to speak with Hipparchus…we have some, er…some unfinished business to set-tle."

"Your name?" the shrill-voiced cohort challenged.

"Harmodius…"

"Harmodius…" the guard repeated, "well, yes…I suppose it is. I believe the Lord Hipparchus is expecting you." Without removing his spear point from Harmodius' chest he looked over at Leonidas, "Search him for weapons, boy."

Resting his own spear against the wall, Leonidas felt inside the visitor's chiton, reaching under the folds of the linen skirt to check for any hidden blades. "Nothing…" he said with a timid shake of his head.

The guard eased his spear back and, grabbing the lad named Harmodius roughly by the arm, half-walked, half-pushed him on through the open gate. Over his shoulder, he called back to Leonidas. "Stay at your post, boy. I may be occupied for awhile…"

Something in the coarse tone and swagger of his fellow guard sent a shiver up Leonidas' spine. There were things about this job that he didn't fully understand yet…things that left him with an uneasy feeling about his newly chosen career. Watching as the two silent figures disappeared into the brightly lit main house, Leonidas retrieved his spear and, with a weary sigh, took up his rigid position at the side of the gate.

It was well after dark before Aristogiton, grimy and exhausted from his long day at Piraeus, finally arrived at Harmodius' front door. Once their precious cargo had been safely stored away in the company's warehouse, he'd made a beeline for his lover's home, sure that he would find a hot bath and welcoming smiles waiting for him…Harmodius' family lost in rejoicing over his safe return home from Egypt.

What he found there instead left him sick with fear…

Ushered by a softly weeping servant girl into the private back rooms of the eerily quiet house, Aristogiton found Harmodius' mother and sister deserted and alone, clinging to each other in the night-darkened weaving room, sobbing as they lamented their missing son and brother. Lighting a lamp, he carried it over and set it on a small trunk—Baobil's unopened ebony gift chest—resting on the floor between the two grieving women. Kneeling down at their sides, he waited with his heart in his throat as, between their choking sobs and moans, he heard the entire story of Helena's disgrace.

At the first mention of the Co-Tyrant Hipparchus' name, a sickening wave of panic washed through Aristogiton…even as Cleisthenes' unheeded words of warning resounded like an ache in his head. As soon as the whole truth sank in—that his beloved Harmodius, his reasoning blinded by a vengeful fury, had left in search of satisfaction hours before…and hadn't been seen nor heard from since—Aristogiton jumped to his feet. Vowing not to return until he'd found his lost eromenos, he grabbed a torch from a pile stacked against the kitchen wall, lit it in the smoldering hearth fire, and raced out into the empty streets in search of Harmodius.

✤   ✤   ✤

Due to the lateness of the hour, it took Aristogiton some time to find anyone who could point him on the way to the Co-tyrant's hilltop villa. When he finally ascertained the right pathway, he could feel his mouth go dry as the race of his heartbeat accelerated in his chest with each apprehensive step forward he took. In the end, the monolithic size of the great house—surrounded by its high stonewalls and guarded by its armed sentry, stalwart and vigilant at the gate—made it nearly impossible to miss.

Suddenly sorry that he'd seized a puling torch instead of the sharpest of death-bringing swords, Aristogiton approached the guard with a growing sense of trepidation. "Hmmm…perhaps not so stalwart after all," he thought with a rush of relief as the guard's slow, shallow breathing and the droop-shut eyes of deep sleep became all too apparent, "…and still just a boy." With a half-formed plan in his head, Aristogiton sucked in his breath and began carefully sidling his way past the dozing guard and on into the deserted compound.

"I wouldn't go in there if I were you…"

Aristogiton froze, the sharp point of a spear pressing painfully between his shoulder blades. With cat-like agility the sleep-feigning guard took a single step forward, careful to keep the razor-sharp bronze tip of his weapon resting in place. Leaning forward, he whispered in Aristogiton's ear.

"You have business with the Co-tyrant?"

Aristogiton could feel a drop of blood forming where the finely honed point pressed against his back. Hesitating, he slowly dropped his hands to his sides as he searched for an answer. "I'm looking for someone" he said, "a friend of mine…a young man…" he had to work very hard to keep the crippling fear out of his voice "…short and handsome…with black hair and brown eyes. I was told that he…er, that he might be here visiting with the Co-tyrant."

"*Visiting?*" This single word was followed by a harsh, bitter laugh…and all of a sudden the pressure of the spear point vanished. "Turn around, my friend."

Obeying the sentry's curt order, Aristogiton turned and found himself face to face with the guard. Holding his torch higher, for the first time he noticed the heavy dark circles ringing the boy's fear-stricken eyes, his complexion sallow and pale in the flickering light. "Your looking for the one called 'Harmodius', aren't you?"

Aristogiton's eyes lit up. "You've seen him then?" he asked anxiously, "You've seen my Harmodius?" Recklessly, he clutched at the boy's arm. "Is he here...is he inside there with Hipp..."

Leonidas shook his head. "No, no...he's long gone from here." Gently pulling his arm free, he did his best to avoid Aristogiton's scrutinizing gaze before adding: "And if you know what's good for you, you'll be gone from here as well."

Something in the sentry's suddenly evasive demeanor brought a cold certainty of disaster home to Aristogiton. "Why?" he asked, stepping forward and wildly grabbing at the boy's tunic top. "Why should I be gone from here? Tell me the truth, boy...what's happened to Harmodius?"

Suddenly looking younger than his years, the shame-faced sentry dropped his eyes to the ground. Unmoving, Aristogiton retained his tight grip on the boy's collar, waiting with mounting dread to hear him out. When the guard finally raised his head, the sputtering torch flame picked out what looked like tears, etching the hollows of the young guard's ashen cheeks. "I...I don't know what happened after they took your friend inside," he muttered, "but it wasn't good...that much I can tell you."

Suddenly conscious of the knotted tunic bunching in his hand, Aristogiton unclenched his fist and released the boy, taking a tactful step backward as he did. Once again, he waited for the guard to find his voice.

Swiping the back of his hand across his dry lips, Leonidas continued: "It was an hour or so after they went inside..."

"Who?"

"Your young friend, the handsome one who came here seeking Lord Hipparchus. He was...er, escorted inside by that lazy turd Pythias," with a jog of his head he pointed across in the direction of the vacated guard post. Carefully avoiding the wild-eyed stare of Aristogiton's gaze, the guard swallowed before speaking again. "Anyway...when they brought him back outside...well, I think your friend was in a pretty bad state."

Aristogiton's eyes narrowed, further twisting the harried lines on his brow. "What do you mean 'a bad state'...how bad?"

Chewing on his lower lip, Leonidas looked away again. "Pretty bad…" he mumbled.

Aristogiton's whole body seemed to sway in the balmy night air as the sympathetic sentry hastened to add: "Oh, I suppose it wasn't all that bad…I mean, he was conscious and everything." Leonidas found himself forcing another swallow, this time against the rising bile at the back of his throat. "It's just that…well, from what I could see in the darkness…your friend was pretty bruised up…especially on his backside." The sentry once again found his eyes wavering off to the side…anything to avoid the stony-cold accusation crying out from Aristogiton's icy glare.

For maddening moments, the only sound echoing through the calm, quiet night was the distant hooting of one of Athena's sacred owls. And then, pushing his face forward until he was only inches from the blacksmith's boy, the oil merchant's son prodded him further: "There's something more…something you're not telling me?"

With the force of a hammer blow, the shame of his disgraceful inaction suddenly hit home and Leonidas' words came rushing out with the force of a river breaching a shattered dam. "He was naked!" he cried out, tears of disgust streaming down his face. "They dragged your beautiful boy out…naked, bloodied and bruised…and threw him like a piece of garbage on the ground right over there!" The sentry pointed to a patch of muddy dirt just outside the Co-tyrant's open gate. "They were all laughing as one of them tossed his torn clothes after him." He spat on the ground. "Pigs!" he snarled in disgust. "They stood there pointing at him and making lewd jokes even as he crawled to his knees and gathered his clothes in his arms." Leonidas choked back a sob before sucking in a high, rasping breath. "When your poor friend finally found the strength to stand…he looked at me and, without saying a single word, stumbled away off down the hill."

Shivering in disgust, the sentry shook his head. "I'm sorry, friend…" he reached out a compassionate hand to Aristogiton's quaking shoulder, "I should have done something…I mean, I…I would have…if I'd had any idea what was going on inside there." His own voice shook with self-loathing as he stared up at the now darkened windows of Hipparchus' silent villa.

Dazed, Aristogiton shook his head in disbelief. "You said 'going on inside there'…" he repeated. "Please…you seem like a good enough fellow…tell me…tell me everything you know…" his ragged voice broke into sobs as he pleaded with the guard. "Tell me what those monsters did to my poor Harmodius!"

Releasing his grip on Aristogiton's shoulder, Leonidas bent his head in shame and returned to his solitary station next to the gate. "I haven't left my post, so I can only guess what happened inside, my friend. But I *can* tell you that the wine was flowing freely inside Hipparchus' house tonight." He nodded across to the empty sentry post, "Too freely, if you ask me...why, that asshole Pythias there, he never even bothered to return...and that can only mean one thing...the lousy sot is somewhere else sleeping it off." His whole body trembled with disgust. "Good sir, I've only been here a week but I've seen things and heard things that...well, let me just say that whenever Hipparchus' men are in their cups, no one—not man, woman, child, nor beast—is safe from their lascivious rampages!"

And then, before Aristogiton could press him for any more painful answers, Leonidas pointed his spear down the road. "Now then, you'd better be on your way, sir...for your own good. I'm telling you...you won't want to be here when Pythias and the others wake up." He nudged his spear in the same direction Harmodius had taken. "Go along now and find your friend. Just follow that road there back down the hill...that's the way he went."

Aristogiton, his mind fogged with visions of Hipparchus and his thugs inflicting their indecencies on his sweet-limbed Harmodius, gave an involuntary shudder. Nodding his head to the compassionate sentry, he started retracing his path down the hillside road. After a few steps he paused and looked over his shoulder. Forcing a stiff smile onto his face, he waved at the young boy and called out: "You know, lad...you really don't belong here with these other louts." Without waiting for a response, he turned away and was quickly swallowed up by the darkness.

"Right you are, my friend..." the blacksmith's son mumbled under his breath, "...right you are."

The next morning, after being relieved at the gate by a painfully bleary-eyed replacement, Leonidas returned to his barracks. As soon as he was alone, he pulled out his mother's old straw basket from underneath his cot and filled it back up with his meager collection of personal belongings...the same few personal belongings he'd brought here—along with all his high hopes for a bright, lucrative future—only one short week before. Throwing a pilfered traveling cloak over his head, he slipped out through a hidden sally port in the villa's rear garden wall.

And so it was that, avoiding any complicating encounters with his fellow guardsmen, he made his impromptu exit from Hipparchus' service. Before nightfall on that very same day, he was well beyond the city limits and on his way westward toward the crystalline shores of Eleusis. Upon reaching this sacred city—long famed for its time honored 'Mysteries'—he kept right on going…turning on to the northern road until he'd crossed safely over the border from Attica into the province of Boeotia.

Eventually finding work in a back street blacksmith's shop on the outskirts of Thebes, he changed his name, married his employer's thick-waisted daughter…and was never to be heard from again.

*   *   *

It was well past midnight before the increasingly panicked Aristogiton finally tracked his missing Harmodius down…eventually finding him sitting alone, crying softly to himself in the darkness of the deserted Kynosarges grounds. As he approached, the shadowy trees took on a more substantial form and Aristogiton, much to his surprise, recognized this lonely spot as that same verdant patch of green along the quiet banks of the Ilissos River where the two men had first made love all those many months ago.

Not wanting to startle his traumatized friend, he stopped a good distance away and called out in a gentle voice: "Harmodius? It's me…Aristogiton."

His lover didn't move. Harmodius remained sitting, staring off into the distance, his eyes fixed and unblinking, yet seemingly blind to the nocturnal sights and sounds around him.

Aristogiton took a step forward. "Harmodius?" he called again. "Can you hear me?" He took another step, this one more cautious than the first. "I promise you…everything will be alright," he whispered. "I'm here with you now, my love."

It was the word 'love' that triggered something in Harmodius' feverish brain. Starting, as if from a heavy dream, he shook his head, slowly turning towards the sound of Aristogiton's voice, searching for the source of the intrusion. Even as his wavering eyes found their focus and he recognized the familiar face of his lover, his tears began to flow. With a painful moan welling up from deep inside his chest, Harmodius swung back around and buried his head in his hands.

Rushing to his side, Aristogiton fell to his knees. Draping his arms over Harmodius' quivering shoulders, he pulled him tight against his chest.

Alarmed by the clammy chill of Harmodius' naked skin, Aristogiton kept his words of solace simple and few. Holding him this way for long hours, rocking his shivering body back and forth while he crooned soothing words into Harmodius' ear, they remained locked together this way until Eos' dawn chariot rose in the east to paint the evening stars from the sky. When the sun was fully up and the early morning gymnasium clients began to appear on the grounds, Aristogiton carefully helped his emotionally and physically spent friend to his feet. "It's time we went home," he whispered in his ear, "your poor mother and sister will be worried to death about you." And that was all that needed saying to get the boy moving again.

As they made their exhausted way along Athens' increasingly bustling streets—early bird shoppers already milling through the well-stocked stalls of the city squares—for the first time Aristogiton took note of the bright red welts ("strap marks", he thought to himself with a shudder) on the backs of Harmodius' legs. Biting his tongue, he worked hard to keep his growing fury in check. "Later…" his mind throbbed the word, "I'll deal with all of that *later*…"

Upon reaching the corner of Harmodius' street they saw that his front door was standing wide open, his mother and sister keeping an anxious vigil from the narrow stoop. As they approached the house Harmodius' tearful womenfolk came running out to crush him in their night-weary arms. After many soothing words and repeated assurances of his well being, Harmodius pled his own exhaustion from the long, nighttime ordeal and, escorted by Aristogiton, retired to his bedroom. There, lying on his narrow cot with a single arm draped over his eyes to block out the intruding rays of light shining in through his open window, he finally broke down and told Aristogiton exactly what had happened when he confronted Hipparchus in his villa.

"A fool," he said bitterly, "I was such a fool…I fell right into his trap."

Aristogiton knew better than to prompt Harmodius along. The words the bruised and battered boy desperately needed to speak would come out in their own good time.

"When I told him he'd been mistaken about Helena…when I demanded satisfaction before the entire city for this vile defamation of my innocent sister's character, he laughed at me and pushed forward a stack of tablets from across his desk." Harmodius lifted his black and blue marked arm off his face and lay staring up at a cobweb hanging from the corner of his ceiling. "I couldn't believe what I was reading. He had *testimony* from all of our neighbors...strangers and friends alike! Each, by itself, appearing quite innocent...but when bundled together like this and presented with his vituperative insinuation and besmirching innuendo..."

Aristogiton reached over and ran a soothing hand through his lover's night-tousled hair. Turning his head sideways, Harmodius met his sympathetic gaze with two haunted eyes. "He set me up, the bastard...I see that now. I came to his villa all innocence and naiveté knowing well what had to be said to the Co-tyrant, to be done to him if need be, to set things right for poor Helena. But all of a sudden, staring down at his foul stack of damning testaments, I was overcome with confusion...I didn't know what to do...what to say." A single tear ran down his cheek and stained the linen pillow under his head. "And that's when he made an offer..."

Aristogiton felt his mouth go dry even as he struggled to keep the expression on his face passively encouraging. "Offer?" he asked.

Harmodius barely nodded his head before turning to stare shamefacedly at his clean, whitewashed bedroom wall. This time when he spoke, his words came so softly that Aristogiton had to crane forward to understand them. "He said that he had admired me that day at the gymnasium...admired the lines of my body when we two wrestled together in the palaestra." Aristogiton felt a dull pain forming in the pit of his stomach. Hesitating over each and every word, Harmodius inched on: "He said that for the longest time now he'd been wanting to 'experience' me...to know the pleasures of my body...to 'breed' me, even if only for a single time...yes, *breed me*...those were the words he used."

With his face turned to the wall, Aristogiton could see his naked shoulder quivering as he revealed these soul-crushing words. His heart racing ever faster in his chest, Aristogiton reached over and pulled the shivering boy back into his protecting embrace. "It's alright, my Beloved One, you don't have to say anything more. I can well imagine what tainted promise he offered you in return for his despicable request." Brushing the damp, black curls off Harmodius' down-turned neck, he brushed his lips against the cold, white flesh. Drawing in a deep breath, he sought to slow his pounding heart before continuing: "And I know that, for the sake of your dear sister...for her reputation and the future happiness of your entire family...you were left with no choice but to accept him." He ran the back of his hand down his lover's smooth, pale cheek. "There is no shame in this, Harmodius." His lips pursed tightly together, "Or rather...the shame to be allotted for this unseemly episode falls solely upon this brute...Hipparchus, our so-called *Co-tyrant of Athens!*"

Harmodius closed his eyes, resting his head back against Aristogiton's broad, muscular shoulder. "No shame, you say?" His breath hitched in his throat. "Oh, Lord of my Heart...if only that were the truth."

Aristogiton felt another twist in his gut. "Fear not, young eromenos. I know that whatever happened, your heart is true to me alone...and that, for me, is all that matters. Surely nothing you did...nothing he might have done to you last night...will ever need words of forgiveness from me." Leaning forward, he whispered in his ear: "Now then, unburden your heavy heart. What happened last night in Hipparchus' villa?"

Feeling his jaws clench together, Harmodius closed his eyes and waited for the pain from these seething memories to dull. Then, proceeding in a somewhat halting voice, he recounted in full detail his experiences at the hands of Hipparchus, Co-tyrant of Athens.

* * *

"I knew when I went there last night that I would do *anything* to salvage my sister's tattered reputation. In my anguished state, Hipparchus' offer seemed a small price to pay when weighed against poor Helena's future happiness. Without a moment's hesitation, I agreed to the Co-tyrant's extortionate demand. But what happened next however...was more than even I bargained for." Swallowing hard, Harmodius wet his bruised lips with the tip of his tongue. "Smiling like some fiendishly hungry cat with a helpless bird trapped under its paw, Hipparchus rose from his chair and clapped his hands together. All of a sudden, the room was filled with a crushing mob of sneering, drunken soldiers. 'Get him ready for me, boys' the Co-tyrant said." Aristogiton felt an icy shiver run up Harmodius spine as he repeated Hipparchus' brittle command. "Before I could protest, two brutes grabbed hold of me, pinioning my arms to the desk, as someone else ripped my tunic in two. Then, without a another word, Hipparchus came around behind and, as he forced himself inside me, grabbed my hair and yanked my head back, hissing in my ear: 'don't fight me, boy...remember your sister's reputation...you agreed to this!'

It was now Aristogiton's turn to shiver involuntarily as he tried to block the gut-churning picture of his lover's violation from his mind.

And still poor Harmodius wasn't finished...

"His men were standing all around us…gawking at me…laughing as he plowed into me over and over and over again. Some busied themselves passing around an open jug of wine; others had their cocks out and were playing with themselves as they watched. It was horrible…something out of the worst nightmare…and all I could do was squeeze my eyes shut so that I didn't have to watch them." Harmodius stopped, his heart pounding so hard that Aristogiton could feel it beating all the way through his naked back. "When Hipparchus finally finished with me, he pulled out and I fell forward onto his desk." Goosebumps covered the boy's trembling arms. "I thought we were through…I thought the horror was over…ended for the night…but I was wrong."

The portent of those words ate a chunk from the fear-frozen heart thudding away in Aristogiton's aching chest.

"'Nothing special about our little wrestling buck after all, I'm afraid.' The Co-tyrant announced to one and all with a bored laugh. 'Either way, I've finished with him.' With a surly laugh, he slapped me on the buttock and turned to his waiting guards. 'Remember,' he said to them with a snide wink, 'whatever happens now, I don't want to hear about it. Take him to your barracks…he's all yours to play with for the rest of the night.' And with that, he left me standing there with this room full of leering, drunken beasts."

The night before, when searching for his missing lover, Aristogiton had imagined that even facing the worst prospect imaginable, he would still be able to keep a check on his raging emotions…if not for himself, then for this one…his beloved eromenos. Now, facing the reality of Harmodius' rape, his body began to rock uncontrollably back and forth on the edge of the bed. Throaty moans—hardly recognizable as human, yet coming from somewhere deep within his gut—came pouring forth even as his arms tightened around the sobbing boy pressed back against his heaving chest.

Eventually the two, overwhelmed by the emotional and physical toll of Harmodius' unspeakable experience, collapsed back onto the bed…there to sleep entwined in each other's arms through the heat of the day.

Later, as the evening temperatures cooled the stifling room and the pale, summer moon rose high in the clear, star-filled sky, Aristogiton carefully loosed his arms and quietly slipped from the cot, leaving the still exhausted Harmodius to sleep out the night.

After snatching a hasty meal in Philippia's kitchen, he left the grieving women and servants alone in the house to watch over their beloved Harmodius, while he went off in search of his comrades from the Thetis.

CHAPTER 10

"Cleisthenes was trying to tell us something! Don't you remember his words? 'Athens will never know true freedom as long as its leaders place themselves above the law…'" Nicias jumped up and began pacing around the brightly lit dining room.

Tylissus leaned forward on his couch and poured himself another cup of his generous host's rich, red wine, careful to add a healthy dollop from the water jar to keep his mind focused and clear. "Nicias is right, Aristogiton…if sanity ruled in Athens, at the very least, Harmodius should be able to drag that cruel bastard into court. I mean…don't we have laws against this kind of thing?" He pounded his fist on his tiny dining table raising a clatter from the half empty dishes. "Co-tyrant or not…this outrage should be exposed and he that committed it…held accountable!"

Aristogiton, two dark circles ringing his bloodshot eyes and a face still drawn and ashen gray from the day's unhappy events, had remained largely silent since his painful recounting of Harmodius' late night run in with Hipparchus and his brutish louts. Now, with a despairing shake of his head, he roused himself from his lonely couch. "Restitution in the courts—could he conceivably get it—won't be enough," he said. "Not for Harmodius…and not for me!"

Diokles, riddled with guilt by the crucial, but innocent part he'd unwittingly played in Hipparchus' scheme for revenge, placed a consoling hand on Aristogiton's arm and turned to his eromenos. "Tylissus," he said. "Even if we *could* find a magistrate to hear the case…it would never succeed."

His lover frowned. "What do you mean 'it couldn't succeed'? At the very least—if we find ourselves an honest jury—Harmodius should be able get Hipparchus sent into exile for years!"

Diokles wearily shook his head. "You weren't listening, my little fool. Technically speaking, Harmodius *wasn't* raped…at least not by Hipparchus…and certainly not in the *legal* sense of the word."

Tylissus, looking around the room for support, caught Nicias' eye…he in turn could manage nothing better than a lame shrug of his shoulders. Seeing their confusion, Diokles rolled his eyes. "Don't you two get it? Harmodius was tricked into making a bum deal. When he offered himself in exchange for Hipparchus vouchsafing his poor sister's reputation…at that instant, any cause for rape against the Co-tyrant was negated."

Now it was Cleon's turn to sputter a protest. "Aren't you splitting a rather fine hair there, my legalistic friend? I think we can all agree—and I'm sure most of your fine legal minds would concur—that if nothing else, Co-tyrant Hipparchus bears at least some responsibility for the depraved actions—actions, I might add, he himself encouraged—of that noxious mob of thugs he employs!"

Diokles templed his fingers together and dropped his head in a thoughtful nod. "You're right, of course. Hipparchus could and should be held liable for any illegal activities committed under his aegis." One of his eyebrows arched in a question. "But when we come right down to it…wasn't Archon Cleisthenes right? The fact that Hipparchus even considered such a despicable action tells us what he thinks of the current state of our legal system…that he and his brother have suborned so many officials, they now consider themselves to be virtually untouchable?" He shook his head. "No, my friends…I'm afraid a lawsuit isn't the answer to this brutal transgression."

Turning to the silent but grim-faced Aristogiton; Diokles offered him another sympathetic smile. "And besides…you didn't really call us together tonight to enlist us in any lawsuit…did you?"

Aristogiton looked down at his empty wine glass and, without answering him, drew in a deep breath and slowly shook his head.

Feeling the sorrow weighing down the entire room, Diokles sought to rouse them all with a shout of encouragement. "You are our 'Captain'…" he cried out to Aristogiton "…and that is how you will always be known to those of us," he opened his arms to encompass the entire company, "fortunate enough to have been shepherded to the very ends of the earth under your watchful eye." There were approving nods and murmurs of agreement from the others.

"Know this then, my friend…all here—each and every one of us—having shared in the deepest bonds of friendship, we are committed to your cause. In this foul business with the Co-tyrant—as in all matters that concern one or the other of us—we are bound together closer than brothers." He paused for a moment, waiting as each man in his turn bowed his head in acknowlegement. Then, boldly adding his own silent nod, he asked Aristogiton one more time: "Tell us then, my Captain, what is your wish…what must we do to exact a fitting retribution for the unspeakable crimes committed against our beloved Harmodius?"

Deeply touched by their loyalty, Aristogiton found himself momentarily at a loss for words. Closing his eyes, he conjured up the image of the bruised and beaten body of his beloved eromenos…the boy still fitfully sleeping on his narrow cot in the darkened room across the hall. Then, slowly holding his two sea roughened hands out in front of him, he opened his eyes and stared at each of them one by one. Finally facing Diokles and speaking in a careworn, gravelly voice he pronounced:

"I won't rest…until these hands run red with his blood."

"No, Aristogiton…"

All heads turned to the doorway where Harmodius—his bruised body covered in a simple, clean white tunic and his hair still damp from a perfunctory wash at the basin—stood gazing proudly over at his lover.

"Murdering Hipparchus would carry too heavy a price…in the very least torture and a horrible death for his assailants. And while I can easily accept this fate for myself…and even for you, Erastes…I can't bring this calamity down upon my friends here." He entered the room and walked over to take a place by his lover's side as the others called out their protestations, vigorously affirming their own willingness to die for their comrade. Taking Aristogiton's hand in his, Harmodius raised the other to silence their shouts.

"No, my friends. I most heartily appreciate your sentiments, but it would be base and selfish of me to accept your lives as sacrifice for my blundering foolishness…my error in judgment." He stopped for a moment, listening with deepening affection as their objections continued unabated. Looking up at Aristogiton—whose face still bore the pallor of love's grief—he gave his hand an encouraging squeeze. With gratitude in his tired smile and tears welling in his eyes, he nodded to the others and waited once again for their silence. "Thank you all…" he finally said, "I am indeed fortunate to count you as friends…truly I am." Pausing for a moment, he reached for the wine jug and filled an empty cup. Picking the cup up in both hands, he held it out before the company. "If you are so willing to set yourselves upon this dangerous course…if you are ready to join me in almost certain death…then let us rather commit ourselves to a cause far more noble than my personal revenge." His eyes suddenly blazed with a cold passion as he allowed his challenge to sink in.

"This evening as I lay upon my cot, my sleep troubled by memories of the bitter profanation of my body at the hands of our cruel Co-tyrant, my dreams suddenly returned to Crete and I came to understand the truth of Cleisthenes' warning words. In that instant, our exiled Archon's hopeful vision of a free and democratic Athens burned away the raging fever of my vengeance." He shook a fist in the air, his eyes narrowing in fury. "I believe the time has come to forever free ourselves and our beloved city-state from the corrupting grasp of the polluted Pisistrade Tyranny!" Lowering the angry fist to his side, he let his voice drop to a near whisper. "For the future of our city…both of them—the Tyrant Hippias and his obscenity of a brother—and as many of their false-hearted followers as can be rounded up…they must all die under the sharpened edges of our swords." Holding out the cup of wine, he cried out: "*Now* I ask you…who will join me in bringing righteous death to these autocrats? Who will join me in this sacred tyrannicide?"

The seeds of rebellion that Cleisthenes had planted in their minds all those weeks before in Crete, now suddenly sprang to life. The small dining room erupted with shouts and cries of boisterous affirmation as each man jumped up off his couch and came forward, each in his turn, grasping hold of Harmodius' cup and sealing his mortal commitment with a heady sip. The sheer volume of noise brought a weary looking Philippia poking her head in the doorway to see if something was amiss. At the sight of the old woman's red-rimmed eyes, the shouting quickly died away and each man returned rather sheepishly to his dining couch.

"It's late, Mother…shouldn't you be asleep in your bed?" said Harmodius, a gentle smile, the placid mask that hid the fevered animation in his eyes.

"I'm overjoyed to see that…that you seem to be feeling better, my son." Her words sounded tentative as she slowly gazed about the room, coolly trying to discern the cause of this sudden uproar. "I remain awake at this late hour to provide your guests with additional refreshment…if that is their desire."

Harmodius walked over to his mother and gently pressed her hands between his. Kissing her on the cheek, he escorted her back to the doorway. "We're fine, Mother. If we need anything, I can forage myself…or if need be, wake up one of the servants." Brushing a loose strand of hair off her cheek, he smiled at her. "Now then, you've had a very distressing couple of days…first with poor Helena…and then with my little mis-adventure." He winked reas-suringly to her. "Go on to bed now…" he purred, "…get some much-deserved rest and we'll speak again in the morning."

A mother's intuition gave Philippia a moment's hesitation. But then, gra-ciously nodding her head to her son and his guests, she backed quietly out of the room and disappeared down the darkened hallway. Harmodius watched until she was safely out of earshot before turning back around…the fever in his eyes, now hardened with resolve.

"And so, my fellow conspirators…to work!"

As each man in the room reflected on his changing fortunes—ripening love affairs and newfound wealth from the profitable venture in Egypt—no one was in a great hurry to toss his life away on a totally reckless and futile escapade. For that reason, on that first somewhat overexcited evening, few of the propos-als considered were practical enough to be agreed upon by all. In fact, as the long hours wore on, the six weary conspirators found themselves in accord on only a single stratagem. And when the dining room lamps began sputtering in their wall niches—their tiny reservoirs of oil nearly burned away—Harmodius and Aristogiton brought the debate to a close, bid everyone a good night's rest, and sent them off to their respective homes.

At breakfast, late the next morning, Harmodius—buttressed by Aristogi-ton's politely compelling complicity—casually informed his mother and sister that they were being sent, along with Mila and the entire household staff, to the family's farm in Araphen. When challenged by his balking womenfolk, Harmodius maintained that to remain in the city during the coming Panath-enaia Festivities would be, at best, embarrassing for Helena. As he so succinctly put it, "…a month's rest in the country will allow plenty of time for the mali-cious gossip and innuendo to die down here in the city." As for himself and Aristogiton…with pressing business concerning the disposal of their much sought after Egyptian cargo, the two would remain behind in the city…at least for the time being. And with the servants away, Harmodius announced that he would be locking up the city house and moving in with Aristogiton until the time came for them to join the others in Araphen.

As eldest male and therefore head of the household, Harmodius' word was law. And so, after putting up a token resistance, Philippia nodded her head in unhappy acquiescence…all the while recalling the absolute terror she'd felt when Aristogiton had returned those few nights ago from 'only the gods know where' half-dragging her badly beaten son at his side. Eyeing the purple bruises and welts still marring his naked arms, she'd had to bite her tongue to stifle the cry of protest clawing at her breasts.

Even now, as she packed her things together, she couldn't help dwelling on possible darker motives for this unexpected exodus—something carefully hidden from her behind Harmodius' well-intentioned considerations for poor Helena's discredited virtue.

Following a hasty noon meal—and without giving voice to her growing fears—she allowed herself to be lifted into the hired cart. The wheels began to turn and, forcing a nervous smile to her lips, Philippia took a last look back at her only son, still standing resolutely in the open doorway with his handsome lover close by his side. With a final wave of her hand, she cracked the little whip over the donkey's head and sent them on their rumbling way down the old cobbled street. With the carefully veiled Helena weeping silently at her side, she led her fractured household out through the city's western gate before turning north on to that very same road that had seen her husband's untimely demise all those sad years ago.

"Ah well…" she thought to herself as she pushed away an ache of regret and urged the donkeys forward "…perhaps Harmodius is right…perhaps we'll find some peace of mind dwelling for a time next to the serene waters of the Gulf of Petalion and the ancient olive groves of Araphen.

Over the next few days, the six conspirators formed a nearly inseparable bond…working out at the Kynosarges together, shopping in the marketplace together, steaming at the public baths together, and dining each noontime and evening at one or another's home. Their only time apart was when they retired in pairs for the night, eromenos and erastes sleeping their dreamless sleep locked tightly in each other's arms.

Using one pretext or another—wheedling, cajoling, and in one case, even resorting to bribery—each had followed Harmodius' lead…finding excuses to send truculent family members and their innocent household servants away from the city. Due to the seasonal festivities, this proved to be an often difficult task...the mere thought of missing all the parades, theatrical events, and drunken parties associated with the weeklong Panathenaia, caused even the most dutiful of household slaves to grumble under their onion-tainted breaths.

Even if they managed to kill Hipparchus and his brother, there was little doubt that in the ensuing melee, some or all of their deaths were a near certainty. But should their attempted coup fail—if, in the end, they were unsuccessful in persuading the populace to rise up en masse and join them against the Athenian Tyranny—an even heavier price would be exacted from the instigators. And it was this fear—that with failure the long arm of Pisistrade vengeance would most certainly be turned against their loved ones—and not concern for their own death or torture, that initially held them back.

And so, before their plan could progress, family members likely to be targeted were sent safely on their way from the city environs.

✤   ✤   ✤

"Who shall host dinner tonight?" asked Diokles, as he vigorously scrubbed away at Tylissus' sweat and dirt coated back with a stiff sponge.

The afternoon shadows were lengthening outside the dimly lit bathhouse at the Kynosarges and the steamy soaking pool was slowly emptying of its usual coterie of muscle-sore athletes and their ever-ogling admirers.

"I believe it's Nicias' turn," said Aristogiton, slowly rolling two knuckles over a persistent kink in Harmodius' powerfully built shoulder. "Even though he bribed his parents to go off on a visit to his aged uncle in Megara and now has that big old house all to himself, he has, so far, neglected to invite his apparently unworthy friends anywhere near the place!"

Nicias splashed a handful of water at him. "That's not fair!" he complained. "My idiot brother is still hanging about here in the city...he refuses to miss even a day of the Panathenaia. He and his dodgy friends are always hanging about the place. Why, the moment my parents left for Megara, the whole group moved right in and took over the very best rooms." He groaned. "You should see it now...it's a pigsty!"

"Not that handsome twin of yours...the clever Demoritus?" prodded Tylissus with a mischievous glint in his eye.

"Handsome? Clever? Ha!" Nicias scowled, splashing him even more vigorously than Aristogiton. "You mean 'too-clever-for-his-own-good', don't you? And any discerning observer with half an eye could see that *I'm* the handsome one of the pair, you blind fool! Everyone says so…" leaning over, he buzzed his patient Cleon brusquely on the lips. "Is that not true, my love?"

Cleon smiled indulgently. "There is no comparison, my little Eros. Aphrodite was smiling down from Olympus on the golden day you slid from your mother's blessed womb."

Somewhat mollified by his lover's honeyed words, Nicias resumed his brotherly invective. "That boy is impossible. I tell you, my poor father is at his wits end. Even after all the trouble Demoritus has caused our family, he persists in living the life of a drunken wastrel! To see him and his wine-soaked friends, you'd think that Dionysus ruled supreme in the heavens. They drink and whore all through the night, *every night*…and then spend the days sleeping it off!"

Patting him sympathetically on his cheek, Cleon turned to the others and offered up a wistful smile. "Never mind, my good fellows…I'll take his turn," he said. "You would be doing me honor to have you as my guests for dinner tonight."

Cleon's not-unexpected invitation brought smiles and nods of approval from the others. Unlike his cautious cohorts, Cleon had had the foresight to keep two members of his family's cooking staff with him in the city. Rather than facing another al fresco meal of bits and pieces purchased on the run from stalls in the marketplace and heated by their own inexperienced hands over the kitchen hearth fire, tonight they could be assured of a carefully thought out culinary experience.

Just then, the last stranger left in the pool—his stomach growling with all this talk of food and dinner parties—lifted his heavy body out of the water, gathered his towel and sandals under an arm and, dripping water across the marble floor, left the bathhouse.

For a few moments, no one spoke. And then, sucking in a deep mouthful of steam-filled air and letting it out in a long, slow whistle, Harmodius lifted his eyebrows and raised the question that continued to plague everyone's mind during all their waking hours.

"Well, my friends…anyone come up with a workable plan yet?"

Much to his surprise, it was his own Aristogiton who raised a hand.

"Uh…the elements of a plan—a good plan, I think—have been coming together in my mind for these last few days." As he scratched at the stubble on his chin, he caught Harmodius' faintly bemused look and hastened to add: "I haven't mentioned anything before now…because I wanted to work out a few nagging details first."

There was a sound of shuffling feet and a careworn old slave—even his loin-cloth discarded in the steamy heat of the indoor bathhouse—appeared backlit in the doorway. Taking a moment for his rheumy eyes to adjust to the dim light from the narrow window slits set high up in the walls, he came slowly padding into the room. Straining under the weight of an enormous jug of hot water held tightly between his two outstretched arms, he soundlessly carried it over to the far side of the room and, kneeling down, carefully added it to the slowly cooling pool. Then, leaning the empty vessel up against the wall, he began discreetly gathering up the dirty towels and discarded grooming articles left scattered about the room by earlier patrons.

"Well…" said Aristogiton, his voice affecting a casual indifference, "I think it's past time we were on our way. We'll talk more about all this over dinner tonight." He raised an eyebrow. "An hour after sunset, then…at the home of our gracious host Cleon?"

Nodding heads and mumbling their agreement the six inseparable friends slowly climbed from the pool, all the freshly scrubbed skin dotting with goose bumps as it made first contact with the modest chill of the early evening air.

❀   ❀   ❀

"But that's too soon…that's the day after tomorrow!"

Aristogiton nodded his head. Leaning forward on one elbow, he dipped a piece of succulent roasted lamb into the thick, honey-sweetened onion sauce before tossing it into his mouth. "As always, Tylissus, your elucidations of the obvious are right on target." He scanned the faces of the others in Cleon's well-lit dining room and noted with a feeling of grim satisfaction that he had everyone's full attention. "As I said, I believe our only chance for success is to make our move during the Great Procession…and that means the day after tomorrow," he affirmed. "The Panathenaic athletic contests finish up with the running of tomorrow night's Torch Race and, as is tradition, most of the city will stay awake throughout the night feasting the victor and his tribe at the Panny-chos." Licking his lips, he stretched them taut in a cold, tight smile. "And you can be sure that thanks to the *largess* of our ever-pandering 'Co-tyrants' they'll be a limitless supply of wine and beer at hand. At dawn, those still clear-headed enough to march in a straight line will gather together at the Dipylon Gate to take part in the great procession to Athena's temple…and I have little doubt that most of these will be pretty far gone from lack of sleep and too much unwatered wine." He tapped the hilt of his eating knife on the tabletop before deftly spiking another chunk of meat off the greasy platter. "If we keep our wits about us…if we remain sober and clear thinking…" he paused, staring at the skewered meat in front of his face, "…with most of our fellows feeling the worse for wear…" his grin took on a sadistic edge "…we can use their confusion to aid our cause."

Diokles excitedly snatched up his napkin and wiped his greasy hands clean before clapping them together. "It's an excellent plan, Aristogiton…excellent. Worthy of our fore thinking Captain!"

Aristogiton smiled, his face flushing with a mixture of the rich red wine and his own embarrassed pride. "We've been going about this all wrong, my friends—trying to think of a way to isolate Hipparchus and his brother at a vulnerable moment—when in truth, the answer has been staring us right in the face."

"Of course! We'll be hiding in plain sight!" crowed Harmodius. "Athena's Birthday Procession is the one day in all the year when every Athenian citizen has the right to parade through the streets in full arms and armor." He squeezed his lover's well-muscled arm. "A masterful stroke, my sweet…we won't even have to hide our weapons! The crowds…all the confusion…it will provide us the perfect opportunity to surprise both Hippias and Hipparchus together as they watch from the reviewing stand." His eyes flashed as he contemplated the bittersweet taste of coming revenge. "Ahh, and how swiftly my sword will strike them down…sending their cowardly shades for eternity to the blackest depths of Tartarus!"

Aristogiton reached a hand around his lover's waist and pulled him closer on the dining couch the two were sharing. For the next few minutes they remained silent, locked in each other's arms, listening intently as the others offered up suggestions and observations meant to fine-tune Aristogiton's superbly conceived plan to overthrow the hated Pisistrade Dynasty. When the excited flow of their words had finally settled down, Aristogiton loosened his hold on Harmodius and, swinging his legs over the edge of the couch, hopped to his feet. Taking his place at the center of the room, he let his eyes travel lovingly from one man to the next.

"This then will be our plan," he said, ticking off each point with his fingers. "Tomorrow, each will spend the day in activities of his own choosing. I for my part will write a letter to Cleisthenes telling him of Hipparchus' intolerable behavior towards Harmodius and his family…and detailing our resolve to overthrow the Pisistrade Dynasty once and for all." He stopped for a moment, soberly gauging their unwavering commitment before continuing on. "As I said, each of you will have the daylight hours to do what you will…take part in the athletic contests…exercise at the gymnasium…enjoy whatever sights and sounds of this great festival you desire. However, at all times we must be on our guard, ever watchful not to draw unwanted attention to our conspiracy." Before ticking another finger he added: "And I suggest that, at some time during the day, you all take time to compose letters to your family and loved ones. Inform them of our coming actions…and why we take them. And be sure to warn them that, should things go awry, they should remain hidden in the country until it's safe to return again."

Rather than give them time to dwell on this somber thought, Aristogiton proceeded right on to his next point. "At sunset tomorrow we'll meet together at the Dipylon Gate for the running of the Torch Race. If any suspicions *have* been raised during the day, it will be good to be seen milling about in the festive crowds. As soon as the runners are off their marks and the crowds begin to disperse toward the Pannychos, we'll use the confusion to retire back to our own homes…" turning, he cheekily grinned down at his Harmodius, "or to the nearby home of a loved one."

Assuming a more serious air, Aristogiton clasped his hands together in front of him and frowned down at his sandaled feet. Raising his eyes a moment later, he solemnly added: "Have no doubt that in striking down these two bullies—these two petty men, Hippias and Hipparchus—we will be striking a blow against the rule of *all* tyrants…and running a sword through the very heart of the Tyranny that stifles the freedom of our beloved city." Reaching behind, he clasped Harmodius' outstretched hand in his. "Tomorrow night should be spent in earnest prayer and ritual preparation. Our weapons, our bodies, and our minds must all be at peak performance for the coming morning's trial."

As the weight of Aristogiton's words sank in, someone suddenly let forth a muffled belch sending the sour smell of spent wine floating throughout the room. The tension for the moment broken, Aristogiton furrowed his brows together in a mock-scolding manner and good-naturedly reproached them: "And of course, from this time forward, they'll be no more drinking…no more wine, no more beer…nothing should pass our lips that might inhibit our singular focus on the difficult task ahead."

Nicias—teetering in mid-sip—sputtered a mouthful back into the half-empty cup, almost spilling the dregs onto his spotless dining couch. With a look of chagrin, he pointedly placed the bronze goblet back on the table and pushed it away.

After the laughter had subsided, Aristogiton held out his hand and ticked off one final finger. "That brings us to the day after tomorrow..." Taking in a deep breath, he sat back against the edge of his couch. "We meet together at the first light of dawn near the Dipylon as everyone gathers together for the Great Procession. When our time is called, we'll take our place with the other citizen-soldiers in the line of armed infantrymen. This will place us behind the ergasti-nai—the sacred weavers of this year's peplos—and before the ordinary citizens following in there demes. From the City's gate we'll march in procession through the Agora and then on up to Athena's temple on the Acropolis." He paused for a moment to settle the growing excitement in his stomach. Lowering his voice to a near whisper, he forged on: "Hippias and Hipparchus should be easy targets standing alone on their raised reviewing stand at the foot of the temple steps." He slowly raised a hand into the air. "When I give this signal..." his hand sliced swiftly down to his side, "Harmodius and I will rush the stand. If the gods are kind, it will be my privilege to dispatch Hippias with a single sword thrust through his scrawny neck..." he turned to his spellbound lover still lying rapt on their twin dining couch, his chin resting thoughtfully on his fist "...while you, my dearest Harmodius..." he smiled fondly at his eromenos "...to you I leave the settling of scores with the contemptible Hipparchus!"

"But what about us?" cried out Diokles, waving a piece of speared lamb in protest at the thought of being left out of the melee.

"Have no fear, my good friend. I guarantee that you—all of you—will spill more than your share of blood on our hallowed Athena's temple steps!" Pointing a finger, he instructed them, "Your job will be twofold," he grinned viciously. "As Harmodius and I charge the platform, it will be up to you four to engage Hippias' bodyguard...thus ensuring us enough time to complete our bloody tasks." His voice ringing with exhilaration, he shook an excited fist in the air. "And all the while you must shout out our cause...exhorting the mob to join with us in toppling the corrupt Pisistrades." His eyes looked almost feverish in the flickering lamplight. "If you can sway even a small part of the crowd with your cries of 'democracy', 'freedom', and 'justice'...we may actually have a chance of succeeding in this wild venture!"

As one, they leapt from their couches, milling around Aristogiton as he stood at their center with one arm wrapped tightly about the beaming Harmodius' slender waist. Holding a hand in the air, he waited until their noisy chatter once again fell silent.

"Very well, then..." he asked, the answer already on their lips, "are we in agreement?"

And, just as they had done on that torment-filled evening one week before, each man in his turn reaffirmed his commitment by taking one last sip from Aristogiton's wine cup.

CHAPTER 11

The yearly Panathenaia was the most highly regarded religious festival in Athens, a city already famous throughout the Aegean World for its Eleusinia, Thesmophoria, Apaturia, and Dionysia festivals. Commemorating the birth of the city's patron goddess Athena, the Panathenaia—or 'all-Athenian festival'—was one of the few times women, freed slaves, and even resident foreigners were allowed to join alongside the male citizen celebrants at the public events. The Festival—lasting a week and taking place during the final scorching summer days of the Athenian month of Hekatombaion—included musical contests, athletic games for boys and men of all ages, ritual competitions between the ancient tribal families of the city, and elaborate boat races in the Bay of Salamis. On the final day everyone in the city joined in a great procession, winding its noisy way through the city streets and leading an unprecedented sacrifice of 100 perfect oxen to the goddess' temple high on the Acropolis.

Following Aristogiton's stirring speech and words of caution from the night before, Tylissus reluctantly withdrew his name from the Pyrrhic Dance contest and contented himself with a long final afternoon spent with his beloved Diokles, discreetly watching the athletic games from the sidelines.

Across town, the lambskin shade still drawn tight over Cleon's bedroom window, Nicias roughly shook his lover awake, half-petulantly demanding that the exhausted man perform yet another of the legendary Baobil's Persian tricks upon his love-starved body.

Meanwhile, sitting alone under the ancient olive tree in the deserted court-yard of his large empty townhouse, a subdued Harmodius picked up his reed pen, dipped it in a black jar of vegetable gum ink, and set to work scribbling on one of his precious pieces of Egyptian papyrus. Before the long afternoon was fully spent he'd composed two carefully worded letters, each filled with tem-pered words of regret, sincere longing, and hope for the future—one to be for-warded to his mother, the other to his beloved sister Helena.

His slaves and employees all released into the city to enjoy the closing days of the Panathenaia, Aristogiton sat down at the warehouse office window over-looking the port of Piraeus and carefully framed his own missive. Trusting that Cleisthenes would grasp the almost certainly fatal ramifications of their fool-hardy move against Hippias and Hipparchus, he began by expressing his disap-pointment that neither he nor Harmodius, in all probability, would be alive to share in the fruits of the democracy so ably championed by his old mentor on their recent visit to Crete. After detailing the abuses and crimes of Hipparchus and his co-ruling brother a goodly portion of the letter was spent expressing his hope that Cleisthenes, on his return from exile, would complete the patri-otic work begun by the six young men. Sealing the letter in an oilskin pouch, he carried it to the office of the harbormaster and paid for its speedy dispatch on the next available ship sailing for Crete.

As the blinding summer sun began it's welcome descent in the west, Aris-togiton mounted his horse and, with one last look back at his beloved Thetis rocking gently at anchor next the other ships in the harbor, he turned the ani-mal north along the now nearly deserted road back toward his madly celebrat-ing city.

"You look exhausted, Cleon," Harmodius chuckled as he slid over and made a space for Nicias and his lover on the rickety tavern bench. "I thought you two were going to be spending the entire day resting up in bed?"

Cleon shrugged his shoulders. "Yes, well…that's what I thought, too." Giv-ing his lover a sidelong glare, he smiled wryly. "Unfortunately, the spirit of that to-be-eternally-damned Persian eunuch 'Baobil' kept intruding on my home-spun Greek dreams!" Everyone laughed as Nicias' face colored a rosy crimson red.

Aristogiton held two fingers up to the hovering innkeeper who quickly scut-tled off, returning moments later with a fresh jug and two more clay drinking cups. "Excellent seats for the start of the race, don't you think?" Aristogiton shouted across to Cleon.

Before he could answer, Nicias leaned over and waggled a scolding finger in Aristogiton's face. "But I thought our pious 'Captain' said we weren't supposed to be drinking any wine tonight!"

Harmodius, grinning widely, patted him reassuringly on the shoulder. "Wait until you see how much water he adds to your cup." He rolled his eyes and shook his head. "Why, I'm surprised the god Dionysus himself doesn't leap down off his Olympian throne and strike us all dead for this desecration to the sacred vine!"

"Nonsense!" said Aristogiton. And with that he grabbed the full jug of wine sitting in the middle of the table and, before anyone could stop him, spilled nearly half of the rich red nectar out onto the dirt floor under their feet. "There!" he said. "A generous libation poured to the goodly god of the vine himself...now that should appease the rapacious Dionysus." Grabbing the two empty cups in one hand, he followed this irreverent display by pouring a bare finger full of the expensive wine into each cup and quickly following it with a healthy dose from the water pitcher. Handing one cup over to the petulant Nicias and the other to the fellow's ever-patient Cleon, he smiled rather rue-fully and whispered, "Sorry, men...but seats like these don't come cheap." He nodded over in the direction of their hawkeyed innkeeper. "As long as we keep ordering jugs of his finest...he'll let us stay here and watch the race." With that, he poured another generous dollop onto the already scarlet saturated ground. Raising his voice, he laughed infectiously, "And that's for the warrior maiden herself! The divine Athena Polias...patroness of our fair city!" Shaking the empty jug over his head, he called out, "More of your best here, Innkeeper!" When a third jug was delivered to the crowded table on the rickety balcony overlooking the congested street below, another handful of silver coins quickly exchanged hands. Grinning, Aristogiton leaned back in and resumed his hushed undertone: "If the old fool ever suspects we're nursing these over-priced drinks of his...it'll be back out in the street with the rest of that drunken mob!"

Nicias took a tentative sip from his cup and almost gagged at the watery fla-vor. "The gods be damned...this muck taste no better than pig swill!" The oth-ers whooped as Nicias, shivering at the off-putting taste, twisted his mouth into a snaky-headed gorgon grimace and emptied his cup down his throat.

As the jokes about Aristogiton's proclivity for over watering the wine died away, everyone's attention turned back to the race that was about to begin on the street underneath them. "I don't think I've ever seen quite this large a turn out for the Torch Race before," said Diokles, his arm casually draped around Tylissus' shoulder. "It looks like the crowd is lined up six deep on both sides of the road all the way from the starting line to the finish!"

Tylissus nodded. "It was nearly impossible getting here tonight...almost like trying to wade through a veritable sea of human flesh!" Grinning, he nudged Nicias in the side with an elbow. "And I could swear that somewhere along the way a good-looking stranger had the effrontery to actually pinch me on the bum!"

Diokles shook his head. "I told you, sweetling...that was me!"

"Oh no, my love..." Tylissus gave his head an emphatic shake even as he patted his doting lover on the cheek, "I know *your* pinch! And this definitely belonged to someone else!"

Rolling his eyes to the heavens, Diokles contented himself with a resigned shrug of his shoulders. Taking a shallow drink from his own wine cup, he sighed: "Whatever you say, my love...whatever you say."

"Look!" called out Harmodius, pointing down toward the end of the street where the ancient Altar of Eros stood just outside the Dipylon Gate. "All the torches are gathering together...it must be the runners lining up...I'm sure of it, they're getting ready to start the race!"

Everyone on the crowded second story balcony jumped to their feet, leaning far out over the wobbly railing in hopes of catching a better view. The sun having fully set scarcely an hour before and its sister crescent moon having yet to rise into the cooling summer night sky, the massing torches near the distant gate seemed to burn as one giant beacon in the darkness. Below the balcony—as word of the impending start of the race passed from mouth to mouth—the teeming multitudes fell silent.

A few minutes passed as the jumbled torchlight seemed to straighten itself out into an even line stretching across the width of the street. A moment later, the echoing sound of a lone priestess' voice pierced the night with a joyous cry of "Athena Nike" and the line of torches began to move forward down the street.

The race was on!

*   *   *

While the culmination of each year's Panathenaia came with the Great Procession of the city's entire populace marching and dancing their frenzied way along the Panathenaic Road to the Goddess' temple high on the Acropolis, for the city's numerous gamblers—and that constituted a goodly portion of this same population, both freeman and slave alike—the climax of the festival came the night before with the running of the Torch Race.

A relay competition with four-man teams entered from each of the city's traditional founding tribes, the object was to be the first to cross the finish line on the Acropolis with your torch still alight. Running from the Altar of Eros in the northwest corner of the city, all the way to the Altar of Athena in her ancient wood-columned temple, the ten racing teams had to contend with drunken mobs, overly-enthusiastic opposition cliques, and haranguing gamblers bent on extinguishing the torches of their rival's teams...along with the risk of stumbling and twisting an ankle on the narrow pitch-dark cobblestone lanes and alleys of the old city.

The winning tribe, after using its triumphant torch to re-ignite Athena's sacrificial fire in anticipation of the morning's massed sacrificial offering of 100 consecrated beasts in honor of the goddess' birthday, collected its hard-earned prize of a perfect bull and a purse fattened with several hundred drachmas. Setting off to the Pannychos—the all-night carnival of drinking, dancing and carousing that followed the frenetically paced relay race—the victor's bull was sacrificed and its tender, if hastily cooked flesh distributed to the poor of the city. All through the long night of orgiastic merrymaking, as gloating winners met up with crestfallen losers along the swirling maelstrom of overcrowded streets, hefty wagers were exchanged and winning bets paid off...all in the name of the Goddess' honor.

The street narrowed precipitously as it approached the tavern, forcing the runners to jockey for position as they funneled between the screaming throngs on either side. When one of the runners tripped up in the momentary tussle and went down on one bloody knee nearly extinguishing his torch in a muddy puddle, Diokles had to grab hold of the overly eager Tylissus' belt to keep him from tumbling right over the railing. A moment later the racers passed underneath the tavern balcony, the noise from the crowd swelling to a deafening roar as the runners scrambled for the lead position, only to disappear around a corner with their most vigorous supporters jogging along in their wake.

The race having moved on, the spectators in the street below began thinning out, moving off in their small, noisy groups by any number of circuitous back alley routes toward the finish line high on Acropolis Hill. The over-priced tavern with its prime viewing balcony emptied just quickly as people emptied into the streets, heading off in the same direction in hopes of eventually catching up with the victors and the awarding of the prize bull. Following along in the midst of the churning mob, the six friends kept up their jovial speculations about the ultimate outcome of the evening's heated race until they reached the street that led off to Diokles' house. The once noisome crowd having thinned out to a few drunken stragglers, Diokles and Tylissus were saying their 'farewells' when Harmodius pulled his one-time suitor aside and, holding tightly to his elbow, pressed a small scroll into his unsuspecting hand.

"If you still have feelings for my sister...and I think that you do, my friend..." Harmodius gave his old suitor a most cunning grin, but even that couldn't hide the wistful concern in his eyes, "...if things should go wrong in the morning...if I should die without ever seeing her again..." Seeing the distress in Harmodius' manner, Diokles felt his mouth go dry.

"What I mean to say is that...well...no matter how things turn out for us tomorrow, I'm asking you, Diokles...*please* have a care..." Harmodius abruptly shook his head, his voice growing fierce with resolve "...take no foolish risks, don't needlessly throw your life away." He bit his lower lip, staring shamefacedly down at the ground. "Diokles..." his voice fell to a whisper and he refused to look up, "I *need* for you to survive...for Helena's sake." He curled his fingers around Diokles' hand, wrapping the note even tighter in his fist. "And, if the gods should choose to spare you, I'd be grateful if you'd give her this message from me."

Diokles sputtered a protest, "I can't do that, Harmodius. I've sworn an oath with the others..."

Harmodius, his lips curled in an understanding smile, cut off the dissent with a single finger pressed firmly against Diokles' lips. "You swore an oath to obey your 'Commander'," he pointed with his chin over to where Aristogiton stood waiting with the others. Diokles' eyes followed his, meeting Aristogiton's confident gaze with his own doubts. Wordlessly, his 'commander' responded to the unasked question in Diokles' eyes with a simple nod of his head. "You see..." said Harmodius, "It's also my Aristogiton's wish that, no matter what happens on the morrow, at least one of us should survive." Diokles' frowned, his face clouding over at the perceived shame of continued existence. But before he could launch another protest, Harmodius tightened the grip on his arm, nearly hissing in his embarrassed frustration: "Don't you see, my foolish friend...this is not just about Helena? No matter the outcome, whatever dreams we may have of a free and just Athens must be kept alive! And that's why, if things don't go as planned tomorrow, someone must remain to tell our story…to counter the vicious lies sure to be spread by the avenging Pisistrades." This time when he smiled an unexpected serenity entered Harmodius' eyes as he peered longingly over Diokles' shoulder at his patiently waiting lover. "And of course, that same hero must remain to work at the side of the Archon Cleisthenes when he returns in triumph from his exile." Loosening his grasp on Diokles, he took a step back. "And I…we…we all want that person to be you, Diokles." Staring down at the tiny papyrus roll left behind in Diokles' fist, Harmodius' voice choked up as he whispered: "And for our Helena's sake, my old friend."

Flustered, Diokles stared down at the note burning in his hand as he mumbled a taciturn acquiescence. "Very well, Harmodius…if that is truly your wish." A moment later, his lips tightened in a stubborn line and he couldn't resist adding: "But, rest assured…I *will* discharge my oath-pledged duty tomorrow…" tears glistened in his eyes as his voice softened, "but I pledge to you on my love for your sister…that I will also have a care while I'm about it…and that's all I can promise you." Holding the scroll up, he nodded his head as he carefully slipped it inside the sweat-wrinkled folds of his tunic. "And if by some miracle I survive…the precious Helena will be as a sister to me for the rest of my life. I swear this by all the gods on Olympus!"

Seeking to lighten the sober moment, Harmodius slapped the surprised Diokles rather roughly on the arm and laughed aloud. "A sister?" he cried in mock amazement, "I'd rather thought you might someday take her on as a blushing bride!" And like the sudden passing of a blustery thunderstorm, the tension broke. Diokles, blushing a fearsome red and fidgeting as he rolled his eyes in the air, could only smile shyly as the others joined in the playful banter.

Exchanging kisses on each cheek, Harmodius and Aristogiton sent Diokles and Tylissus on their way home to bed with a final word reminding them to meet again at sunrise near the Dipylon Gates. A few blocks further along, Cleon and Nicias took their own weary leave of Harmodius and Aristogiton.

Continuing on alone through the nearly deserted outlying streets, Harmodius wrapped an arm around Aristogiton's waist and pulled him in close. "Are you tired yet, Beloved?" he asked.

Aristogiton shook his head, "No…not really. Are you?"

"No…not tired," tickling him on the side, Harmodius crossed his eyes in a clownishly lascivious ogle, "…but that's not to say that I couldn't be coaxed into bed!"

Shivering in anticipation, Aristogiton wrapped an arm around his lover's neck and playfully tousled his hair. A few moments later they disappeared around the corner up the silent, dark hill that led to Harmodius' empty house.

❧   ❧   ❧

Some time later, the six conspirators were sleeping dreamlessly in each other's arms, their physical energies largely spent on earlier frenetic embraces heightened by a pervading sense of finality…whilst elsewhere in the city the night-long debauchery of the Pannychos carried on in full swing.

As the chaotic hours passed, the city's more temperate residents retired to their homes for a few hours of much needed sleep before rousing, hung-over and exhausted, to prepare for the morning's Great Procession. Meanwhile, the local rowdies and die-hards continued with their unfettered carousing and drinking, determined to celebrate throughout the long night until golden Apollo came riding forth in his mighty Sun chariot, ushering in the sacred birthday of the city's Patroness.

❧   ❧   ❧

"Here…give me another swig of that…"

A half-full wineskin was passed over to the wobble-legged red head. Snatching it between both hands, he held it high over his head and with mouth stretched wide to catch the warm spray of cheap red wine, Demoritus swallowed down gulp after gulp as his friends watched in amazement. No sooner had he emptied the skin, then he tossed it aside and sank to his knees, vomiting the whole stinking mess back into the gutter.

"Maybe you've had enough, Demoritus," said a half-drunk crony as he pounded ineffectively on his back.

"Enough?" mumbled the handsome young red head even as he weaved from side to side, trying to stand back on his own two feet. "Never enough wine, my friend…never enough!"

"Hey look here!" shouted a fat balding man, his flabby chin resting on a thick stone pillar with the mute head of some bearded god resting benignly on its top. "Look at this one!" He pointed to the erect phallus jutting out and up from the center of the pillar. "It must be over a foot long!"

The others wandered over for a closer look at the impressive herm, leaving poor Demoritus doubled back over and vomiting once again in the gutter.

"Hipparchus has really outdone himself with this one!" quipped the fat drunk as he jokingly fondled the hard stone penis.

"No surprise there," answered a buck-toothed youth as he compulsively brushed at a greasy strand of black hair hanging down in the middle of his face. Pointing to the high wall surrounding the multi-leveled mansion fronted by its imposing edifice of marble columns, he sneered: "Isn't this one of those dandified villas belonging to the Tyrant Hippias?"

That name alone was enough to send a mood-dampening chill through the intoxicated group. Demoritus and his gang of hooligans had each—at one time or another—suffered the remorseless justice of the Co-tyrant's court. The fat man's copulating hands suddenly released their fondling grasp on the stone penis, dropping nervously to his side as the others took an uneasy step back from the oversized herm.

Ten years earlier, Hippias' brother Hipparchus had introduced the first herm to the people of Athens. Meant to imbue good fortune on passing travelers, the first of these stone pillars dedicated to the fleet-footed Hermes were sited at important crossroads and in the central marketplaces. Later, as Hipparchus' architectural fad caught on, 'herms' began sprouting up in front of the palatial homes of Athens' more ostentatious nobility.

Representing the dual nature of the god, the herm began as a squat pediment topped by a bearded 'erastes' bust of the god with a flaccid 'eromenos' penis hanging from the front of the pillar. Soon, larger fully erect organs—hinting at the virility of the herm's owner—supplanted their more modest predecessors. And in time, well-wishers and admirers began a tradition of hanging flowers, wreaths and small tokens of affection from these imposing phalli.

Muscling his way through the drunken pack bunched together in front of Hippias' great herm, Demoritus snatched another wineskin from the hands of the greasy black-haired youth and, holding it to his lips, squirted, swirled and spat the foul vomit taste from his mouth. Taking another deep swallow, he eyed the great stone herm, reaching out and lasciviously running his hand along the moonlit shaft of the nearly foot-long marble penis. "It's not so big…" he said with a crooked smirk on his face. Lifting the wineskin, he guzzled some more before belching loudly and tossing the empty bag back to the buck-toothed youth. Looking thoughtful for a moment, Demoritus stretched his mouth wide and slowly began working his jaw from side to side. His eyes drooping in a reflective haze, he waved a hand in the air and grandly announced: "This is nothing…I've taken bigger ones before!"

With skeptical murmurs of derision ringing in his ears, Demoritus—steadied by the flaccid arm of the fat balding man—grabbed his purse and spilled a pile of silver coins into the palm of his hand. "Very well then. Who'll take my bet?" he cried out.

"Shhh, Demoritus!" whispered the fat man, "Not so loud! You'll wake up the entire neighborhood."

The lanky boy with the stringy black hair raised his thick, fuzzy eyebrows in amazement. Stepping forward on two unsteady legs, he poked Demoritus in the chest. *"You're gonna go down on that monster…on Hippias' giant herm?"*

Demoritus brushed his hand aside with a laugh. "No problem!" he bragged.

"All the way down?" asked one of the others, greedily eyeing the silver in Demoritus' hand.

Demoritus curtly nodded his head, all the while steadying himself on the fat man's arm. Another noisy burp came belching forth and he clutched at his rumbling stomach for a moment. Steadying himself, he threw his head back and proudly confirmed in his wine-soaked, leering voice: "All the way down, my friends! All the way! Either I rub the point of my nose against the base of that damned thing…or all this silver is yours!" He poured the coins back in his purse, shook it in the air so they could all hear the tempting jangle before placing it deferentially on top of Hermes' enigmatic bust.

As bets were quickly swapped to the merry sound of obscenity-laden jokes and taunts, Demoritus managed to work his way through yet another wineskin. Tossing the empty bladder into the air, he whooped and hollered as his supporters encouragingly rubbed his shoulders. One by one they fell silent, watching in amazement as he opened his mouth wider and wider, his jaw nearly reaching the point of dislocation in preparation for this phenomenal swallow. Everyone took a step forward as Demoritus bent over and lovingly wrapped his lips around the tip of the cold stone pudenda, his bleary laughing eyes rolling in feigned ecstasy.

"Mmmm…" he crooned, always a tease for the boys…and ever confident in his sexual prowess.

Before beginning in earnest, he looked over and gave his fat friend a warning scowl. "Don't you dare breath a word of this to my family…especially my damned brother, you hear me?" he snarled, "…or I'll be finished in this city for good!"

Returning to the work at hand, Demoritus rubbed his hands together in anticipation. Taking several deep breaths, he stretched his mouth wide and began his slow, careful ingestion.

One inch…two inches…three…

He stopped for a moment, his eyes closed tight in concentration, willing the roof of his mouth to lift even higher. Breathing noisily through his nose, he gently slid down another half inch…then another…and…

All of a sudden the stone member pressing against the back of his throat triggered his gag reflex. Without any warning, a sour stomach-full of cheap wine and effluvia came shooting straight into his throat, ramming itself up against the great stone plug blocking its out-of-control exit. Reflexively jerking back, his foot stepped in the puddle of wine he'd spit so carelessly on the ground just moments before. Everyone watched in horrified amazement as the wide-eyed Demoritus—his feet slipping helter-skelter out from under him—clutched frantically at the stone shaft for support.

With a sickening crack, the great phallus snapped in two and Demoritus found himself lying in a filth-covered heap on the ground. Dazed by his fall—and with his throat still gagging on a goodly portion of the god's late, but still erect, penis—he turned over on his side and, with increasingly panicked fingers, struggled to remove the cold marble stopper from his mouth. As he forcefully wrenched it free, several broken front teeth came out along with it…all lost on the ground in a final retching rush of vomit.

"*Who's there…who's out there, I say?*" a stern voice called from the front gate of the mansion. "*What is all this? What's going on here?*"

Struggling to his bloody knees as wave after wave of nausea and pain threatened to trounce him back down, the first thing Demoritus noticed with any clarity was that all of his so-called 'friends' had vanished from sight. Reaching out and using the irreparably damaged herm as a crutch, he pulled himself upright and stood for a moment dizzily shaking his head from side to side, a disgusting mix of blood and vomit, broken teeth and stone splattering off in all directions.

A lantern was held up to his face and he had to shield his eyes from the sudden glare. "Who are you?" called out an elderly voice from somewhere behind the lantern. "And what in the name of all the gods have you…" The lantern suddenly swung over in the direction of the shattered herm. "Oh dear me…may the fleet-footed messenger have mercy on us all…what have you done to my master's…"

Before he could finish, Demoritus lashed out with his fist, knocking the old man and his lantern to the ground.

Sobering in an instant and realizing that death would be assured if he remained in Athens to be apprehended on yet another charge of 'sacrilege',

Nicias' delinquent brother took off at a run…stumbling into the sanctuary of the dark night's shadows.

And in his wild, panicked retreat he never heard the aged servant calling out after him: "I know you, boy…I know who you are! Don't think you'll get away from my master so easily! I've seen you in the marketplace…you and that red-headed twin of yours!"

CHAPTER 12

It was still dark when a pregnant young woman pushed her husband roughly awake, telling him that her time had surely come. Groggily lighting every lamp he could lay his hands on, the anxious husband tied the bedroom curtain aside in a vain hope that a breath of fresh air would cool the stifling room. Across the alleyway, a half-blind rooster mistook this unexpected surge of lamplight for the first rays of the morning sun and let out an earsplitting crow. Fortunately for this astigmatic bird, most of its nearby neighbors were lost in deep, wine-sodden sleep and never heard his ill-timed wakeup call. A scant two doors away from the laboring woman's house however, this screeching cock-a-doo-dle-do did awaken one boy with a sudden start.

Feeling the breath rush out of him in a blind panic, Nicias' sat up in bed, his befuddled mind clutching at the elusive thought that had been nagging his restless dreams ever since drifting off to sleep hours before in the arms of his beloved Cleon.

"My armor...my sword...I...I forgot to...I left them at...oh gods, I'll never make it on time!"

Somehow, in all the excitement of the previous night's Torch Race and the confusion of the noisy celebrations that followed, he'd neglected to retrieve his armor and sword from the chest in his bedroom back home. With a muffled sigh of regret, he edged away from the tempting warmth of Cleon's snoring body, quietly slipping off the bed and creeping on tiptoe across the room to the covered window. Lifting the corner of the shade, he squinted his eyes, fully expecting to be blinded by the first light of dawn. To his amazement, he saw that the star-filled sky was still dark with night. Feeling an overwhelming sense of relief, he looked up at the setting moon and whispered a silent prayer of thanks to Cleon's neighbor and his shortsighted rooster.

Now fully awake, he stole about the room collecting scattered bits of clothing together before leaning over Cleon and gently touching his shoulder.

"Huh...what...who is it?" Cleon, still more than half asleep, mumbled up at the shadowy face hanging over him. "Is it already time to get up...time to go?"

Nicias smiled and shook his head. "No, my love. It's not yet dawn. Foolish me...I forgot my armor...my sword. I'm going home now to fetch them...I promise I'll be back here long before it's time to leave for the Gates."

"Oh...oh, alright then..." Cleon settled his head back down on the pillow and then started to raise it up again. "Do you want me to come along with..."

"No, no, no..." Nicias gently pushed his shoulders back down onto the pillow, "...it's early yet. You stay here, keep the bed warm, and get some more sleep. I'll be back before long."

In the darkness, Nicias thought he saw Cleon nod his head. A moment later, to the sound of his gentle snores, Nicias quietly backed out of the room. Dressing himself in the hallway, he lit a torch in the kitchen and set out across town to retrieve his arms.

❈   ❈   ❈

Even thought the streets were empty and Nicias made quick time on his way, the first pinkish hint of dawn was already streaking the eastern horizon when Nicias finally arrived at the family home. Expecting to find the hungover remnants of Demoritus and his drunken band of hooligans scattered about the place, he was surprised to find the entire house vacant. "Well, that's just fine," he muttered to himself, "they never made it home last night...probably sleeping it off in a gutter some place." And with that he dismissed them from his mind. Fetching a taper from the kitchen, he ran back to his bedroom at the rear of the house and unlocked the door (he always kept everything locked these days...no telling what mischief that fool of a brother and his good-for-nothing friends would get into). He was just lighting the little lamp in the niche over his clothes chest when a furious pounding began at the front door.

Blowing out the taper and tossing it in the recess next to the other discarded ones, he snatched up the lamp and scurried all the way back to the front of the house, the whole time angrily cursing his wayward brother. When he opened the door, he was surprised to see that it wasn't Demoritus after all...but a wizened, old man staring back at him with flinty eyes and a bright red, swollen bruise on his cheek.

Pointing a bent finger right in Nicias' face, the old man cackled: "That's him all right...that's the one!"

And before Nicias could utter a single word in protest, several guards with drawn swords stepped forward, snatched him from the open doorway and dragged him roughly out into the street. The sour-breathed old man, jigging about at his side, poked him in the ribcage with a sharp, bony fingertip as he cackled: "Oh, my little fire-haired devil, what a lucky boy you are today...*you have a date with my lord Hippias!*" He clucked his tongue and then spat in the gutter.

Overwhelmed by a rush of panic, Nicias' desperate eyes darted about the street looking for a friendly face. Finally spying one of his nervous neighbors peeking out at the ruckus from a crack in his doorway, he opened his mouth to call out for help but, as soon as their eyes met, the man disappeared back inside, slamming his door behind him and leaving the confused Nicias alone with his mounting fears.

"Bind him tight!" the old man hooted, "He's a tricky one, he is!"

Cutting off any futile cries of innocence with a torn linen gag, the guards stripped Nicias naked, his hands were quickly bound together in front of him and his feet hobbled with a coarse braided rope. As he was led stumbling away up the deserted street, the old man pranced about at his side, singing out: "You're a naughty one...you've gone and made our Co-tyrant very angry this morning...and on the day of the Sacred Procession!" He shook his head at the sacrilege. "Yes, yes, yes..." he giggled, "my Lord Hippias will want a word with you before this day is over, my boy...with you and all your...associates!" Savoring the sweet taste of his vengeance, he squealed with delight, pinching Nicias' cheek until he drew blood.

Lost in confusion and doing his best to ignore the old man's vicious taunts, Nicias struggled to keep from tripping over his own feet...and all the while, a single unnerving thought kept running through his desolate mind.

"Our plan...they've discovered our plan to overthrow the Pisistrades. Oh gods, can it be...has our nascent conspiracy been discovered? Oh, my Cleon, my Cleon...flee from here, my love...flee!"

❧   ❧   ❧

Even as the fettered Nicias was being hauled through the empty streets of Athens to spend a long, hot day lost in oblivious despair in a lonely, rat infested cell of the guardhouse deep under Hippias' palace, his compatriots—ignorant of this unfortunate turn of events—were coming awake to begin their careful preparations for the day's ordeal.

❧   ❧   ❧

At Diokles' house Tylissus was standing in front of a wide, polished bronze mirror admiring the reflection of his new silver-embossed breastplate—a surprise gift from his ever-solicitous erastes. Turning around, he found the doting Diokles holding out a new leather-lined helmet complete with ornate, hinged cheek guards and a long, dyed-red, horsetail plume sweeping down off the crest.

❧   ❧   ❧

Back at the house two doors down from the pregnant woman (who—after a blessedly short confinement—had delivered a healthy, squalling boy-child on this, the Goddess' own birthday) Cleon waited, sitting naked on the edge of his bed, methodically sharpening his sword with a well-worn whetstone. The curtain was pulled all the way back from the window now and he watched with a growing sense of unease as the morning sun came edging up over the eastern hills. Shaking his head, he stood up and tossed the sharpened sword back on the bed. Heaving a sigh of frustration, he slowly set about his morning toilet, any hope that Nicias would've returned in time for one last foray into Baobil's titillating realm of earthly intimacy—dashed.

Now, it looked as if they would barely have enough time for a quick kiss and a cuddle before rushing off to the Dipylon in time to meet up with the others. A kiss and a cuddle…

If only that damned imp gets his ripe little ass back here…and soon.

❧   ❧   ❧

"Do you remember this?" Harmodius gazed thoughtfully at his father's old, dented war helmet before holding it out to Aristogiton. Knotting the laces on the metal greaves that molded exactly to the musculature of his legs, the gentle-faced warrior looked up, took the helmet from his lover, and sat cradling it in his hands. Slowly, a nostalgic smile spread across his face. With a crook of his finger he signaled for Harmodius to bend his head forward. Standing, Aristogiton pulled the metal chin guards wide and slipped the well-worn bronze helm down over the long black curling locks of his lover's hair.

When Harmodius started to right himself, Aristogiton placed a restraining hand on his shoulder.

"Whoa there…hold still my brave Achilles," he whispered in his ear. Harmodius' eyes responded with a devotion-charged glint as he recalled that happy day in the vinyard at Araphen all those many years ago.

"I'd say it's a much better fit now, Harmodius." Aristogiton ruffled the plume with the palm of his hand. "You're no longer the undersized Patroclus playing at soldier in his father's borrowed armor," his voice swelled with pride. "You stand before me, the very image of the brave Achilles…a true warrior with the heroic heart and stature of the invincible Myrmidon overlord." With a practiced hand, he tucked a few stray locks of hair under the helmet's leather lining before leaning forward and kissing his lover full on the lips.

As they finished helping each other into their last few pieces of freshly cleaned and polished armor, Harmodius' thoughts returned again to his happy childhood years spent in the countryside…the vine covered fields and lush olive groves of his family's homestead. With a melancholy pang in his heart he realized just how much he'd cherished those precious years growing up along the sapphire blue coast of the sparkling Gulf of Petalion. He closed his eyes for a moment, summoning forth a well-remembered picture of the rustic, well-stocked dinner table with his proud father presiding at one end and his delicately beautiful mother patiently beaming at him from the other. Sitting on the bench opposite him, his elfin-eyed younger sister glowed with the unsophisticated energy of childhood, her mischievous expression hinting at trouble ahead as she kicked his shins under the table.

"Ah, Helena…dearest Helena…"

And with those unspoken words still ringing in his ears, the face of this roguishly smiling nymph-child suddenly morphed into the tear-streaked young woman whose tattered reputation had been laid waste by his sadistic antagonist...the brute Hipparchus.

Across the room, Aristogiton turned from the mirror, took his helmet off his head and, with a soldier's grace, swung it up under his arm. As he did so, he glanced over and noticed that the color had drained from his lover's face. The boy's steely eyes seemed to be locked in some far-off contemplation as his whitening knuckles gripped the pommel on his sword with an ever-increasing strength. Calmly stepping up beside him, Aristogiton reached around and lovingly wrapped his hand over Harmodius', waiting patiently as the natural color returned to his face and the anguished grip on his sword relaxed. Leaning forward, the loyal erastes whispered in his wounded eromenos' ear:

"That's right, my love, call him to your mind...evoke the hated image of your enemy Hipparchus...the monster of your nightmares. Think of him now and use that hatred to fortify your resolve. For one way or another...today will see an end to it." He stepped around and stood facing Harmodius. Holding his own sword out, he rested it for a moment in his lover's hand, kissing the leather wrapped hilt as he did.

"This I, your faithful Aristogiton, swear to you!"

❧   ❧   ❧

Something felt wrong about the day...

The participants in the Panathenaic Procession of 514 BC looked forward with growing trepidation to the coming parade as they gathered near the Dipylon Gate. The sun had been visible above the horizon for more than an hour and already the late summer heat had grown oppressive to the fidgeting crowd. Suffering from wine-induced hangovers, short on much needed sleep after a week of festivities, and already sweating uncomfortably in their suits of heavy plate armor and elaborate religious costumes, the celebrants waited impatiently for someone in authority to line them up and start them on their way to the Acropolis.

In past years the Co-tyrant Hipparchus—as chief organizer of the event—had always assumed responsibility for this onerous task. But for some reason, on this sweltering morning it was his brother, a grim-faced Hippias, who finally arrived more than an hour late to get things moving. Shouting bluntly worded instructions to the loutish soldiers in his bodyguard; he soon had the lengthy procession lining up in their predetermined order.

At the lead, as always, came the four chosen maidens carrying between them the newly woven *peplos* meant to adorn the ancient wooden statue of Athena Polias. Following them in a place of special honor came the many priestesses who'd dedicated their lives to serving in Athena's numerous temples. Next in line came the noblewomen of Athens, their arms laden with flowers, freshly baked breads, and small ceramic figurines of the goddess, all to be left as name day gifts on the temple steps.

With a suitable gap in between, 100 flawless oxen—the sacrifice of choice for Athens' fearsome war goddess—led off the next section of the procession. The unfortunate groups that immediately followed—the city's metics wearing their finest purple robes and carrying tiny silver trays covered with sticky cakes and fresh honeycombs in honor of their civic hosts, and a gently swaying line of aulos and kithara playing musicians—would be spending their morning dodging the great piles of ox excrement.

It was a firm belief in Athens that 'beauty accompanies every age' so, following behind the tinkling strains of the musicians, came a small cluster of handsome men in their senior years, each carrying an olive shoot representing their longevity.

Now it was time for the great formal masses of Athenian citizenry to march in their dignified but noisy groups. Mighty four-horse chariots of the cavalry led them off, their hooves clattering loudly on the cobblestone pavement; next came the city's most talented craftswomen, a place of honor kept at the center for the gifted weavers of Athena's peplos. Behind the craftswomen, in two great lines, marched the soldiers of the city's well-drilled infantry. And bringing up the rear of the parade came the already well-rewarded victors of Athena's games, each wearing a ceremonial olive wreath on his head.

And this was the end of the official procession.

On cooler festival days, the ordinary citizens of the lower classes—not to be left out—would have gathered together in their own tribal groupings and followed behind in an informal procession of their own. But on this particular day, with the shimmering heat already rising off the streets, most of the Athenian hoi polloi chose to stay coolly sequestered behind their thick, mud-daubed walls.

❧   ❧   ❧

"Look…he's leaving," said Aristogiton.

Four heads turned in unison and watched as Tyrant Hippias—the earlier confusion of crowd control remedied by his brutish bodyguard—remounted his horse and cantered off in the direction of the Acropolis. "Why not Hipparchus…" Aristogiton asked uneasily, "…and why so late a start to the procession?" He looked nervously over the heads of the other soldiers.

"Wherever he is, we'll meet up with him…and soon enough," murmured Harmodius as the anxious boy stood twisting his fingers around the hilt of his sword.

"And what in Hades happened to Cleon and Nicias?" asked Diokles, wiping the sweat from his helmeted brow with the back of his hand.

"Listen to that…can you hear it? The musicians…they're starting to play." Tylissus craned on his toes, trying his best to peer over the helmeted heads of the massed infantrymen crowding around on all sides. "Damn…the infantry will be moving forward soon…Cleon and Nicias better get here soon or we'll have to carry on without them."

Aristogiton uneasily rubbed his hands together as he continued to scan the crowd for their two missing friends. "What could have happened to them?" he nervously asked himself. "Where are they? Why are they so late? Without Cleon and Nicias, we'll be too few…we'll never have a chance to get close enough to the Co-tyrants." Just then Diokles tapped him on the shoulder and Aristogiton turned around to see Cleon, looking quite out of breath as he strained on tiptoe over the milling crowd, trying to recognize a familiar face. Waving his arms in the air, Aristogiton caught his attention and was surprised when, instead of plunging on through the multitude to join up with them, Cleon remained standing where he was, anxiously signaling for them to leave their places in the processional lineup and join him on the fringe.

Feeling their trepidation grow with each step, Aristogiton, Harmodius, Diokles and Tylissus—ignoring the grunts and protests of their crowded fellows-muscled their way through the sour-smelling troop. Gesturing with his eyes, Cleon pointed off in the direction of a deserted alley at the opposite end of the teeming square. When Aristogiton acknowledged him with the slightest nod of his head Cleon turned away, casually strolling across the street before slipping from sight. A few moments later, the others joined him in the tight but blessedly shady confines of the deserted alleyway. With everyone moving to speak at the same time, Aristogiton held his hand up for silence. Holding a finger over his lips, he quickly surveyed the surroundings, making sure that all nearby doors and windows were bolted up tight for the holiday. Reassured that they wouldn't be overheard, he turned to Cleon and, resting his hands firmly on his shoulders, asked the question that was preying upon all their minds: "Tell us, Cleon…what's happened? Why are you so late and why isn't Nicias with you?"

Cleon's usually placid eyes dissolved in a flood of tears as he quickly told the others what had happened when Nicias didn't return from retrieving his sword.

"I think he said he'd forgotten his sword…I don't know…I was barely awake. Anyway, it was still dark outside when he left my house to go home and fetch it…that and his armor…" Cleon looked miserable, "at least, well…I *think* that's what he told me. I was still half asleep." Cleon stared down at the ground for a moment before continuing. "When I woke up a bit later and saw that he still wasn't back yet…well, I waited for him as long as I dared." He shook his head in dismay. "When he didn't return I realized that something must have gone terribly wrong. Knowing that you'd all be here waiting for us, I finally grabbed my armor and ran as fast as I could all the way across town to Nicias' house."

"Did you find him there? Is he all right…had he fallen ill?" asked Tylissus with a quaver in his voice. "Was Nicias there, Cleon?"

The distraught man shook his head. "No…no one was there. The house was empty. I banged on the door and then stood in the middle of the street calling out his name…but no one ever came out…nothing."

"Nothing?" repeated Diokles.

Cleon shook his head. "Nothing. That is, until a neighbor across the way peeked out of his door and told me to be quiet…that my shouts were waking up the entire street." For a moment he fretfully chewed on his lower lip, his face reddening in shame as he stared at each of them one by one. Finally, drawing in a deep breath he told them what the neighbor had added before disappearing behind his locked door:

"Then the little weasel said something about Nicias having gone off to see Hippias…"

"*Hippias?*" Everyone was suddenly talking at once. Aristogiton's grip on Cleon's shoulders tightened. "Gone off to see Hippias!" he cried. Fighting to regain control, he loosed his hands and forced himself to take a step back. "Tell me, Cleon…tell me now…this nosy neighbor…what were his exact words?"

Cleon rubbed his tear-stained eyes with the palms of his hands. "His exact words?" He shook his head. "They are seared on my brain like a red-hot poker on flesh." Licking his cracked lips, he rocked back unsteadily on his feet before repeating the neighbor's fateful taunt: "He told me, 'You'd best forget your pretty boy, he's found someone else…some old man came here from the palace and escorted him off on a *date* with the Lord Hippias'" Cleon could still see the way the crude man rolled his eyes, licking his lips and leering at him before disappearing behind his door.

Aristogiton grabbed him by the arm and shook him until he had Cleon's attention. "What do you mean, 'a date with Hippias'…I don't understand. Was he a prisoner or did he go willingly? Has something happened between you two?"

Cleon lamely shrugged his shoulders. "I don't know. I…I don't think so. Everything was fine last night." He blushed at the memory of their energetic lovemaking. "I was so taken aback by what the neighbor said, that all I could think of was to come straightaway here to you."

Aristogiton released him and stared down at the ground for a long moment, the wheels in his head spinning furiously as they sought to fathom this unsettling turn of events.

It was Tylissus who finally spoke up. Braving the ridicule of his friends and the wrath of Cleon, he whispered the certain question upon which all their lives turned. "Do you think he's betrayed us?"

Still gazing at the ground, Aristogiton shook his head. "I can't believe that…" he said, "at least, I hope not." Looking up, he shrugged his shoulders in frustration. "Unfortunately, right now there's no time to find out what really happened to Nicias…and what this might mean for our plan."

Biting his lip he turned to Harmodius who'd remained uncharacteristically silent throughout the entire exchange. "Well, my love…and what is your opinion of all this? What do you think we should do now?"

Harmodius sighed, smiling sadly as he took silent note of the uncertainty in Tylissus' eyes and the increasing desperation with which the younger man clung to Diokles' hand. Without any hesitation, an answer came readily to his lips. "Nothing…" he said. "We should do nothing today." He slowly shook his head. "Without knowing if our secret's been broached…and without our full complement—as few as that may be—our position is too weak to harbor realistic hopes of starting any kind of uprising today." Raising an eyebrow to his attentive Aristogiton, he admitted with a dejected shake of his head: "I think we should call it off…at least for the time being."

Aristogiton frowned. "Call it off? Are you sure, my love?"

Even as Harmodius nodded his head for the benefit of the others, his astute *erastes*—recalling the conviction of his lover's earlier distraction—could plainly read the hidden thought behind his words.

"But what of Nicias?" asked Diokles, "What if he *has* gone over to Hippias?"

Cleon, his hand instinctively reaching for the hilt of his sword, cut him short. "That's not possible, I tell you! Nicias would never betray us...never!"

Aristogiton placed a restraining hand on his arm. "Take no offense, good friend...I'm sure you're right. We all know that dear Nicias would never betray us." He rubbed his chin in thought for a moment. "If, however, the Co-tyrant has somehow gleaned word of our plot...if this is why he had Nicias brought to his palace this morning..." his frown deepened "...well then, I must agree with Harmodius. It would be a foolhardy waste of lives to attempt anything further today." Taking in a deep breath, he pushed his helmet back off his forehead and wiped at his brow. "And as long as this cloud of uncertainty remains hanging overhead, I fear the city is no longer a safe place for us to remain. For the time being at least, we should make ourselves scarce...retreat to the temporary anonymity of the countryside." Before anyone could protest, Aristogiton turned to Harmodius and, acknowledging his deceit with a slight lifting of his own brow, continued Harmodius' charade. "Harmodius and I will leave at once to join his family on their farm at Araphen." Turning, he stared at Diokles, waiting for him to speak up next.

Confused and somewhat flustered by this abrupt change in plans, Diokles looked to Tylissus and felt relieved when his lover piped in with: "I think it would be best if Diokles and I hire horses and go west to Megara. My mother's sister has been widowed for many years now and she takes in the occasional boarder to keep her company. She'll happily put up with us for a few weeks."

"And what about you, Cleon? Will you also leave the city?" asked Aristogiton, already painfully certain of his answer.

Cleon, feeling his jaw stiffen, brusquely shook his head. "I won't go anywhere until I know for sure what's happened to Nicias." When the others sought to change his mind he waved them off. "And don't any of you go offering to stay behind with me either. If it's true that the little fool *has* betrayed us, I won't have anyone else's blood on my hands.

Squeezing the faithful man's shoulder, Aristogiton acknowledged his dilemma with a shake of his head. "Very well then, my good friend..."

Turning back to the others, he tugged on his cheek plates, slipping the heavy helmet from his head, all the while keeping his voice low. "When you get to wherever you're going, send word to us at Araphen. Once things have settled down in the city and this business with Nicias has been cleared up, we'll arrange to meet back here in Athens and finish this..." his always-genial smile couldn't diminish the snake-like coil in his menacing eyes "...this matter of the black-souled Pisistrades."

Pointing back the way they'd come, their reluctant captain issued his final orders. "We should separate now. Diokles, you and Tylissus take the alley and make your way from the Dipylon square..." he waved off in the opposite direction, "Harmodius and I will go this way." He looked Cleon squarely in the eyes. "My friend, wait here until we're all well away before returning to your home." He patted him on the arm. "And have a care, old man...don't go rushing off to Hippias' villa looking for trouble! After all, this may be nothing more than a simple mistake. Give the good Nicias a chance to explain."

Feeling a rush of gratitude for Aristogiton's bid of confidence, Cleon smiled tightly as he grasped him by the arms and grimly nodded his head.

For a moment they all stood staring at one another and then each man in his turn took the other's hand in his and squeezed it with a heartfelt affection. Their final words spoken, a moment later Cleon found himself standing alone, watching in thoughtful silence as Diokles and Tylissus turned one way, and Harmodius and Aristogiton the other, each pair jogging quietly off in their opposite directions.

❦   ❦   ❦

"We're not really going to Araphen, are we?"

Harmodius smiled and shook his head. "Well, no...I'm not," he answered, meticulously avoiding the bemused look in his lover's eyes even as he peeked back over his shoulder to make sure that no one was following them. With most of the city marching in the Panathenaic procession, the morning streets were largely empty as they hurried around the corner that brought them to the very edge of the Agora. Tilting his head in thought, he pointed across the eerily empty town square to the wide, tree-lined lane that wound its way up the steep side of Areopagus Hill. Near the top, brooding over the Agora like some garbage-fattened crow, sat the Co-tyrant Hipparchus' well-appointed villa. "Plan or no plan...I have unfinished business to take care of." He searched his lover's eyes for understanding. "And you know as well as I...that it can't be put off any longer." He took hold of Aristogiton's hand and smiled hopefully. "Of course, I'd feel a good sight better doing what I have to do...if I knew that someone was left to look out after my mother and sister."

"Ha!" Grinning back at him, Aristogiton grabbed him by the arm and pulled him in tight. "Not on your life, you little rascal! You've already set up your 'old beau' Diokles for that lucky job!" When Harmodius didn't react to this good-humored retort, Aristogiton found himself chewing nervously on the edge of his lip. Looking away, he silently cursed the day's ill fortune. Turning back, he stared deeply into his lover's eyes, insisting in a heady whisper:

"Don't think for one moment that I'm leaving you to face him all alone."

There was an awkward silence as each man pondered the finality of destiny and the looming certainty of death.

And then, his lips curling up in a sunny smile that filled his eyes with love, Harmodius reached over and gave the hand still clutching his arm a reassuring squeeze. "It was just a passing thought, my steadfast one. Here in my heart..." he tapped his chest "...I never doubted that when this moment came, you would be anyplace but at my side."

Aristogiton pushed him up against the wall of a building with an urgency that surprised them both, kissing him with a full on passion that curled his toes and sent a dizzying warmth all the way down to the very bottom of his gut. The two soul mates lingered over these precious moments, each staring deeply into the other's eyes, memorizing every inch...every cherished feature on the other's face, until finally Aristogiton released him and slowly backed away.

Reaching out to gently slide his fingers down the smooth hollow of his cheek, Harmodius sighed. "I must confess my great relief...at not having to sail the black River Styx alone."

Aristogiton, carefully squaring the helmet he'd knocked back off Harmodius' forehead in the heat of the moment, laughingly saluted him. "One very experienced sailor...at your service." Righting his own helmet, he drew out his sword—staring hard at the burnished blade as it dazzled in the morning light—before turning toward the Agora and, in a voice filled with bravado, pointed the way. "And now, my sweet Harmodius...I believe we have a date with Hades?"

As he was about to step out into the great quadrangle that housed Athens' central marketplace and many of her most important civic buildings, Harmodius suddenly grabbed him by the arm and lurched him back into the shadows.

"Look over there..." he hissed in his ear "...by all the gods, is that Hipparchus?"

Aristogiton felt his heart skip a beat. "Great Zeus on Olympus," he whispered back "he's stopping in to take a piss!"

❋   ❋   ❋

A fat fly buzzed around the snoring head for several moments before settling hungrily near the corner of the sleeping man's grape-stained lips. It had
just rubbed its two front legs together in greedy anticipation of the meal to
come when a sweaty hand reached up and swatted it away.

With a groggy groan, Hipparchus sat up in bed.

The moment he opened his sleep-encrusted eyes, even though the bedroom
was still plunged in darkness, it felt as though a thousand daggers had suddenly plunged into his throbbing brain. As he waited for his aching eyes to
adjust to the warm, stuffy darkness, he reached out for a pitcher always kept
close at hand next to his bed. Almost knocking it to the floor, he grabbed it
with shaky fingers, fumbling for a moment before finally holding it safe in his
two hands. Bringing it to his lips, he tilted the pitcher back and sighed with
delight when cool, clear water—not more warm, rancid wine (the thought of
which nearly sent his churning stomach into convulsions)—dribbled down his
parched throat.

Setting the pitcher in his lap, for a long moment he savored the eerie silence
of the night. "It must still be quite early," he pondered to himself as he torpidly
looked about the room.

With the exception of a naked, still unconscious form lying on the mattress
next to him, the room was empty. He nudged the sleeping boy with his elbow
and wasn't too surprised when he got no response. On closer inspection, he
could just make out several thick, red welts rising in angry stripes across the
boy's freshly whipped backside. Grunting his indifference, Hipparchus threw
the soiled sheets back and, with a laborious sigh, rose to his unsteady feet.
Picking up the broken birch switch that, in the evening's tussle had fallen to the
floor, he tossed it back on the bed.

Reaching over for the empty chamber pot, he suddenly noticed a narrow
band of light creeping out from under the floor length window coverings. Any
thought of relieving himself fled with a sickening panic as he stumbled across
the room and pushed back the heavy purple drapes. As the bright morning
sunlight came flooding into the room, Hipparchus thought he would faint
dead away. "Damn the gods, damn them all…it's already daybreak!" His hysterical words came choking out in a garbled scream. Shielding his bloodshot
eyes from the blinding light, he tried to peer out the window, desperate for
some estimation of the lateness of the morning.

"My brother will have my hide for this!" he mumbled to himself as he scrambled about the room looking for some kind of wrap to throw around his filthy, sweat-covered body. "Why didn't anyone come and wake me?" his voice rose to match his growing anger even as he located a discarded chiton on the floor and yanked it over his head. Several sizes too small, it ripped wide open at the side. "The boy's..." he thought with a chagrin that turned to fury a moment later. "Damn them all! I'll hang 'em up by their thumbs, that's what I'll do...and then I'll whip each of them to within an inch of their useless lives!" He was growling as he kicked open the door and stumbled out into the silent, empty hallway.

The second floor seemed to be deserted...no servants, no bodyguards...no one at all.

He ran about examining room after room, calling out in an ever-growing panic for someone...anyone...to come and attend him. Reaching the stairs, he almost tripped headlong over his own feet, frantically clutching at the polished marble railing as he scrambled down the wide stone steps to the first floor of his strangely silent villa.

With mixed feelings of relief and annoyance, he stumbled over the prone body of a sleeping sentry seemingly lost in dreams as he cuddled up to the cool, marble tread of the bottom step.

"Wake up, you fool!" He gave the soldier a nasty kick in the side. Still half asleep, the man pressed closer against his cool marble pacifier, responding with a grunt as he tried to shoo Hipparchus away. The Co-tyrant, in an absolute fury, responded by kicking him again and again until he finally had the bleary-eyed fellow's full attention. "Where are the servants...my bodyguard?" he screeched, slapping him hard across each cheek as he grabbed him by the collar and shouted in his face: "Answer me now! Where is everyone else?"

When the still half-drunken soldier shrugged his shoulders and insolently suggested that they were probably sleeping it off somewhere else in the house, the enraged co-tyrant punched him in the face, his heavy onyx ring drawing blood from the stunned man's cheek.

Ordering the cowed soldier to roust the rest of his lazy troop and get them ready to march, he pushed him out of the way, screaming: "You have exactly five minutes to pull yourselves together or I'll have your head along with all the others skewered on a fish platter!" With that, he clambered back up the stairs to clean and dress himself, muttering all the way about how 'things are damn well going to change around here'.

When he came hustling back down the stairs—his face freshly scrubbed, his hair neatly combed, and the finest Cretan embroidered himation draped rather chaotically over a wrinkled but clean white chiton—he narrowed his eyes in disgust at seeing only ten rather bedraggled soldiers standing in a haphazard formation at the front door.

"Ten?" he snarled at the soldier who'd already experienced his nasty temper at the foot of the stairs. "Ten men? That was all you could find in the entire house?" Sober and awake, the poor man quailed, deferentially lowering his eyes to the floor…sure that *any* response would bring about another painful beating.

"Never mind now, I'll deal with the others later!" Hipparchus pulled open the great bronze studded, oak front door and led his troop out into the glaring light of day. "Straight away now…to the Acropolis!"

With that he was off—half running, half walking—out through his unguarded front gate and on down the dusty road toward the city's agora…his sadly depleted bodyguard jogging valiantly along behind him, doing their loyal best to keep up with the still fuming Co-tyrant.

When they reached the deserted Agora, two thoughts met at once in Hipparchus' aching brain. The city's main square was still empty which could only mean that the Panathenaia ('thank the gods'…) hadn't passed through yet.

And damn his haste…why hadn't he used that chamber pot when he had the chance? He still had to pee!

Spying the four low walls of the Leokoreion—the modest sanctuary in front of the Agora's public well that for many years now had been used (rather sacrilegiously) as a latrine by passing travelers—he couldn't resist the temptation. Halting his troop with a brusque hand flung in the air, he told his men to stand at ease while he took care of 'business'.

✿   ✿   ✿

Harmodius couldn't believe his eyes.

Or their good fortune…

When Aristogiton's carefully thought out plan to provoke a rebellion against the Pisistrade oppressors had collapsed under the weight of Nicias' sudden disappearance, Harmodius' disappointment had hit him like a punch in the gut. And it came as no surprise when, moments later, an overpowering desire for personal revenge against his foul defiler had returned even stronger than before. Knowing that Aristogiton would understand this unappeasable need for score settling, Harmodius shrewdly colluded with his lover to relieve their friends of any suicidal sense of obligation…sending them off to hoped-for-sanctuary in the countryside.

As for dealing with Hipparchus…

Harmodius had no real plan other than to lie in wait at the Co-tyrant's villa until later that evening when the vile blackguard returned home from the day's Panathenaic festivities. With any luck it would be dark, he and his troop would arrive home 'the worse for wear' and, with surprise (and the trusty Aristogiton) on his side, one of them might just manage a successful sword thrust to end Hipparchus' despicable life.

That is…before being slain by his erstwhile protectors.

At least, that *was* his plan…until Hermes, the ever-wily god of 'good fortune', chose to smile on them.

❦   ❦   ❦

"If we can just get past those few guards, we can take him down like the dog he is in that cesspit, the Leokoreion…and a more appropriate end for the bastard I can't imagine!" he whispered ecstatically in Aristogiton's ear.

"Yes…but we still have to think of a way to get past those guards…and quickly, too!"

"Why don't you leave that…to me!"

The voice behind them caused both men to jump in surprise. With a dry chuckle Cleon stepped in front of them, his sword already drawn and ready. Before they could utter a single word, Cleon took the sharp edge of his blade and sliced a long, bloody gash in the fleshy part of his own right thigh. Throwing his helmet and the sword to the ground, he rubbed his hand through the blood and then smeared it across his face. Grabbing hold of Aristogiton's arm, he smiled through his painful grimace. "Be ready, Captain…you won't have much time!"

Aristogiton squeezed his hand knowing this would be the last time their eyes would meet in the world of the living. "I didn't have you fooled for one moment did I, you old goat?" he asked, a crooked smile beaming from his own flushed and ready face.

Cleon spit on the ground, grinned and shook his head. "No time for words now…" he said as he pushed himself off Aristogiton's arm and went stumbling out into the Agora. Keeping close to the shuttered-up shops that bordered the vast public square, Cleon removed himself as far away from Harmodius and

Aristogiton's alleyway as he dared before raising his bloodied hands into the air and screaming out in a loud, croaking voice, "Help me! Help me! Murderous thieves have stolen my purse. They stabbed me…and robbed me…oh, gods…I've been robbed!" Waving his arms about in the air, he hobbled a few steps forward out across the dusty open space and straight towards Hipparchus' astonished bodyguard. As soon as he saw them begin to break ranks and move in his direction, he swung himself around in a vividly theatrical circle—catching Aristogiton's eye one final time as he did—before collapsing to the ground in the semblance of a dead faint.

The acrid urine smell bleaching up from the yellow stained walls of the airless enclosure was enough to make one gag. Even so, Hipparchus hiked up his chiton with one hand, held his nose with the other, and set about adding his own mark to the wall. The sour stream had just begun to puddle in the dirt at his feet when he thought he heard the sounds of shouting coming from outside. Not enough of a disturbance for his bladder to forgo its much-needed release, he shut his mind to the distraction, confident in his bodyguard's ability to deal with whatever situation might arise. With a satisfied sigh, he closed his eyes and leaned up against the wall, savoring his too long neglected 'call of nature'.

The cold tickle of steel pressing against his exposed throat abruptly brought Hipparchus from this piddling reverie. Someone grabbed him roughly by the hair and yanked his head back. Opening his eyes wide, he found himself staring into a face that, for a fleeting moment, he had trouble placing.

And then it came to him…

"Harmodius…"

As he spoke the name all color drained from his face.

The pitiless assassin stared unsmilingly into Hipparchus' fearful eyes, his vile malefactor at last helpless before him. A thousand words came to Harmodius' lips, each demanding to be spoken—curses and revilements, condemnations and profanities, harsh chastisements and clever rebukes. But with the painful awareness that even now brave Cleon was most likely sacrificing his life for these few precious moments, he said only:

"This, for my sister…"

And with that, he pulled back and drove the full length of his deadly sword blade straight into the Co-tyrant's belly. Screaming like a woman, Hipparchus' pupils dilated with shock as his perforated body—kept upright by Aristogiton's pitiless hand holding tightly to his hair—attempted to sag at the knees.

"And this for me…"

Harmodius twisted the hilt of his sword and, seizing it with both hands, wrenched it straight up slicing brutally through Hipparchus' ropy intestines which came spilling out in a steaming heap—spoiling the elegant Cretan embroidery on his fine himation—only to land with an unceremonious splash in the Co-tyrant's own puddle of piss. Hipparchus thrashed helplessly from side to side, wailing in agony as the razor sharp edge continued its relentless passage up through his bleeding chest cavity, slowly sawing the rib cage into two grisly pieces and only coming to a stop when it sliced through Hipparchus' black, dead heart.

Hearing the sound of running feet, Aristogiton dropped the lifeless corpse to the ground and turned with his unblooded sword out at the ready. "They're coming…" he called over his shoulder even as his revenged lover, his sword stuck fast in the gristle of Hipparchus torso, planted his foot against the fallen co-tyrant's shoulder and struggled to yank his jammed blade free.

At the sound of that first high-pitched scream echoing from inside the roofless Leokoreion, Hipparchus' bodyguard looked up from the wounded man feigning unconsciousness at their feet. Turning as one, they grappled with their swords even as they began running back to their master's defense. In a futile effort to even the odds for his two friends—and forsaking his only chance of escape—Cleon reached out and grabbed the two closest soldiers by their ankles. With reflexes natural to trained killers, two blades came whistling down in frightening unison, each severing one of Cleon's hands at the wrists. On the back swing, one sliced the heroic Greek clean though his neck, the decapitated head bouncing across the Agora like a child's ball.

The first guard to reach the Leokoreion ran right into Aristogiton's waiting sword point. Mortally wounded, the guard grabbed hold of his assailant by the wrist even as Aristogiton struggled to free his sword from the man's punctured groin. With a final moan bubbling from his bloody lips, the guard fell to his knees, blocking the doorway and forcing his cohorts to jab vainly around him at the two cornered assassins. Eventually collecting their wits together, two of the guards grabbed their lifeless partner by his legs. As the dead man, his vise-like grip still encircling Aristogiton's wrist, was pulled clear, Aristogiton was dragged with him out into the open. As he fumbled to free himself, Aristogiton's sword slipped from his bloody hand and fell to the ground.

Scrabbling desperately about on the ground for his sword, a hobnailed toe connected with Aristogiton's jaw and sent him sprawling. Someone grabbed him by the hair and hauled him to his feet, while two other brawny louts pinioned his arms behind him, roughly dislocating one shoulder as they did. Swooning, Aristogiton could only watch in helpless horror as the other soldiers rushed the Leokoreion. Cornering his sweet Harmodius—still standing triumphantly over Hipparchus' filth covered body—they cut him down in a hail of slashing blows even as he raised his gore-covered weapon to defend himself.

❧   ❧   ❧

"What do we do now? Shouldn't we slit this one's throat and leave him there in the shit hole with his friend?"

That very same guard who less than an hour before had been on the receiving end of his master's wrathful foot looked over the bloody mess in the Leokoreion and thought hard for a moment. Two bodies: one hacked to pieces and virtually unrecognizable, laying on top of the other—their master, the late Co-tyrant himself...and gutted like some discarded fish cast up on the beach at Piraeus. The guard felt his mouth go dry...Tyrant Hippias wasn't going to be pleased at this turn of events. Whatever Hipparchus' bungling bodyguards did at this moment might very well determine their fate. After a long pause he turned back to the soldier and, with a flick of his head toward the quietly weeping Aristogiton, responded: "No...better keep him alive."

"You..." he pointed to the men standing watch over him, "...you two take him along to the city prison and see that he's locked up tight. I suspect the Lord Hippias will want to deal with him personally." Barely pausing for a breath, he began issuing orders. "You four...take the Lord Hipparchus' body back home." When one of his cohorts, grimacing at the gruesome task, dared to open his mouth in protest, the guard turned a withering eye in his direction, "...and take those loose guts along as well...everything goes back to the villa. See to it that the slaves do a proper job putting him back together and cleaning him up for the funeral!" He gave them another threatening glare. "And you can tell them for me that they'd better do a decent job of it...or else!" With a shiver he muttered, "Lord Hippias will be expecting nothing less!"

Turning to the remaining guards, he pointed with his sword to where Cleon's decapitated corpse lay unmoving in a fly-covered pool of bloody mud.

"Bring what's left of that one over here and toss him into the cesspool with his friend there…" he motioned toward Harmodius' barely recognizable remains. As they turned to obey his orders he grabbed one by the arm and held him back: "I want you to remain stationed here in front of the Leokoreion until someone comes to relieve you." Narrowing his eyes he added: "No one is to enter…do you hear me? Under no circumstances is anyone to touch these two bodies!" The man's head bobbed smartly and, sword at the ready, he immediately assumed his position.

Their self-appointed leader was about to turn and head off at a run for the distant Acropolis—the morning's most delicate task still to come—when the unnerving sound of distant chanting accompanied by massed flutes and kithera came floating into the Agora.

"Gods! The procession is coming!" he groaned to himself as he felt his heart skip a beat. "Can anything else go wrong today?"

"You there…" He pointed to the man who'd first questioned him about Aristogiton. "Take as many men as you need and block off that street! I don't care how you do it, but I don't want anyone coming into the Agora before Hippias gets here."

Relieved to at last be answering to the controlled voice of authority, the still anxious guard curtly nodded his head. "And what shall we tell them, sir?"

"Tell them nothing! Not a word." And then a desperate idea sprang into his head. "Hold a moment…on second thought, tell them there's been an unexpected delay and that they should turn around and reassemble back at the Dipylon."

As the music grew louder, for the briefest of moments everyone-seemingly frozen in time—remained in place, listening nervously as frightened eyes darted from one fellow to the next.

"Well, get to it!" shouted their new commander hiding his uneasy panic. And at the resounding clap of his hands everyone sprang into action. "I myself will run on to the Acropolis and bring this…the tragic news of the murder of our beloved Lord Hipparchus to his poor brother the Co…er…the Tyrant Hippias."

In a sour mood from the oppressive weather and his brother's annoying tardiness, Hippias stood alone on the temporary platform erected in front of the Temple of Athena Polias, impatiently awaiting the arrival of his brother's much-delayed Panathenaic procession. For some reason, the sudden appearance of a lone soldier running breathlessly up the wide steps of the Acropolis mount sent a shiver of foreboding through his body. With a nervous flutter of his fingers he had the pale-faced man intercepted by two members of his bodyguard and brought straight to him on the dais.

Falling to his knees, the frightened guard—his eyes fixed rigidly on the ground in front of him—quickly relayed the horrifying news of his brother's murder. Stunned beyond words, Hippias—now sole Tyrant of Athens—stood motionless, listening in shock to the news of his brother's unseemly demise.

In a daze, Hippias had the entire story repeated over again before the reality of the gruesome episode finally began to sink in. The clever soldier—hoping to turn the grieving Tyrant's mind away from the dismal failure of Hipparchus' bodyguard—peppered his story with wild fabrications, half-truths and outright lies. In his retelling, Harmodius and Aristogiton's act of personal retribution became nothing less than the vanguard of 'a carefully organized assassination plot' against the Pisistrades.

"Assassination?" Hippias looked up; panic visibly radiating from his saucer-round eyes. "An organized plot, you say?"

The guard nodded his head. "Yes, Lord. Three of them—infantry men from the procession—they lay in wait for your poor brother inside the Leokoreion and fell upon him at his most private moment…"

"*Infantrymen?*" Hippias' eyes narrowed, a chilling note of skepticism creeping into his voice, "…and only three of them?"

Blanching at this sudden change in tone, the guard repressed an urge to turn and flee. "Their leader…" he whispered, his voice crackling with feigned urgency, "…he called out '*Run! Warn the others…*' right before we cut him down."

Now it was Hippias' turn to pale. "Others…" he repeated, the strangled word barely audible as he brought a hand protectively up against his throat.

The guard vigorously nodded his assertion. "Yes, Lord. But we captured him…the one who tried to flee and warn 'the others'. He's been taken to the central prison to await your pleasure." The guard let his words sink in for a few moments before daring an optimistic glance up at the Tyrant. "I beg you, most high and gracious Lord, give me the privilege of personally tearing the names of the other conspirators from this foul traitor's screaming lips."

Hippias, his eyes hooded in thought, smiled sadly as he slowly shook his head. "I think not, my good fellow. That *pleasure* most certainly belongs to me." He looked about for one of his own guard and then, almost as an after thought, turned back to the kneeling soldier. "I would, however, be most grateful if you would return posthaste to your poor master's home and see to the care of my brother's body...that he is made decent for his funeral." Catching the eye of his own captain of the guard, he crooked a finger and signaled him to come forward. "An important task, my fine fellow..." he continued appreciatively to the kneeling guard. "And one that I wish to be handled with utmost discretion and care." Looking away a second time, he dismissed the man with a curt nod of his head. "As for any *conspiracy*...my own guard will deal with that."

Around the ceremonial platform, the shocking news of Hipparchus' murder spread with the speed of Borealis' wind. A guard standing close to Hippias on the dais mumbled word to the Priests of Athena watching over the flaming high altar...who then passed it along to their curious acolytes forming a human barricade around Athena's sacred precinct...and from there the tale quickly traveled from mouth to ear among the sweaty, impatient mob scattered over the Acropolis hilltop.

"Worse than useless fools! I want them all dead before the sun sets in the sky, Captain...do you hear me? All of them!" Hippias glared after Hipparchus' departing bodyguard. "They failed miserably in their duty...lazy fools, they failed to protect my dear, dear brother...and for that they must pay with their lives!"

Wanting to twitch his shoulder blades as a line of sweat trickled down between them, Hippias' Captain remained at rigid attention, his face blank as one extraordinary command after another issued from between his lord's tightly pursed lips.

Grimly canceling what was left of the Panathenaia, Hippias had announced a month long period of mourning for his brother...and in the same breath, sent his merciless guard to put everyone in Hipparchus' unfortunate household—bodyguards, servants, and slaves alike—to death.

As night descended over Athens the cries of the grieving could be heard from every quarter of the city. A day that should have seen the joyous culmination of the boisterous festivities honoring their patron goddess, ended with the senseless executions of hundreds of innocent citizens.

And that was just the beginning...

❦   ❦   ❦

Hippias used the freshly sharpened edge of his paring knife to cut a juicy wedge from the golden apple clutched in the palm of his hand. Popping the slice into his mouth, he turned the point of the short blade and pressed it, ever so slowly, into the hairless chest of his naked prisoner. As another thin line of blood ran down the length of the young man's bruised torso, his tormentor smiled at him, amiably chewing away at his crisp, tasty fruit. With the skill of a practiced sadist he twisted the blade first to the left and then to the right, pulling the point back before it could do any serious damage. After slicing himself another apple wedge, he moved the bloody, juice-covered blade over by an inch before starting again.

Aristogiton, his black-and-blue wrists attached painfully over his head to a rusty iron ring fixed in the ceiling of the basement prison cell, flinched with each of Hippias' probing jabs. Ever since his beloved Harmodius fell beneath the killing blows of Hipparchus' guard, one thought alone had occupied his pain-wracked mind—an unremitting longing to join his waiting beloved's shade on Hades' Elysian Fields. And so it was with mixed feelings of relief and trepidation that he approached this final confrontation with the hated Tyrant...for he had little doubt that it would be this same Lord Hippias who would provide him his longed-for release from life.

"They're all dead, you know...your accomplices...all of them!"

Aristogiton stirred, his eyelids fluttering open.

Diokles...Tylissus...Nicias...Cleon...the names drifted over and over through his tortured mind like a numbing litany recited by the high priests on a holy day. Aristogiton moaned, his eyes rolling back in his head. "Are they then..." he asked himself "...also among the dead?" The question throbbed in his head. Confused, his disoriented psyche suddenly conjured a grisly picture of four stiff, decapitated corpses all lined in a row...the golden dust of the Agora drenching red with the blood pouring from their open neck wounds.

Hippias' knife pierced his chest again and with an involuntary shudder, brought him out of his nightmarish reverie. "No...it was only Cleon I saw...poor, faithful Cleon." He pushed the lurid vision of Cleon's headless body, left to rot in the city square, out of his head."

"Didn't you hear what I said?" Hippias screamed in his ear. "We caught them all...your murdering friends...all your fellow assassins. They are being executed this very night...even as we speak!" The paranoid shrillness in Hippias' voice caused Aristogiton to look up with a jerk. Staring straight into his tormentor's unfeeling eyes, Aristogiton looked for any sign of exultation but saw only confusion and fear.

"I won't suffer traitors in my city! Do you hear me?" The quivering man shrieked with feigned delight as he dug another shallow hole—this one just below Aristogiton's left nipple—into the already blood-soaked chest. Mistaking the sudden dilation of his prisoner's pupils for a desperate glimmer of hope, Hippias grinned and quickly yanked back his knife. "Oh no, my fine fellow...not so fast. Your death won't be *that* easy." This time he fastidiously wiped the blade on his tunic before cutting himself another apple slice. "Oh yes...that I can promise you!"

A hollow knock on the oaken cell door interrupted the interrogation and a soldier—a damning reddish tint coating both of his arms all the way up to the elbows—came striding in. Never taking his restive eyes off his dangling captive, Hippias acknowledged the man with a brusque tilt of his chin. "Have you finished, Captain?"

The soldier stood at attention and curtly nodded his head. "Yes, my lord. As per your instructions, the Panathenaia celebrants waiting at the Dipylon Gate were dismissed back to their homes...with the exception of the uniformed infantrymen."

"Ah yes...*the Infantry*...yes, that's right." Hippias nodded to him before turning his attention back to his stubbornly mute prisoner. "Go on, Captain..." he whispered as he teasingly ran the razor-sharp knife blade up along one side of Aristogiton's elongated ribcage, stopping to jab the point in when he reached the sensitive hollow of his armpit.

"Well sir, we stripped the whole lot of them naked and set about inspecting their kits. Those found with 'any weapon other than the regulation sword, shield, or spear' (he was careful to quote the Tyrant's exact words), they were all kept behind. The others we sent on their way."

"And did you find many of these *hidden weapons* among my 'oh so loyal' troops?" Hippias spoke through gritted teeth as he prodded and poked the raw underarm of his silently squirming captive.

For a moment, a look of confusion crossed the soldier's face. Staring at the small knife in Hippias' hand, the disgusted man found himself thinking, "Of course we found weapons, you idiot...we found hunting knives, fishing knives, even a few cursed apple-coring knives!" But given a moment's pause, he thought better of these words and simply replied: "Yes, my Lord…we found 172 personal knives, a number of small daggers…and 28 slingshots."

Hippias licked his lips and smiled. "And how many of these *traitors* confessed to being a part of this cabal to murder my brother and I, Captain?"

There was another uncomfortable pause before the soldier, clearing his throat, muttered, "Well, none…my lord."

"NONE?" screeched the Tyrant. "Not one?" He pulled the blade out of Aristogiton's armpit, swung around and pointed it in the wide-eyed soldier's face. "But you gave them warning, didn't you…you told them of my generous offer of exile for any who, confessing to this heinous crime, would simply name their co-conspirators?"

Red-faced, the Captain nervously chewed on his lip as he slowly nodded in reply.

Stunned, Hippias sucked in a noisy, rasping breath. "And not a single of these festering tyrannicides would accept my merciful offer?"

This time the captain looked down at the floor before repeating, "None, my Lord. Each of them to the very last man professed his innocence to the end."

Hippias frowned, for the first time uncertain about the stubborn brutality of his paranoid response. The oppressive silence of the torch-lit room grew almost unbearable until the sullen Tyrant finally asked, "Very well then Captain, tell me now…how many did you execute?"

Startled, the soldier looked up. "I, my lord?" The color suddenly drained from his face. "I…I personally slit the throats of thirty Athenian infantrymen." He couldn't keep his eyes from straying down to the fading stains on his hands. "My men executed another 178…"

"Two hundred and eight…you put two hundred and eight men to death?"

"Yes, my Lord."

Even Hippias found himself astonished at the number.

Dropping his half-eaten apple to the dirt, for several long seconds the Tyrant stood staring vacant eyed down at the bloody blade locked in his fist. His Captain of the Guard was sorely tempted to use this opportunity for a discreet withdrawal, but fearing his master's temper more than the unpleasant news that still remained, he waited for Hippias to regain his composure.

"Two hundred and eight men…" the Tyrant repeated, each word enunciated with a practiced rhetorician's flourish.

The Captain coughed. "There's…er, one other thing, my Lord."

His eyes narrowing to angry slits, Hippias swung his head up with a jerkiness that caused the soldier—a man of unquestioned bravery—to take a nervous step backward.

"Speak!" Hippias' voice boomed in the enclosed space of the prison cell. "What else do you have to say to me?"

"It's just that…" the soldier found his gaze moving past the Tyrant's icy glare to the blood-spattered assassin hanging half-conscious from the ceiling ring. Silently he cursed the doomed man for the reckless calamity he'd brought down on them all.

"Well?" Hippias scowled impatiently. "Speak up man!"

"I'm afraid that word of the…er, the mass execution has spread throughout the city, my Lord. Violence and unrest are already breaking out in many quarters. I'm afraid there may be rioting before long…"

"Yes, yes…I can well understand that." Hippias stepped away from his prisoner, the expression on his face growing increasingly distant. "The people of Athens are a fickle lot, Captain. At one time they worshipped my family…my father was a veritable god to them!" His eyebrows shot up. "And me…they loved me, as well Captain!" He shook his head in dismay. "But now…" his voice turned bitter "…now they have betrayed us…betrayed the entire Pisistrade clan." His fist tightened around the apple-coring knife. "But mark my word, Captain…there will be a heavy price to pay for this disloyalty!" With an angry gesture he dismissed the uncertain soldier, muttering: "Never mind…I'll deal with all that in the morning." As an afterthought he called after him, "But see to it that my escort is doubled, Captain. When I've finished up here, I wish to return to my home…in safety."

Alone again, he turned his attentions back to his captive, sure that the truth about this entire assassination plot was still locked away inside the taciturn fellow. Much to his surprise, Aristogiton had apparently shaken off his pain-induced haze and even now was staring back at his tormentor with belligerence-filled eyes. The tortured man opened his mouth to speak:

"You foolish man." His head wobbled from side to side. "You've slaughtered two hundred and eight innocents…senseless murders all…and now there's rioting in the city…"

Hippias raised an open hand to strike the insolent man across his face but the look of sheer hatred blazing from his adversary's eyes took his breath away. Struggling to regain his composure, he smiled savagely at the man and leaned forward to set the point of his knife blade right up under Aristogiton's chin. Reeling with fury, he spit in the face of the man who this very morning had murdered his brother. Pushing the blade in until the blood flowed freely down over his hand, he hissed: "Tell me their names, damn you...tell me now or I'll bleed you like a stuck pig! I'll bleed you until you cry out begging me for a quick death...and then I'll bleed you some more! Don't make me ask you again! Who were your compatriots? Who in Athens dares to conspire against the Pisistrades?"

A sour apple smell filled Aristogiton's nostrils as Hippias' foul spittle dripped slowly down along his handsome cheek.

"Rioting in the city..." his last thoughts even as he forced a scornful grin to his lips "...goodness, won't dear Cleisthenes be pleased!"

And with that, using the full force of his thick, gymnasium-trained neck muscles, he drove his chin down hard on Hippias' blade, severing the carotid artery that carried the life-giving blood to his brain and ensuring himself a quick end.

As Aristogiton's thick, hot red blood went spurting out across the room drenching the enraged Tyrant from head to toe as he vainly scrambled out of the way, the dying man released a final sigh. With the single word 'Harmodius' falling lovingly from his parted lips, the light forever left his eyes.

Epilogue

"As news of Hipparchus' murder spread throughout the city..."

The gentle morning breeze fluttered a single long strand of Helena's raven hair across her face. Discreetly pulling it back behind her head, she tucked the errant lock into the single twisted plait Mila had so carefully prepared earlier in the day. Smiling over at her husband, she turned her attention back to Cleisthenes' passionate oration.

"That very same night, spared from certain death by Harmodius' foresight and on their way to a safe refuge in Megara, Diokles and Tylissus first heard of Hipparchus' assassination while stopping at an inn for a hurried meal."

Cleisthenes, alone on the temporary platform erected just that morning in the center of the Agora, found himself somewhat dwarfed by the sculptor Antenor's latest masterpiece. Leaning forward, he made a sweeping gesture toward the seats of honor down front.

Blushing when his name was called out, Diokles clutched at his wife's trembling hand and squeezed it with pride.

"Unaware of the fate that had already befallen their comrades in Athens—but remembering well his pledge—this very same Diokles turned his horse north and rode straight for Araphen hoping to ensure the well-being of Harmodius' sadly widowed mother and sister...even as his beloved Tylissus bravely retraced his hapless path back to Athens."

Helena felt a gentle nudge as Mila's ancient head tottered over on one side to rest against her shoulder. Quickly and with discretion—before the old woman's robust snores could drown out Cleisthenes' words—Helena tickled her on the arm. Waking with a start, Mila stifled a snort with the palm of her hand as she looked about in a bewildered daze. Leaning over, Helena whispered in her ear, "It's all right, my dear...I fear you nodded off again."

Seeing that Cleisthenes was still deep in his oration, Mila felt the color in her cheeks rise even as she stifled another yawn. "A thousand pardons, mistress…" she mumbled behind her hand. "I was just thinking back to our dear, sweet boy and…well…you know how the Lord Cleisthenes' voice falls so harmoniously on the ear that I'm afraid I…"

With a sympathetic pat of her hand, Helena smiled. "Never mind, old girl. His long-winded speech will soon be over and then we can return you home for a nice afternoon nap."

Having reached the turning point in his story—that moment when the harried citizens of Athens finally cried 'enough' and rose up against their Tyrant Hippias—Cleisthenes hit his oratorical stride. *"And what of young Nicias…"* he cried out to the enraptured crowd, *"…the boy whose innocent misadventure with the law became the unsuspecting catalyst for their aborted coup?"* Cleisthenes frowned and shook his head. *"In all the tumult following Hipparchus' death, I fear the poor fellow languished forgotten in his prison cell for nearly a month before finally being summoned to trial on the charges of gross sacrilege and…"* he didn't bother trying to repress the smirk on his face, *"…and defacement of private property."*

Forgetting the solemn nature of the occasion, several older members in the audience laughed outright at the memory of the great stone cock on Hippias' herm…snapped in two by some drunken—and never apprehended—fellator.

"Fortunately the goddess Dike—'Justice' herself—was watching over our boy that day. When the prosecution presented two broken front teeth as their primary piece of evidence in this spurious case, Nicias—whose own teeth were quite intact—was immediately released from his shackles…and, I might add, to the ridicule of all involved."

Cleisthenes paused, his hand scratching thoughtfully at the scraggly beard hanging from his chin. Looking out over the crowded Agora, he waited patiently for their nodding murmurs to subside. When a hush had finally settled, his voice rose up once again, quickly reaching its well-practiced rhetorical plateau as the famous Cleisthenes of Athens sought with all his oratorical might to elevate this moment of history into one of legend.

"Yes, citizens…inspired by the sacrifice of Harmodius and Aristogiton, Nicias and his compatriots enjoined our neighbor Sparta for their military support against the capricious villainies of the Tyrant Hippias…and, in the forthcoming struggle, along with hundreds of your fellows," his two hands shot straight out at the now-agitated crowd, *"gave his life that this cruel despot might forever be exiled to Persia's distant shore."* Cleisthenes paused here, turning slowly to point

a single condemning finger toward the far eastern horizon. Across the wide Aegean expanse, the coastline of Ionia—once a prosperous land dotted with rich Greek colonies—now sat captive under the iron fist of Persia's Great King Darius. And at the mere mentioning of 'Persia' the entire multitude fell into howling growls of hatred and derision for their new enemy.

Mila took this opportunity to tug on the pleated sleeve of her mistress' chiton. "Mistress?" she whispered, her fingers discreetly covering the hectoring movement of her lips.

"What is it now, Mila?" At times the old woman could be even more exasperating than Helena's small children.

"The statue..." she pointed a bony finger up behind the speaker's podium at the two towering figures striding forward side by side from their great stone base. "Of course I recognize the likeness of our young Harmodius, Mistress...but that other one...his friend?"

"Aristogiton..." Helena prodded, her own voice muffled carefully behind the sleeve of her chiton.

"Yes, him...Aristogiton." Mila bit her lip for a moment as she pondered the niggling question that bothered her so. "It's that beard," she finally said with a frustrated sigh. "My memory may have faded with the years...but even so, I don't recall that young man having such a fine beard."

Helena's carefully plucked eyebrows came together in a furrow. "He didn't," she answered with an exasperated sigh. "Hush now, dear Mila...I believe our noble Cleisthenes is about to introduce himself into his own story. I'll explain the beard to you later."

Shielding her eyes against the mid-morning glare Helena peered past Cleisthenes' vigorously gyrating shoulders, her mind wandering—even as the demagogue extolled his own praiseworthy part in the improbable restoration of Athenian democracy—to the recently unveiled statue of her brother Harmodius and his lover Aristogiton.

Was it really just a year ago that she and Cleisthenes—standing in the middle of Antenor's bustling studio, ankle deep in marble and bronze shavings—had squabbled so over that damnable *beard*?

"But think, my dear...Aristogiton was an orphan when he died..." she could still hear his inveigling words ringing in her ears *"...after all, who will ever remember what he looked like?"* Before she could protest that many peo-

ple—she and her husband among them—still carried vivid memories of the beardless Aristogiton in their hearts, he'd lifted the foot-high model of the statue in his hand and held it aloft, gazing with wonder at the two figures. *"But with this beard..."* he pointed at the tiny red clay smudge that had recently appeared on Aristogiton's chin *"...the clean-shaven youth and his older bearded companion. Yes, this beard will forever identify them as erastes and eromenos."* He'd smiled persuasively as he held the miniature figurines out to her. *"And for centuries to come, people will marvel at this great statue, speaking in hushed voices of 'the tragic lovers who, through their sacrifice, brought democracy to Athens.'"* Oh, how he'd prattled on that day. *"It will be the first of its kind in all the Greek world,"* Cleisthenes had said, *"the only portrait statue ever sculpted at public expense!"*

His very words...

Now—sitting here considering the cold, chiseled face of her beloved brother—Helena squeezed her eyes shut and tried with all her heart to invoke his true image. In all honesty, even though she'd spent countless hours in Antenor's studio carefully describing her brother's every feature in the greatest possible detail, the final likeness wasn't particularly faithful.

She sighed and mentally shrugged her shoulders. "Ah, well. What matter?" she asked herself. "What matter...as long as they all look to this beautiful work of art and remember my brother and Aristogiton as the saviors of their sacred city-state...the hallowed fathers of Greek democracy. These two magnificent 'Tyrannicides' who inspired the uprising against the hated Pisistrade brothers."

Burying the bitterness in her heart, she smiled to herself and sent a silent prayer of thanks to the Underworld. "Dearest brother...I know you gave your life to avenge my slighted honor. Even so...find peace in Hades' sacred realm with your beloved Aristogiton forever at your side. And know that you're precious sacrifice has ignited a flame that will be remembered until the end of time."

Afterword

Following the assassination of Hipparchus in 514 BC, Athens fulminated for four more years under the increasingly harsh and capricious rule of his brother Hippias. Deposed in 510 by a timely Spartan invasion (prompted in secret by the rival Alcmaeonid clan and their exiled leader Cleisthenes), Hippias was given safe conduct to his son-in-law's court at Lampsacus in Asia Minor. From there he made his stealthy way to Persepolis, the Persian capitol of King Darius I. Capturing the High King's ear, Hippias relentlessly plotted his vengeance against Athens until finally, twenty years later, he found himself in charge of Darius' ill-fated invasion fleet that met its destruction on the fabled plains of Marathon.

Having appealed to the Spartans for aid against Hippias, the Athenians found their avaricious allies reluctant to leave the comfort of their city. For nearly two years Athens suffered under the thumb of their handpicked puppet Isagoras—a nobleman who saw it as his duty to undo the democratic reforms put in place by his more notable predecessors Solon and Pisistratus. In 508 BC, after staging one final uprising, Cleisthenes and the Alcmaeonids finally swept the Spartans from Attica and took control of Athens. Under Cleisthenes guidance numerous reforms were undertaken that eventually enfranchised all the free male citizens on the Attic peninsula. Seeking to remove the remaining stigma associated with Athens' traditional hereditary divisions, Cleisthenes reorganized all Athenians into ten regional tribes. And it was from these ten tribes that the city's chief lawmaking body—the Council of 500—was elected.

By 500 BC, Athens had firmly established the democratic traits that would be the pinnacle of her coming Golden Age.

※   ※   ※

Mention of Harmodius and Aristogiton can be found in many of the writings extant from the ancient world. Thucydides and Herodotus both relate the tale of Harmodius and Aristogiton's assassination of Hipparchus (although from diverging points of view) in chapters of their famous 'Histories'. The portrait sculpture—the first such statue erected at public expense—is described at length in the writings of the Roman naturalist Pliny, as well as in Pausanias' witty travelogue: "Description of Greece".

As for this first-of-its-kind statue...

The original, sculpted by Antenor and installed in the Athenian Agora, remained in place only a few short years before being carried off as booty when Xerxes and the Persians—seeking retribution for his father Darius' humiliating defeat at Marathon—sacked the city in 480 BC. Following the astonishing Athenian victory over the Persian navy at Salamis, a new statue was commissioned—this one by the sculptors Kritios and Nesiotes. And it was most likely a description of this statue, copied any number of times in later centuries by art-loving Hellenes and Romans, that comes down to us today.

Legend has it that when Alexander the Great—in his turn conquering the Persian Empire in 330 BC—found the original statue stored in the city of Susa, he immediately had it shipped back to a grateful Athens.

Glossary

Agora—the market place and central square in Greek city-states where political, commercial, and legal business usually took place.

Anakrisis—the preliminary hearing of a lawsuit held before a single magistrate.

Archon Basileus—a religious magistrate who officiated at trials involving sacrilege or religious impiety.

Archons—aristocratic magistrates who ruled the central Greek city-states following the deposition of the earlier monarchies.

Amphidromia—traditional ceremony where a newborn is placed under the protection of the household gods. The Amphidromia, meaning "the running around", culminated when the father carried the child around the family's hearth, placing him under the protection of Hestia, goddess of the hearth.

Apaturia—the Athenian festival honoring 'fatherhood'. New members were usually enrolled into their family clans on the last day of the feast.

Attica—the peninsula/state controlled by Athens.

Aulos—a blown reed instrument similar to the oboe, usually made from bone, wood, or ivory and played in pairs by a single instrumentalist.

Chiton—a belted garment made of linen. A woman's chiton was usually ankle-length, while a man's stopped above his knees.

Chlamys—a cloak usually worn over the left shoulder and pinned on the right. In Winter the chlamys could be pulled up over the head against poor weather.

Deme—a small population center, often a village or suburb near a larger city.

Dionysia—a popular five-day festival featuring processions and theatrical performances dedicated to the fertility god Dionysus.

Elaphebolion—the month corresponding with March on the Athenian calendar.

Eleusinia—an Athenian religious festival of athletic games held at Eleusis over four days in the month of Metageitnion (July-August).

Ephebeon—the training area for young men and adolescents in a Greek gymnasium.

Erastes—in the idealized Greek form of love between two men prior to marriage with a woman, the erastes was the instigator of the relationship. Often the elder of the two, the erastes was also known as "the lover".

Ergastinai—craftswomen responsible for weaving the sacred peplos carried in the Panathenaic Procession.

Eromenos—in the idealized Greek form of love between two men prior to marriage with a woman, the eromenos was the receiver of the admiration and affection of the erastes. Often, but not always, the younger of the two, the eromenos was also known as "the beloved".

Gamelion—the Athenian month corresponding with our month of January.

Hekatombaion—the Athenian month roughly corresponding with our month of July. The Panathenaia is celebrated on the last days of this month. The term Hekatombaion probably refers to the '100 oxen' sacrificed to the goddess during the great festival.

Herms—Stone representations of the god Hermes, usually a pillar featuring his bearded head and an erect penis, set up for good fortune in front of homes and public places.

Hetaera—the courtesan class in Greek society; prostitutes.

Himation—a rectangular cloth or cloak that draped over the left shoulder and under the right, with the remainder hanging loosely from the arm. The himation could either be worn over the chiton or by itself and could be of plain material or dyed, often adorned with embroidery.

Kithera—a harp like instrument similar to a lyre. With seven strings of equal length, the fingers and, at times, a plectrum plucked it.

Knucklebones—a children's game played with the anklebones of a sheep...somewhat similar to our modern game of 'Jacks'.

Krater—a large bowl used for mixing wine with water.

Leokoreion—a small sanctuary situated near the center of the Agora where the Panathenaic Road crossed the main road to Piraeus. Fronted by a public well, the Leokoreion had four short walls inside which modest travelers often relieved themselves.

Metic—a foreigner, a resident-alien of a Greek city-state

Myrmidon—the legendary Achaean warrior clan led by Achilles in the Trojan War.

Noumenia—the first day of the month (new moon day) and sacred throughout the Greek world.

Paidagogus—a family slave whose job it was to accompany his young master to school each day. The modern word 'pedagogue' comes from paidagogus.

Palaestra—a wrestling school; also the word sometimes used to describe the structure housing the gymnasium.

Pannychos—a wild, all-night celebration during the Panathenaic Festival when all of Athens lost itself in a frenzy of feasting and dancing before the Great Procession and Sacrifice on the morning after.

Peplos—The garment favored by women in Ancient Greece. A single rectangle, usually of wool, doubled over above the waist, the peplos was fastened at the shoulders with decorative pins and cinched together with a girdle.

Petasos—a wide brimmed traveling hat used to cover the head and face from inclement weather. Usually made of felt or leather.

Phratry—one of the traditional clans usually made up of one or more aristocratic families.

Plynteria—a solemn spring festival dedicated to the washing of Athena's statues and the cleaning of her temples.

Pyanopsion—The Athenian month that corresponds with our October.

Rhyton—a one handled drinking cup or horn, often shaped like an animal's head.

Satrap—a Persian province.

Sophist—a professional teacher who traveled from town to town offering practical lessons for a fee. The range of topics taught by sophists included oratory, law and politics, music, mathematics, astronomy, and ethics.

Stoa—a long, colonnaded building, often serving as one boundary of the agora. A popular meeting place in the Greek city-state.

Strigil—a dull-edged, curved metal blade used by athletes to scrape off sweat and oil following a workout.

Thesmophoria—a three-day women's festival dedicated to the goddess Demeter who brought fertility to the crops. Celebrated in Athens and throughout Greece.

Tyranny—the rule of a single man, often for life, with the support of the common people. Maligned in later times, the Greek tyrannies often served as transition points between the aristocratic rule of the archons and the democracy of Greece's golden age. Often hereditary in nature, tyrannies usually lasted as long as they retained their popular support.

Tyrant—a type of monarch who seized power with the support of the common people.

Xystos—the training area for adult men in a gymnasium.

0-595-30198-3